Flutter

by
Amanda Hocking

Second Paperback Edition: September 2010

For information:

http://amandahocking.blogspot.com/

Flutter — Book III

ISBN 9781453816905

For John Hughes.

Jack smiled at me from across the glass chessboard, and any thoughts I had about the game were completely lost. Since I made the transformation from seventeen-year-old girl to full-fledged vampire three weeks ago, the ability to focus on anything had become much harder.

My new senses made Jack even more amazing. When he moved his hand to touch a pawn, the light, tangy scent of him and his blood made my mouth water. He was even more attractive than I'd ever known, and I'd spent far too many hours just gaping at him.

"Ahem," Milo cleared his throat more loudly than necessary, considering he could grab my attention by just changing the way he breathed.

Every sound was so much more magnified than it was before. While I couldn't hear a butterfly flapping its wings, my hearing had greatly improved. When it comes to heart beats and blood, I'm particularly sensitive.

"I thought you wanted to learn to play chess," Milo said.

He sat behind us, perched in an over stuffed chair with one of his legs hanging over the arm. In human years, he was a year and a half younger than me, but he'd been a vampire longer than I had. With dark, wide eyes, he managed to look deep and mysterious, while as a human, he had just looked innocent and naive. The change sat with him immensely.

"I know, I know," I said, and my embarrassment amused Jack. "Just go over what a rook is one more time."

"You're not even trying at all, Alice," Milo sighed.

"Be serious," Jack chimed in, his tone very dutiful.

Our relationship currently bordered on unhealthy obsession, but that had to do with me turning and our recent bonding. Everyone assured us that it would eventually lessen to an acceptable level.

Without any effort on my part, my body would automatically tilt towards him. Under the glass chess table, he had started brushing his foot against my leg, trying to get me to pay attention to him. His touch, even through a sock against my calf, did insane things to me. My heart fluttered unabashedly, but at least I could hear his for a change.

"Okay, I totally know what you're doing." Milo sounded disgusted.

"Sorry!" I pulled my leg back.

"You're no fun," Jack grumbled but made no attempt to touch me again.

Jack's brother Ezra insisted we keep some distance for awhile. My emotions tended to get the best of me. Anything passionate, like hunger or lust, overpowered everything, and I could actually kill Jack if we got frisky. So, we almost constantly had baby-sitters, in the form of Milo, Ezra, or Ezra's wife Mae.

Jack decided that he wasn't the best one to teach me chess, so he bowed out and let Milo take his place. Milo explained the rules to me again while Jack made himself comfortable on the couch.

His giant white Great Pyrenees, Matilda, brought her rope over to him so he would play with her. Even though he had moved away from us, my attention remained fixed on him.

"Alice!" Milo snapped his fingers in front of my face, trying to draw my eyes away from Jack. "I'm going to send him out of the room if you don't knock it off."

"Sorry!" I repeated.

Jack laughed, and that did nothing to help the situation. With sandy, disheveled hair, dancing blue eyes, and flawless, tan skin, Jack was attractive in his own right, but it was his amazing laughter that always got me. It was the clearest, most perfect sound I had ever heard.

Milo stood up, preparing to make good on his threat, but Ezra walked into the living room.

Ezra's presence was like no other. Handsome in a way that only a vampire could be, his blond hair fell across his forehead, and his warm, russet eyes were unnaturally anxious.

Mae followed close behind, and her usual happy demeanor vanished. She wrung her hands as they walked into the living room.

"There's been some trouble," Ezra said in his deep voice, edged with his faded British accent. "I've got to go take care of some things."

"What trouble? What are you talking about?" Milo asked, and his voice raised an octave, the way it did when he was nervous. When he had first turned, I'd been afraid he would lose some of his human traits, but for the most part, they seemed intact.

Ezra exchanged a look with Mae, but she shook her head. Jack had dropped the rope, and Matilda kept pushing it against his hand to get him to play with her again, but he ignored her.

"Peter," Ezra answered finally.

At the mention of his brother's name, Jack's entire body tensed so much he frightened Matilda away.

I was still surprised at how little I felt when the topic of Peter was brought up. The painful bond I had with him no longer existed, but I doubted that I could ever entirely sever my feelings for him.

"Is he coming back?" Milo moved closer to me, as if I still needed protection.

Jack dropped his eyes to the floor, and he battled to keep his anger under control. He'd never forgive Peter for nearly killing me when I'd been mortal. Somehow, I had never really faulted Peter for that.

"No, he's not coming back." Ezra shook his head but kept his eyes on Jack, gauging his reaction to the news. "I don't think he'll ever come back."

"He won't if he knows what's good for him," Jack growled in a voice so low it barely sounded like his own.

"Jack, he's still your brother," Mae reminded him, her gentle accent trying to calm him.

"He was *never* my brother!" Jack rolled his eyes and leaned back in the chair.

Peter was 150 years older than Jack, so they weren't related in the human sense of the word. Peter had been the one to turn Jack, so his blood had fused to Jack's, creating a bond between them that was much stronger than any normal familial relation. Before that,

Ezra had turned Peter, making a steadfast bond between the three of them. Until I came along.

"It doesn't matter how you feel about him," Ezra told Jack, but there was an underlying hurt. "He's in very real danger, and I've got to go help him."

"What kind of danger?" I asked, and I felt Jack's eyes flit over to me but I refused to look back at him.

"He's..." Ezra furrowed his brow. "He's killing vampires."

"Yeah, that sounds like Peter," Jack muttered.

"I thought he'd gone off the grid," I said, and Jack scoffed at me.

Three weeks ago, Jack turned me into a vampire, and Peter took off. Peter did that frequently, but usually Ezra had a way of getting in touch with him. This time, Peter disappeared, and despite his best attempts, Ezra had been unable to reach him.

"He has. Word travelled down about Peter," Ezra elaborated. "I just got a phone call that vampires are seeking revenge on him. So I'm going to try and find him and see if I can't reason with him."

"He can handle himself," Jack sneered at everyone's concern. "Peter has killed vampires before, and he's fought in wars. If there's one thing Peter knows, it's how to fight."

"This is different." Ezra's eyes grew sad. "There's reason to believe he's on a suicide mission."

"Good," Jack grunted under his breath.

"I'll go with you." I stood up abruptly and knocked over the chess board. My mind hadn't caught up to what my body could do.

"You'll what?" Jack raised an eyebrow but looked at me evenly.

We hadn't talked about Peter at all since I had turned, but he incorrectly assumed that my feelings for Peter mirrored his own.

"I'll go with," I repeated.

I bent down to pick up the chess pieces, but Milo swatted my hands away.

"I'll do it," Milo said, pulling glass pawns out of my hand. "You get busy letting them talk sense into you."

"Alice." Jack's expression remained mostly quizzical, but his breathing got heavier.

Part of me did still care for Peter, and not because it was ingrained in me. Peter hadn't done anything wrong in all of this, but he'd been ostracized by his family and gone through a terrible heartbreak because of it - because of *me*.

"Alice, you don't need to go with," Mae shook her head.

"I know I wouldn't be any good in a fight, but maybe I could reason with him. Maybe I could convince him that it didn't need to get to that point," I said.

Mae turned to Ezra, waiting for him to shoot me down, and I think that's the only reason that Jack hadn't freaked out yet. They all expected Ezra to thank me for my sentiments but tell me that it was better if I stayed home.

"She has a point," Ezra said carefully, and that's when everybody decided to get upset.

Mae touched his arm and tried to plead with him that I was far too young to go anywhere, let alone on a crusade to save Peter from a suicide mission. Jack jumped to his feet, but he couldn't seem to decide whether he was angrier with me or Ezra, or maybe Peter. Milo finished setting up the chess set and smacked me on the arm.

"Ow!" I scowled, rubbing my arm. "What'd you do that for?"

"Because you're an idiot and I can!" He'd always been a rather over-protective younger brother, but he was the mature one, the sensible one.

I knew it was stupid, but as soon as Ezra had said that Peter was in danger, my heart flipped. If anything bad happened to him, it was my fault. If I left his family alone, the way he repeatedly begged me to, then he wouldn't have run off into the mess that he's in.

"Ezra, you can't seriously be thinking of taking her with you," Jack said.

His fists clenched at his sides, and his eyes were frightened. It killed him that I cared anything for Peter, and it would literally kill him if anything happened to me.

"I won't let anything happen to her, but she might be the best chance I have for talking Peter down." Ezra held his hands palm out towards Jack, trying to calm him. "I have to try anything."

"I am so sick of this!" Jack shouted. "I should've just killed him when I had the chance!"

"Jack!" Mae yelled. "You don't mean that! Don't say things like that!"

"I would love to stay and have this argument with you, but we really need to get on a flight out of here," Ezra boomed over us all. "Alice, if you're coming with, you need to pack for the cold. I'll go book the flight and get our passports ready." He turned to walk down the hall to his den, ending the conversation.

"Ezra!" Jack made a step after him, but Mae stopped him.

"I'll talk to him. You take care of her." Mae nodded towards me.

She hurried after Ezra, and Jack turned to me. He looked at me for a moment, trying to think of precisely what he wanted to say to me, and I took a deep breath before he could mount his argument.

"You're not going to talk me out of this, Jack."

I brushed past him so I could run upstairs to my room, to *our* room, but both he and Milo followed right on my trail. With my quick, clumsy steps, it was amazing that I didn't fall down the stairs, and if I had, that would've done very little for my case.

Jack had been sleeping in Ezra's den downstairs since I had turned, but all his things were still in here. The closet was full of both our clothes, and my wardrobe had expanded since I had moved in. Ezra and Mae had set me up with an expense account and credit cards a few weeks ago, and my new, trimmer vampire body required all new clothes.

I went into the massive walk-in closet, rummaging around for bags. Jack had hot pink luggage, but I didn't have time to question it and pulled them out. Jack stood in the doorway, and Milo was behind him, both of them glaring at me.

"You're actually packing?" Milo asked. "You can't really be considering going with Ezra."

"He's right. This is stupid," Jack agreed. "It's ridiculous and dangerous, and you don't even know where you're going. How can you even pack for that?"

"Ezra said to pack for the cold," I reminded them.

I loaded my bag with sweaters and jeans and socks. Vampires didn't really feel cold, and in fact, we preferred it to heat. But if we were to walk around in a blizzard wearing a tee shirt and shorts, humans would question it, so we dressed to fit in.

"Jack, just forbid her from going or something!" Milo said.

"I can't *forbid* her from doing anything," Jack replied tiredly, but he definitely wished he could. "And if I tried, it would just make her want to do it more."

I threw a pair of boots in the bag and then struggled to zip it up. Obviously, I was much stronger than the stupid metal zipper, but I hadn't figured out how to use my strength at all.

"Here." Jack knelt on the floor next to me so he could zip up my bag for me.

"Thank you."

"Alice, why do you even wanna go?" Jack asked.

"He didn't do anything wrong," I told him quietly, and he rolled his eyes.

"He tried to kill you, Alice!" Jack shouted.

"He didn't *mean* to," I insisted, and that was only half a lie.

Peter never really wanted to hurt me, but he didn't know what to do about anything. When I asked him to end my life, he refused, so I bit my lip hard enough to draw blood, and I knew that he wouldn't be able to reject biting me then. I had forced him into it, and Jack rushed in to stop him from finishing the job.

"But he did, Alice! All he ever did was push you away and treat you like crap and almost kill you! What about that is so endearing to you?"

"He didn't ask for any of this, Jack! He didn't ask to feel the way he did about me, and he just wanted it to stop! And now he's alone and suicidal somewhere because of me! I can't just let him die!"

My intensity only hurt and bewildered Jack more. He leaned back, resting against a row of shelves filled with his Converse. His face had gone lax, and I knew he had resigned himself to me going, but that didn't mean he felt okay about it.

"Jack, listen to me." I took his hand, and his sad, blue eyes met mine. "Ezra's not going to let anything bad happen to me. And I love *you*, okay?"

"I don't want you to go, Alice," Jack said simply. "Please, if you love me, don't go."

Seeing him like that, so desperate for me to stay, broke my heart. I never wanted to hurt him. If Ezra shot me down, I wouldn't have fought to go, but he agreed, so he thought that I could help. If causing Jack a few moments of misery would save Peter's life, then so be it.

"I'm sorry, Jack."

Downstairs, Ezra called my name and said we had to get going. I pursed my lips, watching Jack. Part of me expected him to yell and demand that I stay, but that was never his style. He lowered his eyes and rubbed his thumb along the back of my hand, making my skin tremble.

"I'll drive you," Jack whispered and got to his feet.

"What?" Milo asked incredulously. "You're just letting her go?"

Jack still held my hand, so he helped me to my feet. He leaned over and picked up my bag so he could carry it downstairs.

"What am I supposed to do?" Jack gave Milo a helpless shrug as we walked past him.

"I told you! Forbid her from going!" Milo grew nervous and fidgety, traits that were increasingly uncommon with his new-found vampire confidence.

"Yeah, you try forbidding her," Jack muttered.

He held my hand as we went downstairs where Mae and Ezra waited with his luggage. On the table, a small duffel bag was full of special containers.

We survived mostly on blood donations, thanks to a set of clinics they ran similar to the Red Cross. People donated blood thinking it was for blood transfusions in humans, but really, they were sustaining almost the entire species of vampires.

When traveling with blood, we used special equipment. Airport security would find it suspect if Ezra boarded the plane with bags of blood. He used metal cans that looked like shaving cream, lined to make it impossible for dogs to sniff out. We could each only take one can with us, but it just had to be enough to last me the flight. We'd get more when we landed.

Ezra stood next to Mae, sifting through the papers to make sure they were all in order. As soon as I had turned, he got all the documentation set up so I could live my life with them without any suspicion.

That had been a source of contention since I had insisted on keeping my last name Bonham instead of changing it to Townsend, like the rest of them. Nobody had actually cared except for Jack, but he didn't understand why I wouldn't want his last name, especially since that was Milo's last name too.

Someday, I'm sure it would change, but for now, I wanted to hang onto every part of myself that I could, even if it was just my name.

On the plus side, Ezra changed my age to eighteen, so it'd be easier for me to do things if I wasn't a minor. They did the same thing with Milo, even though he was only sixteen, but he looked closer to nineteen.

All of Ezra's information said that he was twenty-nine, even though he had actually been twenty-six when he turned, but it was that way with all of them. Jack was really twenty-four, but his license said he was twenty-seven, and Mae's said that she was thirty-one, even though she was three years younger than that when she turned.

They'd lived this life, this name in this house, for four years already. They wouldn't be able to pull off their ages for much longer, though, which meant that they were going to have to move very soon. As it was, Jack didn't really pass for twenty-seven, and he would never make it as thirty.

"When was the last time you ate?" Ezra asked me but didn't look up from my passport. It was brand new, and he inspected it for any mistakes. As soon as I'd turned, Ezra had gotten me all the paperwork I might need, including a driver's license, birth certificate, and passport.

"Um, yesterday," I said.

There was a constant thirst with me, but it wasn't the same as being thirsty when I was human. My mouth wasn't parched, and my stomach didn't feel empty like I was hungry, either. I just felt this need inside me, coming from everywhere and nowhere all at once.

The closest feeling I could recall is when I ran too fast in gym, and my muscles would start to ache from the oxygen depilation. It would be this slow, swelling cramp that permeated through me. Except now the relief came from blood, accompanied by frantic lust.

I managed to have reasonable control over my bloodlust. Both Milo and I had a stronger grasp of that than most vampires, something that bewildered Ezra and Mae. Our relationship to vampires constantly surprised them, and Ezra thought there was something deeper going on than merely my bond with Peter and Jack.

"Hmm." Ezra eyed me over. "I don't want you to get tired just yet. We'll have to wait until you're on the flight. Do you think you can handle being around people that much on an empty stomach?"

"I think so," I nodded, but I wasn't as certain as I tried to sound.

Since I was so newly turned, blood had a very strong effect on me. Eating felt amazing, but after, I'd be very drowsy and out of it. Usually, I'd just pass out and sleep it off for awhile. Eventually, drinking blood should give me more energy instead of knocking me out, but that was awhile off yet.

On top of that, I had very little experience being around people. I found myself attracted to Jack's blood, and his pulse is significantly weaker than humans. Their blood smelled stronger, pounded harder, and would be far more enticing. I had shown a lot of self-control so far, but in all honesty, I'd had very little temptation.

"Good." Ezra nodded once, then looked at Mae. "Is everything packed then?"

"Yes." She bit her lip when she met his gaze, and she didn't want him to go anymore than Jack wanted me to.

"Well, then." He smiled wanly at me. "Are you ready?"

"Yeah," I nodded again.

He put all the papers in the front pocket of his suitcase and grabbed his bags. Up until that point, I think Milo expected Ezra to tell me that I had to stay behind, but when he saw that we were really serious, he balked loudly.

"You can't really be going!" Milo flared with agitation, and Mae put her hand on his back, rubbing it to ease him down before he went berserk. "This is the dumbest thing I've ever heard! You're going to get her killed!"

"Milo, that's enough," Mae said.

"But... but..." Milo stammered and turned to her for help. "You know this is stupid!"

"Milo." Ezra cut him off decisively, and Milo's face crumpled. "Just say goodbye to your sister before we go."

He cried when he hugged me, which didn't make things easier. He didn't want me to go, and he didn't want to be left behind, but there was very little in the way of options. The one time that he had actually met Peter, it hadn't gone over well, so he wouldn't be able to do anything to help the cause of rescuing Peter.

Mae kissed Ezra with tears in her eyes, and once again asked him if there was anything that could get him to stay. He didn't say anything, but that was as she had expected. Sniffling, she hugged me and made me promise to be safe, to always run at the first sign of trouble, and to call her constantly, whether anything was wrong or not.

When we left, she had her arm wrapped around Milo, and they stood in the entryway, looking terribly forlorn. Jack hadn't said anything as we left, and he continued his silence on the car ride to the airport. He took Ezra's Lexus, and Ezra seemed lost in his own thoughts, trying to figure something out.

The Minneapolis airport was a bustle of human activity. The cold October air felt good on my skin as we walked from the parking lot to the airport, but everything was already filled with the warm, tantalizing scent of blood.

My heart sped up a little, and Jack took my hand, squeezing it to reassure me. Once inside, the feeling only got worse, and I tried to think of sad things, like dead bunnies, to keep my appetite under wraps.

Ezra went to the desk to pick up our tickets while Jack stood with me, waiting in the crowd. Jack was unusually still, but that was for my benefit. I felt everything he felt, so he tried to be calm and soothing so I wouldn't get agitated or hungry.

"I'm going to have to go soon," I said, looking up at him sadly.

"I know."

The crowds around us paused to stare. Before, when I had been out with Jack in public, it drove me crazy the way everyone fawned all over him. Now, I had the same power, and it was incredibly odd having a private moment in front of an audience.

Jack touched my face, his hand warming my cheek, and I leaned into it. Leaving, even for a short time, would be so painful, but it was the only thing I could do. I couldn't live with myself if I didn't do everything to help Peter.

Gently, he pressed his lips against mine, and his luscious heart beat through my skin. He kept it soft and very PG, because I didn't want to get out of control in a crowded airport. Still, nothing was sweeter than his kisses, and I couldn't help but want more.

"The plane is going to board soon," Ezra interrupted us, not unkindly. "We need to get through baggage claims and security."

Reluctantly, I pulled myself from Jack. His eyes locked on mine, and my heart screamed. It'd just finally dawned on me what I was about to do. Separating myself from Jack to sleep was uncomfortable. Being miles and miles away for I don't even know how long... that sounded unbearable.

"I'll take good care of her," Ezra promised when Jack seemed unwilling to let me go.

Ezra took my hand in his, partially to help coax me away from Jack and partially so he could keep tabs on me. This was not the most ideal place for a new vampire's first big outing, and everyone knew that.

Jack let go of my hand, and as Ezra carefully guided me through the crowds past the first set of metal detectors, my eyes never left Jack's. He just stood in the middle of the airport, staring after me, like some tragic music video, and I wondered what exactly I had gotten myself into when I became a vampire.

- 3 -

My transformation from human to vampire had been so incredibly brutal that the English language isn't fit to describe it.

My body died and ate itself. My organs shifted around, feeling as if my intestines had been replaced with living, moving snakes that squirmed inside of me. I spent hours upon hours vomiting. I was in a constant state of fevered delirium. My body ached on a cellular level. Even touching my hair would cause excruciating pain.

It wasn't until I finally drank blood for the first time, cold from a bag, that everything began to take a turn for the better. The pain subsided and was replaced by pleasure.

All my senses were heightened, and I couldn't believe how glorious everything really was. There were more colors, tastes, and textures in the spectrum than I ever imagined.

I felt Jack when he entered the room, and not like before. My heart always knew exactly how far he was from me. The way plants strained for the sun, I strained for him.

I had changed. My skin was smoother, my hair silkier, my eyes brighter. While I hadn't exactly been fat before, I had a new elegance to how I looked.

The change wasn't as drastic as it had been with Milo, more like I had simply gone through a makeover, but I definitely looked better. And I had shot up from 5'3" to a whopping 5'5" feet tall.

Once I was fully conscious, fed, and the pain had gone away, I wanted to fill in the missing gap. The last thing I remembered before surrendering into the transformation was that I had just drank Jack's blood, and he was about to battle Peter.

But here we were, in Jack's room, with him by my side, and we both seemed alright.

"What happened?" I asked, forcing myself to sit up in his bed.

"When?" Jack played dumb. He sat at the end of his bed, watching me.

"How are we both alive?" I asked, and he laughed, completely distracting me.

His laughter, which had always had power over me, rippled through me. It was almost too miraculous to really comprehend the actual sound.

"You look totally in awe right now," Jack smirked at me.

"I am but... don't change the subject." I blinked to focus myself. "How are we alive? Is Peter..."

Jack's lips tightened into a thin line at the mention of him. Maybe it wasn't the sound of his name quite as much as my underlying concern, but he pushed aside his feelings and decided that I deserved an explanation.

"No. He's alive." He let his words hang in the air, and I waited for him to elaborate, but he didn't.

"How? How are you both alive?" I asked.

"I broke the bond." The glimmer returned to his eyes and an easy smile spread across his face, enchanting me. "When you drank my blood, whatever tie you had with Peter was severed."

That should've been obvious. As soon as I thought of Peter, I didn't have that physical ache for him or that fluttery feeling in my heart. While I had concern for his well-being, the only things I felt physically were a dull bloodlust and a pull towards Jack.

"So we're... bonded now?" I spoke cautiously, afraid it was too good to be true.

After all this time trying to figure a way around it, around Peter, it almost seemed impossible to believe that while I was sleeping, it had happened.

"What do you think?" Jack smiled crookedly at me. Breathing him in, feeling the way my body felt magnetized to his, I knew we were bonded.

My first big clue was when Jack had opened his veins in the den, and I had been unable to resist the scent of his blood. It tasted wonderful, and my mouth watered at the thought of it. But no vampires' blood should be that appealing to humans. People aren't meant to have bloodlust, but I did, for Jack.

"So then what happened?" I continued, ignoring the delirious happiness taking over me. My heart sped up and my thirst intensified, but I wanted my curiosity satisfied before I dealt with my other pressing needs.

"I don't know." Jack furrowed his brow, but more out of displeasure over the subject. "I was in the den with you, and Peter went crazy in the other room. I was afraid he would hurt you, so I ran out to find out what happened. He was destroying the house, and Ezra could barely contain him. But he didn't seem to care about me when I came out."

"But why? If he didn't want to hurt you, why was he so angry?"

"He felt it break." He lowered his eyes from mine. "The bond. If you hadn't been out, you would've felt it. And if you hadn't bonded with me, you'd still be feeling it. Apparently, it's... incredibly painful."

"Why?" I asked.

"I don't know." He shifted and hesitated before continuing. "Physically, I guess it's similar to turning, but on a smaller scale. But... something happens emotionally too. And Peter was so riled up from everything else that had been going on."

Jack didn't like talking about the fact that Peter had actually cared for me. He didn't want to believe it because of how Peter treated me and how much Jack loved me. If he admitted that maybe Peter did truly love me, then what Jack had been doing with me suddenly became a betrayal, and Jack did not see it that way.

"So where is he now?" I asked.

"Nobody knows. He's just gone, for good this time." Jack shrugged, as if it was of no consequence to him.

"Good," I lied and hoped he didn't notice. Then I swatted his arm, probably harder than I meant to from the surprised grimace on his face.

"Thanks?"

"That's for being the biggest idiot ever! How could you do something so stupid?" I yelled at him, and it was a tough decision not to hit him again. "You were going to kill yourself! If the bond hadn't been snapped or whatever, you would've been murdered!"

"I didn't have a choice," Jack said, and he suppressed a laugh at my mini-outburst. "There was a good chance that I would die no matter what I did. In case you haven't noticed, I'm a lover, not a fighter."

"That's not an excuse," I said, but a smile started to curl up at my lips.

"I just needed to know you were safe. That was the only thing that mattered to me," he said earnestly and placed his hand on mine.

Heat instantly spread through me, making my heart flutter. I lunged forward, kissing him and pressing my body against his. He gave into it for a moment, but hunger threatened to completely take control of my body. Just when I was about to let it, he pushed me back from him, and that's when I got the big sex talk.

After a few days of getting my bloodlust under control, Ezra thought it would be good if I went about cleaning up what was left of my human life. That meant doing fun things, like going with Jack to my mom's house so we could have this incredibly intense fight when I said that I was moving in with Jack, again. She tried to convince me to stay, then cried a lot, called me names and told me she loved me.

When it was all said and done, she stormed off into the night. I packed up my things, and since I felt incredible guilt, I "borrowed" money from Jack to leave her. Maybe she wouldn't have to work so hard, and at least that would be something.

Milo called her after I left, as he had been infrequently doing since he moved out. He got to make up all sorts of fancy stories about a boarding school in New York, and that seemed to cheer her up a bit.

I formally dropped out of high school, which I enjoyed. Milo insisted that we both take our high school equivalency later so we could go to college if we wanted, and I agreed to it, but I didn't really have any intention of doing it. As far as I was concerned, I could spend the rest of my life as a trophy wife, and that was fine by me.

There was the issue with my "best friend" Jane, but I didn't know how to resolve that. When I went to the high school, she saw me and instantly figured out what had happened. I still looked like me, but I was hotter than I had been before, maybe even hotter than her.

It was during the day, so I was incredibly tired. We exchanged a few heated words, and she ended the conversation with the flippant, "I hope you have a good death."

Meanwhile, my life as a vampire was pretty damn awesome. There were missteps of getting the handle on walking, moving, breathing, eating… all the basic skills I had taken for granted before. But I was completely and totally in love with Jack, and I had just started spending the rest of eternity with him.

What could I possibly have to feel bad about?

- 4 -

When the plane started to take off, I thought I might throw up. My fingers squeezed the arms of the seat so tightly that I'd break them if I wasn't careful. I'd never been on a plane before, and it scared the hell out me.

This amused Ezra endlessly. He chuckled warmly at my stricken expression as the engines came on, making all sorts of whirring and clicking noises that sounded like death to me. I looked out the window at the dark night around us and imagined the plane crashing into the runway and bursting into flames.

"First time flier?" A woman across the aisle looked over at us.

"She'll be fine," Ezra cut her off shortly, and I was too busy being terrified to comment on his rudeness. When he looked back at me, he smiled.

"You could say something comforting," I suggested in a thin, anxious voice.

"Why? This is distracting you from thinking about other things going on around you," Ezra said. "It's less than a three hour flight to New York, and I'd like to wait for you to eat until the next flight."

By "other things" he meant the other passengers, who flooded the red-eye with the scent of their blood, and the plane wasn't even that full. I'd had just eaten yesterday, which meant I wouldn't need to eat for another five or six days, but I wasn't great at controlling my hunger.

"Mmm, sounds great," I muttered. Unfortunately, he had a point. My current level of fear made it almost impossible to notice my thirst.

"Really, you should be enjoying this," he said with a wry smile. "There's only a small window left where you'll be able to feel fear like this."

"Oh, yeah, this is totally awesome."

"Let me give you a little tip." He leaned in towards me, lowering his voice so it would be inaudible to anyone around us. "Even if the plane does crash, you'll survive. You're immortal now."

It hadn't dawned on me yet. I was a vampire, and I wasn't going to die in a plane crash.

My fingers relaxed on the arm rest. Still, whenever we hit turbulence, I'd grip onto Ezra for dear life, but he'd just chuckle.

I tried to enjoy the rest of the flight, but it was dark, and even with my improved vision, there wasn't much to see out the window. Ezra brought some books on tracking, and he went through them, even though I'm sure he'd read them before. He'd probably read everything ever written.

"Where are we going anyway?" I asked him quietly. Most other passengers were sleeping, and I didn't want to wake them.

"New York City," Ezra replied without looking up from his book. "And then to Finland."

"Finland?" I raised my eyebrow, completely caught off guard by his answer. "Peter's in *Finland*?"

"I believe so." He flipped a page. "Scandinavia has always been his favorite place to hide out, especially in winter. There's hardly daylight for months, and the temperatures are usually below freezing."

"So we're just going there because that's where he usually goes?" I still couldn't wrap my mind around Peter hanging out in Finland. That just didn't sound… exotic enough?

"No. Peter's had a run-in in Finland. I don't know exactly where he is, but I'm certain he's there," Ezra said.

"A 'run-in?' What happened?"

"I'm not entirely sure," he said at length. "And I'd rather not speculate."

"You'd rather not speculate?" I repeated. "I'm on a plane flying half-way across the world, and not only do you not know where we're going, but you'd rather not even speculate on *why* we're going?"

"Finland is not half-way around the world," Ezra corrected me.

"Whatever." I sunk down in my seat and crossed my arms over my chest. "I can't speak Finnish."

"You don't need to. I can." He flipped another page in his book, and I sighed.

"You're gonna be a hoot to travel with if you're like this whole time," I muttered, and he laughed to himself.

I borrowed a book from Ezra so I had something to do with the rest the flight. After a couple hours of reading about native Finnish wildlife, I vowed to get as many magazines and books as I could when we landed at JFK. That was my plan until we actually started de-boarding the plane, and Ezra grasped my hand in his.

"There's a layover here," Ezra told me quietly as we walked.

"You can't eat until we get on the next plane, because you're a mess when you eat. I need you to stay by me and never let go of my hand, no matter what. Is that clear?"

"Yeah but…." I was about to ask him why, but then we were stepping beyond the plane, and the smell hit me for the first time.

There hadn't been that many people in the Minneapolis airport. In fact, I would go so far as to say there weren't even that many people in Minneapolis. JFK terminal is a city unto itself, full of hot, sweaty people pressed up against each other.

Suddenly, my thirst appeared with a vengeance.

Waiting in the airport was torture. Most of the time, I had to grip Ezra's hand so tightly, I don't know how I didn't break a bone or something. I sat rigidly, my eyes locked on my shoes in front of me.

Ezra sat next to me, a leg crossed over his knee, with a magazine open on his lap and telling me all about Martha Stewart's recommendations for making Halloween treats. He was trying to keep me calm and focused, but hearing about making Rice Krispies treats orange made me want to vomit.

Going through security was very hard, but Ezra told me to keep saying the alphabet backwards in my head. It didn't really soften the burning thirst inside of me, and I kept my eyes locked on the throbbing pulse in the security guard's neck, but I didn't bite him. So I counted that as a success.

Ezra gave me the window seat and belted me in, which made both of us feel better. I closed my eyes and tried not to think of Jack. He lurked painfully in my thoughts and only made my bloodlust increase. The whole situation felt very precarious, and I started to think that I wasn't ready for this trip.

When the engines of the plane revved, Ezra leaned over and whispered, "If the plane crashes, it'll be in the ocean. The ocean's full of sharks, and they can kill us. You actually have something to be afraid of this time."

"Is that supposed to comfort me?" I asked through gritted teeth.

"No, not at all. I wanted to scare the hell of out you so you'd stop thinking about... things." He squeezed my hand back, and that felt reassuring somehow. "But it's still true. Sharks are brutal."

The instant we were free to move about, Ezra grabbed the cans of blood from the overhead bin and led me back to the restrooms. We got a lot of weird looks from the other passengers and the flight crew, but nobody stopped us. I doubted that any humans ever stopped Ezra. He was too beautiful and confident.

There was hardly enough room in the bathroom for one person, let alone two, so he swiftly lifted me up and set me on the sink. He set the cans on my lap, and I imagined that I could smell it and trembled with hunger.

"You are so pale," Ezra murmured to himself. He pushed a strand of hair out of my face and looked at me fully in the eyes, inspecting them for their level of hunger. "I'm going to give you two cans, okay?"

"Yeah, whatever, fine," I nodded quickly. I didn't care at all what he said as long as I got the blood.

"This is gonna hit you hard, but I need you to walk back out to your seat, okay?" Ezra said. "And you can pass out as soon as you sit down."

"Okay!" I snapped.

He pursed his lips but unscrewed the can. The small room instantly filled with the scent, and I ripped it from his hands and guzzled it down. As soon as it slid down my throat, ease grew in my muscles. Even though the blood was very cold, it spread hot through my body.

Before I even finished the first can, Ezra opened another one. He wanted me to get them down me as fast as possible, so we had a chance of me making it back to my seat before I blitzed out.

After I drank them both, he shoved the empty cans in the garbage. I licked my lips clean, but he inspected me for any blood on my face. The world already had that hazy glow to it, and a wonderful tranquil feeling wanted to take over.

With Ezra so close to me, I had the strangest urge to kiss him. That was just the blood talking, so I lowered my head before I could act on it.

We walked back to our seats, him with his arm on me to steady me. It took all my strength to keep from stumbling or doing anything ridiculous. All the colors seemed to shine brighter. My green sweater looked like grass, and I wanted to pet it, but Ezra was sliding me into the seat.

"How are you feeling?" he whispered as he buckled me back in.

"Dreamy," I murmured with a dazed smile on my lips.

Before he could put the bag back in the overhead compartment, I passed out. Even with his new threats about sharks and the gnawing ache for Jack, I slept soundlessly the entire way to Finland.

Ezra shook me awake, and while I'd been sleeping, he'd gotten me a pillow and blanket. He had a blanket folded on his lap, and I wondered if he'd slept at all.

"We're about to touch down in Helsinki," Ezra informed me.

"Really?" I yawned and stretched, then looked out my window. It was dark out, but the city was aglow with twinkly lights. "What time is it?"

"It's ten o'clock, Wednesday," he said.

"Oh." My brain scrambled to figure when we left, but it didn't seem right. "Wait. Didn't we leave at ten on Tuesday?"

"There's a time difference. You might suffer a bit of jet lag," he said.

"I hope not." I didn't even really know what jet lag was, but it didn't sound like something I'd want to suffer from.

A flight attendant came to collect our blankets, and the captain came on, saying things about making the descent into Helsinki. He repeated the same message in Finnish, or at least I assumed he did since I didn't understand a word of it.

As we got closer, the city looked much more stunning than I expected. In my mind, it had been more of a cold, desolate place, but in reality, it was glamorous and historical, the way I imagined Paris or London might be. Not that I had ever seen either of them to have any real comparison.

"This is where Peter went to live off the grid?" I asked as I admired the architecture.

"No, he's not here." Ezra shook his head. "We have one more flight to make."

"Really?" I wrinkled my nose. Even though I had slept through this flight, my body felt stiff.

"Just up to northern Finland, in the Lapland," Ezra said as if that meant anything to me. "I'll explain more once we land. We have another layover."

"Fantastic," I sighed.

We got off the plane, and Ezra got everything sorted for the next flight. I made sure to hang out by a large window. I was determined to admire the view of Helsinki. Not that there was a view from the airport. It was mostly planes, landing strips, and traffic. But that was more than I had seen in New York.

"It really is a beautiful city," Ezra said, coming up to stand next to me.

We watched a plane taxi down the runway. He knew I was trying to catch a glimpse of something I would miss entirely. I sighed but refused to leave my post at the window.

"You've stayed here before?" I asked.

"Many times, mostly before Mae." He nodded. "I've managed to drag her out here a few times, but she doesn't like to leave Minnesota very much. But Peter loves it here."

"How come?"

"The cold, the dark, the wilderness, the seclusion. He stays further up north. They have a few national parks and some ski resorts. And Helsinki, Stockholm, Amsterdam, they're not that far away, whenever he requires bustling city life."

The way he said "*life*" I knew he meant more than dinner and a show. Actually, he just meant dinner. Peter might enjoy isolation, but he needed a population to eat, preferably a mixture of vampires and people. Vampire bars and blood banks made eating so much easier, and the fewer the people, the less the options.

"So that's where we're going? Up north?" I turned to Ezra. "What'd you call it? The Lapland?"

"Yeah. It's the northern most territory in Finland." He took a deep breath, and he sounded reluctant when he continued. "There's something I haven't told you."

"There's lots of things you haven't told me."

"This is important." He licked his lips and shifted his gaze. "You've heard stories of werewolves, right?"

My stomach dropped. Sure, I may be a vampire, but there were certain things I couldn't take. Like finding out an endless stream of monsters and folklore were real. After this, maybe we'd roll with a Yeti or go swimming with the Lochness Monster and a Leprechaun.

There had to be some point where fiction remained fiction, and I was determined that it ended immediately after vampires.

"No, no, no." I shook my head. "Jack told me there weren't any werewolves. There's no such thing."

"No, there's not," Ezra agreed. "Shape shifting of any kind is an impossibility. Or at least as far as I know."

"So..." My heart slowed a little, but he was still holding something back. "Why even bring them up?"

"You've heard the stories about them, though, haven't you?" His deep brown eyes looked at me intently.

"Yeah," I answered uncertainly.

My knowledge of werewolves was very limited, and mostly based on Michael J. Fox's portrayal in *Teen Wolf*. I had never thought the film was very factual, because I couldn't imagine how surfing on a van could be possible, werewolf or not. The only thing I carried from it was that wolves were good at basketball. This information did not seem pertinent to the situation.

"How the full moon makes them come out, and they attack without reproach?" Ezra went on. "They turn into vicious animals, unfettered by remorse or logic."

"Okay, sure," I nodded, hoping he would just hurry and make his point.

"Do you remember when I told you about the vampires I had encountered when I first turned?" He grew more solemn. "They were … rabid animals."

"You're not… they're not…" I faltered. "What are you saying exactly?"

"Sometimes, some vampires, either by choice or just by design, don't ever fully civilize," he explained carefully. "The ones that are entirely primeval are killed quickly. Even vampires can't stomach rampant monsters. But some willfully seek out a different life, one separate from people and humanity.

"We believe the early stories of werewolves are based on vampires living like this." He took a deep breath and looked out at the night sky. "In small packs they hunt together, living more like animals than people. By necessity, they can't kill most of their food, but they want to hunt and kill. They hunt big game, like bears and elk, even wolves. Not for food, but for sport."

"People do that too," I interjected, but I'm not sure what point I was making with that.

"We call them lycans. It's short for lycanthrope, which just means werewolf. It's a little inside joke for vampires." Ezra smiled at me with that, but I didn't really think it was funny. "Lycan, I think, just means wolf in Greek."

"This was a roundabout way of giving me a lesson in Greek?" I asked dryly.

"There's a pack of lycan that live in the Finnish Lapland," he ignored me. "I've come across them before, but it's an ever changing group, with only the leader remaining. He's a sadist, and the life expectancy for his pack isn't anywhere near what it is for the average vampire, or even for other lycans. They're known for their brutality, and they've killed people and vampires indiscriminately."

I swallowed hard and focused on the bright lights flashing outside of the window. By now, I figured out how this story ended up with us here, waiting for a plane to take us to the lycan. Our destination was very much connected with theirs.

"Last week, Peter killed a member of their pack. They want revenge, and they won't stop until they get him. And, Peter, in his current state, seems happy to offer himself up," Ezra said quietly. "We have to find him before they do."

I could barely control my own bloodlust, but we were going out to the wilderness to track down a pack of crazed werewolves-cum-vampires so we could save a vampire that tried to kill me before. It all made perfect sense.

"Alice?" Ezra asked when I just kept staring out the window. "Do you have any questions?"

"Nope." I shook my head. "But Jack's gonna be so pissed when he finds out what we're doing."

- 5 -

The hotel was a cross between a Holiday Inn and a hunting lodge, with fireplaces and antlers hanging on the wall, but I was still pleasantly surprised by the set up. After another flight, followed by a short drive in a rental car and a brief stop at a local blood bank to stock up, we checked into the hotel.

Our room had hardwood floors, and it had that same nice, generic look any other hotel would have. They had internet access and a television. Based on the amount of cars in the parking lot, it was relatively busy.

Ezra busied himself with unpacking, while I had just dropped my luggage on one of the beds. I claimed the double bed closer to the window.

"I'm going to take a shower," Ezra said and gathered up his change of clothes and toiletries. "Then we'll get some rest and have a go at finding Peter tomorrow."

"Do we really have time to waste?" I tried to ask without accusation. We left in such a hurry, and I wasn't sure how imminent the danger was.

"We have to rest, or I'll be of no use to Peter." He shrugged, as if he couldn't see any way around it.

Once he'd gone in the bathroom and I heard the shower running, I changed into my pajamas. They felt tremendous after spending the past twenty hours or so stuck in jeans and a sweater.

I had gotten sleep on the plane ride over the ocean, and with the time difference, I'd just be getting up in Minneapolis. Plus, Ezra had amped me up when he dropped the news that we were really chasing after werewolfian vampires, so I didn't feel like sleeping.

I pulled out my cell phone, and I was surprised to find that I had a signal (subconsciously I guess I had been thinking that Finland was in the stone ages).

Crossing my fingers, I sat down on the bed and hoped Jack'd be awake. This had been the longest we'd gone without talking to each other since I'd turned, and it felt very strange. Like the chemicals in my body were off-balance without him.

"Hello?" Jack sounded frantic when he answered the phone. "Alice? Are you okay? Is everything okay?"

"Yeah, yeah, I'm fine." Irrational tears welled up in my eyes. It was stupid how much I missed him. "We just got to the hotel. I was calling to let you know that we got in alright."

"Good. Good." He was genuinely relieved but didn't relax. "How was your flight?"

"I slept through most of it," I said. "This is my first time being out of the Midwest, though, and it sucks. I was in New York City, and I didn't see any of it. I barely got a glimpse of Helsinki when we were coming in."

"You're in *Finland?*" Jack yelled, and I realized that I might've said too much. "That's where Peter's in trouble with vampires?"

"Um…" I shifted on the bed, thinking of a line to feed him.

"They're not really vampires, are they? It's lycan." He sighed when I didn't say anything, and he held the phone away from his mouth. "Mae! Mae!"

"Why are you yelling at Mae?"

"Because. If she knew that's what you guys were doing-"

"What?" I interrupted him. "What would she do?"

He grumbled something under his breath but didn't have a follow-up for that. Even if Mae had known about it before we left, she would've tried just as hard to talk Ezra out of it. Ezra hadn't told anybody where we were going for that reason. He had made up his mind, and he didn't want to waste time fighting about it.

"I should get on a plane right now," Jack said.

"Don't be silly. Ezra wouldn't let anything happen to me. I'm just here to try to talk Peter into coming back, not to fight any stupid vampires," I said.

"Peter doesn't *need* to come back," he muttered.

"Have you been to Finland?" I quickly changed the subject. I couldn't make him feel good about me being here, but maybe I could distract him enough where he worried a little less.

"Yeah, once, a few years back," he said disdainfully. "We went skiing, and it was terrible. I broke a snowboard and rolled down the hill. It wasn't that fun. Finland's not that great. You should just come home."

"Jack." I smiled when I pictured him tumbling down a hill, but it faded when he went back to trying to convince me to leave. "You're wasting this call. My phone's going to die, and I don't have a charger. Do you really wanna spend this time arguing with me, when you know you're not going to change my mind?"

"Yeah, I kind of do," he replied. "Besides, I'm sure Ezra has a charger that'll work there, and you can use that."

A few weeks ago, Jack bought me an iPhone. It was the exact same phone that both Ezra and Jack had, so if Ezra had a charger, it worked on mine.

"Ezra speaks Finnish," I said, keeping the subject away from Peter or coming home. "It's pretty fancy, although I can't understand a word of it."

"Ezra is fluent in like every language known to man, even the dead ones. He thought he was so cool when he watched *The Passion of the Christ* without subtitles because can he speak Aramaic, but I'm pretty sure that's the *only* time that'll ever come in handy." Jack lightened up, just a tad, and it made me smile.

"Can you speak any other languages?" I asked.

"Spanish and German," he informed me with pride. "I learned Spanish in high school, and German in college, so I'm not fluent in either. But I can ask if you speak English in both languages, and I think that's the only thing I really need to know."

"Yeah, that sounds helpful," I laughed, but my happiness made fresh tears in my eyes. "I miss you."

"I miss you too. You can come home, Alice, whenever you want. No pressure."

"I know. But I have to help. It shouldn't be that long, I don't think. We'll find Peter, and then come straight home."

Jack started saying something about the Finnish wilderness being complex, but Ezra came out of the bathroom, distracting me. He had changed into flannel pajama pants and a tee shirt, and he ruffled his hand through his damp hair, looking at me questioningly.

"It's just Jack," I told him, holding the phone a little way from my mouth.

"Ezra's there? Let me talk to him!" Jack demanded.

"You don't need to talk to him," I sighed.

"I take it he knows we're in Finland then?" Ezra asked me, and I nodded sheepishly. "Oh well. He'd find out sooner or later."

"Look, Jack, I should get some sleep anyway. I'll call you soon and let you know how things are going," I said. Ezra rolled down the teal bedspread, meaning he was getting ready for bed and I should probably do the same.

"Alice..." Jack was almost whining, and he realized it so he stopped. "Just call me soon, really soon. And take care of yourself, okay?"

"I will," I promised.

When I hung up the phone, I fought the overwhelming urge to sob. Hearing his voice only made things worse. My heart ached in my chest, and my body felt completely out of whack. I hated that I could barely even survive being away from Jack.

"You didn't have to get off the phone because of me," Ezra said.

I swallowed back tears, staring down at my phone, and heard the rustle of blankets as he settled himself into bed. Even though I'd just gotten off the phone, I thought about calling Jack back. It wouldn't do any good to make me feel better, so I decided against it.

"I know," I said. Setting my phone on the nightstand, I crawled underneath the covers myself. "Are you going to call Mae?"

"Not until I know anything. Jack can fill her in." He rolled onto his stomach and rested his head on the pillow. "Are you going to be okay with all of this?"

"Yeah, I'm fine," I nodded, and I wasn't sure if I was lying or not.

Rolling over so my back was to him, I allowed a few silent tears to slide down my cheeks. He didn't say anything, and eventually, his breathing had the regulated quality that comes with sleep. Unfortunately, sleep wouldn't be as easy for me.

Ezra tore open the shades while the sun was still up, and I squinted and pulled the blankets over my head. The little experience I had with the sun so far made me tired and cranky, and I had no urge to relive that. Fully dressed and whistling an old Neil Young song, Ezra went about the room, and I knew it was time to get up.

"What time is it?" I mumbled, still buried underneath the thin hotel comforter.

"It's a little after one, but we need to get going. We're burning daylight." He chuckled at his own joke, and I was starting to think that I didn't agree with his sense of humor.

"You're actually expecting me to get up now?" I poked my head out, braving the blinding light that filled the room.

"We do need to get going." He checked something on his phone, then he glanced back at the open window. "I can close the shades, if that helps."

"You know it does," I yawned.

Ezra complied, still fiddling around with his phone, and I hoped that meant that he had a lead on something. His half of the room was already completely straightened up, the bed made and everything, and

I wondered what time he had gotten up.

"I wish I still drank coffee or Red Bull or something," I said as I stumbled out of bed and made my way to the bathroom. (Fun fact: Vampires still pee. Blood is a liquid, after all.)

"Just take a cold shower. That'll perk you right up," he said.

Following his advice, I took a quick, cold shower, and it helped some. I dressed in a hurry and blow dried my hair so it wouldn't freeze outside.

The hotel was alive with people today, and I pulled my scarf over my mouth and nose to muffle it. When we were walking out, I noticed the décor in the hotel was distinctly green. Potted plants were everywhere, probably to counteract the long winters and oblique white window views. I enjoyed winter, but it would be odd to live in a place that had snow eight months out of the year.

It really wasn't that cold out, only in the low thirties, but I bundled up in a winter jacket and boots, like any normal person would. There wasn't that much snow yet, only enough to crunch underneath my feet.

"So what's the plan?" I followed him out of the building, and he walked towards the silver Range Rover he'd rented yesterday.

"We're going for a drive," Ezra answered vaguely, and I wondered if he was purposely infuriating or if it was just force of habit. He got in the driver's side, so I hopped in.

Without looking, he whipped the Rover into reverse and sped out away from the hotel. Usually, he was a mild driver, but it became apparent where Jack's driving skills came from. As he sped down the road, I pulled my hood up over my head and sunk lower in my seat, hiding myself from the sun's rays as much as I could.

"How is this gonna work?" I yawned when we'd been on the road for ten minutes. Already, I felt like napping, and I knew as the day wore on, I would only get sleepier.

"We'll be in tree cover most of the time." He motioned to the thick pine trees that filled the world around us. "You have your hood and sunglasses, and when we get back in the morning, we'll both eat. We'll be fine."

We traveled about a half hour or so when he turned off the road and parked in a small clearing. I'd been dozing a bit, but I sat up when the vehicle stopped. I leaned over to inspect the GPS system in the dash, hoping to find a clue about where we were. Finnish words and names looked like gibberish to me, so I didn't gain any insight.

"Okay. What's going on?" I asked, but Ezra turned off the car and jumped out in response. "Thanks."

I scrambled out after him, and I slipped on an icy patch of snow. When I tried to catch my fall by grabbing onto the car, I only succeeded in denting the side. It was pretty awesome having almost no control over my body. I couldn't wait for the grace and strength to really kick in.

"Are you coming?" Ezra paused long enough for me to collect myself and scurry after him.

"Yeah. Where are we going?" I asked when I caught up with him.

"The woods." We were already walking into a very thick patch of trees, so he was doing nothing more than stating the obvious.

"You're really becoming my least favorite person," I muttered as

I nearly tripped over a fallen log.

"I don't know exactly where we're going," he reluctantly admitted. "I just know the area we're supposed to be in, and this is it."

We were in the shadows thanks to cover of trees, so at least that was something. Looking around, though, everything appeared the same as everything. Evergreens blanketed the area, and somewhere up ahead, I could hear a river flowing.

Other than that, I had no idea how Ezra could tell one tree from another, or how he could possibly have any clue where we were. He was much more familiar with the area than I was, but I couldn't see what distinguished these trees from the rest.

"Where are we?" I stopped walking and stared up through the trees at the sky.

"The lycan live around here."

I would've liked to press him further about it, but he didn't want to talk. Ezra didn't even slow down for me, so I learned my lesson about stopping for no reason. We trekked through the trees all afternoon, and while the sun didn't directly shine on me, I felt a burst of energy when it finally went down.

Once night closed in completely, Ezra started to wait for me and insisted I stay close to him. During the day, other vampires were much less likely to be out, which was why he wanted to check things out then.

The biggest excitement of the night was when we saw a few reindeer walking in front of us. Ezra explained that many Europeans say that this is where Santa Clause lives, not the North Pole, partially because of the large reindeer population. We weren't that far south from the North Pole anyway, so it wasn't much of a stretch.

By the time the sun started to rise, I was completely exhausted. There's a myth that vampires don't ever get tired or run out of energy, and Ezra did seem to exemplify that. Maybe I'm just a wuss. I don't really know. We made the long walk through the trees back to the car, and I was incredibly relieved when I sat down inside the Range Rover.

The gnawing hunger set in a few hours ago. Ezra's pulse had gotten more noticeable, and my hands exhibited a fine tremor. The early morning light that filtered in through the windows only made it worse.

When we got back to the hotel, I must've been jonesing noticeably because Ezra put his arm securely around me when we walked inside. It was after seven in the morning, so the breakfast crowd filled the dining room. The scent of eggs and deer sausage made me sick. Over that, I smelled the delectable scent of blood, and I was grateful for Ezra's strong arm steering me towards our room.

Once inside, I peeled off my jacket and kicked off my boots.

"That was a total waste of a day," I said, squirming about the room. My clothes felt too heavy and uncomfortable, and it was hard not to take them off.

Ezra turned the temperature down low and filled the bathtub with ice and blood bags before we left last night, so the blood was still cool and intact. While I was in the room twitching and not taking off my clothes, he was in the bathroom getting food for us.

"We figured some things out." Ezra came out of the bathroom

with a several bags of blood. "Tomorrow we'll have a better idea of where we need to go."

The blood was in sight so any petty complaint I had didn't matter anymore. I practically ripped it from his hands. I downed it, and Ezra watched me with an odd look of fascination on his face. That wonderful warming effect spread over me, and I held out my hand for a second bag.

"Get ready for bed first," he shook his head. "I'm not getting you in your pajamas after you're passed out."

"Fine. Look away."

He did as he was told, and I took off my clothes as quickly as I could. That didn't end up being all that fast because that tired, loose feeling took over me, and I almost fell over just taking off my shirt. When putting on my pajama pants, I fell back on the bed and didn't bother to get up again.

"Done," I announced and held out my hand to him.

"You're going to have to learn to take it easier on these. I don't think I packed enough for you to keep going at this rate," he warned, but he handed it to me.

"I thought you'd be an over packer," I said before gulping it down.

"I am." He looked at me severely and sat on his bed across from me.

"It's the sun." My words already slurred. "The sun is super draining. I don't think I can go back out in it again, not like that. And then walking around for like seventeen hours? It's just too much for me…"

"It's not too much for you." He shook his head as he watched me struggle to stay conscious. "You have almost infinite power, Alice. You've got to stop thinking like you're human."

"You are!" I spouted, but clearly, that didn't make sense.

"Yes, of course, I am," he rolled his eyes.

I started to ask him a question, but I didn't even know what it was. Pleasure rolled over me, and I didn't want to fight it anymore. Ezra wanted me to express more self-control, but then again, he claimed that I *was* expressing self-control.

If this was me under control compared to other vampires, then I'd hate to see what they were like.

"Oh… the lycans are worse than this, aren't they?" I groaned.

"I don't really understand the question." Ezra got up and walked over to me. "Why don't you get some sleep, Alice? You've had a long day. Get under the covers."

If Ezra had been driven on his pursuit of Peter the first day, the next day he was relentless. I refused to go out in the sun, so he let me sleep until four in the afternoon, but I'm not sure how much sleep he'd gotten. Using his phone and his laptop, he'd been busy trying to get coordinates for where he thought Peter would be.

When I got up, I responded to a couple text messages from Jack, got ready, and we left. Over ten hours later, I found myself in the middle of the Finnish Laplands, staring up at the spectacle of lights above me.

Dazzling green lights flashed across the clear night sky. We had crossed a river when I happened to look up and notice the aurora borealis dancing above us. I stopped on the frozen shore and stared at them in awe. They were breathtakingly beautiful, and even Ezra paused and looked.

My attention shifted from the Northern Lights when I heard a rustling sound coming from the woods. I could see something dark shifting through the trees, and I caught a whiff of the familiar farm-y smell of reindeer. A few yards down the river from us, six huge reindeer came barreling out through the trees and charged across a shallow part of the river.

"Alice," Ezra whispered. He took a step back towards me, holding his arm out in front of me.

"What? They're just reindeer. Did you have a run in with Blitzen once?" I teased, but he hissed at me.

"They wouldn't be running like that at this time of night unless something was chasing them." His words were nearly drowned out in the splashing as they tore across the river.

I moved closer to Ezra, and strained to see what could be following the reindeer. I crossed my fingers for wolves, but I had a feeling that it was a something a little more anthropomorphic than that. Once the reindeer plummeted back in the woods, other than the sound of their depleting hooves, there was an odd silence.

Straining, I realized that wasn't exactly right. There was silence, but not silence. I could see things, but not things. It was like every time I almost caught something, it was gone before I could even register it. Almost as if there was a ghost spooking the deer, and I thought hopefully, maybe it was just the run-of-the-mill ghost.

"Alice!" Ezra shouted suddenly and grabbed my arm.

- 6 -

The river splashed directly in front of us. Literally out of nowhere, a man leapt into the river. When the black water settled around him, I got a look at him under the glowing green lights.

He was shirtless, revealing well-muscled arms. His black hair went past his ears, and he was very attractive. But something in his black eyes unnerved me.

He stared at us, making my heart hammer nervously in my chest, and I was about to say something to break the tension, but I saw movement behind him.

Across the river, walking deliberately slow, two more vampires came out from the trees. They stood on the shore opposite us, flanking the one in the water, but they looked less imposing.

They were barefoot and wore ragged clothes. The blondish one on the right looked amused.

The other one appeared to be embarrassed about this little confrontation. He kept his dark brown hair shorter than the other two, but he had a thick stubble on his face. While he was well-toned, he was smaller than the others.

His eyes were the thing that caught me the most. They were gentle and large, reminding me of a puppy.

In the water, the first vampire crouched down lower, poised for an attack, and my mind raced to think of a way out of it. Mae and

Jack warned me to run, but I couldn't outrun him. I wasn't even sure if Ezra could. He had to have some kind of super speed to appear out of nowhere like that.

"We don't mean to bother you," I said weakly, and Ezra squeezed my arm.

From the water, the vampire growled at me, but the one with the kind eyes stopped him.

"Stellan!" he snapped, and the vampire in the water made an argument in Finnish, but he cut him off.

"You're American, yeah?" the amused blonde vampire asked, his tone lilting with an accent.

"Yes, we are," Ezra responded. "I'm Ezra, and this is my sister, Alice."

"I'm Dodge," he smirked at us. "I'm from Boston."

"Leif," the kind vampire gestured to himself, and then to the vampire in the water. "That's Stellan." Stellan turned back to him and retorted something in Finnish, but Leif shook his head.

"What are you doing out here?" Dodge cocked an eyebrow at us. "It doesn't look like you're on a friendly hike."

There wasn't really a good answer to the question. We didn't look like vacationers or skiers, and these were probably the lycans after Peter.

"She's never been here before," Ezra chose his words carefully. "She wanted to explore."

"I like exploring," I added, and Ezra shot me a look.

Dodge chuckled but that only infuriated Stellan. He stood up straighter, making himself larger and more imposing. To Dodge and

Leif, we appeared to be a curiosity. Leif especially looked at us with tolerance, but Stellan seemed threatened.

Glancing back at Leif, Stellan shouted something in Finnish. He kept talking to Leif, but he didn't take his eyes off us. Ezra could understand everything he said, but he played dumb.

"Did you know this was our territory?" Dodge asked when Stellan finished his rant.

"No. This is a National Park, isn't it?" Ezra pretended to be confused.

Leif and Dodge exchanged looks. They seemed skeptical of our intentions. But based on Dodge's casual shrug and Leif's nod, they didn't think we were a danger to them. We probably weren't, so that made sense.

"This is lycan territory." Leif looked gravely at us. "It's best if you don't wander around here."

"We'll be more careful in the future," Ezra apologized.

"Make sure that you do," Dodge said, abandoning his earlier humor. His face and voice hardened, resembling Stellan's. They were threatening us.

Ezra nodded at them and ushered me away, back the way we came. The lycans didn't move, and I felt their eyes on us as we hurried through the forest. Ezra kept his hand on my back, pushing me to go faster. I started to say something several times, but he shushed me until we got to the car.

"What are we doing?" I asked when he unlocked the Range Rover and got inside.

"Get in," Ezra commanded and slammed his door shut.

"It's only one-thirty." I climbed in after him. "We have plenty of time to look for Peter."

"If they caught us in the woods again tonight…" He trailed off.

He made sure the doors were locked before racing down the snowy road. He kept glancing in the rearview mirror, and I turned around, half expecting to see a pack of wolves chasing after us. But there was only an empty road.

"What's going on? They didn't really seem that bad. In fact, other than the Finnish one in the river, they seemed like ordinary vampires," I said.

"That's not the whole pack." His eyes flitted back to the rearview mirror. "They were following us, and that's why I wouldn't let you say anything in the woods. Now they've seen us, and they know our vehicle. We can't do anything more tonight."

"You're just being paranoid." I shook my head, but his certainty was unnerving.

The road had patches of snow and black ice, and the signs on the side warned of reindeer crossing. In spite of that, Ezra sped up faster, and his eyes rarely stayed on the road in front of us.

"I don't want to scare you," he confessed randomly.

"Thanks," I said.

"I'm not sure how many lycans are in his pack anymore. At times there were as many as fifteen or twenty, and other times there were as few as four. It depends on what kind of mood he's in. He'll wipe out his entire pack for the hell of it, and start over fresh," Ezra talked as if he was explaining something to me, but he started in the middle of the idea.

"Who are you talking about?" I looked over at him.

"Gunnar." His eyes went to the mirror again, as if saying his name summoned him. "He's led a pack in the Lapland for the better part of three centuries. They winter up here, and summer in Russia and Siberia."

"How do you know that he's still the leader?" I asked.

"It's been fifty years or more since I saw him last," Ezra admitted. "But when I was told of Peter's troubles, Gunnar was mentioned by name."

"So you knew *exactly* what you were getting into when we came here?" I narrowed my eyes at him, and he pursed his lips. "Then why are you so freaked out by this? If you knew that's who were dealing with."

"I was hoping to avoid him entirely. I thought we'd find Peter and depart, before they knew we'd been here," he sighed. "And that's how I know Peter's on a suicide mission. He was with me the last time we encountered Gunnar."

I sank back in the seat and finally grasped what frazzled Ezra so much. They outnumbered us, and they were pissed off. We had just very narrowly escaped death.

"How do you kill a vampire?" I breathed.

With my murder becoming increasingly imminent, I wanted to know possible methods for my demise. Ezra once mentioned starvation lasting for months or years led to death, but that seemed unlikely here. I imagined something more instant, more violent.

"Head. Heart." He shifted uneasily, but the car slowed, meaning his initial panic ebbed. "Our bones are nearly unbreakable, but another vampire could do it rather easily. We're our only enemy in this world."

The imagery of my heart getting ripped out was enough to keep me silent for the rest of the car ride back to the hotel. When we parked, Ezra didn't check behind him for lycan, but I did.

The clerk behind the desk made googley eyes at me when we came in, but I barely even noticed. There were far more important things on my mind. Like how I planned on surviving.

We made our circles wider around the lycan territory, but after three days, we had no choice but to move in closer. Besides that, everything Ezra heard said Peter was imbedded in lycan land. It was all part of his suicide plan, I guess. Hang out around them long enough until they slaughtered him.

Since we saw the lycan, Ezra became hesitant about bringing me with him. His whole plan for getting Peter rested on my ability to convince him, but that wasn't fool proof. Neither of us were sure how he'd respond to me.

Except... the last kiss we shared, the only time Peter truly kissed me, I felt something different.

Peter tasted Jack on me, he knew Jack had bitten me, but Peter didn't come back to kill him. Everything inside him, the insistent bond in his blood, screamed that he should kill Jack, but he hadn't.

Instead, he planned on really letting me go, not because of his own fears or what his body demanded, but because he knew that would be what made me the happiest. The one true kiss we ever shared had been a kiss goodbye. Underneath all of his chemicals and reservations, Peter had to have genuine feelings for me, otherwise he never would've let me be with Jack.

That just happened to be when Jack walked in, and he set off an entirely different chain of events than what Peter had in mind.

That's what kept me coming back out in the woods, even with the full understanding of what we were up against. I thought that Peter might really listen to me, and even if he didn't, I had to try.

We walked through the woods in silence, but I knew when we got closer to the lycan homeland. Ezra walked faster but made sure his steps matched mine. He looked around more and kept incredibly close to me, so sometimes I was almost tripping over him.

Ezra would risk anything for Peter, but he didn't feel the same way about me risking everything. In the hotel today before we left, he asked if I wanted to stay behind. I said no, but he continued recommending it until I refused to talk about it anymore.

We were going back to the exact area the lycans had warned us away from, but that had to be where Peter was, assuming that Peter was still alive.

"Shouldn't we be calling his name or something?" I asked when the silence and the search became too much for me.

Ezra shook his head, and I ducked underneath a low-hanging branch. The one thing I could say for this was that I was getting a lot more nimble and agile. I wasn't getting as tired out as I used to, and I hadn't been quite as hungry. If nothing else, this would get me through vampire boot camp.

"I just don't think we're doing that much," I said, keeping my words hushed. "We're just wandering around the trees. How are we supposed to find Peter? You have this carefully calculated plan of where to look, but when we get here, we don't even do anything."

"They can't know we're looking." Ezra was barely loud enough to be heard over the crunch of our boots in the snow.

"I get that, but Peter has to know. Or how else will we find him?"

"Smell him. Hear him. See him." He shrugged but slowed, almost pausing to look at me. "Can you still… feel him?"

Whenever I had been around Peter before, my body automatically pulled towards him. My natural inclination had been to be with him, and that would be really helpful in a search party.

"I don't know," I said, although I didn't think so.

If I thought about Peter or talked about him, I didn't get all fluttery and intense anymore. I have a bond with Jack, and I feel things like that for him, which means that I probably can't for Peter anymore.

"Oh well." His pace picked up again, and I scampered behind him to catch up. "We'll find him anyway."

We passed over the river where we had met the lycan, and my heart skipped. He glanced back at me, and I hated that he could hear my heart. I could tell he was about to ask me if I wanted to turn back, but I shook my head and insisted we plow ahead.

Hopefully, Ezra tracked better than I did, because I couldn't even smell the lycan anymore. They smelled of animals that lived outside, like reindeer but not. There was something edgier about the lycan scent, like livestock and… road kill.

A branch cracked loud enough that even a human could hear, and I whirled towards it. Ezra moved in front of me, his posture defensive.

It had been an hour since we passed the river, so we were well into their territory, and we had yet to see any animals. I inhaled deeply, but I could only smell the cold. Snow. Trees. Dirt. Maybe an owl...

A flap of wings followed by the rustle of branches, and I saw a large owl take flight in front of the moon. Relief washed over me, but Ezra didn't relax at all. If anything he tensed up more, and then I heard something else too.

The soft crunch of footsteps in the snow, softer than hooves, softer than shoes. *Barefoot.*

In the moonlight, I saw the lycan. Several yards ahead of us, he walked towards us with his hands held up, the sign of surrender.

It was Leif, the kind one with large brown eyes. He wore the same clothes he did the other day, and they appeared even dirtier. Ezra, on the other hand, looked dapper for a midnight hike. He wore a black cashmere sweater with a thick collar, but in most ways, Ezra appeared to be an entirely different species than Leif.

"I'm alone," Leif announced as he got closer to us.

Leif stopped a few feet in front of us, but that was still much closer than I'd like. Ezra kept his body partially blocking mine, shielding me.

"I am alone. I know you don't trust me, but it's the truth," Leif said.

He sounded American or maybe Canadian. He pushed a strand of his thick hair off his forehead and chewed his lip. His eyes roamed around us, unsure of where to let them settle, and he glanced up at the moon.

"They're in Sweden, hunting," Leif continued, as if we had asked. "Dodge was convinced that we'd scared you away, so they left."

"But you weren't?" Ezra asked, and his stance grew more rigid. Leif shrugged in response and lowered his eyes to the ground. "Is that why you stayed behind? To see if we came back?"

"Maybe," Leif said, then quickly added, "But not like you think."

"You don't know what I think," Ezra said evenly.

Leif shifted and looked at the moon again. Rubbing his arm, he looked like he wanted to say something but couldn't find the words.

"You're after Peter, aren't you?" Leif asked, and I stiffened. "I'm not out to get him. He killed my brother, but it was self-defense. Krist had a temper and…

"Peter had no business being here," Leif went on. "He was 'trying out' for the pack, but that's not how it works. Gunnar put him through all these tests, and Krist was one of them. But Peter started winning…" He looked apologetic, his eyes wide and sincere. "It wasn't fair what they did to him. What they're *still* doing to him."

"Still?" The fear in Ezra's voice made me wince.

My head swam with images, and Ezra had seen far worse than I had. He knew what true torture could be for a vampire.

"He's alive. He's okay." Leif's voice cracked on the last word.

"What are they doing? Where is he?" Ezra demanded in a low growl, and Leif shrunk back. Any pretense that Ezra had of submitting to the lycans was over.

I didn't think scaring Leif worked to our benefit, so I put a hand on Ezra's arm. Reluctantly, he responded and took a step back. Leif nodded his appreciation and stood up taller.

"I don't know exactly," Leif said. "They've been hunting him."

"He's in Sweden?" I raised an eyebrow.

"No, he's still here," Leif shook his head. "The pack is in Sweden."

"I don't understand. Why is he still here? If they're gone, why didn't he just come home?" I asked, and Leif and Ezra exchanged a look. "What? Why won't Peter leave?" I looked at Ezra since Leif didn't answer.

"Us," Ezra said thickly. "The pack will track him if he leaves and follow him back to us."

"If they're so good at tracking, then why haven't they killed him yet?" I asked, ignoring the implications.

If they could follow him across the Atlantic, then they could find one vampire in their own territory. Why would they leave him alive, especially after all this time?

"They like to play with their food," Ezra said, and Leif looked at the ground. "They want him to wait in fear, wondering when they're going to strike, jumping at every noise. Eventually, he'll either go mad or come home, which is a prize itself."

"What are you talking about?" I asked as nausea welled up inside me.

"Why don't you explain it to her?" Ezra growled at Leif.

"It's not my idea." Leif looked ashamed. "I'm here, telling you this, at risk to myself."

"You didn't do anything to stop it, did you?" Ezra took several steps toward him. This time, Leif didn't back down. "You wouldn't have said anything to us if you hadn't seen us."

"I couldn't stop it! I can't go up against them." Leif shook his head. "This is *my* pack. Peter's just a stupid, arrogant..."

Leif rubbed his neck, and Ezra sighed, repressing his urge to fight him. Regardless of what Leif had or hadn't done, he was the only one trying to help now. If we were going to find Peter, he'd be our best bet.

"I still don't understand what you want with keeping Peter alive," I said.

"Peter has a death wish, otherwise he wouldn't be here," Leif explained. "Killing him would give him satisfaction, and they want him to suffer. They'll make him watch as they kill everything he cares about. That's his real punishment. Gunnar won't even kill him in the end, because sometimes, living forever is worse."

Jack, Milo, and Mae were sitting at home, alone, unguarded. Ezra and Peter were here, thousands of miles away from them. A cold shudder ran through me.

"Are you sure the pack's in Sweden?" I asked, hearing my voice tremble. "They didn't go anywhere else?" Ezra caught onto what I was saying and narrowed his eyes at Leif.

"Yeah, I'm sure," Leif looked bewildered, but then it dawned him. "No! They didn't think you had anything to do with Peter. If they did, they would've killed you already, and left your bodies for him to find."

"We need to get out of here," I said. Even if he was telling the truth, the thought had been put in my head, and I was desperate to see Jack, to know he was safe.

"Where is Peter?" Ezra asked.

"I can tell you the area he's in, but I can't take you there," Leif said. "They'll smell my scent mixed with yours, leading you to him."

"Where is he?" Ezra repeated.

"He's about a kilometer and a half east, past a small lake. He's been hiding in a little cave in the ground." Leif pointed in the direction he'd told us, the direction he'd been walking from.

Without waiting for me, Ezra raced towards Peter. I knew I'd have to rush to keep up with him, but I paused. Leif looked so apologetic and forlorn, I couldn't help but feel drawn to him.

It wasn't until that moment, when I looked directly at him, that I realized what it was that I liked so much about him. He had eyes just like my brother's.

"Thank you," I told him earnestly.

"Just go. Get him. Get out of here."

Ezra was already a blur in the trees ahead of me. He had a far better sense of direction than I did, so I had to catch up with him.

I'd made great strides in grace lately, but at this speed, it became impossible to maintain. I slipped and stumbled over everything and hit my head on several branches. By the time I came to the small lake, I was covered in snow and pine needles.

Ezra stopped sharply, and I didn't notice him until it was too late. I slid on the ice and slammed right into him, which was like running into a brick wall. Bouncing off his back, I fell to the ground. I crouched, preparing to stand up, but then I glimpsed something through Ezra's legs and I froze.

His eyes were unmistakable, but they were even greener than I remembered. Peter stood a few feet in front of Ezra, looking mangy. His chestnut hair hung down to his shoulders, growing several inches in the last few weeks. Thick stubble covered his face, but wasn't quite a beard. His clothes were filthy and ragged, and Peter had always prided himself on his appearance.

He still looked gorgeous, and somehow, I had expected that to fade. But it turned out that he was just plain stunning, and that had nothing to do with whether I was bonded with him or not.

I waited, expecting that intense pull at the sight of him. But nothing happened. Even when his eyes briefly met mine, I never had to remind myself to breathe. He no longer captivated me.

"You brought her?" Peter asked Ezra, but it wasn't lined with that familiar disgust and contempt he tried to hold for me. Instead, he sounded nervous and concerned.

"She insisted on coming," Ezra said.

An odd tension brewed between them. I had thought Ezra would just come up and say something like, "Alright, that's enough Peter, let's go home" but he barely said anything. He almost seemed afraid of Peter.

I stood up and brushed myself off. Hiding on the ground behind Ezra just didn't feel right.

"She can't fight them," Peter said. When I came around Ezra, he avoided looking at me

"We're not here to fight," Ezra said.

"Did you come here to die then?" Peter looked pained and pale under the moonlight, and his words echoed off the trees around us. Somewhere, the owl hooted and took flight again, sending shivers down my spine.

"Peter," Ezra tried to reason with him, but Peter wanted nothing to do with it.

"I can't believe you did this. I've been staying here, going through all of this, so they would stay away from you. They're going to *kill* you, Ezra! Do you understand that? They're going to kill you and Alice and everyone!" Peter paced, and he'd started to unravel.

"No one is going to kill anyone," Ezra's impassive baritone overrode everything else.

"You don't know what they're like." His pleas bordered on whining. "It's been too long since you've seen them in action!"

"We have been here for days, searching all over the lycan territory, getting our scent on *everything*. We've already ruined your attempts at self-sacrifice. Let's go back to the hotel, get you cleaned up, and figure a way out of this mess," Ezra said.

Peter groaned, but more at Ezra's stupidity than at the thought of going to the hotel with us. Running a hand through his dirty hair, he scanned the forest.

"We probably won't even make it back to the car," Peter said at length.

"The lycan are in Sweden. We have a few days to sort things out." Ezra took a step back, gesturing to the way back.

"Come on," I said, speaking to Peter for the first time since we had kissed, since I had been mortal. "Come back with us."

Peter looked at me, eyeing me up the way that he had before. I wasn't in love with him anymore, but something about it still made me blush, and I lowered my eyes.

Finally, he nodded, and with Ezra leading the way, he followed us to the Range Rover. In the long, silent walk back, I often felt Peter's eyes on me, but I tried to ignore it.

- 8 -

Peter had gone without eating for a long time, and he gulped down four canisters of blood when we reached the hotel. That was enough to make even the strongest vampire woozy, and he lie down on Ezra's bed and instantly fell asleep.

Ezra leaned on the dresser, watching Peter sleep, with a sublime look on his face, and I stood next to him.

"So what's the plan?" I whispered, looking up at Ezra.

"There isn't much of one at the moment."

In my hand, I had my phone, and I twirled it around. It contained fifteen text messages and two missed calls from Jack, along with seven messages from Milo. They wanted to know what was going on, but I had nothing to tell them.

"So..." I shifted my weight. "Peter's gonna sleep and rest up, and then what? We're gonna hide here? We're gonna go home? We're gonna fight?"

Ezra chewed the inside of his cheek and chose not to answer me. Peter stirred in the bed, moving his head against the pillow, and Ezra tensed up. He felt over protective, and I didn't blame him. But his paranoia should've left him plotting escape plans instead of just gazing at Peter.

"We should just get some rest. We'll come up with a plan tomorrow," Ezra said at length.

"There's no way I can sleep after this."

"Eat." He nodded to the bathroom, where he stored the blood.

I had a million questions I should be making him answer, but as soon as he mentioned eating, I could think of little else. I decided it'd be better to give in and get some sleep. It wouldn't do me any good to stay up all day worrying.

I ate quickly, and it hit me hard. I staggered like a drunk person, and I was thankful I'd already changed into my pajamas. Within seconds of hitting my bed, I fell asleep.

When I woke up, Ezra slept on the bed next to me, pressed so close to the edge he nearly fell off. I sat up, careful not to wake him. I looked over his shoulder and saw Peter sitting on the other bed, staring over at us. I gasped, and even though I caught the surprised yelp before it escaped my lips, Ezra's eyes shot open.

"Sorry," I smiled guiltily at Ezra.

He waved me off as he sat up. His eyes searched the hotel room, appraising it to make sure that nothing was out of place. He had slept on the covers, fully clothed, and he was much more alert than me.

"How long have you been awake?" Ezra asked Peter, studying at him.

"Not long." Peter tried to tuck his hair behind his ears, but it was filthy, almost to the point of being matted.

"So what's going on?" I asked.

They sat across from each other. Peter lowered his eyes, but Ezra kept staring at him. I wrapped the comforter around my shoulders and scooted across the bed, so I was sitting next to Ezra. He glanced over at me and sighed.

"So... what?" I asked when neither of them said anything. "The plan is a staring contest of some kind? Cause that's not a very good plan."

"I have an idea," Ezra said finally, and Peter gave him a hard look. "I can make an exchange."

"What kind of an exchange?" Peter narrowed his eyes. "There's nothing that you have that they want."

"That's not true," Ezra shook his head. "They don't enjoy money, but they require it. They have to travel to the larger cities to eat, and they can't walk around in the rags they live in."

"They won't take money. You've been gone for too long. You don't remember what they're like," Peter said.

"There's got be something that they want," Ezra said. "These aren't self-sufficient creatures. Gunnar is power hungry, and there is always something he can use to make himself more powerful."

"Yeah, because we really wanna make him *more* powerful," Peter scoffed and stood up. "No. I appreciate the rest and food, but I have to face them myself."

"It's too late!" Ezra got up and blocked Peter's path. "They've already seen us. They know we're after you. Just taking you won't be enough anymore."

Peter looked at the floor and tightened his lips into a thin line. His jaw clenched tightly, and his mind worked furiously to find fault with Ezra's logic. The lycans had to put the pieces together soon, if they hadn't already.

"Let me go talk to them," Ezra said. "I'm certain that if I talk to them, we can arrange something."

"There's nothing they want. Except to hurt me."

"Well, then I'll convince them that whatever I'm giving them is hurting you," Ezra said.

"You can't talk to them. They'll just kill you!" Peter was almost pleading with him.

"They won't hurt me," Ezra assured him. "Gunnar won't kill me. Not now, not like this."

Peter shook his head again, growing irritated with Ezra's certainty. They stood next to each other, trying to change the other's mind and unwilling to back down themselves.

"Maybe we should just come up with something better," I said when they had been standing for an uncomfortable length of time.

"She has a point," Ezra softened.

Peter crossed his arms over his chest and shifted his eyes between the two of us. He was skeptical about Ezra's conceding so easily, even momentarily, and so was I. Ezra had seemed absolutely certain about his intentions, until I chimed in.

"Why don't you take a shower and clear your head? We'll talk after," Ezra said.

Despite being suspicious, Peter was in dire need of a shower. He was a rather particular person to begin with, so his current level of hygiene had to be driving him insane.

"Alright." Peter looked at Ezra severely. "I'll get cleaned up. But we'll talk after."

"Of course," Ezra agreed.

Peter gathered clothes Ezra brought for him and went into the bathroom. As soon as we heard the water running, Ezra rushed about the room. He grabbed the keys to the Range Rover and his cell phone, and I jumped off the bed as he slipped on his shoes.

"What are you doing?" I asked.

"I have to talk to them." Ezra glanced at the bathroom, making sure that Peter couldn't hear us. "Stay here and don't let him leave."

"But Peter doesn't think you should go," I said, and I kept my voice low.

"He's just paranoid." Ezra brushed it off. "But he needs to stay here. They will kill him. Our best chance of getting out of here alive is bartering with them. And they won't hurt me."

"How can you be so sure?" I asked.

"I just am," he said simply. "You're just gonna have to trust me."

I bit my lip and looked over at the bathroom door. If I yelled for him, Peter would rush out and stop Ezra. But Ezra had never given me any reason to doubt him. And I had to think about more than just Ezra, Peter, and myself. We had a family back at home that could be hurt if we didn't put a stop to this.

"Hurry. And be careful."

"I will." Ezra smiled wanly at me. "I'll be back as soon as I can. But you both need to stay here until I get back. Understood?"

I nodded, and he disappeared out the door. I stood in the middle of the hotel room with the comforter wrapped around me, wondering if I did the right thing letting him go.

When I heard the water shut off in the bathroom, I winced. Peter came out of the bathroom, shirtless, and I tried not to be wowed by the perfection of it. He wore drawstring sweats that were a little too big and ran a towel through his long tangles of dark hair. As soon as he looked over at me, still standing in the middle of the room, he knew.

"He left?" Peter growled.

"He said everything's going to be fine."

"Bullshit." He tossed the towel aside and searched for a shirt.

"Okay, Peter, you can't go!"

"Watch me," he said as he tore through one of Ezra's dresser drawers.

I put my hand on his arm, attempting to physically stop him. Some part of me still expected that electrical jolt I always got from touching him, and when there wasn't one, I felt oddly lacking. His skin still felt warm and soft under my hand, but it was nothing spectacular.

"Alice." Peter rolled his shoulder and pushed my hand off.

"You can't go," I repeated and let my hand fall to my side.

"You keep saying that but you're not telling me why."

"Because of me!" I shouted randomly.

It got his attention, which is all I really wanted. He held a shirt in his hands, but instead of putting it on, he turned back to me. The shower, along with eating and sleeping, had done wonders for him. He hadn't shaved yet, but he actually looked really good.

"What do you have to do with anything?" Peter eyed me dubiously.

"If you go, they will kill him to spite you," I said as calmly as I could. "But by himself, he has a shot at reasoning with them. This is the *only* chance we have of all three of us getting home alive. But if you go after him, we're all dead, and you know it."

"But if they kill him, and I do nothing-"

"If that happens, we'll do something," I cut him off, ending that train of thought. "Okay? But we have to believe he can do this."

Peter scoffed and sat back on the bed, tucking his hair behind his ear. Unsure of what else to do, I leaned back against the dresser and watched him. I was afraid that if I did or said the wrong thing, I would accidentally change his mind, and he'd rush out the door after Ezra.

"It's ridiculous how much influence you still have over me," Peter muttered.

"What are you talking about?"

"I shouldn't even be listening to you!" He said it like it should be incredibly obvious, and he wouldn't look at me.

"Yeah, you should. Cause I'm right."

I wasn't sure what he was insinuating, but it made me feel strange inside. Like somehow after all of this, broken blood and all, he managed to have feelings for me. And somehow, that seemed to matter to me, when it most definitely should not.

"Maybe." Abruptly he pulled on the tee shirt and stood up. "I should go after him."

"What? Why?" I asked. "

"I don't know!" He sounded exasperated and rubbed his temples. "It just doesn't feel right! Sitting here, with you, while he's out there."

"I agree with your sentiments, except for that random dig at me," I said.

"Oh, come on, I didn't mean it like that. I meant that I should be out there, with Ezra!"

"And not sitting around acting like me," I finished for him.

"Being impossible doesn't make me want to be around you more," he said, casting me a look.

"Who says I want you to be around me?"

"Why are you here?" Peter asked honestly, looking at me.

"Um, well..." I stammered. "Ezra told us that you were in trouble, and um... I offered to go with."

"But that doesn't explain why you're here," he said, sitting back on the bed.

"What do you mean?" I asked.

"You can't still care about me."

"Of course I do. Not like before, but I still care," I said. Then I floundered, feeling embarrassed. "I mean, don't you? Like... a little bit?"

"I don't know that we were ever truly bonded anyway," Peter answered brusquely, ignoring my question entirely.

It was such a ridiculous statement, like saying that the sky was purple, I didn't even know how to argue with it. There was no other way to describe what we had gone through together, and he knew it.

"Why did you come out here then?" I asked.

"I like Finland."

"Yeah, right." The blanket slipped off my shoulder, and I readjusted it. "You came out here to join a crazed pack of vampires cause you like Finland? That sounds a lot more like you were trying to get yourself killed."

"Why would I wanna do that? Over you?" He stood up quickly, smirking down at me. "That's what you think, right? That I couldn't possibly live without *you*? That's a little bit of an ego trip you're on, isn't it?"

"Well… no… that's not what…" I stammered out some kind of response, then I straightened my shoulders. "After you lost Elise you almost-"

"Don't talk to me about Elise!"

"Peter, I am just trying to help you! I don't know why you're so angry with me for that," I said.

"This is you helping?" Peter laughed darkly.

"How do you want me to help? What do you want me to do?" I shouted at him, frustrated.

"I want you to-" He looked pained and surprisingly vulnerable, but he stopped and shook his head. His face fell, and he sat heavily back on the bed. "I don't want anything from you. Not anymore."

On the night stand, my phone started ringing. The tone was familiar to both of us, and Peter eyed up my phone with disgust. It was Jack calling, and since I didn't really have anything helpful to tell him, I didn't want to answer.

"Aren't you going to answer that?" Peter asked.

"Not right now. I'm busy."

"Doesn't he have you on some kind of string?" he asked pointedly after the ringing stopped.

"You mean like you did?" I gave him a harsh look, but he stared back at me, unaffected.

"Yeah, I do," he nodded. "If I had called you before, you would've answered no matter what you were doing. It just seems odd to me that if you're bonded-"

"That I'm capable of still thinking for myself?" I raised an eyebrow. "Yeah, I still can. And I did with you too, otherwise I never would've been able to be with Jack." His eyes flashed hard again. "But I thought you said we weren't really bonded anyway."

"I don't know what to think."

"Why did you come here?" I asked gently, attempting to really talk to him. "If it wasn't because of what happened-"

"Of course it was because of what happened," he sighed. "Of course it was because of you." He looked back up at me, his eyes uncertain and exposed. "Is that what you want to hear?"

"I don't want anything from you except the truth."

"Everything with you has always been so complicated." Peter ran a hand through his dark hair, which looked amazingly silky after the shower.

He chewed his lip and stared off at my empty bed. He would've said more if my phone hadn't started ringing again, and I had to do something about it. If Jack called repeatedly in a short time, that meant that he wants something. Or that something was wrong. Either way, I didn't feel right about just letting it ring.

"I should get that."

"Don't let me stop you," Peter said, but his expression had gone stony.

I had barely even hit the answer button when I heard Jack yelling anxiously, "What the hell have you been doing, Alice? Are you okay? What's going on? I've been trying to reach you for days!"

"I've been busy, Jack." I tried to sound irritated. My heart ached for him, but with Peter sitting on the bed behind me, I didn't want to show it. "We've been looking for Peter. Remember?"

"Why can't you call? Or answer a text message? Or let me know that you're still alive?" Jack demanded.

"I'm sorry." I swallowed back tears, and Peter got up off the bed. "Where are you going?"

"What? I'm not going anywhere?" Jack was bewildered on the phone.

"No, not you," I told him and nodded at Peter. "What are you doing?"

"Going to the bathroom. Is that okay with you?" Peter tried to make a joke, but I could tell that he was distressed.

"Yeah. Just don't leave the room, okay?" I didn't really trust him not to sneak away.

"Whatever you say." Peter saluted me, then went into the bathroom. A few seconds later, I heard the water running, drowning out the sound of me talking to Jack.

"Who is that?" Jack's voice had gotten icy, so he knew exactly who it was.

"Peter." I sat down on the bed, thankful for the bit of privacy.

"You found him?" Jack shouted incredulously. "Why didn't you tell me? Why are you still there? When are you coming home? Are you okay? Did you get hurt?"

"I'm fine, he's fine." I was tempted to say that Ezra was fine, but at that moment, I didn't know if that was true. "We just found him last night. He needed to rest, and now we're getting some things sorted out. We should be leaving soon."

"What things sorted out?" Jack asked. "Why don't you just get on the next flight out of there?"

"Peter's still in pretty bad shape. He needs some more time to recuperate. He's had a rough go of it here."

"I thought that was the whole idea. That's why he went there." Jack tried to keep the edge to his voice, but it faded a bit. As angry as he was with Peter, he wasn't a hateful guy.

"We'll be home soon. You don't need to worry anymore." That actually hurt to say. I knew there was still a good chance we wouldn't make it out alive, but I couldn't tell Jack that. So I lied, and tears welled in my eyes.

"You better be," Jack said. "Things are going crazy around here."

"What do you mean?" I asked.

"Your brother and *Bobby*."

"Who's Bobby?"

"He's... I don't know. You'll have to make Milo explain when you get back," Jack answered vaguely. "All I know for sure is that he's around all the time now."

"All the time?" I asked. "I've only been gone for like ten days!"

"It's been a pretty wild ten days around here," Jack said. "And Bobby showed up like the day after you left. So yeah. It's been eventful."

"I don't understand."

"You'll see when you get home," Jack said. "It'll give you more of an incentive to get here quicker. As if I weren't incentive enough."

"No, you're definitely enough," I laughed sadly. Laughing at his silly jokes made me want to sob.

After I hung up, I knocked on the bathroom door to let Peter know the coast was clear, and he came out a minute later. He was much more subdued, so we said very little to each other.

I showered and got dressed, and after that, there wasn't much else to do. Peter lay on the bed with his fingers laced behind his head, staring up at the ceiling. I paced the room and frequently peeked out of the curtains.

We just waited for Ezra to return.

Sun filtered around the edges of the curtains, and that scared the hell out of me. The lycan were even more strict about their nocturnal habits than we were, so the odds of them continuing a discussion into the daylight didn't seem likely. If Ezra weren't back soon, he probably wasn't coming back.

"He's still not here." I peered out the curtain, letting the warm morning light stream in, burning my overly sensitive retina, and then shut it. I looked behind me, where Peter laid immobile, the same way he had all night. "Peter?"

"I'm aware that he's not here, Alice."

"Don't you think we should do something?" I glowered down at him. Lying in bed did not seem like the right answer for this situation.

"I'm thinking." He closed his eyes, as if that could block out my voice.

"You've been thinking all day! We knew that Ezra might not come back, and he's obviously not going-"

"I have been thinking, Alice!"

"Well… you should let me in on it!" I crossed my arms over my chest. "I could help!"

"You mean like pointing out the obvious and peeking out the curtain?" He pushed himself up into the sitting position, letting his legs dangle off the edge of the bed.

"I don't know what else to do!" I felt powerless and on the verge of tears, and I didn't like it at all. I took a deep breath, and pushing a strand of hair behind my ears, I decided to start over. "What did you come up with?"

"Nothing useful. I just can't see a way around anything." He sighed, then muttered to himself. "I suppose that's why he brought you."

"What are you talking about?" I stiffened, as if he claimed something derogatory.

"Ezra brought you with because he knew how utterly useless you would be," Peter explained. "And I've been going back and forth between it all day long, wondering what I would finally do when it came down to it."

"What?" I asked, filled with an aching sense of uselessness.

"If I go after Ezra, and I bring you along, you'll get killed. If I leave you here, they'll follow my scent back, and you'll get killed. If I try to put you on a plane to get out of here, you'll probably do something horrible in bloodlust, and get yourself killed. There's nothing I can do except stay here and baby-sit you!" Peter growled.

"I don't..." I started to stumble out some kind of protest about needing a baby-sitter, but everything he said was true. After the initial sting of that wore off, I thought of something even stranger, especially given the way that Peter talked to me. "What do you even care if I die? So what? Let's just go out there and give them hell."

"Like you could really give them hell," he laughed hollowly. "You'd just slow me down."

"Maybe," I admitted. "What you're saying ... or thinking... If Ezra isn't coming back and they're only going to come after us... Why don't you just go? I don't want to slow down your fight. But it's better than the both of us waiting here to die."

His expression changed instantly into something foreign. It took me a minute to realize that it resembled concern for me. Even when we had been bonded, he'd never looked at me like that.

"That's an idiotic plan," he shook his head.

"That's pretty much what your plan is," I said.

"I'm not gonna just *leave* you here."

"But you're saying they'll kill me no matter what. At least this way you can get in a few good punches, take out some of the bastards that-" I stopped myself before I said anything about Ezra being dead. It was too terrifying to say aloud.

"You'd be completely unprotected. You wouldn't even stand a chance," he shook his head again, sounding tired of the conversation, and stood up.

"So what? You almost killed me once before and now you're suddenly my body guard?" I wrinkled my nose at his hypocrisy.

"Oh, god dammit!" Peter rolled his eyes. "I'm so sick of having that thrown in my face! I did that because I loved you, Alice!" He immediately regretted saying that and stared off anywhere but at me.

"Yeah, cause that's a healthy way to express love! By killing another person!" I was purposely pushing his buttons. If the only chance at a rescue mission was Peter going off without me, then I had to piss him off enough to leave me.

"I wasn't trying to kill you! I was trying to kill *me*!" He rubbed his eyes, looking as if he'd said too much and not knowing how to take it back. "Jack was in the house. I knew he was tuned in to your heart. When I grabbed you in the kitchen, he came flying in to save you. I thought if he found me, draining the life from you, he wouldn't hesitate to kill me." Tiredly, he exhaled. "I knew he was a better match for you than I was, and I didn't see any other way out."

I was too stunned to say anything. I'd always suspected Peter hated me. But he loved me so much, he'd been planning to die for my happiness. My heart thumped dully in my chest, and I tried to think of something say to him.

"Stop looking at me like that," Peter snapped when he finally met my eyes again. "I don't know why it's so shocking that I wouldn't want you to die. Do you really think Ezra would be so willing to sacrifice himself for me if I was such a psychopath?"

"Peter, I am so sorry," I whispered, unable to muster the full strength of my voice.

"Stop!" Peter repeated. "Ezra is the one out there! We need to be worrying about him, not us! Because there isn't even an 'us' to worry about!"

"You're right." I shook my head, clearing it of any confused thoughts about Peter.

It was hard, though. It changed the way I thought about *everything*. All the time I had been messing around with Jack, falling in love with him, the one thing that had given me the green light was that Peter had tried to kill me.

But when I thought about it as his own suicide attempt, that he had loved me so much he had been willing to give me up... We had been bound together, and he had truly loved me, but I had run off with his brother instead.

Peter didn't say anything, and neither did I. I'm not sure if he was really trying to come up with another plan, but I certainly couldn't. Part of me was really trying to, but I felt like all the wind had been knocked out of me.

The door to the hotel room thudded softly, interrupting my thoughts. Not a knock exactly, but more like something falling into it. I looked to Peter, his eyes already fixed on the door. He moved in front of me, blocking me in case the lycan announced their entrance.

When the door slowly swung open, we were greeted by something almost as bad.

- 10 -

Ezra leaned on the doorframe, looking worse than I could ever imagine him being. His clothes, the same black sweater and jeans he had worn the night before, were torn and dirty. His skin was gaunt and pale. He staggered into the room and Peter rushed to him.

Bite marks covered his neck and wrists. The lycan territory was nearly an hour drive away, plenty of time for a vampire to heal, but his bites were red and swollen. Ezra had been so drained he didn't have the strength to heal.

"He needs to feed," Peter told me and attempted to hand Ezra off to me. He hurried to the bathroom to get blood for Ezra, leaving me alone to struggle with the situation.

I'd been frozen in shock, but I put my arm around Ezra and helped him on the bed. His deep brown eyes were glassy. I'd never seen a vampire look so ill before. It had never even occurred to me that they could even look like this, especially Ezra.

When I sat down next to him on the bed, he collapsed back on the bed and rested his head on my lap. He gripped my thigh with a painful desperation, like he needed to hang onto something.

"I brought blood," Peter said when he walked back into the room. He looked down at Ezra, clinging onto me, and pressed his lips into a thin line.

"I can't eat. Not right now." Ezra grimaced, as if he was in too much pain to even think of eating.

I brushed his hair from his forehead, his skin feeling clammy. After blood loss, I'd think eating would be the only thing that would make him feel better. Then it dawned on me what was going on.

The lycan had fed on him. That was something vampires never let other vampires do, unless they were lovers. There was something sexual about the exchanging of blood, but it was more than that.

When Jack bit me, I felt him flow through me, and his love and kindness consumed me. Ezra had been bitten by a pack of rabid monsters. All their pain and rage burned through him now. Physically and emotionally, they drained him.

Ezra made a pained sound but fought to suppress it. He gripped me so tightly, that had I been human, he would've broken bones and ruptured organs. Despite his weakness, his muscles felt like concrete underneath my hands. He tensed so tightly, his body was completely rigid, and his legs curled up a bit, closer to me.

"My blood..." Ezra forced a few words, but he barely managed that.

"Just rest. We don't need to talk." I tried to reassure him, running my fingers through his blond hair.

"No," Ezra said, his voice tight and weak. "My blood for your blood. It's over. We need to get out of here. Peter, can you..."

"I'll make all the arrangements," Peter said when Ezra trailed off. He tried to keep his composure as much as possible, but his eyes burned. It killed him knowing Ezra had exchanged his own blood for Peter's life.

After a moment of staring remorsefully at him, Peter went into action. He got his cell phone and started making calls, most of which I couldn't understand because they were in Finnish.

"I shouldn't be burdening you with this," Ezra said and tried moving away from me.

"No, you're okay," I insisted. "Don't worry."

"No. I …" Ezra trailed off again, and a spasm went over his body. He gripped even tighter and I could barely breathe. It passed, and he relaxed, as much as he could. "I'm sorry."

"Ezra. It's okay."

When Peter got off the phone, he watched Ezra for a moment as he struggled to keep his breaths even. I could feel Ezra biting back screams, and I looked to Peter for help, but he wouldn't meet my eyes.

"The best thing for him to do is rest," Peter said. "The feelings will fade, with time. Our flight leaves in seven hours. He can get some rest and eat, and then he ought to feel good enough to at least make it home."

Peter packed our things and got us ready to go. I felt like I should help him, but I didn't want to leave Ezra alone. Eventually, Peter suggested we get some sleep. Ezra went in and out of consciousness. I managed to doze off a little bit, but Ezra woke me frequently with moaning or writhing.

When Peter woke me in the evening, Ezra was still tangled up with me, but the fierceness in his grip had disappeared. Peter helped him to the bathroom to eat and get cleaned up, and I got up to stretch. My whole body ached terribly from the way he had held me.

Just comforting Ezra had been exhausting, and I couldn't

fathom what he was going through. I stood next to the bed, feeling more emotionally drained, and Peter came out of the bathroom to give Ezra privacy. He looked at me with concern, but I didn't deserve any, so I busied myself with straightening up the room.

"Alice." Peter placed his hand on my arm, stopping me. "How are you holding up?"

"Better than Ezra," I gave a hollow laugh.

I looked up at him, and I couldn't hold it in anymore. Unwanted tears streamed down my cheeks, and roughly, he pulled me into his arms. Burying my face in his shirt, I sobbed hard.

"Thanks. And sorry," I mumbled when I got myself under control and pull away from him. He kept his hand on my arm, as if severing contact would reduce me to tears.

"Don't worry about it. I saw how hard that was on you," Peter said.

"He's not even crying." I wiped the tears from my face and hated myself for being a baby.

"It's different for him. He's been through this before, although I don't think it's ever been this bad." His eyes got hard, no doubt thinking about how this was his fault.

"What do you mean he's been through this before?" I asked.

"That's what his old 'master,' Willem, used to do and he was a bad, bad man." He stared off into space. "But Willem was just one man, not a pack of sadists. I've been bit before, by something less than them, and it's..."

"What?" I pressed when Peter trailed off into silence.

"My blood burned in my veins. My body tried to reject it, and I was so drained of blood already. And on top of the physical pain, which is excruciating, it gives you emotions. It makes you want things you don't want. You feel disgusting and ...." He shook his head, unwilling to elaborate further. "It's torture, absolutely."

"Will he be okay?" I asked.

Ezra came out of the bathroom, changing our attention. He wore fresh clothes, and the marks on his neck and wrist had finally healed. His skin was still pale and his expression grave, but he moved around okay.

He barely said anything to either of us on the way to the airport. I saw how rigid he was, and he struggled to hold back what pain was left. On the plane, he mumbled several apologies to me, all of which I brushed off. I had barely done anything for him, and it was nothing that he wouldn't do for me.

This made me gain even more respect for him. Whatever made him feel this bad would've killed anybody else.

On the rest of the flight back to America, he kept his eyes shut tightly and his lips pressed together. I couldn't stop staring at him, terrified he would fall apart or die if I did.

- 11 -

By the time we landed in Minneapolis, Ezra returned to something that resembled his normal self. A very subdued version, but he could talk and walk without grimacing. Thanks to my preoccupation with him, I hadn't texted anyone to let them know that we were here. We took a cab home, deciding a surprise return was better at this point.

As soon as the plane had touched down, I felt a pull in my heart. After days and days of a dull ache at being away from Jack, it screamed with pleasure, knowing how close he was. The cab had barely stopped at the house when I jumped out .

I dashed through the front door, and Jack rounded the corner to the entryway, his blue eyes wide. He broke out in a gigantic smile, and I dove into his arms and wrapped my arms around his neck.

I could feel his heart beating through my chest, and that was the connection I had been so sorely missing. For the first time in what felt like an eternity, I felt complete and contended again. Squeezing my eyes shut on happy tears, I wanted to stay that way forever.

Jack's muscles tensed around me, and I realized Peter walked in the house. I could hear Mae and Ezra talking, but Peter didn't say a word.

As close as Jack was, I didn't feel close enough. I wanted to cover him in kisses and... and well, a lot more than that. Instead, I would have to untangle myself with Jack and act in a civil manner around people. I opened my eyes and looked over Jack's shoulder to a different problem. Standing behind Jack were my brother Milo and some kid I had never seen before, looking curiously at us.

I use the term "kid" loosely. He looked older than me, with black hair falling across his forehead and almost an olive skin tone. Shorter than even Milo had been as a human, he had tattoos visible on his chest below the low v-neck of his shirt and all down his arms. If I hadn't been so distracted in my excitement over Jack I would've noticed him sooner.

His veins were pulsing with hot blood, *human* blood. I realized belatedly how long it had been since I ate. Spending all that time with people lately had left me with more self-control than before, but I wasn't accustomed to it in my own home.

"Who is that?" I asked, finally releasing Jack so he would lower me to the ground. Milo moved protectively in front of the kid, which made something flare inside me.

"That's Bobby." Jack put me down but he kept an arm looped around my waist, and I doubt it was just because he missed me. Tension from Peter along with my confused reaction to this Bobby person made the room feel unstable. "I told you about him on the phone. Remember?"

"You didn't tell me he was human," I sniffed, crossing my arms over my chest.

"You were human like ten seconds ago," Milo rolled his eyes.

Bobby peered around Milo at me, and it wasn't his species difference that offended me so much. This was the first time Milo had ever brought a guy home. On top of that, I had been away when it happened, and this kid was older than Milo and had tattoos.

"I couldn't tell you very much about anything since you wouldn't answer my calls or return my texts," Jack pointed out icily, and he glanced back at Peter.

Peter held our luggage and stood awkwardly by the front door. Matilda sniffed him, wagging her tail, but nobody else acknowledged him at all.

Ezra looked much better, but he was still clearly unwell. Mae had to smell the other vampires on him. Even I could still smell it - dank and musty and unpleasant. Touching his face gingerly, she had tears in her eyes, oblivious to the growing unease in the room.

"Come on." Milo gestured to the other room. "You've all had a long trip. I'm sure you guys wanna relax for a bit, and fill us in with all the juicy details."

Milo led the way to the living room, deliberately putting himself between Bobby and me. It was weird thinking of myself as a threat.

Jack's arm was still around me, and I remembered with some delight that I was with him. I smiled up at him, but he was slow to return it. His heart beat too loud, meaning something distressed him.

"I would love to catch up with you. I missed you all so much," Mae said when we reached the leaving room. She smiled and squeezed my arm lovingly. Ezra stood behind her, his expression drawn. "But Ezra and I are going to have to excuse ourselves. He needs some rest."

"I understand," I said.

As I watched them walk away, I felt Jack's eyes settle on me. Ezra's anguish made Jack wary about what had gone on in Finland. I avoided his gaze, because I wasn't ready to explain it to him, especially not in front of Milo and his new friend.

Milo flopped back in an overstuffed chair. Bobby remained glued to his side and sat on the arm of the chair next to him, so he was half on Milo's lap. Something about that sent a ripple of agitation through me. When Bobby put his hand on his thigh, I wanted to slap it away.

"So…" Milo asked me. "How was your trip?"

"It was okay," I shrugged, unwilling to give up anymore right now.

Peter walked over to lean against the wall, and Jack moved smoothly around me, putting himself between Peter and me. This was the way things would go for awhile, and it was too early to already get annoyed by them. I went over and sat on the couch.

"Since you brought Peter back, I assume it was a rousing success." Milo looked at Peter out of the corner of his eye. He'd only met Peter once, and that hadn't gone that great.

"You could say that," I said

Jack sat next to me, and Peter glanced around the room diffidently, managing not to look happy or upset. I pulled my knees up to my chest and leaned in closer in the crook of Jack's arm, but he was unnaturally tense.

I would've loved to ease his fears, but I was preoccupied by this Bobby character that was all but sitting on my little brother's lap.

"It looks like you've had a pretty busy time without us," I said as casually as I could.

"You could say that," Milo laughed.

Milo shared one of this disgustingly sweet looks with him. Bobby leaned down and kissed him on the lips, and I could hear his heart race faster. My stomach twisted in knots, out of disgust and hunger, and I didn't appreciate that combination at all.

It wasn't the fact that Milo was kissing a dude that I found so upsetting. It was that he was kissing *anyone*.

"I think I'm gonna crash," Peter said. He looked to Jack, who tightened his arm around me, as if he expected Peter to tear me from him. "Is my room in the same place?"

"It's exactly as you left it," Jack said as evenly as he could.

"Alright." Peter nodded at Jack, then he turned and went upstairs.

"That guy has weird vibes," Bobby said, speaking for the first time since I'd met him.

He stared after the space where Peter had been and shook his head to toss his bangs out of his dark eyes. To comfort him, Milo rubbed his back, and Bobby smiled, settling back into the chair with him. Is it too early to say that I really hate Bobby?

"So Bobby," I said, and he smiled clumsily. "Are you gay?" Jack laughed, filling me with a familiar glee. Once Peter left, he relaxed a bit.

"Alice!" Milo snapped, embarrassed.

"What?" I asked.

Nothing was overly gay about Bobby, other than the fact that he had kissed my brother. His clothes were fashionable scene apparel, skinny jeans and slip on Vans. He might be wearing eyeliner, but he might just have dark eyelashes too.

"No, it's okay," Bobby laughed. "Yeah. I am gay."

"How old are you?" I asked pointedly.

"Twenty," Bobby said, and I bristled.

Milo was a vampire, and thanks to their rapid maturation, he looked about nineteen or so. In actuality, he was barely sixteen, and he was making out with a twenty-year-old guy. Not cool. In fact, it was so not cool that I planned to freak out on Jack for letting this happen while I was away. (At this point, it had not occurred to me that Jack was born over 40 years ago, and I wasn't yet eighteen.)

"Alice, you were in Finland for weeks!" Milo exaggerated, sensing my growing anger. "I'm pretty sure you have more exciting things to do than interrogate my boyfriend."

Boyfriend? They were already up to that terminology? It had been months and months until I started referring to Jack as my boyfriend. In fact, in conversation, I still don't think I would use that word. It sounded too weird to say about him. Once you're over the age of twenty-five or you're no longer human, the word "boyfriend" no longer fits.

"Yeah. What happened in Finland?" Jack turned to look at me.

"It's too much to talk about right now," I brushed him off.

"Seriously?" Jack raised an eyebrow. "*That's* what you're giving me? After weeks of this? You're gonna come home and tell me it's too much to talk about?"

"Well, I just don't want to upset you needlessly."

"You were in Finland with Peter! And you wouldn't answer my calls!" Jack was all but yelling. "You've upset me plenty already, and it didn't bother you then!"

"Of course it bothered me." I pulled away from him. "I thought about you constantly. But I knew if I said anything you would rush over there and get yourself killed."

"I would get myself *killed?*" He turned to face me more and his expression got even more severe. "What the hell were you involved with, Alice? And what happened to Ezra?"

"Yeah, what is the deal with him?" Milo asked unhelpfully.

"It's all very complicated." I shook my head, afraid that if I told Jack what had happened he would... I don't know. Yell at me a lot and then try to beat up Peter and Ezra.

"I know you were with lycan. That's who had Peter." Jack bit his lip, looking down at me. "I should've gone over as soon as you told me but..." If he had gone there, everything would've turned out much worse, and I think he kinda knew that.

"Lycan?" Milo sat up sharply, almost knocking Bobby off the chair. "You mean werewolves?"

"Not exactly," I sighed. "Not at all, really. They're just vampires that live in the woods. They were after Peter, but Ezra made an exchange with them, and we came home. End of story. Most of the trip was spent just looking for Peter."

"What was the exchange?" Milo asked, but by Jack's expression, he'd just figured it out.

"Peter let them do that?" Jack whispered.

"He didn't have a choice. Ezra... did what he had to do," I explained as best I could.

"What are you talking about? What happened?" Milo demanded.

"Nothing. Never mind," I said. Jack stared at me intently, his blue eyes full of too much anguish. "Nothing happened to me. Okay? I barely even left the hotel room. Nobody tried to hurt me. I never got in any fights. Everything was fine. Honest."

Jack wasn't completely convinced, but he wrapped his arm around me, so I would curl up to him. Milo was perplexed, but he dropped the subject.

Milo had never been out of the area, either, so he pressed for more information about traveling. I told him what little I had seen and how terrified I had been on the plane.

Once Bobby started falling asleep, Milo decided it was time to excuse himself and head up to bed. He scooped Bobby up in his arms, carrying him upstairs to *their* room, and I gaped after him. We had to have a very long talk about all of this as soon as I had the chance.

I would've loved some time to catch up with Jack, but I felt drained from the trip. Being away from home had been much harder than I had thought. Jack wanted to go to bed with me, and even with my exhaustion, I would've been happy to oblige.

Except I knew the only reason he insisted so hard was because Peter slept across from me, and I refused to let his paranoia control our relationship. He had to get used to Peter being around, and I needed to get some rest before trying to be *alone* with Jack.

Jack walked me up to his room, kissing me on the forehead before going back down to the den to sleep. I curled up in his unmade bed, falling asleep in his mass of blankets almost immediately. It felt so good to be home.

When I woke up, I felt an instant relief being in my own bed.

After a long trip away, nothing felt better than that. Well, almost nothing.

I stretched, working the stiffness from my limbs. My reunion with Jack had been anticlimactic. I allowed myself to get distracted by my brother's new boyfriend and Jack's worry over Finland. I'd have to have a very long talk with Milo about this Bobby fellow, but I had more pressing needs in mind.

Along with that familiar thirst burning just below the surface, I had a desperate ache for Jack. A bit of jet lag and stress made it too bittersweet for me to greet him the way he deserved, and I had to rectify that immediately.

When I walked out into the hall, I could smell Bobby. That sweet, delightful scent of hot blood coursing through his veins. His heart pounded quickly, like a frightened rabbit.

I tensed up, thinking he was in some kind of danger, but I realized he was just excited. This was confirmed by a happy moan from him, and a throaty laugh from Milo. My stomach tightened with nausea and anxiety as I thought about what Milo was doing in the room next to mine.

It was completely unforgivable that he would have a sex life before I did. The "talk" was becoming more imminent, but I did not want to walk in on whatever they were doing right now to administer it.

Peter's bedroom door opened, making me jump. I'd brought him home, but it was still a shock to see someone in his room. It had been shut off for so long, like a shrine for a dead loved one, even though it was the exact opposite of that.

"Oh. Hey," Peter said, nodding at me.

"Hey," I replied. We stood across from each other, staring awkwardly, so I assumed I should make conversation. "Did you sleep okay? I bet its nice being back in your own bed."

"Yeah. It is." Peter nodded again and shifted uncomfortably.

"You're up!" Jack announced too loudly from the bottom of the stairs and raced up to us. He was happy to see me, but the arm he threw around my shoulder was too tight to be anything but for show. "I thought you were going to sleep all day!"

"Sorry. I guess I had sleep to catch up on," I smiled at him. His grip around my shoulders was borderline painful.

"I'm just gonna... go," Peter said. He turned and walked down the stairs, ignoring the look on Jack's face.

Once Peter was out of sight, I wriggled out of Jack's arms. It felt weird to pull away from him, but I wasn't a big fan of his jealousy. Jack realized what he was doing, and his expression changed to one of a little boy that got caught with his hand in the cookie jar. He shoved his hands in his pockets and looked apologetically at me.

"Sorry," Jack shrugged. "I'm just getting used to this. You've had all this time to readjust to Peter but the last time I saw him..." He shivered and looked away from me. I'm not sure what he was thinking about exactly, but it was either Peter kissing me or trying to kill him.

"It's okay." I put my hand on his chest. His muscles felt warm and strong, and his heart beat gently. I leaned in towards him, preparing to give him the kiss I had been wanting to give him for ages, but a fresh scent completely diverted my attention.

Just down the hall, Milo had apparently drawn blood from Bobby, and the scent of his blood was so strong and intoxicating, my mouth instantly began to water. My stomach didn't exactly growl, but it was suddenly ravenous. Bobby's heart rate quickened even more, and I could associate the sound with the smell, making it irresistible. My body flushed with heat, and all I could think/hear/feel was his blood, and how badly I needed it.

The bloodlust had taken me over entirely.

- 12 -

I had my hand on Jack's chest, and the next thing I knew, I was racing down the hall, to Milo's room in the turret. I awoke in the moment with Jack's hand tightly clamped on my arm. He stopped me from getting very far, but it was disturbing that I had blacked out for a second and had no control over myself. I'd been in a trance, and I wasn't completely out of it yet. At least now I was aware of what was happening, but my desire to feed didn't lessen.

"You need to eat," Jack said.

"Yeah, no kidding." I went towards Milo's room again, but he stopped me.

"No, not him."

He pulled me in the opposite direction, away from the blood. The rational part of me understood what he was doing, that I did not want to feed on my brother's boyfriend. But my thirst made me irate that he would take me away from the blood.

"Come on, Alice. There's food downstairs."

"Not good food!" I protested.

I'd never had fresh blood as a vampire, so I didn't have anything to compare with it. But fresh blood smelled so much better than bag blood. My body craved it far more intensely, making it almost impossible to resist.

Jack was stronger than me, and at least some of me knew he was right, so I let him drag me away.

Mae was just coming up from the basement when we got downstairs, her arms overflowing with cold bags of blood. Apparently, Ezra was eating more than normal too. She saw the look on my face and gave me a bag before I changed my mind about sparing Bobby.

As I gulped it down, loving the exotic rush of pleasure that ran through me, I overheard her talking to Jack. Ezra was still weak and required lots of rest and food, and Peter had left to do something. She was vague on the details, but I'm not sure if that was for Jack's sake or because she really didn't know.

By the time I finished my bag, she disappeared back into her bedroom to tend to Ezra, and that deep wooziness hit me. I'd just woken up, and I was preparing to pass out again.

I grabbed onto Jack, hoping that hanging onto him would make me more alert. He laughed at my struggle against sleep, and it resounded through me. He kissed my forehead and held me in his arms, and that was too comfortable for me to fight to stay awake anymore.

I was curled up in the crook of his arm when I woke up, and the faint sounds of Depeche Mode filled the bedroom. Jack had one arm around me, and the other one held a graphic novel, *The Killing Joke*. It was one of his favorites, so it was battered and beaten. He was so into it that he didn't even notice when I opened my eyes.

"Hey," I smiled up at him. He pulled his head back so he could look down at me, already setting the book aside. "Sorry I just passed out like that."

"No, it's cool. I understand," he grinned.

"I missed you." I snuggled closer to him, pressing my body against his, and his heart sped up.

"For awhile there, I wasn't sure if you'd ever come back." When he pushed a strand of hair from my eyes, his face went stormy, re-imagining all the horrible things he had thought happened to me in Finland.

"But here we are!" I hurried to erase his dark thoughts, rubbing my hand over his chest. "In your room, in your bed, *alone*." My expression faltered, and his face fell with concern. "We are alone, aren't we?"

"What do you mean?" His arm tensed up around me, and his voice had an edge to it. He incorrectly assumed that I was thinking of Peter, but he was the furthest thing from my mind.

"Milo and his new 'friend.'" I nodded to the thin wall that separated our rooms.

Listening to Milo and Bobby fool around earlier had been rather nauseating, and I didn't like the idea of them overhearing me messing around with Jack. I was really, really hoping to *finally* take things to next level with Jack, and I wanted it to be as intimate and private as possible.

"Oh, no, they're long gone," Jack smiled and relaxed next to me. "They went to a club a few hours ago."

"A club?" I arched my eyebrow and knew I was ruining the mood, but I couldn't shake my concern. "Is that safe?"

"Yeah," he shrugged. "Milo is a vampire. He can handle himself."

"What about Bobby?" I didn't really care much for his safety, but Milo would, and if other vampires moved on him, I wasn't sure how wisely Milo would respond.

"They're okay," he said. "And if they weren't, they have cell phones, which they know how to use. Unlike *some* people." So he hadn't entirely forgiven me for not calling him from Finland, but that was okay. I planned on making up for it.

"So what you're saying is that Milo is gone, Peter is gone, and Mae and Ezra are too preoccupied to notice anything? And we are completely, entirely, alone?" I said, sliding my leg up over his.

"It would appear that way," Jack smiled wickedly.

I tilted my head up towards him and his mouth pressed softly against mine. The kiss was only gentle for a minute, though. As soon as I felt his lips searching mine, this frantic need took over me.

Throwing one leg over him, I moved so I was sitting on top of him, straddling him between my legs. Jack moaned, but it was barely audible through our kisses. His hands searched my body, and his skin was already smoldering. My temperature would soon match his, and I felt the warmth racing through me.

I pulled away long enough to tear off my shirt, and he smiled appreciatively at me. He looked like he wanted to say something, so I silenced him with kisses. I loved talking to him, but right now, words weren't enough.

We'd been forbidden from being together almost since day one, and even after I turned into a vampire, we'd been forced to stay at arm's length.

After he slipped off his shirt, I took a moment to take him in.

His skin was tan and soft over the smooth muscles of his chest and stomach. Jack was completely perfect. A painful happiness spread over me as I thought about how lucky I was that he wanted me. I leaned over, peppering him with kisses, on his mouth, cheeks, chest, everywhere.

When my lips came to his neck, a delicious heat surged through me. I could feel and smell and *taste* his blood through his skin, and I remembered how wonderful it felt when I drank it to turn. All of his love and pleasure had coursed through me, filling me with the most intense heat. Every other emotion paled in comparison.

"Alice, no," Jack breathed heavily, but he sounded reluctant to stop me.

If I pushed it, I knew he would let me drink from him. It'd feel almost as amazing for him as it would me, but it was dangerous. As much as I wanted Jack, it would be nearly impossible for me to stop once I got started.

"Sorry," I whispered, using all my strength to pry my lips from his neck.

His hands on my back slid below my pants, pressing me even harder against him. His kisses had gotten hungrier and more aggressive, and I knew it was a battle for him to keep from biting me as well. It would be too easy for me to get out of control, even if I was the one being bled.

Jack started pushing down my pants, and my body started to tremble with excitement.

I heard the bedroom door open, but it was a secondary sensation. My hunger for Jack blotted out everything else. He was slightly more grounded than I was, and thinking quickly, he pulled the covers up to hide me, since I was almost entirely naked.

He had stopped kissing me, but there was a fog over my mind where I could still taste him. It took a moment to clear, and I realized Milo and Bobby were standing in the doorway. Bobby looked embarrassed, but Milo just looked grossed out and disapproving.

"What the hell are you doing?" I was almost screaming. I had probably never been as pissed at my brother as I was then.

"What are *you* doing?" Milo countered, crossing his arms firmly over his chest and glaring down at us.

Jack sat up so he could shield me somewhat, and I wrapped his comforter around me. Bobby snuck an admiring glance at him, and I moved closer to Jack.

"I don't think that's really any of your business," I snapped.

"Whatever." Milo rolled his eyes. "You both know you're not supposed to be alone like this. And for once, its not you I'm worried about, Alice. You could kill him, and he'd be happy to let you." His words stung as true, and feeling ashamed, I pulled the blankets more securely around me.

Jack noticed my discomfort and rubbed my back, but I pulled away from him. The heat of the moment faded, and I hated knowing how close I had come to hurting him just because it felt good. He sighed and turned to my brother.

"So, what exactly did you want?"

"We came home to tell you something, but then I heard you guys," Milo wrinkled his nose in disgust, and Bobby made a nervous giggle. He chewed at his black nail polish, and when he caught me

116

glaring at him, he cowered more behind Milo.

"So what's this big news?" I asked, sounding bored.

"Jane was at V, and she's a blood whore," Milo said.

"A blood whore?" I asked.

"It's like a whore, but with blood instead of sex, and usually there's no monetary exchange," Milo explained.

"Well, if there's no money, than what is she getting for it?" I asked. Milo lowered his eyes, but I didn't understand. It was actually incredibly obvious, but I was still under the fog of my lust for Jack.

"They get hooked on the feeling they get from having vampires drink their blood," Jack said carefully. He'd never liked my former best friend Jane, but he wasn't eager for bad things to happen to her, and he knew that I still cared about her.

Milo became shifty and uncomfortable. A few months ago, he'd been wounded protecting Jane and me from vampires, and he'd been forced to drink her blood to compensate for a blood loss. Well, he hadn't really been forced. He just hadn't resisted, and it was one of the most disturbing things I've ever seen. He had been like a wild animal, and she moaned with pleasure. So if Jane was addicted to being bitten, Milo had gotten her addicted.

"Milo-" I was about to tell him that it wasn't his fault, but Bobby put his hand on Milo's back, comforting him. I narrowed my eyes at him. "Wait. Is that what you are?"

"No, of course not!" Bobby protested quickly.

"Alice!" Milo yelled.

"What?" I asked. "That's not an unfair judgment to come to, especially after whatever it was you two were doing earlier." Bobby's olive skin burned red with shame, but Milo just glared at me.

"That's a horrible thing to say to him," Milo said.

"Imagine how you would feel if someone had called you a bloodwhore," Jack looked at me with something veiled in his eyes. It made me think that somebody had probably called me a bloodwhore, and I wondered if that somebody had just been rescued from Finland.

"Sorry," I said without looking at Bobby. "I'm just looking out for Milo's best interests."

"Whatever," Milo said, but he didn't sound as angry as he had before. "Just get dressed. I'm not a big fan of talking to you when you're naked."

Milo put his hand on Bobby's back and ushered him out of the room. He gave us a warning glare before closing the door behind him. Jack and I just sat in silence for a minute, letting the weight of what we had almost done and the news about Jane settle in.

"So what exactly does being a bloodwhore entail?" I asked. I pulled my shirt back on, and I watched sadly as Jack did the same. "I understand the basic concept, but like… I don't know. How does it work?" Running my fingers through my hair to smooth out the tangles, I thought of something that made my stomach twist. "I mean… you've had bloodwhores before, haven't you?"

"Most vampires try it once or twice at least," he replied evasively. He got out of bed and readjusted his clothing, purposely avoiding looking at me. "It's fairly common."

The word "whore" made me the most uncomfortable. And I knew how amazing it felt when Jack drank my blood, how I could feel him, and how he could feel *everything* I felt. It was the most intimate act on earth, and he casually did it with random whores he picked up at a bar. I swallowed hard and refused to think about it.

"Alright." I remembered that I had to take it all in stride when dating a vampire. "So how do you go about that? You just... what?"

"Bloodwhores usually hang around the club. They know what the scene is." He began pacing the room, pretending to do things like readjust a picture on the wall or move something on the night stand. "You can just go there and find a girl. Or a guy. Whatever you're into. Then you, y'know, bite them. When it's done, you go on your way, and they sleep it off."

"So how would Jane find out about a place like *V*?" I asked.

"If she hung around downtown long enough, and she knows what to look for in a vampire, it's only a matter of time." He fixed a piece of tape on his *Purple Rain* poster and looked back at me. "It's like it is with any other drug."

"What are you talking about?" I asked.

"Bloodwhores are addicted," Jack said. "Letting a vampire bite you is pretty dangerous, but it's not the worst thing you can do. And they'll crave it more and more. There's only so much blood loss the human body can take."

As soon as Milo had mentioned that Jane had gotten involved with vampires, I hadn't been thrilled by the idea. But I had gotten so used to Jane being reckless and her name associated with being a whore that I hadn't thought much of it. If Jack was showing even an ounce of concern for her, it meant things were pretty bad off, and he was looking very gravely at me.

"You're saying that Jane could actually die?" I sat up straighter in bed, and my mouth suddenly felt very dry.

"No. I'm saying that... unless she gets out of that lifestyle, she *will* die," he said quietly.

Time seemed to stop. It wasn't until somebody threatened to take her away that I realized how much she meant to me. Jane was vain, self-absorbed, and a bitch most of the time, but underneath that, she had always been my friend. No matter who was at a party or what they thought of me, Jane always brought me along, and most of the time, she stood up for me. When vampires attacked us a few months ago, she saved my life.

Jane just never believed that she was more than a pretty face. And even through all the things she did, she had been my best friend since I was seven years old, and she'd been there for me as much as she was capable.

Now she was in serious trouble, and it was all because of me.

"We have to go get her," I said.

I jumped off the bed, scrambling to pull on my jeans as I did. Panic started taking over, and I flew around the room. Grabbing my shoes and my brush and a sweater and thinking that I had to do something to my hair before we went to a club or Jane wouldn't even speak to me... and then Jack grabbed my wrist.

"Alice. Slow down," Jack said. "She's not dying right now."

"You don't know that!"

"I'm pretty sure if she was in immediate danger, Milo wouldn't have left her there," he pointed out.

"Maybe." My heart slowed a bit. "But we still have to go get her."

"I agree, but you need to take a minute to calm down. We're going to a vampire club, for the first time since you turned, and it would be helpful if you were in control of yourself." Jack smiled wryly.

"Okay," I nodded and looked down at myself. The casual jeans and top combo I was going for would never work at a club, or at least Jane would say it didn't. If we were going there, I might as well fit in. "I'm gonna go get ready. Why don't you let Milo know, and we can get out of here?"

"Sounds good." He kissed me gently on the lips, sending tingles through me so much that I almost forgot about Jane. "Everything will be okay."

I smiled like I believed him, and I went into the closet to look for something to wear. What exactly did one wear when going to rescue their former best friend from an underground vampire club?

- 13 -

Milo and Bobby took the Jetta down to the club because Jack called dibs on the Lamborghini. Jack was a notoriously speedy driver, but the trip downtown had never seemed so long.

Since it was after two in the morning, most of the clubs and bars had cleared out, and he found a parking spot a block away from *V*. Milo pulled up behind us a minute later, meaning he had sped as well. I considered launching into a speech about the importance of driving safely, but then I saw a vampire walking towards us.

After becoming a vampire, other vampires are a lot easier to spot. A vampire's heart beats much slower and much quieter than a human could and still walk around.

The one walking towards us was tall and slender and pale, reminding me of the way Tim Burton would design a vampire. The human girl at his side looked even shorter and chubbier in comparison to him. Her skin had a blotchy ashen quality to it, a symptom I associated with recent blood loss, and her eyes were glassy with overly dilated pupils.

Her Tim Burton companion led her along carefully to keep her from stumbling or simply passing out right there, and while he smiled, there was an offhand way that he treated her. Like he was leading a cow to the slaughter.

I shivered involuntarily, and she smiled dazedly at me, her pudgy cheeks dimpling. She couldn't be more than sixteen herself, if that, and I wanted to steal her away from him. He wouldn't be eager to part with her, though, and even if I could get her away, she wouldn't appreciate it.

Besides that, the horrible truth of it was that this was the way of life. *My* way of life. Vampires are going to drink from people, and at least this way they're both willing participants. This is probably the best I can hope for.

"Come on," Jack said, putting his hand on my back. He saw me watching after them, and while he empathized with her, he knew there was nothing we could do. "We should get going."

"Yeah, come on. Before Jane leaves," Milo agreed. He held Bobby's hand and walked ahead of us.

Milo turned off Hennepin Ave onto a darkened street. The nearest streetlamps had gone out, and I suspected that was a constant occurrence. Vampires liked night as dark as it could be, which was why the doorway of the club was hidden on the darkest street in Minneapolis.

Bobby held onto Milo more tightly, probably because he couldn't see where he was going and didn't want to trip over anything. Jack and I followed directly behind them, and Milo glanced back at us before opening a nondescript door.

The bouncers stood inside the door. They were two massive vampires, and they barely looked at any of us, but they sniffed at Bobby. We squeezed in between to them to the narrow hall lit by a single red bulb.

At the end of the hall, a steep set of cement stairs led down into black nothingness. The only light came from the red one upstairs. It was more than enough for me to see the way down, but Bobby went down slowly and carefully, and Milo kept his hand on him to catch him if he fell.

As soon as we had opened the doors upstairs, I had been able to hear the faint sound of the music, but I'm sure that Bobby was just starting to hear it when we hit the landing. The hall went on forever, but we stopped at a pair of massive doors.

Milo pulled them open, bathing us with a blue light that was almost blinding after the darkness of the hall. To all the people dancing inside, it seemed dim and reasonable for a club, but it was different for vampires.

A long, metallic bar ran along the far side of the room, and bottles lined the back wall, full of alcoholic drinks for the humans. Several very attractive vampires stood behind it, bartending. The stools in front of it were full, and a line of people were waiting to get drinks.

The ceilings of the room were amazingly high for a basement. Electronica filled my ears, blotting out any sound of heartbeats, which was a relief. Nothing could be done for the smell. At least five-hundred people were smashed onto the floor, dancing wildly. And they all smelled deliciously of blood and sweat. Jack squeezed my hand tightly, drawing me back to him before bloodlust hit me.

The dancers were a mixture of vampire perfection and people, but the bouncers sifted through the humans to make sure only the more attractive specimens made it down here. Every one of them was beautiful and delectable. For Bobby's part, he seemed just as entranced by the vampires. I wanted to be angry with him for it, but they were still captivating to me.

"She's probably in the other room," Milo leaned in closer to us. He didn't raise his voice at all, but I could hear him above the echo of the club.

Wrapping his arm around Bobby's waist, Milo waded through the crowd. Jack looked down at me, checking to make sure I could handle crossing the floor. It required me to push up against lots of people, to physically be able to feel their rapid pulses beating against me, but I had to learn willpower sometime. Swallowing, I nodded and gripped his hand, and we followed Milo.

Everyone was hot from dancing, and I could feel it radiating from them. Jack pushed headily through, purposely being rough to get them out of the way. He wasn't a threatening person, but he was strong, and they parted for us. It was still a fight to keep back my thirst. I had no idea how Milo had been able to handle himself so well after he first turned.

We made it across the room, where the blue lights started to fade and a doorway led into the next room, glowing warm under the dim red lights. Milo waited at the door for us, Bobby pressed up close to him, his head resting on his shoulder.

Just before we reached them, I heard something disturbingly familiar. Jack and Milo didn't seem to notice it, buried in the sounds of the club, but I froze in my tracks. The sound was sweet yet fragile, like a tinkling bell... on helium. I pulled away from Jack, scanning the crowd for bright purple hair.

The last time we had gone to the vampire club, I had been

introduced to a pair of vampires, Lucian and Violet, who became intent on capturing me. Peter took care of Lucian, but she had gotten away. Violet seemed less interested in pursuing me, but like her boyfriend, she had been a caricature of vampirism. Her hair had been dyed purple, her eyeliner was thick black, and she capped her teeth to make them more pronounced fangs.

"What?" Jack asked, watching me search the dance floor.

"I don't know." I shook my head. I had been positive I had heard Violet's distinct laugh, but I couldn't see her anywhere.

I was just about to give up looking when a girl at the bar caught my attention. Her blond hair hung down her back, shimmering like silk under the blue lights. She tilted her head back, laughing at something a drunk guy said to her, and I shivered. That was Violet's laugh.

Absently, she looked back over her shoulder, her odd purple eyes landing on mine, and they flickered with frightened recognition. She traded in the thick black eyeliner for something subtler, making her prettier and younger, more innocent. Turning into a vampire made her look around nineteen or twenty, but something in her eyes led me to believe she was younger than that.

"Violet?" I said, but she instantly looked away, shielding her face with her hair.

"You know her?" Jack was at my side, looking at her quizzically. He had only met her very briefly when she looked much different, so he didn't recognize her.

"I think that's Violet." I walked towards her, but Jack put his hand on my arm.

"Wait, wait. That's the girl that was stalking you before? Why are you going to talk to her? Are you gonna…" His face darkened. "What are you gonna do?"

"I don't know. I wanna talk to her." I shook my head, unable to explain myself.

"What's going on?" Milo asked. He stood in the doorway, his arm around his boyfriend. He hadn't seen Violet, and that was for the best. He would take running into her much worse than I would.

"I'll be right back," I said and hurried over to Violet before she hid or escaped. Jack was right behind me, but he didn't try to stop me.

The drunk guy talking to her was mid-sentence, and she stood up without explanation. I know I should've felt angry. She had almost gotten me, Milo, and Jane killed, but I wasn't out for revenge. I just wanted to talk to her.

"Hey. Violet." I blocked her path, and she looked at me with wide eyes. All of her former cockiness was long gone, and that probably had to do with the death of her boyfriend.

"I don't know what you want but…" She trailed off, her eyes flicking from me to Jack. "I don't want any trouble."

"Neither do I." I glanced back at Jack to make sure he wasn't glaring at her or anything. Jack had such an open face, it was pretty hard for him to look threatening unless he was really pissed off.

"What do you want then?" Violet tried to look strong and angry, but without the confidence behind it, she just looked like a whiny child.

"I don't know." I chewed my lip. "Before, when you were

chasing after me, what did you want?"

"I didn't want anything with you," Violet said. "I mean, at first, I went after you as a joke because you were so tasty..." She lowered her eyes. "But Lucian, he wouldn't let it go. I think he liked the idea of stealing you from another vampire."

"Well, now he's gone and she's a vampire, so that's settled then," Jack interjected with a clumsy smile.

"How old are you?" I asked, ignoring Jack.

"I don't know why that matters," Violet said, but she looked flustered. "I was fourteen when I turned, and that was like two years ago.

"Look, it wasn't my idea." A strand of blond hair fell into her eyes, and she looked at me, as if daring me to defy her. "Not going after you, not turning into a vampire. It was all Lucian. He thought this was all some great big fantasy, and he had somebody turn him, and then stupidly, I had him turn me.

"But he's dead. And I'm over it. So..." Blinking hard, she tried to keep me from noticing the tears in her eyes. "Are we through?"

"Yeah. Sure," I nodded, unable to think of a reason to keep her talking to me.

Violet brushed past me, disappearing into the dance floor. Even after everything she had put me through, I felt this strange sadness for her. To be so powerful and young, and yet so confused and alone. She had been a dumb kid playing around with Hot Topic makeup and got in way over her head.

"You okay?" Jack touched my arm.

"Yeah." I remembered we weren't here to check up on my

enemies. Jane was here somewhere, probably losing blood as we spoke. "Sorry. Let's go."

"Who was that girl you were talking to?" Milo asked when reached them, and Bobby craned his neck around to see.

"Nobody. Where's Jane?" I asked.

"I haven't seen her yet, but we've just been waiting here." Milo gave me an irritated look, so I pushed past him into the adjoining room.

The light above glowed dull red, the kind of lighting that was most pleasing to vampires' eyes. This room was smaller than the last and dressed more like a coffee shop than a club. Soft couches filled the room, and a small bar in a dark corner served drinks, but only ones of the type AB variety.

A lot of doors and darkened hallways led out of it, and while I had never been in one of the rooms, I knew exactly what they were for. Some vampires required more privacy when they were with the bloodwhores, while others were camped out on the couch, drinking openly from their human donors.

With one quick scan of the room, I knew Jane wasn't there. Her heart and her scent were almost as familiar to me as Jack and Milo's, and they were nowhere in this room. I turned back to Milo, and he had come to the same conclusion.

"She was here before," Milo said.

"She was with a guy," Bobby added.

Jack walked around to look more closely, in case we missed something. I had taken too long getting ready or staring at the people outside or randomly talking to Violet. I had been wasting time when I should've been tracking down Jane. I still had her phone number, but she hadn't answered my calls since I turned into a vampire.

"Alice! He finally did it!" a voice purred, and a vampire got up off the couch and walked over to me. She left a girl discarded on the couch behind her, a thin trail of blood drying on her neck, and she moaned softly, reaching out in the empty space where Olivia had been.

With long black hair past her knees, Olivia had ageless beauty, but she had been in her forties when she had turned, which had probably been a very, very long time ago. Her clothing was entirely tight black leather, and I had never understood how she was able to move.

While we weren't exactly old friends, Olivia had been the vampire who had first rescued me from Lucian and Violet. There seemed to be a wisdom lurking below her hazy grin, and even though she had the slow, slurred movements of an aging junkie, she still had the killer instincts of a vampire.

"What?" I tried to return her smile, but I was too frustrated over not finding Jane.

"He turned you," Olivia said, and she reached out, caressing my cheeks. Her eyes were glazed, but her voice was low and surprisingly seductive. "And what an exquisite creature you are."

"Thanks," I replied uncertainly, and Jack appeared at my side.

"Maybe you can help." Milo walked over to us. Bobby trailed after him, and Olivia looked at him with disdain. Her interest apparently didn't go past human girls, or probably girls in general. "We're looking for a girl, a friend of Alice's."

"She's a bloodwhore, we think," I said. "She's tall and thin, and very pretty, like a model. Her hair is short and dark, and she's always dressed to the nines. Her name is Jane, and I think she's in trouble."

"If she's the girl I'm thinking of, she definitely *is* in trouble," Olivia nodded gravely. She licked her lip and pointed down the hall. "She's been coming around here a lot more than any one person should, and she went down that hall an hour ago with a vampire."

"Thank you," I smiled and turned down the hall.

The hall was pitch black, but I saw the outlines of the doors. I smelled the blood and heard the erratic heartbeats and happy moans, and I had to concentrate on it without thinking about it. I had to find Jane without giving into my own thirst.

Jack was a few steps ahead of me listening for her. Bobby complained about being unable to see anything behind us, and Milo tried to reassure him.

Before I could even smell her, I heard her overly sultry moan. Unfortunately, in my years of friendship with her, I had heard it far more than I had ever cared to. Without thinking, I threw open the door, and a figure flew at me.

- 14 -

I didn't have a chance to react, and Jack was already in front of me, shielding me from the vampire coming at my throat.

Jack threw him back, slamming him against the wall and holding him there while he gnashed his teeth. Jack managed to hold him in place, but Milo rushed past me to help him restrain the seriously pissed off vampire.

Jane was lying on a bed stained dark with blood. She wore some tiny piece of clothing that passed for a dress, revealing her pale skin. While she had always been thin, her arms were bony and her face was gaunt. Her heartbeat was almost nonexistent.

The room was filled with the scent of her fresh blood, and it was impossible to ignore. She moaned and stirred in the bed, and somehow that let my urge to protect her override my urge to eat her.

"Jane!" I ran to her, leaving Milo and Jack to contend with the thrashing vampire on the wall.

I got on the bed, ignoring how disgusting and tantalizing the blood stained mattress was, and I slapped her cheek. I had meant for it to be gentle, but the panic mixed with my unmastered strength made me slap her a little hard, not that she even noticed or woke up.

"Is everyone okay? What's going on?" Bobby asked. He couldn't see anything in the darkness, and he only heard the sound of struggling.

"Everything's under control!" Milo shouted as the vampire tried to bite his throat.

"What the hell is going on?" the vampire growled, and when he saw me tending to Jane, he stopped fighting. "You're after the whore?" We interrupted him in the middle of feeding, the time when vampires are most animalistic, and he seemed to be coming down from that.

"Her name is Jane!" I snapped, trying futilely to rouse her. She was completely out, and I knew how impossible blood loss was to wake up from.

"I know her name!" the vampire shouted. "I want to know what you want with her!"

"What do you care?" Jack countered, doing his best to sound tough. It would be comical if he wasn't trying to hold back a vampire from slaughtering us.

"Jonathan," Jane murmured, still mostly asleep.

"No, it's me, Alice," I said. She moved her head, and I turned it towards me, trying to get her to focus on me. "Jane, wake up. We need to get you out of here."

"She's talking about me, you silly twat! I'm Jonathan!" The vampire pushed against Jack. "Will you let me go? I'm not gonna fight you! I don't have to. She's not gonna go with you."

Jack lessened his grip, and when Jonathan didn't attack him, Jack took a step back from him. Milo did the same but more hesitantly. Jonathan smoothed out his shirt and glared at them.

"Jane, honey, wake up," I said and shook her.

"No, Jonathan, let me sleep." Jane swatted at me.

"She's not going with you," Jonathan repeated. He stepped closer to me, and Milo growled and moved in between him and the bed. "I'm not gonna stop you. What do I care if you take the whore?"

"I think it might be better if you just shut the hell up," Jack said.

"Jane, come on." I grabbed her shoulders and pulled her so she was sitting up. Her head lolled back, revealing the open wounds on her neck. Then she opened her eyes and lifted her head. "Jane, come on. Let's go."

"Alice?" Jane squinted. "What are you doing here?"

"Taking you with me." I put my arm around her to pick her up, but she pushed back at me. She was much weaker than me, but I didn't want to force her. "Jane, you've gotta come with me."

"No! *No!* Why would I wanna I go with you?" Jane pushed away from me so she could lie down on the filthy mattress. "Get away from me. I'm staying with Jonathan."

"I told you," Jonathan said and crossed his arms over his chest.

His hair was cropped short, almost shaved, and he had that perpetual unshaven look. He was undeniably foxy, the way all vampires seemed to be, and I was fairly certain that I had seen him on a billboard modeling men's underwear before.

"What are you even doing here?" Jane sounded incredibly irritated, because I was ruining her buzz. She was awake now but not entirely alert, and she ran her fingers through her hair in an offhandedly sexy way. Her reflexes were even seductive.

"We came to get you. We're worried about you," I told her as sincerely as possible. I put my hand on her arm, but she pulled it back from me.

"*We?*" Jane squinted harder in the darkness, trying to see who I brought with me, and pushed herself to sit up. Her skeletal arms were stretched out behind her, holding her up precariously so she didn't fall back on the bed.

"That *was* your little brother I saw grinding up on some boy on the dance floor! I thought that was him, but I didn't believe you were letting him date yet." She gave a laugh, and Milo scowled at her. "That's just like him to narc on me anyway. I bet you just ran home to tell her right away, didn't you?"

"This isn't the kind of life you want to have," Milo said, his cheeks reddening.

"Tell that to your boyfriend," Jane laughed again, but it was a tired, hollow sound.

"Jane, come on. This is enough. Let's get you home." I got up off the bed and reached out for her, planning to throw her over my shoulder if I had to.

"No! I'm not going with you!" Jane yelled. "You've barely even talked to me since you got Jack, and you have the balls to condemn me for doing the exact same thing as you?"

"I *never* did this!" I shouted. "And I was avoiding you to protect you, and then you avoided me. I called you like a million times but you wouldn't answer!"

"Doesn't that tell you something?" Jane smiled darkly at me. "I don't want to be your friend anymore, Alice! You don't need to save me from myself! I am just fine without you!"

"You are not fine! And I'm not saving you from *you*! I'm saving you from vampires!" I knew that sounded really dumb since I planned on bringing her back to a house full of vampires, and Jane laughed at the stupidity of my argument.

I bent down and scooped her up. She yelped in protest, but I tossed her easily over my shoulder. I was much stronger than before, but it was almost too easy. As soon as I had her, she hit at my back and screamed at me.

"Put me down, you stupid bitch!" Jane shouted, pounding her tiny fists as hard as she could against my back. Of course, it didn't hurt at all, but that didn't stop her from trying.

"She doesn't want to go with you!" Jonathan made a step towards me.

Jack and Milo moved closer to him. Jonathan held his hands up in a gesture of peace, but his face contorted with contained rage. If I tried taking away food from a starving wolf, I imagine that he would make a similar expression.

"What's going on?" Bobby asked, terrified.

"Everything's fine," Milo told him unconvincingly.

"You can't kidnap her," Jonathan said.

I hadn't moved towards the door yet because I hoped Jane would calm down, but he was right. I couldn't take her kicking and screaming onto the city streets.

"Just put me down!" Jane shouted. Sighing, I set her on her feet next to me. She slapped me once more for good measure, and I had to remind myself that she was my best friend. "You are such a control freak, Alice! Just because you're a prude doesn't mean I'm wrong!"

"I don't want any trouble but she is *mine*," Jonathan exchanged a look with Jack, and Jane puffed up.

Jane misinterpreted his use of the word "mine." She saw it as something resembling love, like he cared so she belonged to him. All he really meant was that he had bitten her first, so he laid claim on her until he gave her up.

She reached out in the darkness, feeling around for Jonathan to protect her. Milo moved, allowing Jonathan to walk to her. He put his arm around her in something that she perceived as affection, but it was nothing more than ownership.

"We'll talk later," I said finally.

"Fat chance," Jane scoffed.

Milo comforted Bobby, who frantically clung to the door. Jack put his arm around me, escorting me from the room.

I looked back over my shoulder at Jane. Thin and frail, she hung onto Jonathan just to keep from falling over. Before we had even left the room, he tilted her head back and sunk his teeth into her neck. She moaned and her blood filled the air.

Jack tightened his arm around me to prevent me from rushing at Jonathan and getting myself killed. He pulled the door shut behind us and drug me down the hallway, past all the rooms where vampires were feeding on other people's best friends.

I spent the entire car ride home sulking and glaring out the window. Jack tried to talk to me and cheer me up, but I wanted nothing to do with it. It wasn't his fault that Jane wouldn't come home with us, or that vampires were such horrible creatures, but he was the only one I had to take it out on.

When we pulled in the garage, I slammed the car door behind

me and stormed into the house, noticing that Milo and Bobby hadn't returned yet.

"Alice!" Jack called after me, but I didn't slow down.

Matilda waited at the door for us, but when she greeted me, I pushed past her. Jack indulged her more than I did, but he was trying to keep up with me so he made it quick.

"Alice, come on. I know you're upset, but you didn't really think you could swoop in there like Batman and save the day, did you?"

"I don't know what I thought," I muttered.

I reached the kitchen and stopped. I wanted to eat something. Not that I was actually hungry, not for human food, but whenever I had come home frustrated, Milo always fed me. It was probably for the best I turned into a vampire, otherwise I would've ended up as a very fat stress eater. Out of habit, I opened up the refrigerator, which actually had food in it again, thanks to Bobby.

"What are you doing?" Jack asked.

"Making Bobby a snack."

Since I'd never had a conversation with the kid, I had no real clue what kind of foods he might like, but Mae stocked the fridge for him, so it was a safe bet that anything in it would work. I hadn't really meant to make him anything, and it was a well known fact that I couldn't cook, but it would give me something to do.

The crisper was filled with fruits, so I grabbed them all, thinking that chopping them up for a fruit salad might go a long way to alleviate my anger.

"Do you need any help?" Jack asked, watching me drop the armload of fruits onto the island.

I shook my head and searched the kitchen drawers until I found a large butcher knife. I couldn't tell the last time anybody had used it, so I rinsed it off. Then I realized I hadn't washed off any of the fruit, either, so I grabbed it all and dropped it in the sink to clean.

"Are you mad at me?" Jack leaned against the island with Matilda rubbing up against him so he could scratch her head.

"No," I said, but that wasn't exactly true. "You and Milo could've taken that Jonathan idiot. And I'm sure Jane would've followed you out of there. We could've taken her if we really tried."

"Maybe," he admitted.

I picked the fruit up out of the sink, but they were wet and slippery, and the grapes and strawberries tried making their escape onto the floor. He came over and caught what was falling and helped me carry it back over to the island.

"Thank you," I muttered, not ready to give up on my anger yet.

"If we had to kidnap Jane, what good would it have really done?" Jack looked at me. "You watch that *Intervention* show about junkies. What do they always say? You can't make a person change, and they can't quit for anybody else. Jane has to *want* to stop."

"Then why did we even go down there?" My hands felt shaky when I started chopping a pear, but I ignored it. I couldn't forget the image of how sickly Jane looked, and how content she was with that.

"I thought maybe you'd be able to talk some sense into her." He shrugged. "But now she knows that you still care, and if she has a change of heart, she'll talk to you."

"Jane's never listened to me about anything, and you know it."

"Maybe so, but this is her choice, and you have to let her make it." He was on the other side of the island from me, leaning across it.

My body was naturally pulled to him, and I pretended like pears and apricots were more interesting. Unfortunately, I'd never been a coordinated person, and I didn't do much better as a vampire. I was distracted by Jack and thoughts of Jane, so it was only a matter of time before the knife sliced my finger.

I yelped and pulled my hand back, sustaining my first real injury as a vampire. The pain was much sharper and more intense than any I had felt as a human, but it died away instantly. The cut was nasty, hitting the bone in my index finger. If my bones hadn't been so strong, I probably would've sliced the tip right off.

I stared down at it, watching the blood seeping from my wound with some amazement. This was my blood, and I could smell it, warm and strangely exotic.

"You do smell *really* good," Jack said in a hushed tone.

The pink edges of the cut were already healing, right in front of my eyes, and I glanced up at him. His eyes had gone translucent, and I heard his heart speed up. Nothing in the world was more enticing to him than the scent of my blood, and that hadn't changed when I became immortal.

"Want a taste?" I offered my hand to him, knowing how wonderful it felt when he tasted me and how crazy it drove him. I imagined him throwing all the fruit off the island and pushing me back down on it, kissing me ferociously until his mouth found my neck...

"In the kitchen?" He raised an eyebrow, his breath shallow.

With great effort, he managed to pull his eyes from me to look around the room, pointing out how completely exposed we would be. At any minute, Milo and Bobby would come home, and Mae and Ezra had to be somewhere around here

"Suit yourself." I shrugged, pretending it meant nothing, even though I knew he could hear my own ragged heartbeat. The cut had healed completely, and the blood dried on my skin. I put my finger in my mouth, cleaning it off.

"You're horrible." He shook his head and took a step back from the island, trying to clear his head of me.

Within seconds, Milo and Bobby came in from the garage. They both eyed up the fruit spread on the island with confusion, but Milo's face contorted into something different. He sniffed, giving me an evil look that was somehow hungry as well.

"Why does it smell like your blood in here?" Milo demanded, then shot a glare at Jack.

"I just cut my finger," I sighed and held up the knife that still had my blood on it. A few droplets were on the island, and I wiped at them with a rag.

"Oh really, Alice." Milo rolled his eyes and came over to me. "Do you want me to do this for you? What are you doing anyway?"

"I thought you didn't eat," Bobby said. A strand of his black hair fell into his eyes, and he pushed it back, walking over to the island to inspect what we were doing.

"I thought you might be hungry," I said. Milo had taken over chopping up the fruit, and he looked back at me with surprise.

"Thanks," Bobby said and blushed lightly. Everyone clearly assumed that I hated Bobby, and they weren't that far off base, but I did like distractions.

"Milo always used to cook for me when I got home," I said lamely.

Tucking hair behind my ears, I caught Jack smiling at me. He knew the whole snack thing was about busy work, not Bobby, but he was glad that I made nice with Bobby. Jack liked Bobby, which for some reason, made me angry with Jack again, so I sighed and leaned back against the kitchen counter.

"Milo is a very good cook." Bobby smiled at me before looking adoringly at my brother.

"He was gonna be a chef," I said.

"I still can be," Milo cast me a look. "I'm not dead." Jack laughed at that sentiment, and Milo rolled his eyes again. "I have lots of time to become whatever I want."

He finished cutting the fruit, and he went to the cupboard to get out a serving platter. Once he brought it back to the island, he arranged the fruit. Bobby smiled and delicately picked at grapes, afraid of disturbing the masterpiece that Milo had created.

The bedroom door to Mae and Ezra's room slammed loudly, followed by quick footsteps, and Mae repeatedly saying the word no. She appeared in the kitchen, looking haggard. Her cheeks and eyes were red from crying, and her honey curls were pulled back in a very messy bun. Tissue was wadded up tightly in her hand, and she glared at us.

- 15 -

Ezra followed close behind Mae, looking better than he had in days. He didn't appear as upset as her, but his expression was grim. When he reached out for her, she pulled away from him.

"Where have you been?" Mae demanded, her warm voice more shrill. Bobby had been in the middle of chewing, but he gulped it down whole and moved closer to Milo.

"Why? Did something happen?" Jack asked carefully.

"Just answer the damn question!" Mae shouted, making us all jump. Her hands were balled up at her sides, and stray curls stuck to her tear stained cheeks. "You think you all can just come and go as you please. This isn't a hotel. We are a family, and this is our home!"

"Sorry?" I apologized uncertainly. I looked to Ezra for help, but he was too busy watching her to give us any hint about what the hell was going on.

"Yeah, we're really sorry," Milo said, more sincerely than I did.

"We didn't mean to not tell you," Jack said. "We just left in kind of a hurry, I guess."

"Where did you go that was so important you couldn't let me know?" Mae fixed her gaze on Jack because he had offered the most up, and he shrunk back from it, wrapping his arms over his chest. He shifted uneasily and glanced at me, but I shook my head. I didn't want any part of her hysteria.

"We just, uh, went to the club to look-" He'd barely gotten out the word "club" before her eyes widened and she cut him off.

"The *club*? Not the vampire club? None of you would be that stupid to do something as risky and dangerous as that without even letting me know." Mae was completely aghast, and Jack looked at his feet, so she turned to the rest of us. "What were you thinking? Do you all have a death wish? Just because you can live forever doesn't mean you will!"

"We were going there after Jane," I said quietly, hoping to appease her some.

"If you all want to die, I can't save you!" She threw her hands up in the air. "I can't save anybody!"

A fresh tear slid down her cheek, and I wanted to hug her or comfort her in some way, but I didn't know how. I was afraid that anything I did would just set her off more.

"We're really, really sorry," Milo said.

"I can't save *anybody*!" Mae wailed, her voice cracking.

"Mae," Ezra whispered. She sobbed, doubling over and holding her sides. He wrapped his arms around her and held her up. "Mae, love, it's all right."

"It is *not* all right!" Mae tried pushing him away, but he held steadfast. "This is not how it's supposed to be!" She cried harder, her words lost completely in her tears, so she turned and buried her face in his chest.

They stood that way for a minute, and the rest of us stared at them. We weren't really sure if we should leave or stay there or speak or what, so we just stared.

"I don't mean to be rude," I said carefully when Mae seemed more composed. "But, um, what is going on?"

"Mae went to visit her human family," Ezra explained.

Even though his words were meant to be soothing, I heard the disapproval in them. He didn't think that Mae should have anything to do with the humans she had left behind when she turned, but she insisted on driving out to check on them, although she never interacted with them.

"Tonight, she found out that her great-granddaughter is terminally ill, and she only has a matter of months to live," Ezra said, and he held her more tightly. Just hearing him say it aloud devastated her.

Mae had been twenty-eight when she turned, leaving behind a young daughter. Her change hadn't been entirely by choice, and she had to leave a family that meant everything to her. She had been forced to watch her daughter grow up from a distance, and then her granddaughter, and now her great-grandchildren.

Ezra tolerated her fondness for them because he loved her so much, but he had given her a deadline. They were going to have to move away from them soon, because she couldn't spend her entire existence watching her future generations getting old and dying.

The hardest part for Mae was that she had had an infant son that died several years before her daughter was born. It almost killed her, and Mae swore that she would never outlive any of her other children. Unfortunately, she had become immortal, so she would have no choice.

But nothing could've prepared her for losing her five-year-old great-granddaughter. I doubt she could even wrap her mind around losing her adult daughter, let alone a small child.

I went to her, and she pulled away from Ezra just enough so she could hug me. As much as she loved him, at that moment, she wanted a child, and I had become a surrogate daughter for her. She held onto me so tightly it was painful, but I said nothing.

Eventually, she calmed down and apologized for her behavior. By then, Milo and Bobby had snuck up to their room, much to my annoyance. Ezra stayed by her side, in case she might need him, but Jack had ventured into the backyard with Matilda to give us space.

When Mae could speak clearly, she explained that Daisy, her great-granddaughter, had been looking under the weather the last few months, but it wasn't until tonight that she was able to overhear them talking and found out exactly what was going on.

Ezra was convinced that rest was the best solution to her current state, and he looked rather drained himself. He helped Mae back down to their room, looking apologetically back at me as he did. He cared about her very much, but he was still upset she had any contact with them. Nothing good came from keeping humans in your life.

I thought of Jane at the club, and Bobby upstairs with my brother, and shook my head. Eventually, everyone would die, except for us, and I could never tell if that was comforting or terrifying.

Jack was outside, wrestling in the fallen leaves and frost with Matilda. The moon was fat, but thin clouds hazed over it. I stepped out the French doors, relishing the chill in the air. Breathing in deeply, I tried to let the freshness from the outdoors cleanse everything else. All of Mae's tears, and all the horrible images of Jane in the darkened rooms of *V*.

Jack grinned when he saw me and got up from a pile of leaves he and the dog had been demolishing. Matilda had twigs and leaves imbedded in her fur, and she loped around the lawn carrying a big stick in her mouth. He ran a hand through his hair, freeing a few leaves himself and walked over to me.

"How are you holding up?" he asked.

"Great." I was exaggerating, but I did feel a lot better being outside.

"You sure?" He looked at me seriously, and I picked at some of the foliage that clung to his tee shirt. His bare arms were dirty and cold from the ground, but I doubted he noticed.

"Yeah. Mae is the one having the rough night, not me," I said.

"How is she?" He looked past me at the house, worrying about her.

"I really don't know," I admitted. "Ezra took her back to their room to get some rest, but…" I trailed off and shrugged. It was hard to say how she would hold up.

"I'm sorry we couldn't help Jane more." He returned his concern to me.

"Me too, but you're right. She has to want to help herself, and she'll probably never want to," I sighed and rubbed at my arms, even though they weren't really cold.

"You've had a really long night. You should probably get some rest, too."

"That is true." It was early for me to go to bed, but I hadn't felt completely rested since before I went to Finland. I yawned and

149

thought longingly about curling up in bed.

"Do you want any company?" Jack asked, wagging his eyebrows.

"You know I do," I chewed my lip. I always wanted Jack in bed with me, especially after we had started earlier, but my heart wasn't really in it just then. "But we probably shouldn't. I'm probably not in control enough to handle what you would do to me."

"That is true," he smiled a little sadly. "You go in and go ahead to bed. I might come up in a bit to grab some clothes, but I gotta get the dog cleaned up before I can take a shower and crash on the couch."

"I feel so bad about kicking you out of your own bed," I said for the millionth time since I had moved into his room.

"Hey, I'm nothing if not a gentlemen, and I couldn't sleep knowing you weren't absolutely comfortable." He leaned down and kissed me. His lips were cool from the night, but the kiss was brief, stopping too soon. Still, my skin felt warm and flushed when he straightened up. "Go on and get to bed. I'll see you later."

Reluctantly, I turned to walk back into the house. Matilda chased after me, planning to sneak into the house, but Jack stopped her. Her big white paws were covered in cold mud from running around by the lake, and her fur was full of debris from rolling around. I don't know what his plan was for getting her clean before they went into the house, but I left him to it.

I watched them for a minute before heading up to his room. Matilda leapt happily over piles of leaves, and Jack charged after her, laughing and egging her on. He was dirty and his clothes were getting ruined, but he didn't notice at all because he was having too much fun with his dog.

It was weird how things like that could make me love him so much. My heart swelled at the sight of him, and I turned to go upstairs before I changed my mind about inviting him to go with me.

In the middle of a horrible dream about crocodiles chasing kittens, Jack came in and gave me a kiss. I stirred a little in bed and invited him to join me, but he declined for reasons that remain a mystery. I'm sure he told me, but as soon as the words were out of his mouth, I was asleep again, but thankfully, I managed to save all the kittens from the crocodiles.

When I did wake up for good, I realized that one of the things that Jack had said to me had been goodbye. Not "good night," not "see you in the morning," but "goodbye," which had way too much finality in it for my taste.

I raced downstairs to find the den, a.k.a. Jack's current sleeping quarters, deserted, with all his blankets folded up neatly, and he never folded up blankets or made his bed. I thought about checking in with Mae, but I didn't want to disturb her.

That left me hurrying back upstairs to check with Peter on the off-chance he knew something, and Matilda trailed after me, another sure sign that Jack was gone. Peter was gone, too, but I wasn't even sure if he'd come home yesterday.

In truth, I'd known Jack was gone the second I opened my eyes. I could always feel when he wasn't around me, like the thread between us got pulled painfully thin. I couldn't tell exactly where he was at or anything; I just knew that it wasn't close by.

Before knocking on my brother's bedroom door, I listened

carefully. After hearing what he'd been up to yesterday, I didn't want to walk in on them in the middle of something. From the sound of it, Milo was still asleep. It wasn't even six at night, and in vampire time, that's pretty damn early. Usually, I'm not up before eight pm.

"Milo?" I knocked cautiously but didn't dare open the door. This was weird considering Milo and I usually just burst into each other rooms. We had never any reason for propriety before this Bobby character had come into our lives.

I was about to knock again when Bobby opened the door. He wore pajama bottoms and nothing else, revealing his heavily tattooed torso. Something in Latin was scrawled across his chest, and ivy wound about just above his pubic area, not to mention about a million others that I didn't have a chance to study. He hadn't flat ironed his dark hair, so it stood up in a crazy mess, but he looked to have been awake for awhile.

"He's still asleep," Bobby whispered and crept out of the room, closing the door quietly behind him so we wouldn't disturb Milo. "Is there something I can help you with?"

"Uh, maybe, I guess," I said. He crossed his arms over his chest, trying to protect his bare skin from the chill of the house, and I wondered why he hadn't just put on a shirt. "Do you know where Jack is?"

"Kinda, actually," Bobby nodded, looking pleased to be able to help. "They had some emergency business thing. I didn't understand exactly, but the stocks were going crazy and they had to go fix it. Ezra and Jack left a few hours ago, and I think Peter was already on his way there. They should only be there for a day or two."

"How do you know all this stuff?"

"Oh, cause I have insomnia," Bobby smiled a little. "It kinda works out having a vampire for a boyfriend, but he still sleeps, and I don't." He shrugged at the humor in it, but I wasn't sure if I found anything about him fun or charming.

"I see."

Matilda finally decided neither of us were Jack nor were we suitable replacements, so she wandered down the hall. I watched her walk away, then went back to staring awkwardly at Milo's half-naked boyfriend.

He smelled delicious, but I didn't really want to eat him. I counted that as a good sign, but I didn't like him. Still, I didn't really want to go back to my room just yet.

"So, are you up for the day?" Bobby asked.

"Yeah, I think so."

"Cool. Let me just get a shirt," he said, as if I had invited him to do something. I nodded and waited for him, like I thought I had invited him too.

Bobby disappeared briefly into the room before coming out with a slim-fitting zippered hoodie hanging open. I tried to peer around him to see what Milo's bedroom looked like now that he was sharing it with someone else, but Bobby barely opened the door. I'm not sure if he was trying to hide something, or if he was just trying to respect Milo's sleep. Either way, I decided that I didn't trust him.

- 16 -

"I was gonna get something to eat," Bobby said, zipping up his hoodie. He didn't do it all the way to the top, but from what I could tell about his penchant for low V-neck shirts, he was a big fan of showing off his chest tattoos.

Not that I blamed him really. Bobby was actually very attractive. If I was still human and didn't have Jack and didn't know that he was shagging my brother, I'd probably think he was hot.

"I wasn't, but that's probably better for you." I was kind of joking, but I was also trying to sound kinda threatening. Just as a reminder that if he hurt my brother, I could totally kill him.

"Right." He gave a small laugh and went downstairs. I went with him, because really, I had nothing better to do. "So... do you ever miss food?"

"Not really," I shrugged, following him into the kitchen. "It's hard to explain. I remember the way food tasted, and I kinda crave it. But when I think about eating it, I feel nauseous. Besides that, blood tastes a million times better than any food ever could."

"I'll take your word for it." Bobby crinkled his nose at the thought of drinking blood, which I found distasteful. I knew he let Milo drink his blood, and he enjoyed it. It seemed kind of hypocritical.

"Whatever." I pulled a stool up to the kitchen island and sat down while he rummaged around in the fridge.

"I've always been partial to a bagel with cream cheese." He got said foods out of the fridge and popped the bagel in a toaster. "I don't think I could ever give it up, so I guess being a vampire is out for me."

He was trying to make a joke, I'm sure, but it sounded like a stupid thing to be a deal breaker for immortality, especially considering that eternity would be with Milo.

Bobby leaned against the counter, waiting for the bagel to pop up, and an uncomfortable silence settled over us. I was thinking my day would be much better spent watching the newest season of *Dexter* on DVD in Jack's room. I had been slowly working my way through the whole series since Jack constantly raved about it.

"So… you don't really like me," Bobby said after his bagel popped up. He spread cream cheese thick all over it and didn't look at me. "I don't blame you."

"Why? Low self-esteem?" I said flippantly.

"Kinda, but that's not what I meant." He took a big bite of his bagel and turned to face me. He swallowed it before continuing. "I get it. Milo is your little brother, and he's pretty young and inexperienced. And I'm older, and I do kinda have that bad boy vibe, even though I am clearly not a bad boy."

With the tattoos and dark features, Bobby did have a rebel without a cause thing going on, but after the way I had seen him cowering around Milo in the club last night, I could say with complete certainty that Bobby was not a bad boy in any real sense of the word.

"Those things are true," I said carefully.

"And I am human, which is dangerous in a way for vampires," Bobby said. "I mean, he's stronger and more powerful than I am, but I complicate things for him in a lot of different ways, and I know that."

"If you know that then why are you with him?" I asked, not unkindly.

"That's a good question." It was such a good question that he had to finish the entire bagel so he could think it over. Finally, he swallowed the last bite and leaned back against the kitchen counter. "I don't want to tell you."

"I don't like the sound of that," I warned him icily.

"No, it's not..." He shook his head. "You'll think I'm just under the spell, that one that vampires put humans under, and it's not that." He paused a second. "It sounds cheesy and like an easy excuse and everything... but we're in love."

"He's sixteen! What does he know about love?" I don't know why that was my go-to argument, and it was Bobby's turn to think that I was hypocrite. "Okay, yeah, I get that I'm not much older than Milo, but..."

"You understand where we're coming from," Bobby said with a wry smile, and I shook my head, unwilling to admit defeat. "The situation is difficult, but the heart wants what it wants."

"What a stupid thing to say," I scoffed. "My stomach wants what it wants, too, but you don't see me ripping out your throat to get it, Bobby." He shrugged, unfazed by my veiled threat, and I wasn't sure if it made me hate Bobby more or less. "What is that about?"

"What?"

"You're like twenty-one, and people call you *Bobby*. Isn't that a little boy name?" I wrinkled my nose, and he laughed.

"People called Robert Kennedy 'Bobby' his entire life."

"And look at how well that turned out for him," I countered, referring to his untimely assassination.

"Maybe. But my name actually is 'Bobby,' not 'Robert' or 'Bob' or anything," he shrugged. "So it's just what I go by, since it is legally my name."

"Was your mother like a hippie or something?" I asked.

"Something like that."

"Okay, so fine, you and my brother are crazy in love," I said, and it left a bitter taste in my mouth just playing devil's advocate. "Let's say that I buy that. How did you two meet? And how did you come to know our particular lifestyle?"

Lifestyle wasn't exactly the right word, because it implied that there was a choice in this. I had chosen to become a vampire, but I could never choose not to be one, not unless I died. Even then, I'd just be a dead vampire.

"Um... well..." Bobby fidgeted with the zipper on his hoodie. "I used to frequent the gay clubs, especially right after I turned 18. I wasn't a slut, exactly, but I wasn't... not a slut, either.

"One of the gentlemen pursuing me turned out to be a vampire. We 'dated' for awhile, but I'm using the term loosely. We'd just fool around, and he'd bite me. But it took some time before I figured out what was going on. I mean, even after I realized that he was physically biting me, it was still a hard concept to buy that he was a vampire."

"Yeah, I know what you mean," I said. The supernatural could be a very hard pill to swallow. Sometimes, I still found it hard to believe in vampires, and I was one.

"I was never a bloodwhore," Bobby said quickly. "I did like the way it felt, being bitten." He looked at me. "You've been bitten, right?"

"Only twice."

"It's pretty wonderful," he smiled. "But it's even better when you're in love. All their feelings rush over you, and if the guy biting you is a douche bag, it can feel pretty dirty and terrible, even when it feels so good."

That was exactly why Ezra had been in such horrible shape in Finland, but I wasn't eager to think of that, so I nodded for Bobby to continue.

"Anyway, I started hanging out around *V*, looking for vampires, and then I met Milo." Bobby looked at the ground. "It was like love at first sight. That sounds like a line, but it's true."

"So you just saw him, and that was it?" I asked.

"Pretty much. He just walked over to me and we started dancing, and kissing, and talking, and we've been together ever since." Bobby smiled wider. "Milo's a pretty great guy."

He ran his hands through his hair, trying to smooth out his side bangs. His dark eyes had that weird wistful quality to them and his cheeks were reddening lightly, so I knew he was thinking about Milo. I didn't doubt that he really did care about my brother, but I just couldn't seem to like him.

Well, that wasn't even it exactly. I actually did kinda like Bobby, or I was starting to at least. I studied him closely, trying to figure out what about him was really bothering me. Was it just that he was Milo's boyfriend and I wouldn't like anybody he dated?

That's when it finally dawned on me. I didn't like Bobby because I didn't like him. My first reaction to him had been suspicion. That had just been because I was surprised he was human, and I was protective of Milo. Dislike was perfectly reasonable, but I shouldn't have been able to feel that way. Not if Milo and Bobby were really supposed to be together, the way my blood had been meant for Peter.

The reason everything had gotten so complicated with Jack and Peter was because of how fluid the bond is. Jack, Peter, and Ezra, and now Milo and I, were held together by a similar blood bond.

Milo and I were especially bonded because we were siblings in real life as well as in vampires. That meant I should have a great affinity for whoever he was bonded with. It would be impossible for me to hate who he was meant for, and yet, I had instantly disliked Bobby.

I understood transference in all of this. I had broken my bond with Peter, and I knew that love could be stronger than blood. But that probably wasn't the case with Bobby. He was just a nice guy that Milo would be into for awhile, but not forever.

I suddenly felt sorry for Bobby, because, Milo would break his heart. Not the other way around.

"And you don't have to worry about us," Bobby was saying,

drawing me from my thoughts. He tired of trying to straighten out his hair and flipped up the hood of his sweater. I hadn't really been listening to him, so I just stared, hoping he would elaborate. "I mean, Milo, I guess. He's not like that guy Jane was with, and I'm not like her, either. That's not our thing."

"No, I get that," I nodded. Maybe at first the idea had crossed my mind, but I didn't think so anymore.

"I understand the appeal of her lifestyle. It's something that you can fall into pretty easily." Bobby twisted the drawstring to his hood around and looked at the ground.

I had a feeling that despite all his protests, it was a lifestyle that Bobby had come precariously close to getting into, and when things ended with Milo, there was an even greater chance that that's how he would end up. Thanks to Milo, he'd be even more hooked on the feel of being bitten.

"So, you know what it's like, probably better than anyone in the house." I leaned across the island, looking at him more intently. "You get where Jane is coming from. If the situation were reversed, if you were a bloodwhore, what could somebody say to get you to stop?"

"That's a good question." He exhaled and stared off, thinking. "I don't know really. As long as it still feels good, it's a pretty hard thing to convince somebody to stop. I think it has to start hurting her, and then you have to keep reminding her how much it hurts."

"How does it hurt her?" I asked. "I know that it's killing her, but she's unaware of that. Like, any time she feels like crap, she just gets bit, and then feels better, right?"

"Not exactly," Bobby shook his head. "Immediately after, you feel really good. But shortly after that is when you feel the worst. The loss of blood really damages your body, and you start to feel what it's going through. And you have the residuals of the vampire you're with, and if she is picking up random guys at the club, they're probably dicks. Meaning she's left with none of the euphoria but all of their emotions and how they feel about you, which is usually pretty shitty.

"It's after that, after the bad feelings fade and you get your strength back, that's when you go back to the club," he went on. "You forget how bad they made you feel, how incredibly weak you were, and for some reason, all you can remember is the pleasure of the bite."

"Huh." I eyed him up, and he noticed, so he shrugged sheepishly. "Not that your information hasn't been helpful, but I'm starting to think you picked up a lot more vampires than you let on."

"It's different with Milo," Bobby insisted with a wounded look in his eyes. "Honest. You don't have to believe me, but it's more than biting and fooling around. So... Please don't tell him, okay? He knows that he's not the first vampire I was with, but he doesn't know how many were before him. I don't want him to think that's what this is about, because it's not."

"I won't tell him unless I think it's relevant. So just don't make it relevant," I said, staring at him evenly. He nodded, realizing that was about the most he could get from me.

"This is a pretty awesome place," Bobby said, changing the subject. He moved onto making coffee, and the coffee maker looked brand new. Mae had probably bought it especially for him, so he must not be all bad if she approved of him. "And Mae is amazing. How is she doing today?"

"I haven't seen her." I looked over my shoulder toward her room, and I tried to listen for the sound of her over the coffee pot gurgling, but I couldn't hear anything. "Have you?"

"No, but if Ezra left, I didn't think it would be that bad," Bobby said.

The kitchen smelled completely of coffee, and I felt an odd pang of knowing I couldn't have any. I had never really liked coffee, but I loved the smell of it. My stomach gave me a sharp pain, reminding me that I didn't want any of that anyway.

Bobby suddenly seemed to smell stronger, and I pushed it back. This was just my body's attempts to convince me I was hungry, but I shouldn't be yet, and even if I was, I had to learn to get control of my hunger instead of letting it control me.

"You okay?" Bobby asked.

"Yeah, yeah, I'm fine." I shook my head to clear it. "I think I'm just gonna get a shower. But, um, it was nice talking to you, and I'll see you later."

"Yeah, alright," Bobby said, but he still looked worried.

When I went upstairs, Matilda followed me again. She assumed that every time I went anywhere, Jack would be waiting. Maybe I spent too much time with him.

Although lately, it wasn't really feeling like I spent *any* time with him. I had just gotten back from a trip, and then he left. In his room, with all his things, my heart throbbed at the thought of him. Matilda jumped on his bed, covering his blankets with her white fur, and

163

sniffing about, as if he was hidden amongst them.

I sighed and started rummaging around the room for something to change into. I'd most likely spend the day watching TV or reading or something. Nothing worth getting gussied up for. Maybe if I was lucky, I could get Milo and Bobby to hang out with me, if they weren't too busy with each other.

What kind of cruel world was it where my little brother got to have sex and mess around with his boyfriend any time he wanted, and my boyfriend was stuck sleeping in the den every night? Sure, I was still sorely lacking in self-control, whereas Milo had always been a master of that, but come on!

While Jack was gone, I vowed to work on getting myself under control, so when he came back, we could move onto the next phase of our relationship. Namely, the really fun stuff.

Instead of doing anything fun, I spent my time curled up in Mae's bed with her. She was unnaturally quiet, so we mostly sat in silence. Milo came in her room later on, and that helped. He was always much better in a crisis than I was, and for some reason, he was incredibly close to her. I think that maybe he was her favorite, but that didn't bother me so much. I was Jack's favorite, and that's all that really mattered.

Bobby didn't feel comfortable hanging out with Mae when she was like that, and that made sense. She was nearly inconsolable, and he hadn't known her that long. I ended up making an escape once Milo had her sitting up.

He put on *Houseboat* starring Raquel Welch on her TV, and that got her talking about her plans to buy a houseboat someday. Her cheeks were puffy from crying, but I hadn't seen a real tear in hours. With Milo there, she had even hinted at a smile a few times.

That left me to further bond with Bobby. We played some war game on the Xbox, which I seriously sucked at, but he didn't yell at me once. When I played with Jack, he could usually manage about twenty minutes of it before suggesting that I sit out a turn and let Milo play instead. It was nice being tolerated and killing Nazis.

Before going to bed, I called and texted Jane a few times. She didn't answer or reply, but I hadn't expected anything different. I'm pretty sure she was pissed at me, although I didn't know why.

Maybe she hated me for introducing her to vampires, or maybe she hated me for not introducing her sooner. I don't know. She was usually easy to get a read on. Her life revolved around boys, clothes, and getting drunk or high. I hadn't interfered with any of those things before today, so she didn't have anything to hold against me.

Jack texted me letting me know he loved me and they'd be getting on a plane soon. I thought about staying up to wait for him, but then I figured that falling asleep would make the time go faster. I crawled in his bed and couldn't wait for him to get back.

I felt him the instant he came in the house. My heart pounded with happiness, and I opened my eyes.

As soon as I stepped out of my room, I heard them arguing. They weren't shouting, but they weren't doing anything to be quiet either. I wanted to run down and greet Jack, but I decided to wait at the top of the steps, eavesdropping.

"Oh, come on, Jack!" Peter said, sounding frustrated. "I did not take your pillow!"

"You did too!" Jack insisted. "You were flirting with the stewardess and conned her into giving you the last pillow on the plane, which happened to be mine."

"Even if that is true, I didn't know it was the last pillow. And she shouldn't have given it to me if it was *your* pillow," Peter said. "And I think they prefer the term 'flight attendant.'"

"Or, maybe, just maybe, you could've given me that pillow when you realized what she had done," Jack said, ignoring Peter. "Maybe she was a shitty stewardess, but you saw what happened. You could've done the right thing for once in your life."

"Why? I wanted the pillow, and I had the pillow. It didn't have your name on it. Why should I give it to you?" Peter asked. "Or are you the only one allowed to take things?"

"I didn't take anything!" Jack snapped. "I had one blanket and no pillows. What exactly was there for me to take?"

"I don't know, Jack. What in the world could you have possibly taken that didn't belong to you?" Peter replied icily, and I could hear both of their heartbeats speed up.

"Will the pair of you knock it off?" Ezra asked warily. From the sounds of it, they were somewhere near the bottom of the steps, in the kitchen maybe, but Ezra was walking past, going to his room. "People are sleeping, and I am so sick of hearing about the damn pillow."

"It's not about the damn pillow," Peter said.

"Why don't you tell me what this is *really* about?" Jack asked, but he knew exactly what it was about. I was getting a hint myself, and it made me nervous.

"I know you two are having some kind of ... scuffle, but so help me, if either one of you wake up Mae or disturb her in any way, you'll be sorry. Do I make myself clear?" Ezra warned them.

There was silence, then I heard Ezra walking down the hall to his room. Jack and Peter waited until they heard his bedroom door shut before speaking.

"You're an asshole," Jack said when Ezra was gone.

"You're the asshole!" Peter whispered fiercely.

"I just wanted a pillow!"

"I just wanted you to leave *her* alone!" Peter shouted.

The silence felt too thick, and my heart was barely beating, which was good, because I didn't want them to know I was listening. I thought that maybe I should interrupt and stop them from whatever they might do, but they had to hash this out eventually. They hadn't really spoken through everything that had transpired, and they had to have a lot of things bottled up.

168

"But I didn't. Now what do you want me to do about it?" Jack tried to keep his voice calm, but there was a definite edge to it. "Is stealing my pillow really making it even?"

"God dammit, Jack! Will you shut up about the fucking pillow?"

"What do you want me to do? What's done is done!" Jack started shouting but remembered Ezra's warning and quieted down. "Seriously. I don't know what you expect me to do at this point. I can't change what's happened, and frankly, I don't want to. So... that's what it is."

"I don't want anything from you," Peter sighed, sounding defeated. "Just never mind. Next time I'll make sure you get a damn pillow on the plane."

I had expected them to continue talking for longer, but I was wrong. Peter turned to climb the stairs, his bag slung over his shoulder, and I didn't have a chance to hide. When he saw me, his expression was blank. I smiled sheepishly at him, but he just exhaled and came up the stairs.

"Good morning, Alice," Peter said louder than he needed to, letting Jack know that I had been spying on them. "You should've come down and said hello."

"I just woke up."

"Mmm, yes, I'm sure you did." He opened his bedroom door, but I stopped him.

"Peter, I'm really sorry," I said.

"You're not the one that needs to apologize." He looked at me for a minute, his eyes uncharacteristically vulnerable, then he glanced down the steps. The French doors off the kitchen suddenly slammed shut as Jack went outside with the dog. "If you'll excuse me, I need to get some rest. It was a very long flight."

"It sounds like it." I attempted to make a joke, but he just turned and went into his room, closing his bedroom door quietly behind him.

I sighed and went downstairs. Jack's irritation was no longer just directed at Peter. Somehow me apologizing to him was a slight against Jack. I hated the idea that they were two teams, and I always had to pick one side or I'd be deemed an enemy.

Jack opened the shades over the French doors to step outside, and bright sunlight streamed in. I hadn't slept very much to begin with, and the sight of the sun made me want to curl up in bed again.

Outside, Jack ignored his own fatigue. He stood on the stone patio, his hands shoved in his pockets, and watched Matilda root around for some long gone animal. It was wonderfully cold when I stepped out, contrasting with the warm fall day depicted out the window.

"So it was a long flight?" I asked, wrapping my arms around me as I walked up to him.

"Yeah, but I'm sure Peter feels much better now that you apologized to him."

"He deserves an apology," I bristled.

"How can you even say that?" Jack whirled on me, his face contorted with pain and confusion. "After everything you've been through-"

"We both know what happened. You don't need to rehash it every time I mention Peter's name." A cool breeze picked up, blowing my hair across my face, and I pushed it back behind my ears.

"This is just so ridiculous!" He shook his head. "Shit happened, stuff that I apparently can't talk about, but it happened. And still, you wanted to go off and risk your life to rescue him, and I said fine. For some stupid reason, I let you go."

"You don't 'let' me do anything, and you know it," I glared at him.

"Whatever. I didn't protest. You said you wanted to go, for… God, why, Alice? Why would you want to do that? Why are you always defending him? He doesn't deserve any apology! He doesn't even deserve to be alive! And you just bring him back here like nothing ever happened? And for that, *I* am supposed to apologize to *him*?" Jack looked at me incredulously. "That is so fucked up! I love you! Why do I need to tell him I'm sorry for that when I'm not?"

"Because he loved me too, and I wasn't yours!" I shouted, and he flinched.

He looked away from me, squinting up at the sun, and I wasn't sure if that was the right thing to say. Rubbing the back of his neck, he fell silent for a minute.

"I saw you first," Jack mumbled.

"You cannot use that as an argument." I rolled my eyes. "I'm not the last piece of pizza. I'm a person, and I chose you. You have me. He doesn't. Peter has nothing, and he's your brother. And I know before all this, you cared about him, too. So now he lost me *and* you. I'm not sorry that I love you, but I am sorry that he had to get hurt in the process."

"I know you're right," Jack said thickly. "But I can't forgive him.

171

Fighting for you, I understand. Trying to kill me, I totally get that. But when he tried to kill you... I can't ever forgive him for that, and I shouldn't have to."

I touched his arm gently, and his blue eyes were swimming when he looked at me. I chewed my lip, trying to decide whether or not I should tell him. I felt like I was breaking Peter's confidence, but if it could get the two of them to stop hating each other, then maybe it was worth it.

"Peter never tried to kill me."

"I was there!" Jack was irritated. "You can't tell me that didn't happen."

"No, it did, but not exactly the way you think. When Peter bit me, he knew you were in the house. You had fought before when you thought he was going to hurt me. He knew you'd never let something happen to me," I explained quietly. "He was counting on you to rush in and save me, and he thought that you'd be too angry to let him live. Peter wasn't trying to kill me; he was trying to kill himself."

"No..." Jack shook his head and his face completely fell. "No. That's not... Because if he did that, that would mean he..."

Realization flashed across his face, and he looked at everything in a new light. All the things Peter did had seemed cold and cruel were all really for me, and even Jack. Peter had been trying to let me go since the day he met me because he thought I'd be happier without him.

Jack never let himself believe that Peter loved me because he loved Peter. He respected him and never wanted to go against him.

172

Then I came into the picture, and the only way Jack could reconcile his own feelings for me was by assuming Peter could never feel the same way.

Jack truly believed he was the one that was meant to be with me, not Peter, and that made all his actions and behavior okay. But if Peter loved me as much as he did, then Jack suddenly became the villain in his story instead of the hero.

"Jack, you know how much I love you."

I reached out for him, and he pulled away. He exhaled shakily, so I reached out for his hand again, and this time he let me take it. He wouldn't look at me, so I moved so I was standing in front of him.

"I really do love you, and this is the right choice. And we didn't do anything wrong, not really. I mean... I don't know. What else were we supposed to do?"

"I don't know," Jack admitted quietly. He was still looking down so his eyes wouldn't meet mine, and I touched his cheek.

"I'm sorry. I didn't mean to hurt you like this. I just..." I trailed off. He felt so sad and *guilty*. I hated to see him this way. "I just wanted you to go easier on Peter. You two should be able to get along."

"No, you're right." He forced a smile at me, but it barely counted as one, so he let it go. "I will try."

"Why don't you come inside with me?" I asked. I wanted to stay with him all day, but the sun was really starting to get to me. It was this heavy sort of weakness that just barreled down on me like a wet blanket.

"No, I wanna stay out here just a little bit longer. Matilda's still having fun," Jack said. Matilda had actually sprawled out on the patio, basking in the sun for warmth, but I didn't argue with him.

"Are you sure you're okay?" I asked and wished he would just look at me.

"Yeah, I'm fine," he nodded, but he was lying.

"I love you," I whispered, hoping that would help somehow.

"I know, and I love you, too." Without looking at me, he gave me a quick kiss on the forehead, and stepped away from me. He had never kissed me so brusquely before. "Mattie, come on! Where's your ball?" Matilda jumped up to start searching for it, and Jack went to help her.

I glared up at the sun before going back in the house. If it wasn't for the stupid light, I would've stayed out there with him. But the bright noon sun was too draining, so I walked back into the house. The dark sanctuary of the kitchen brought relief, and I sighed. I had no idea if I had done the right thing, but anything that made Jack that upset was probably bad.

I spent more of the afternoon pretending to sleep than actually sleeping. To fill the time, I texted Jane and tossed and turned a lot. I listened for Jack to come in the house, but he never did. Bobby got up to eat, but everyone else was sound asleep. Except for Jack, who was gone.

Finally, I gave up on getting anymore rest and got out of bed. I texted him to ask where he was, but he didn't answer. I was starting to think I was a pariah the way nobody answered my calls or texts.

When Bobby walked by on his way to his room, he smelled

overly delicious. My bedroom door was shut, and the scent of his hot blood wafted in. It had been a few days since I ate, and vampires could go much longer than that. I had to get my hunger in control if I ever planned on being with Jack.

So as hungry as Bobby made me, I swallowed it back and decided to clear my head with a nice long shower. I had just started gathering my clothes when I felt the warmth in my chest, meaning Jack was nearby, and a moment later I heard him bounding up the stairs.

"Hey." Jack poked his head in, still hanging onto the bedroom door. "Are you up?"

"Yeah, I was just about to take a shower," I held up my clothes for him to see. "Unless you wanted something?"

"No, go ahead and shower. But do you wanna watch a movie after?"

"Yeah, sure," I shrugged. "Have you slept yet?" It was after six, and as far as I knew, he hadn't gotten any sleep since he got back.

"Nah, I'm okay," he shook his head. "I'll talk to you after your shower then."

"Uh, yeah, okay?"

With that, he left, shutting the bedroom door behind him. I stood there, holding my clothes in my arms, trying to figure out what was going on. I heard him knocking on the door across the hall. He got more nervous, which made me nervous, so I decided to wait to see how this turned out before I got in the shower.

"Yeah?" Peter opened his bedroom door sounding crabby, but that was Peter.

"I went to the video store and I, uh, rented *Brideshead Revisited*. I know you really like it, and I thought you might want to watch it with us. Me and Alice, I mean," Jack said.

"Um... sure." Peter sounded taken back, and so was I.

"Alice's taking a shower, so it'll be a little bit," Jack said.

"Okay."

"Okay." There was kind of an awkward silence. Jack must've finally excused himself because Peter shut his door, and I heard Jack running back down the stairs.

In the shower, I sing very loudly (today it was the theme to *Golden Girls*), but even over the sound of my voice and the water running, I could still hear Mae screaming. This would later prove to be a godsend, when Peter explained to me that *Brideshead Revisited* is an eleven-hour long period piece that originally aired on the BBC in the 1980's.

At the time, however, Mae's desperate pleas were enough to scare the hell out of me.

- 18 -

Once I got out of the shower, I could hear well enough to ascertain that Mae wasn't in immediate danger, and Ezra was trying to calm her. But something was the matter and I didn't like it. I threw on a pair of my sweats and one of Jack's oversized tee shirts, and hurried out the door.

"I wouldn't go down there if I were you." That was Bobby's word of advice. He stood just outside of Milo's door with a hoodie wrapped tightly around him. "It doesn't sound pretty."

"You aren't bloody listening to me, Ezra! You never listen to me!" Mae shouted from downstairs.

"What's going on?" I asked Bobby, hoping to gain some insight on the situation before diving into it.

"I don't really know. Milo and Jack left on a blood run about fifteen minutes ago, and Mae and Ezra started fighting a few minutes after that," Bobby shrugged.

A blood run meant that we were getting low on bag blood at the house, and they had gone to get some from a blood bank. My stomach grumbled at just the thought of blood, but Mae was yelling so much, I ignored it.

"Don't tell me to calm down! I am not going to calm down!" Mae continued after Ezra mistakenly suggested she relax a bit. "This isn't something that we should be reasonable about! This is life and death, Ezra!"

"I know that, Mae! That's exactly why we need to think about this!" Ezra raised his voice, but there was nothing angry about it. He was just trying to be heard over her. "But everyone else in the house doesn't need to hear us yelling."

"I don't care who hears anything!" Mae yelled, followed quickly by the sound of something glass smashing, like a vase. Matilda barked in response, and Mae snapped at her to shut up.

"See?" Bobby whispered, but the things that made him cower were exactly the reasons I felt like I had to intervene. Peter was still in his room, trying to sleep from the slow sound of his heartbeat, so that left me as the only one to help out.

I went downstairs and found Matilda looking as worried as a dog can look. Mae stood to one side of the living room, and she was even worse than yesterday. Her hair was a frizzy mess, and her skin was blotchy from yelling and crying so much. She hadn't changed her pajamas in days.

Glass was shattered all over floor in front of her. A heavy glass statue of a swan had sat on the mantle, and she would've had to have thrown it very hard to make it shatter like that.

"You've woken Alice," Ezra told Mae, almost tiredly. He stood on the far side of the room across from her, wearing silk pajama pants and a tee shirt. Apparently, they had started fighting immediately after waking up.

"No, I was awake. I just got out of the shower." I tugged at my hair to demonstrate. It dripped wet down my back since I hadn't had a chance to dry it.

"I don't care if I wake her! I don't care if I wake anybody!" Mae raised her head to the ceiling as if to wake anybody else that might be sleeping.

"Will you knock it off? This isn't about them. This isn't their fault," Ezra said.

"How is it *not* about them?" She pointed at me, but she refused to look at me. "This is completely about them! They're why you won't do this!"

"No, that's not true. They have no bearing on this," he shook his head.

"Bloody hell they don't! They have everything to do with it! You wouldn't even turn Alice because her brother had just turned, and I *know* you wanted her to turn!" Mae gave him a knowing look that I didn't understand, and he shook his head. "Don't be so damn condescending, Ezra! I know you turned her brother for her! So why won't you do this for me?"

"This is an entirely different situation, and I won't do this. Absolutely not." He was quiet, but his voice was so firm and finite.

"Dammit, Ezra!" Mae wailed, tears streaming down her cheeks. "You can't deny me this! You have no right! *No right!*"

"I cannot allow this, Mae, and I am sorry." He pursed his lips tightly but didn't budge.

She looked ready to collapse, but he made no move towards her. I wanted to help, but I was afraid of how she might react to me. If Ezra wasn't going to tend to her, then I didn't think that I should either.

"You are not sorry! You are cold and you are cruel, and I cannot spend my life with you!" She was sobbing so hard she had to grip onto the back of the chair to keep from falling over. "I will not let you make this decision for me! You can't!"

"You're right. I cannot make this choice for you, but I will not tolerate it, either. You can do whatever you like, but you will not be allowed in my house with that abomination," Ezra said coolly.

"*Abomination?*" Her voice cracked. "We are the abomination! She is merely a child, and I want to save her!"

"You cannot save her, Mae! You can only turn her into a monster!"

"Like we're monsters?" Mae brushed a strand of her hair from her eyes and looked down at the floor. "Maybe we are, and maybe she would be too, but she would have a life. And it wouldn't be a bad life. She could have everything that we have to offer."

"We have nothing to offer her," he said.

"How can you say that?" Mae gaped at him, then she looked at me with hate for the first time, and I flinched. "Is it because of her? Because of Alice? She gets everything you have to offer? You let Jack turn her and gave him no repercussions, even though you had just turned her brother. For her.

"She is not the only thing in this life that needs you, Ezra! In fact, I don't think she even needs you! You aren't that indispensable to her!" Her lips quivered, and she glared at him. "You aren't that indispensable to me either!"

"If I'm some kind of burden, I can leave. I don't want to cause any problems between you two," I said quietly. I hadn't completely figured out what their fight was about yet, but I certainly didn't want to be the source of it.

"You're not a burden," Ezra said, looking apologetically at me. "Don't worry yourself with this. You can go up to your room."

"What if she moves out?" Mae latched onto an idea, and her entire demeanor changed. She took a few quick steps closer to Ezra, deftly missing all of the broken glass on the floor. "She and Jack could move out. He can take care of her, and Milo is already self-sufficient. Peter is gone most of the time anyway. We have the room, and we have the time."

"Alice and Milo are not ready to be on their own like that," Ezra said. "And it isn't about them! You keep trying to solve something that isn't the problem. Even if everyone moved out, and it was just the two of us, I would still say no. This cannot be done, Mae, no matter what anybody else does or doesn't do."

"There has to be something!" She knelt on the ground at his feet. She was literally begging him, and when she took his hand, he didn't pull away, but he wouldn't look directly at her. "Ezra! *Please*! I have never asked you for anything like this before!"

"You've asked me for plenty like this before, and I have indulged you too much," he sighed. "But I cannot do this. I won't."

Mae let go of his hand and sat back on her heels. Closing her eyes, she rubbed at her forehead, and I knew she was trying to think of something.

"What if *she* wanted it?" Mae looked up at him, but she was talking about me. I was getting increasingly uncomfortable with the way she talked about me like I wasn't standing right here.

"I don't know why you have this idea that I have some special

181

relationship with Alice." He sounded tired by the idea, but he wouldn't look at me.

"Because you turned her brother for her! I know you were against adding more vampires, but you did that for her anyway!"

"Yes, and I did the same with Jack, for *you*." Ezra looked severely at Mae. Her face darkened with shame, and she looked down at the floor.

I had no idea what Ezra was talking about. From what I knew, Peter had turned Jack in order to save his life. The story that I heard from everyone never made any mention of Mae or Ezra at all. It had been an act of compassion, and for some reason, that made Mae squirm.

"That was different," Mae said quietly.

"Yes, it was. Because Alice actually cared for her brother. He wasn't just some random kid." Ezra looked off at the wall behind her. "And Milo's young, but he is not a child."

"She is innocent! She deserves a life!" Mae twisted a tissue in her hands and turned to look at me, pleading with me. "Alice, tell him! I don't care what he says! He'll listen to you! If you tell him that he needs to do this, he will!"

"I-I don't really know what you're talking about." I turned to Ezra for help, but he just looked grimly at me. "I can't tell him anything if I don't know what you're asking."

"My great-granddaughter Daisy," Mae said, silent tears sliding down her face. "She is only five years old, and she's going to die. She hasn't had a chance to live her life yet. But if we turn her, she can live forever. She can do anything!"

"Except grow up," Ezra reminded her. "She can never fall in love or get married. She'll never be able to live on her own or drive a car or even go to a bar. She'll depend on you for everything, forever, and that may delight you, but she'll hate you for cursing her to this life.

"Other vampires will never accept her, or you, for it," he went on. "They'll try to kill her because she's an abomination against everything we are. And that says nothing to our more perverse underbelly, who thrive on making childlike vampires to live as their slaves or to trade with human pedophiles in exchange for blood. Is that really the kind of life you want for her? Do you think that's what her hopes and dreams amount to?"

"It won't be like that," Mae insisted. "We will protect her and love her, and she'll have everything a child could ever want."

"But she won't really be a child forever! She'll be a woman trapped in a child's body with a child's temperament for all of eternity. That is a horrible thing to do to someone you claim to love so much," he said.

"You don't understand!" Mae looked desperately at him, and he met her eyes. "I cannot let this happen! I swore I would never watch another one of my children die!" He exhaled deeply and matched her intense expression with a calm one of his own.

"Then don't watch," Ezra said.

"Ezra!" I shouted, unable to believe that he would say something that cold to Mae.

"I know she is hurting, but I can't do this!" His collected façade evaporated for a moment, and he was merely exasperated and worried. Mae had gone back to looking at the floor and crying, and for a brief second, he looked completely lost. "There is nothing I can do to rectify this situation."

"So then comfort her! Don't yell at her!" I told him, still in shock over how icy he had been to her.

"No, it's alright, Alice," Mae said wearily and shook her head. "I knew what I was going to get from him. Ezra is many things, but he is predictable above all else." Sighing, she got to her feet. She wiped the tears from her face and tried to smooth out her hair. When she had composed herself a bit, she turned to look at him. "I will do what I have to do."

"I understand that, but you will not do it in my house," he said.

"I know." She nodded once, and then turned and walked back to her room.

For a moment after she left, I stood and tried to catch my breath. I had never seen the two of them fight about anything before, let alone something as intense as this.

I knew that Ezra was right, that turning a child into a vampire was an impossible idea, but I knew how desperate Mae was to do anything to protect her family.

Finally, Ezra started to move, picking up the pieces of broken glass of the floor, and I went over to join him.

"You were too cold with her," I said, picking up a large chunk of glass.

My hair was still dripping cold water down my back, and I tucked it behind my ears. Part of me felt nervous at the thought of contradicting Ezra about something like this, but he had no reason to be that cruel.

"She wouldn't have listened to anything else. She's been pleading me with since she found out about the child being ill, and I decided that being forthright was the best avenue to take." Ezra was incredibly tired, and I wasn't sure if he was over what the lycan had done to him yet.

"Why is she pleading with you?" I asked. "I mean, if this is what she wants, then why doesn't she just do it herself? Why does she need your permission?"

"She's never turned anyone before, and she's afraid to, especially with a child so young. She thinks she'll do it wrong somehow, even though there is no real wrong way."

He picked up most of the large pieces of glass, everything that we could get without a broom, so he stood up and tossed the broken bits into the fireplace. Since he had done it, I followed suit and threw what I had picked up into the fireplace.

"So is she going to do it if you don't?" I asked.

"I honestly don't know." His normal booming voice sounded defeated. "She wasn't really asking my permission, either. She knows my stand on it. If she turns the child, I will not be with her. I won't go through that heartache. Neither of them would survive it, not for long. Child vampires never do."

"What do you mean?" I asked.

The youngest vampire I had met had been Violet, and she was fourteen. I couldn't imagine what one would be like younger than that. Would they look older too, the way that Milo and Violet both looked about nineteen?

"They go insane, or they're killed," Ezra said simply. "They learn but can't mature. They get old but can't grow. They get impulses they can't control. They're volatile and strong and never really understand the consequences of their actions. Other vampires don't like having them around, and they don't like being alive.

"It never ends well." He ran a hand through this blond hair and breathed in deeply. "And if Mae were to change her, to get even more attached to the child than she already was, she would either die trying to protect her, or kill herself after the child died. And I have no interest in being a part of that."

"And Mae doesn't see that?" I asked, even though I knew the answer. She was too blinded by her love for her family to see any rational thought. Her only concern was keeping the girl around for another day, at any cost.

"No." He gave me a sad smile. "She mistakenly believes that I can do anything. But I can't this time." His expression was far away. "I cannot save the child. There is only one type of death versus another. The child will suffer and then die, either way. But Mae cannot accept that."

"Are you going to go talk to her? Maybe you can help her accept this. I mean, she's just going through the seven stages of grief, and it sounds like she's at bargaining," I said.

"Maybe, but unfortunately, she actually has something to bargain with. Most people have no other recourse, but Mae does. Would anyone really move past bargaining if God would actually talk to them and listen to their pleas?"

"Did you just compare yourself to God?" I raised an eyebrow at him.

"Accidentally," he admitted, looking disgusted at his own choice of words. "Sorry. I didn't mean to. But I don't think I have anything to say that can help Mae through this." He sighed heavily. "But... my clothes are in the room, and I should get dressed."

"Are you two going to split up?" I was surprised how nervous I sounded, but really, they were the only stable couple I had ever met. And if they split up, what hope did the rest of us have?

"I will stay with her as long as she'll have me, and as long as she doesn't turn the child," he said, but that was the kind of answer people gave when they weren't ready to tell the kids they were breaking up.

I started to think that maybe it was only a matter of time before things ended between them, and that was terrifying. I loved them both, and I couldn't imagine a life where they weren't both in it.

Ezra went down to his room. For someone who was completely obsessed with the idea of family, I couldn't believe how rigid he was being with Mae. He was right about not turning her granddaughter, I'm sure, but he was inflexible when talking to her. He had been willing to die to save Peter, but he wouldn't allow the same irrational passion in her.

Maybe it was because this was his way of protecting the family. If she did this, it would certainly devastate everything around her, himself included. I don't know what would happen to our family unit. If we would split up between them, like children of divorce, or... I don't know.

I knew I was going to live a very long time, I somehow had

expected that everything would stay the same forever. Ezra had once told me that everyone I know would die, and that I would outlast everything. But I had never believed that I would outlast this family.

- 19 -

When Milo and Jack finally came back from their blood run, I told them about the fight. Milo went to talk some sense into Mae, and we let him. Jack still invited Peter to watch a movie with us, but after all the drama, we decided to watch something lighter than an epic British mini-series. So we went with the opposite and put in *Futurama.*

As the night wore on, I decided to go to bed, and I wanted to invite Jack to stay with me. The fight between Mae and Ezra had left me feeling shaken up, and I wanted to hang onto something that I knew would be around forever. But Peter was lingering around us, giving me a weird look, and I didn't feel right about asking him.

The next morning, he tried waking me bright and early to take Matilda to the dog park, but I wanted to sleep in. The joke was on me, though. After he left, I couldn't fall back to sleep, but I blamed that on how hungry I was.

It had been a dull ache growing in the pit of my stomach since yesterday. When we had been watching TV with Bobby, I found myself more fascinated by watching the pulse pounding in his jugular than in the images on the screen.

Today was even worse. I had a dryness in my veins and my throat. My limbs felt crackly when I moved them. I had no energy, but I felt strangely frenetic. I knew I had to eat soon, but for now, I decided to just avoid Bobby.

Milo and Bobby were going to have to go to the club again soon to check on Jane, but I didn't feel up to being around humans. In fact, I could hardly stand being this close to Bobby. Heartbeats echoed in my ears, and the faint scent of Bobby permeated through my walls. I was going to have to distract myself before I went insane.

I went about getting ready, but I couldn't find the energy to shower. I just brushed my teeth, got dressed, and pulled my hair back in a messy bun. I tried to call Jane again, but she still wouldn't answer.

I probably should've considered eating, but I really, really had to control myself. Because I really, really wanted to be alone with Jack, and this was the only way I could trust myself. I knocked on Peter's bedroom door and chewed my lip. I stood a better chance of not biting him than I did Bobby, and even if I did bite Peter, he stood a better chance of living.

"What?" Peter opened his bedroom door, looking irritated. "Is the house on fire?"

"No. Can I come in?" I tucked a stray stand of hair behind my ears. His green eyes were bewildered, but he relented and took a step back from the door so I could go in.

When I brushed past him, I inhaled deeply. He smelled so good, and I had almost forgotten that. His blood used to be my favorite scent in the world, before I really knew that's what it was. When I had been human, the tangy scent he left behind always intoxicated me, and I hadn't realized that it was his blood I was lusting after. Now I did, and the smell was even stronger and more delicious.

"You look hungry." Peter shut the bedroom door behind me when I came in, and that might have bothered me if I had a clearer head.

"Yeah, well," I tried to play it off like nothing. For him to notice meant it had to be getting bad. My skin was ashen, and my heart beat too fast.

His room looked as messy as he would allow, which was much cleaner than mine and Jack's room. His large four-post bed was unmade. The French doors that led onto the balcony off his room were slightly ajar, letting in a chill breeze that ruffled his curtains.

Overflowing bookshelves lined his walls. Peter had apparently decided to spend the day reading, and a few books were discarded on his bed. On the white chair by the bookcases, he had a book splayed open, a red ribbon marking his page should it close.

I paced his room, trying to ignore the painful gnawing inside of me, but I stopped when I saw the red stain on his white rug.

"Perhaps you should eat," Peter said, but there was an uncomfortable edge to his words. He had caught me staring at the stain. It was blood, *my* blood, from when he had nearly killed me.

"Why don't you throw away the rug?" I twisted at the hem of my shirt, feeling fidgety, and turned to face him.

"As you can tell, I'm really not in the mood to hang out," he completely ignored my question.

He avoided my gaze and gestured to his room, as if the state of it would signify something to me. Underneath his smooth tan skin, I could see his veins pulsing delicately, and it quickened ever so slightly. I made him nervous, and I delighted in that, even though it

191

did nothing to ease my hunger pains.

"You shut the door behind me." I motioned to the closed door. "I think you're okay with talking. You just want everything on your terms."

"What's so wrong with that? Don't you want everything on your own terms?" He ran a hand through his chestnut hair. He hadn't cut it since we'd come back, and while I had never been partial to long hair on guys, it looked really good on him.

In fairness, everything looked really good on him. Wearing slim jeans and a white sweater that rode smoothly over his muscles, he was still the most attractive vampire I'd ever seen, and that really was saying a lot. I hated him for it. The way he could just be casually spending the day in his room and look like that. More than that, I hated that I was still attracted to him, when I knew I had no reason to be.

"I want things the way I want them, but I don't force other people to live by my rules," I said.

"Neither do I. Am I forcing you to do anything?" Peter looked at me, letting his brilliant emerald eyes pierce through me. They still dazzled me, if not the same way they once did, but maybe in my hunger, they hit me even more. Everything about him just seemed so much more enticing.

"No, but... I don't know." I shook my head and turned away from him, returning to pacing his room again. He leaned against one of the posts on his bed and crossed his arms over his chest.

"Why don't you just eat something instead of pestering me?" he asked.

"No, no, I can't," I waved away the idea. "I'm fine anyway."

"Very convincing," Peter sighed. "Is that what you're doing here? Trying to distract yourself from eating? You're probably fantasizing about ripping into your brother's little boy toy, aren't you?"

"Don't be disgusting!" I scoffed, but he was really close to the truth, and I blushed a little.

"It's not disgusting. It's a fact of life." He narrowed his eyes at me as something occurred to him. "You haven't bitten anyone yet, have you? You're still a virgin to the vampire ways?"

"I'm virgin in every way," I muttered under my breath before I could catch myself.

"What was that?" Peter asked, his eyes widening.

"Oh, never mind." I shook my head and blushed deeper. "I haven't been turned for very long. I need time to get everything under control."

"I see." A smirk twitched on his lips, and I sighed heavily.

"Stop! Don't look at me like that," I snapped, but that only made him chuckle softly. Groaning, I looked around his room, desperate to find something else to talk about.

On his bed, half covered by his blanket in a poor attempt to conceal it, was a book. But not just any book. It was a century old with worn binding and tattered pages, and I had spent a great deal of time reading it a few months ago. Entitled *A Brief History of Vampyres*, Jack had been convinced that Peter had written it himself. I had stolen it from Peter's room until it mysteriously disappeared.

I moved towards his bed to grab the book, but Peter saw where

I was heading and moved to intercept me. He was much quicker, but his attempt was half-hearted since I'd already seen it.

He grabbed my wrist just as my hand touched the cover, and almost the instant his skin hit mine, it started to heat up considerably. I pretended like I didn't notice and jerked my hand away from him before he could feel my pulse quicken in his grip.

"You did take it!" I held the book up in front of his face, as if he wouldn't know what I was talking about. "I *knew* you took it!"

"It's *my* book! You stole it from me!" Peter tried to match my indigence but failed. If I didn't know any better, I'd say he was embarrassed at getting caught.

"So?" I faltered for a minute, since he did have a point. "You weren't reading it, and I didn't 'steal' it. I borrowed it."

"And I wanted it returned." He reached for it but I pulled it back before he could grab it. He didn't look amused, and he held his hand out to me, waiting for me to give it to him. "Can I have it back please?"

"I was reading it. I want to know how it ends." I opened it, flipping the pages and trying to skim through it.

He glowered at me over the top of the book, so I couldn't pay that much attention. It didn't really read like a novel, either, but rather it was part diary, part how-to manual.

"Rosebud is the sled," Peter replied flippantly, giving away the ending to *Citizen Kane* instead.

"Why don't you want me to read this?" I asked and looked up at him.

"It's not that I don't want you to read it," he said, but he wouldn't meet my eyes, so I had a feeling that he wasn't being entirely truthful.

"Then why did you take it from my room?"

"Because I…" He floundered for a minute, a very rare occurrence with him, and rubbed at his eyes. "I just didn't want you to have it anymore." I had never made him this distressed and irritated before, and I enjoyed it. Usually he was the one driving me nuts. "Do you remember when I took it?"

"Yeah, it was the night you snuck into my room," I said. He had done more than just sneak in that night.

"And I bit you." His eyes shifted, and his heartbeat changed. He had deep emotions buried in with biting me, but I couldn't tell what they were. "Your blood tasted of Jack, and… so I didn't want you to have the book anymore."

"This is your book, isn't it?" I stopped taunting him. "I mean, you wrote this, didn't you?"

"Yes," he said quietly. "So you can understand why I wouldn't want you to have it after everything that happened with Jack."

"I do." I held the book out to him so he would take it, but he just stared at it for a moment then looked up at me.

"Do you still want to read it?"

"Only if you wouldn't mind."

"I don't think it really matters to you what I mind." His voice was barely audible, and he turned away from me, leaning his back against his bed.

"That's not fair, Peter! I've been doing everything I possibly can to make it up to you!"

"I know you have," he sighed. "Just take the book. Read it. It'll take your mind off how hungry you are so you can finally fuck Jack."

My jaw dropped. That was what I was trying to do, but he didn't need to throw it in my face like that, making it sound dirty and bad. It hurt and pissed me off, so I threw the book at his chest and stormed past him.

"Alice, wait!" Peter groaned and grabbed my arm, stopping me from escaping his room. "I'm sorry. That was uncalled for."

"You've gotta meet me half way." I was almost pleading with him. "I have been trying and trying. And even Jack is trying. But you gotta help me out here. You've gotta..." I trailed off and looked away.

"Why is it so important to you that I forgive you?" Peter asked.

That really was the question at the heart of it all. Why did it matter to me so much what Peter thought of me? It wasn't even just about getting him and Jack to repair their relationship or making amends for damaging the family. It was something more than that, something that I couldn't quite explain.

"Why did you come back?" I whispered, unwilling to look at him. His hand burned warm on my arm, and I knew that I should shake it away, but I didn't.

"You asked me to."

"No, not from Finland. I mean that night that you took the book. You'd been gone for months, and then, suddenly, one night, you appeared in my room and you drank my blood." I bit my lip, and I didn't know why I was asking. Or why I'd even care about that night. "Did you really want my blood that badly?"

"Your blood is divine," he admitted sadly. "But I always wanted more than that." He exhaled huskily. "What is it about you? You were more than just a human, and even now that I'm not bonded with you..." He trailed off, but I finally lifted my eyes to meet his. "Why can't I resist you?"

I inhaled deeply, breathing him in when I should've been running away. His skin scorched against mine, but I felt my own body hurrying to match his temperature. His green eyes burned so intensely I couldn't look away. The sound of his heartbeat rippled through me.

The air was so thick with the scent and feel of him that I could almost taste it, and I wanted to taste him. I wanted *him* in the most visceral way.

Suddenly his lips were on mine, and I can't say if I moved to him or if he moved to me, but I definitely didn't resist. His kisses were rough and soft all at once. Burying my fingers in his thick, silky hair, I pulled myself as close to him as I could get. His muscles were like granite forming to my body, and he wrapped his arms around me, crushing me to him. His mouth tasted amazingly sweet, and I wanted more.

The blinding hunger surged through me, mixing bloodlust with passion. All my sense were blurring together into one. I could taste what I felt, and I couldn't see anything. My pulse pounded in time with his, heavy and warm.

And he smelled so delicious I could barely stand it. My body literally burned for him, like my skin was covered in flames and the only relief would come if I bit him.

He kissed me ferociously, and almost playfully I pressed my teeth against his lip. I didn't bite him, but I tested the waters to see if I could.

Peter moaned, and the sound of his voice radiated through me. He would gladly let me bite him, let me drink the wonderful elixir that flowed through him, and I wanted him so badly it was painful.

- 20 -

Just before my teeth sunk into him, something inside me had a moment of sanity and screamed *Jack*.

I'd like to say that just like that, I snapped out of it, but I didn't. Thinking of Jack made me hesitate before I bit Peter, but it didn't change how badly I wanted to.

Everything about Peter was designed so I'd want him. His blood, his touch, his smell, really had been meant for me. I loved Jack, but the physical shell of Peter was everything my body had been made to want.

Somehow, I managed to free my mouth from his, but I stayed in his arms, holding him to me. Peter started kissing my neck, and as wonderful as it would feel to have him bite me, I did not want to be bitten. I was starving, and losing more blood would only make it worse.

In the end, it was my intense hunger that saved me.

"No," I moaned and tried to detangle myself from his arms. Either he didn't hear me or he didn't want to listen, because he kept hanging on to me, his lips trailing down the sensitive skin of my throat. "Peter! No!"

When I pushed at him, he let go of me, but I wasn't stable on my feet so I stumbled backwards. In the mess of kissing him, my hair had somehow come free from its messy bun, and it fell around my face, blocking my already blurred vision.

The hunger and the intensity of kissing Peter left me feeling dizzy and strange. It was almost like being drunk. I was weak, and my eyesight was wrong. Everything had this hazy red edge to it, but that was from the bloodlust.

"I can't do that," I shook my head and my voice came out weak.

"I'm sorry." Peter tried to catch his breath, but he wouldn't look at me.

I fought the urge to pounce on him again, and I think he struggled just as badly. To avoid temptation, he turned and walked out on the balcony.

When he was gone, I grabbed onto the bed to keep from collapsing. The actual passion of the moment was fading away, but the bloodlust refused. If I didn't eat something soon, I would go mad and slaughter something. A dark animal part of me threatened to surface, and I had to contain it.

"Milo!" I shouted and stumbled out into the hallway. I couldn't take care of this on my own. My stomach lurched and growled, and my body burned. "Milo!"

"What's going on?" Milo came out of his bedroom, and I wanted to bite him. Thankfully, Bobby didn't follow out after him, because I'm not sure that I could've refused him. "Oh my god! Alice!"

"I need to eat! *Now!*" I fell to my knees, clutching my stomach. My vision blurred even worse, and I could smell Bobby on Milo, making my mouth water. I was on the brink of blacking out, and it scared the hell out of me.

"Oh, hell! Okay! Hang on, Alice!" Milo put his arm around my waist, which really wasn't the wisest move in the world. His throat was completely exposed to me, and I seriously contemplated tearing it out.

I closed my eyes and let him lead me downstairs, trying not to think of anything. The pain was overwhelming, and I moved stiffly, like a zombie. It seemed to take forever, but I don't even really remember moving. The next thing I knew, I was in front of the fridge and Milo was handing me a bag, promising everything would be okay.

The blood ran cold down my throat, and that wonderful searing heat spread over me. Drinking felt good, but it wasn't like it normally was. Instead of being real pleasure, it was more the absence of pain. I swallowed several bags in a very short amount of time, but I don't remember much after that. Almost the instant my thirst was quenched, I passed out.

To make matters worse, I woke up in Jack's bed to find him sitting next to me, looking at me with concern and adoration. I had just kissed his brother, and he was making sure that I was okay. Admittedly, he didn't know that I had kissed Peter, but that made it worse somehow.

And better, too. Because if he did know, there was a very good chance that he'd never want to talk to me again, and I wasn't sure I could handle that.

Once I assured Jack that I was okay, I insisted that I needed to take a long hot shower. He tried to kiss me, but I managed to avoid it without raising too much suspicion. He'd be able to taste Peter on me, and the whole point of this was that he didn't find out about that.

The hot shower didn't really fix things, although it did give me a chance to think. Why had I kissed Peter? Being so hungry had left me more vulnerable and weak, but even when I thought of it now, the way his lips felt against mine, I wanted to kiss him still. My skin flushed warm, and I turned the faucet so the water was even colder.

Of course, I could never kiss Peter again. Nobody could ever even find out about that. I loved Jack, and I do mean really and truly loved him. Whatever I felt for Peter had to be some kind of residuals from the bonding and nothing more.

It was like how bloodlust made my body want things that I didn't actually want, like when I was crazed and wanted to drink Milo's blood or Bobby's. It wasn't the same as actually liking Peter or wanting to be with him. I didn't have any real feelings for him at all... did I? I mean, I couldn't. Not when I loved Jack and I had done so much to free myself from Peter.

This was everything that I wanted... wasn't it?

When I came out of the bathroom, the TV was turned on to shark show on the Discovery channel, and I don't know if Jack was trying to be ironic or not. Sharks were known to go into frenzy when they smelled blood, and apparently, so was I.

Jack wasn't really watching it, anyway. Standing in front of a mirror on the side of the room, he had on Dickies shorts, skater socks, and a white dress shirt with a black tie around it. He stared intently at the tie, struggling to knot it properly, but glanced back at the TV every time the music got dramatic.

"Hey, how you feeling?" Jack didn't turn all the way around when I came out of the bathroom, but he looked at me with concern and a lopsided smile.

"Much better." I forced a bright smile and walked over to him.

I had put on my comfy pants and one of his tee shirts, as was my usual bedtime outfit. The sky would start to lighten soon, which meant that even though I had slept most of the night away, I would be getting tired again pretty quickly.

"You look better. Showers are the answer for everything," he grinned, then turned back to staring at himself in the mirror.

"What are you doing?" I asked.

"Trying to tie a tie." His expression was in deep concentration, even though I knew he was half-listening to the TV too. He would never miss a shark attack. "Ezra usually ties them for me, and he's getting sick of it."

"Any luck?"

"Never." He looked tiredly at his reflection. "You know, vampires are supposed to be smarter and more talented and all that stuff. Can you imagine how badly I'd tie one of these if I was still mortal?" I stifled a laugh at his lack of skills, and he looked at me hopefully. "Do you know how to tie one?"

"Nope," I shook my head. "I never had any need to tie one, and Milo always knew how. You could hit him up. I'm sure he'd be glad to help."

"Maybe. But I think the point of this is that I learn how to do it myself." He undid the mess he made of it, preparing to start over from scratch, but the music on the TV got very loud and ominous, so he turned back to watch it.

On screen, a shark tore into some kind of carcass the camera crew had dropped in the water. The narrator was saying all kinds of things about how perfect the shark's teeth were for eviscerating flesh and bone. "

Holy cow! Do you see that?"

"Yeah, that's pretty intense," I agreed.

While I hated it when they showed sharks attacking things like seals or whales (although, strangely, I never minded watching sharks bite people), I did think there was something beautiful and awe inspiring about the power and grace of sharks.

"You know, sharks are the only natural enemy vampires have," he said, his eyes still locked on the television screen.

"Yeah, Ezra told me that," I said. "But I don't know if they're really a 'natural' enemy. I mean, how many vampires live in the water?"

"That's true." The attack footage ended, and it was just sharks swimming about the ocean, not hurting anything, but Jack kept watching it. "If you stripped away any humanity or real consciousness from us, that's what we'd be. They're just pure muscle and perfectly designed killing machines. Of course, they have more teeth than us, so they're much better at it." The show went to commercial, and he gave me an easy smile before going to back to the business with his tie.

"You really like sharks?" I asked, even though I knew the answer. We'd watched *Jaws* four times last summer, and he'd even made me watch the sequel that was supposed to be in 3-D and *Jaws:*

The Revenge because (and I quote) "this time it's personal."

"Yeah, why?"

"Let's go to the zoo tomorrow," I suggested. "They have sharks down in the aquarium so we don't have to worry about the sun. It won't be super exciting, but it'd be nice to get out of the house for awhile."

"Yeah, sure. That sounds good," he smiled at me.

His smile was so wonderful, and I felt this painful tug inside of me. I walked up behind him and wrapped my arms around his chest, resting my head on his back between his shoulders blades, and hugged him. I just wanted to be close to him.

"What's that for?" He stopped with his tie and put his arms over mine, and he sounded a little concerned. "Are you okay?"

"Yeah, I'm fine. I just miss you, that's all." I did miss him, a lot, and I had a bit of guilt thrown on top, but he couldn't know about that. "I feel like we haven't spent any time together lately."

"We just watched an entire season of *Futurama* together last night," Jack laughed, and I could hear it vibrating through his back. Delighted shivers ran through me, and I squeezed him tighter to me. He loosened my arms and turned so he could face me. "But I guess I can never really spend enough time with you."

He kissed me softly, and my heart swelled happily. Of course, I couldn't completely enjoy the moment, because I couldn't help but think about Peter's kiss, and how different it felt. Jack must've felt it because he pulled away and looked at me, his blue eyes filled with worry.

"Are you sure you're okay?"

"Yeah, I'm fine." I lowered my eyes. "I'm just a little shaken up from today."

"You'll get the hang of it. It just takes time," he assured me. His concern made me feel even guiltier, so I walked back away from him and sat on the bed. The distance helped some.

"How come Milo got the hang of it so quickly?" I asked.

"It just depends on the person, I guess," Jack shrugged and turned back to the mirror. "It took me way, way longer than it took him, but I'm a slower learner, apparently."

Jack kept practicing his knots, and while he eventually managed something that looked semi-professional, he never got it down the way he would've liked. I sat on the bed, watching Shark Week and chatting with him, but the night seemed to end too quickly. I was not ready for him to go when he started yawning, but he'd insist he'd see me very soon.

Even though I'd just eaten, I made sure to eat again before I went to bed. If I was going to spend the afternoon around people, I wanted to be prepared. I was really excited about going to the zoo, so I woke up early and got ready. Jack came up to check on me just as I pulled on my shoes.

"Ready?" Jack grinned at me.

"Always. Are you sure you are?" I eyed up his outfit, which was his standard uniform. Shorts, two-toned neon Converse, and a Boba Fett tee shirt.

"What's wrong with this?" He glanced down at his clothes.

"Nothing, except it's the end of October, and it's like fifty degrees and we're going to be outside. Plus, the sun is out." I had chosen jeans, a long sleeve shirt, and a fashionable scarf that I had looped around my neck. Even though we enjoyed the cold, people didn't, and we were supposed to look like people.

"I'll be fine, and it's not that cold," he shrugged. "Come on. Let's go. I wanna see the otters before it gets too dark."

The sun wouldn't be out for much longer, but I couldn't stand being in it for that long anyhow. If we were going to the zoo, there were a few animals that Jack wanted to see while we had the chance. He was telling me about how he refused to compromise on the prairie dogs as we went down the stairs, but then I saw Peter and completely tuned out.

- 21 -

It might seem pretty weird that I lived in the same house as Peter, directly across the hall, but I had managed to avoid him since we kissed. The reason for that is that I hadn't left Jack's room. I didn't want to see Peter, and that was part of my logic behind the zoo trip.

Unfortunately, when we descended the steps into the living room, Peter happened to be standing right there. He wasn't looking at us, but my initial reaction was to panic anyway.

"Something wrong?" Jack asked.

"No, I'm fine," I shook my head and hurriedly pushed my feelings away.

Ezra hung a new giant flat screen TV on the wall, and Peter and Bobby supervised in some way. I'm not sure what was wrong with the old flat screen, although I would lean towards nothing. Peter stood a few feet back from where Ezra held the TV up, and Bobby was sprawled out on the couch, popping some of the bubble-wrap that had come with the new television. The cardboard box was on the floor by his feet, along with the "old" TV.

"What's going on?" I asked, even though I didn't really want to say anything. I wanted to rush out of the room before Peter had a chance to look at me or Jack, but that would seem odd.

"Ezra bought a new TV," Bobby answered, watching as Ezra handled a TV that would be too big and too heavy for any one man to deal with alone.

"Is it straight?" Ezra held onto the bottom of it and took a step back to look at it. "It better be since I have all the wires hooked up already."

"Yeah, it's straight," Peter said, and just hearing his voice made my pulse change.

"What was wrong with the old TV?" I asked to distract myself.

"Nothing." Ezra stepped back further into the room so he could admire his handy work. "Jack and I just went to Best Buy this morning, and this TV is way better than the last one."

"You went to Best Buy?" I cocked an eyebrow at Jack. "How early did you get up?"

"Early enough," Jack shrugged. "Ezra was going to the store and asked if I wanted to come with, and like I would pass up a trip to Best Buy?"

"I don't see how this TV is any different than the one we had before," Peter said, echoing my thoughts. "It isn't even bigger, is it?"

"It's not about being bigger!" Jack walked away from me, closer to the TV so he could explain all the merits of it. His lingo instantly got technical, which was silly since Peter probably knew less about technology than I did. Ezra and Jack were the ones who were obsessed with all things new and electric.

"It just looks like a television to me," Peter said when Jack finished explaining how awesome it was.

Jack scoffed loudly, and this time, even Ezra defended his purchase. At that point, they were mostly talking to themselves, and Peter looked back at me. Just briefly, and I looked away almost instantly, but his eyes still caught me. It shouldn't even be possible for eyes to be that green, and I shouldn't be thinking about how stunningly attractive they were.

At least he played it cool better than me. If Jack and Ezra weren't so damn excited about their new gadget, I'm sure they would've noticed how frazzled I acted. When I looked away from Peter, he went over to them to pretend to be interested in it.

Bobby sat in the chair, swinging his feet over the edge, and he looked more entertained by the bubble wrap than he did the TV. Milo was missing, which was strange, because he loved this kind of thing. He should be in here gushing all over the TV too.

"Where's Milo?" I asked Bobby, since nobody else would listen to me unless I used the words "HD" or "plasma."

"Helping Mae with the laundry," Bobby said and popped another bubble.

I was tempted to steal the bubble wrap from him, but I had my chance to escape, so I took it. Jack wouldn't be ready to go for at least another ten or fifteen minutes, and I'd rather spend that time waiting somewhere Peter wasn't. At least Jack was too distracted to notice me slipping away.

Down the hall, between the den and the main bathroom was the laundry room, filled with two sets of super powered washers and dryers. Seven people lived in the house, and that amounted to a lot of laundry. I tried to do mine and Jack's, but Mae somehow always got to it before I did. She was magic that way. The laundry room had several racks with hangers.

Most of Jack's overflow clothes ended up down here, hanging

on racks. His suits were in plastic bags, all neatly pressed, and they stayed down here to keep them from getting smooshed and wrinkled in our closet. The room was filled with the clean scent of clothes, but I could still smell us on them, especially Jack. No matter how many times they were washed, clothes managed to maintain some of their owner's smell.

On one wall were the machines themselves, one set dark blue, and the other a weird orange. Apparently, the days of ordinary white machines were gone. Milo sat on one of the washing machines, watching as Mae pulled towels out of the dryer and folded them. I'm sure he offered to help, but she refused. She thought it was her duty to do everything for us.

Milo was dressed and looked good, except he'd painted his toenails, and I blamed Bobby for that. Mae, on the other hand, still wore her pajamas, and I hadn't seen in her in real clothes in days. Her hair was up, but it was more of a rat's nest than a bun.

"How's it going?" I asked, trying for casual instead of concerned. When I walked in the room, Milo gave me a wary look, and Mae barely glanced back at me.

"I'm going to have to buy new towels," Mae said. The usual warmth of her British accent sounded stogy and commandeering, but that was better than sobbing. "You leave the towels in your room for so long they smell of mildew, and I just can't get it out."

"Sorry. I'm working on it," I said. Jack and I were the messiest ones in the house, unless Bobby turned out to be inordinately dirty.

"I didn't say it was your fault." Mae was nearly snapping at me, and she folded towels in an angry huff.

I'm pretty sure Mae loves doing laundry. I've seen her folding and washing things, and it's like meditation for her. That was not how she did laundry today.

"Bobby and I always make sure to take our towels down," Milo told her, and I glared him.

"Why is Bobby doing his laundry here, anyway?" I asked, and I realized I had missed very crucial facts about him. "Doesn't he have like an apartment or a job or something?"

"He's in art school and lives in a dorm," Milo answered, matching my glare.

"Of course he is." When I thought about it, Bobby really had art student written all over him. "So, does he ever go to school or anything? Why is here all the time?"

"He goes when he feels like it," Milo said. "And staying here is better than staying at a dorm, and I want him here."

"Our house has always been open to anyone who needs it." Mae sounded irritated by that as she folded a towel. "Anyone that's ever needed a place, be they vampire or not, has always had a place. You wouldn't believe how many people have stayed with us over the years. Ezra has always had an open door policy. To anyone.

"Literally, anyone," she went on. She put the folded towel in the basket and just leaned on it for a minute, as if she was too suddenly too weary to go on. "Except for my family. Except for what matters to me."

"Mae, you know that's not what it's about," Milo said gently. He tried to put his hand on her shoulder, but she snapped back into motion and pulled a towel out of the dryer. "And you have us here.

Don't forget that. We're your family, too."

"You know that I adore you, but…" She held a towel to her chest and trailed off.

"Have you made a decision yet?" I asked carefully. "About what you're going to do?" As far as I knew, she still had her heart set on turning her great-granddaughter, and Ezra hadn't changed his either.

"No." Mae closed her eyes and shook her head. "Maybe. I don't know." She rubbed her forehead and smiled sadly at Milo. "I mean, if I left, you could all handle doing your laundry, couldn't you?"

"We don't want you to stay because of laundry," Milo said, looking appalled. "You're the heart of the family. I don't know what would happen if you went away."

"I know that, love." She touched his leg gently. She went back to folding laundry, but more like the normal way she did. "I have time to think. There's still time."

"Alice!" Jack called from down the hall. "Alice? Where are you? Are you ready?"

"I should go." I nodded back to the door. "We're going to the zoo today."

"Have fun," Milo gave me a half-wave, but his focus was still on Mae. She chewed her lip and didn't even notice me leaving.

Back in the living room, Ezra was making Peter watch that *Planet Earth* documentary because of how amazing it looked on the new TV. Jack came over to me and took my hand. As he said his goodbyes to the guys, Peter gave me a weird look, and I hurried Jack along. I wasn't sure how well I could hide my emotions from Jack.

Maybe I'd have to talk to Milo about all of this. He'd be really disappointed in me, but he'd help me out, assuming there was a way to help me out.

We got to the zoo in time for Jack to see the otters and the prairie dogs, and he was overly excited about both of them. We spent a long time in the nocturnal exhibit with the bats, and Jack had way too much fun. As usual, his happiness was contagious, and I was having a great time.

The best thing about the zoo was that most of the people there were children, and children didn't react to us the way adults do. Some people still stared at us, and a small cluster of people followed us closer than was polite, but it was nothing that I couldn't shake off. Jack didn't even notice it at all.

The highlight of the trip was the dolphin show. Jack made sure we sat right down in the front row, so when they jumped out or came to the edge, we got splashed. Afterwards, we went down to the lower level so we could see them in the aquarium. I stood next to the glass, watching them swim as if they were dancing with each other.

"You know, I swam with dolphins once," Jack said casually. "Mae had always wanted to do it, so the two of us went down to Florida, and we spent all day in the ocean. It was this thing we paid for, so it wasn't like we randomly found wild dolphins or anything. But it was super awesome. We asked Peter to come with, but he said no, because dolphins are just big fish, and there's nothing exciting about swimming with fish."

"Dolphins are mammals!" A little girl was standing next to me, her face pressed up to the glass, but she sounded completely offended when Jack called dolphins "fish."

215

"Yeah, I know," Jack grinned at her. "My brother thinks they're fish."

"Your brother is an idiot," the little girl said.

"He sure is," Jack laughed.

The girl's mother just noticed her talking to us, and she apologized profusely as she dragged her daughter away, all the while managing to ogle Jack as she did.

"So you and Mae swam with dolphins?" I asked, walking away from the tank and changing the subject from Peter. Even in jest, I was uncomfortable with Jack saying anything about him.

"Yeah, it was a really spectacular trip. We should go again," Jack suggested. We wandered around the aquarium, and he had his hands shoved in his pockets as I admired the seahorses. "Milo would love it, and I know Mae would be up to going. We have to go during the day, and the sun gets pretty hard on you, but if you eat a lot and just crash the whole next day, you should be okay."

"That would be really awesome." I couldn't imagine anything cooler than swimming with dolphins, but the thought of Mae made me less enthusiastic. "But do you think Mae would really go?"

"Yeah, why wouldn't she?" Jack asked, but then it dawned on him what I meant. "Oh. Well... when this is all over, I'm sure she'll want to go."

"You really think so?" I raised an eyebrow. "Because, from the way Ezra makes it sound, there is no happy ending to all of this. She's gonna be miserable."

"I know," he sighed.

In the center of the aquarium, there was a shallow pool full of stingrays and sharks that people could pet, and Jack stopped at it. He reached in the tank to touch them, but he wasn't that into it. I'm sure he actually adored that kind of thing, but I had him worrying about Mae now too.

"I'm sorry. I didn't mean to bring the entire day down," I said.

"No, you're fine," he said, taking his hand out of the water. "Were you talking to her today before we left?" I nodded. "How is she doing?"

"Not so great," I admitted. "But at least she hasn't made a decision yet."

"You mean she's still considering doing it?" Jack looked at me with wide eyes and his skin paled a little. "I thought that after Ezra gave her that ultimatum, she'd just kinda get over it. I mean, not quickly or anything, but I thought that's where she'd be headed."

"You didn't see her when she fought with Ezra." I thought about how she had literally been on her knees begging him. "For her, I don't think there is any getting over this. Ever. Either she loses Ezra, or she loses a child."

"I know Daisy means a lot to her, but she's not really her child." Jack chewed the inside of his cheek. "She didn't give birth to her or raise her or even speak to her. I understand that there's a connection, but I don't get why she's willing to sacrifice everything for it."

"I don't completely get it either, but then again, I've never been a mother," I said. "And that's really all Mae has ever been." I took Jack's hand in mine. "But you don't think she'll actually do it, do you? Or even if she does, her and Ezra won't really split up over this? Will they?"

217

"I honestly don't know," he sighed resignedly. "Once I would've said that nothing could break them up, but the longer I live, the more I realize that nothing lasts forever." Realizing the implications of what he said, he smiled at me and looped his arm around my shoulders.

"Except for you and me. We're in this 'til the end, baby." He kissed the top of my head, and I leaned onto his shoulder, and I really, really hoped he was right.

By the time we left the zoo, Jack managed to cheer me up. On the car ride home, he forced me to sing along with the Backstreet Boys, and he started making threats about taking me to a karaoke bar someday.

When we got home, Matilda was the only one watching the brand new TV in the living room. Jack had bought her one of those pet DVD's that were all images and sounds dogs would like, and this one had wacky misadventures with cats or something.

Matilda was so engrossed in the movie that she hadn't run to the door to greet Jack, so we decided to watch it with her and see what all the fuss was about. He sat down in the recliner, and I sat on his lap, resting my head on his shoulder.

"Maybe we should get a cat," Jack said. Matilda was parked on the floor right in front of the TV, staring intently at a kitten chasing a string. Every time the kitten meowed, she'd cock her head and prick her ears up.

"She would probably eat a kitten."

"Oh, she would not. Mattie would never hurt anything, would you, girl?" His voice got higher when he talked to her, and she glanced back at him and thumped her tail on the floor. "See? Harmless."

"That's hardly an assertion," I laughed. "But still, that's not a reason to get a cat. You don't get cats so your dog has something to play with and possibly snack on."

"Sounds like a good enough reason to me."

When I came home, I hadn't noticed anybody's heartbeats. I was well-fed and less inclined to it. But I was naturally tuned into Jack's and Milo's. Even if I wasn't paying attention, when they were distressed, I'd pick up on it.

Upstairs, I suddenly heard Milo's heartbeat racing in a panic. And on top of that, I could smell blood. I pushed off of Jack's lap, but he got up, so he noticed it too.

Before I could do anything else, Milo started screaming.

"Help! Oh my god, *help!*" Milo yelled at the top of his lungs, and I raced up the steps. Jack flew past me because he was faster, and Ezra and Mae weren't that far behind.

When I reached the top of the stairs, Peter and Jack had already zoomed into Milo's room, but Milo still stood in the hallway. He was shirtless, and all the color had drained from him. His eyes were wide and horrified, and tears already slid down his face.

His cheeks were flushed unnaturally red, contrasting even more with the white of his skin. Fresh blood stained his lips, and a few splatters of it were on his bare chest, most of it smeared. He just stared at his bedroom, until Ezra pushed past me to get to his room, and then Milo turned to look at me.

"I killed Bobby."

- 22 -

Milo looked like he might faint after his confession, and I ran over to him. Mae stood behind me, not moving. I wrapped my arms around my brother and stole a glimpse inside his room.

Everyone blocked the view, but Bobby was definitely immobile on the bed. Peter knelt next to him, and Ezra bent over Bobby. Jack stood in the doorway, his arms crossed.

"Everything's gonna be okay," I lied. He cried silent tears, and he was in shock.

"I need O negative!" Ezra shouted.

"O negative?" Jack repeated.

"Yes! Now!" Ezra barked. Jack rushed past me and leapt down the stairs. "Where's Mae? I need the IV!"

"I'm right here, and I'll get the kit!" Mae sprang to life and darted down the stairs.

"He's alive?" I asked.

"Get Milo downstairs!" Peter growled, glaring at me.

I listened for the sound of Bobby's heart, but over the frantic beating of Milo's and my own, it was impossible to hear. That didn't mean anything, though. If he'd lost a lot of blood, his heartbeat would be really faint, probably too faint to hear over all the noise.

"Alice!" Jack shouted as he came barreling back up the stairs. "Get Milo out of here! He doesn't need to see this, okay?"

Using all my strength, I pulled Milo away from his room. I had no idea where I would take him, but away was as much as I planned. By the time we made it to the stairs, Mae was already bounding back up them.

"Everything will be okay, love," Mae promised with a sad smile, but Milo didn't even notice. After his initial screaming, he'd gone catatonic.

Milo needed to be someplace where he couldn't hear everything, and he needed to get cleaned up. So I took him into the main bathroom downstairs, and I turned on the sink to drown out all the other sounds. Putting the lid down on the toilet seat, I forced Milo to sit down. I got a washcloth wet to start wiping off his chest and mouth.

"Did I really kill him, Alice?" Milo asked, staring off into nothing.

"They're working on him." I evaded answering him. "They saved my life like that before, too. Ezra is really good at giving blood transfusions, apparently."

"I didn't even..." He trailed off, and I stopped wiping at his chest to look at him. "We were fooling around, the same way we had been, and then... I bit him. And I didn't even realize how much.... I didn't know his heart stopped."

"You didn't mean to." That was the best I could come up with.

"The thing is..." Milo became more animated, and his tears got heavier and louder. "I know that he isn't 'the one' or whatever, not like what Peter was to you. But I love him, you know? I really do love him."

"I know, sweetie. It's gonna be okay." I wrapped my arms around him and hugged him.

He was sobbing by then, and I just kept telling him it would be okay. I had no idea if that was the truth, but that was the only thing I could say.

We stayed down in the bathroom for what felt like forever. I folded up towels and laid them on the floor, and I sat down with my back up against the tub. Milo lay down next to me and rested his head on my lap. All I could do was brush his hair back with my fingers, and eventually, he even stopped crying.

When Jack opened the bathroom door, Milo jumped to his feet. I was too scared to move, as if me standing up would have an impact on whether Bobby lived or died.

"He's alive," Jack said, but he wasn't smiling. Milo almost fainted in relief, and he grasped onto the counter to keep from falling. I got up to catch him if he needed it. "But he lost a lot of blood. He's not exactly stable yet."

"Can I see him?" Milo asked and wiped at his eyes.

"Yeah, Ezra's up there, and he'll probably wanna talk to you too." Jack touched Milo's shoulder in an attempt to comfort him, but Milo just sniffled and hurried past him.

"So... how is Bobby?" I walked over to Jack.

"Not good," he said grimly. "He really almost didn't make it. I mean, Milo drained that kid dry. It was *bad*." Then he forced a smile at me. "But his heart's beating, and that's something."

He wrapped his arms around me, and I buried my face in his chest, surprised to find myself crying. Milo would never hurt anyone, and he really loved Bobby. It was terrifying to think that Bobby might die, and it'd be because they were in love and careless.

It scared me even more when I thought about my relationship with Jack, and how I almost lost control with Peter. Milo was way more in control of himself than me, and he nearly killed Bobby.

What would I do to Jack? Even with him being a vampire, I could find myself in the same situation, and that was too much.

Worse still, Jane was still out there, doing that kind of thing all the time with strangers. Most of the vampires she picked up were probably more experienced than Milo and me, but maybe they weren't. She had no way of knowing. And either way, they were still draining her of her blood, over and over again.

Accidentally or on purpose, the odds of her dying were getting exponentially higher ever day that passed. I couldn't let her do it anymore. As soon as things were settled with Milo and Bobby, I was taking Milo to the club, and we were taking her away. I don't care if we had to kidnap her; I wasn't going to just let her die.

The house was incredibly subdued. Mae didn't tend to Bobby. Immediately after he was stable, she returned to her room. Ezra stationed himself in Milo's room to monitor Bobby, but Jack later confided in me that Ezra had been crashing in the den with him the last few nights. Mae has all but kicked him out of their room.

Milo didn't feel right being around Bobby, and he was positive that Bobby would hate him when he woke up. I couldn't convince him otherwise, but he wanted to bunk with me, and really, I didn't mind.

Milo cried in his sleep, but I didn't say anything. After what he'd been through, I didn't blame him. I don't know what I would do if I did anything to Jack, and then I pushed the thought from my mind.

I would *never* do anything to him, even if that meant I had to wait months and years to do things with him. Or maybe never do anything with him. I wasn't going to hurt him, not like that.

Not like that. I had to amend everything with that now, because I was clearly okay with hurting him other ways, as seen by me making out with Peter.

That situation didn't want to resolve itself quite so easily either. When I got up in the morning, I bumped into Peter in the hall. There was this awkward exchange where neither of us knew what to say and just kind of stared at each other.

It was almost a full day after the transfusion that Bobby started to really come around. He'd had some hazy conversations before that, but he hadn't been lucid. Milo was too afraid to go in and talk to him, even after Bobby had started asking for him.

I even went in to talk to him, and Bobby repeatedly assured me that he didn't blame Milo for what happened, and he still loved him. He was pale and tired, but otherwise, he seemed okay.

Milo's plan was to hide away from Bobby, so he went down into Mae's room with her. Mae was abnormally useless in the situation. Jack and I ended up getting Bobby food and clothes and doing all the maternal/nurse things that Mae usually did, leaving him to survive entirely on peanut butter and jelly sandwiches and Campbell's soup.

He mostly slept at first, so I let it slide, but I wasn't going to let Milo just hide while I took care of his boyfriend. I gave Milo another night to sleep on it, but the next day I would make him see Bobby.

When I went to fetch Milo from Mae's room, I brought Jack along with me. Milo was still pretty fond of Jack, and I thought he might listen to him, even if he wouldn't listen to me. Stupidly, I thought Mae would encourage Milo to get up and deal with Bobby, but that wasn't how new sulky Mae rolled. They were curled up in the dark, listening to Norah Jones.

I flicked on the bedroom light, even though I didn't really need it to see anything. I just felt like they needed a flash of something to wake them up. They both squinted at me and groaned, and Milo buried himself deeper in the blankets and pillows. "Milo, come on," I said. "Bobby wants to see you."

"He does not!" Milo pulled the blanket entirely over his head, so his protests came out muffled.

"I'm sure he does, love," Mae sounded almost like her normal self. I don't know if it was our presence or the light, but it momentarily snapped her out of her funk. She scooted a bit closer to Milo and pushed back his blanket. "He loves you, and you know he does."

"I can't see him!" Milo said, fighting back tears. "Not ever!"

"I know it seems major, but it's really not as bad as you think." Jack sat at the down at the end of the bed to coax Milo out. "I mean, it would be major for normal people, but he understood what he was getting into when he got involved with a vampire."

"Well, maybe I didn't!" Milo whined, and he almost never did. Mae pushed back his hair from his forehead, and he rubbed at his eyes with the palm of his hand. "I don't know how I can ever face him again."

"Just face him the same way you did before," I shrugged. "You haven't seen him, but if you had, you'd understand. He really doesn't hold anything against you."

"But he should!" Milo pulled himself out from underneath the covers a bit more, but he just stared up at the ceiling. "I nearly killed him. He should hate me. Something should happen. There should be repercussions for my actions."

"You don't think there are?" I asked. "Look at you!"

"It's not enough," Milo said. "I mean, I'm a monster! I should be locked up and kept away from people forever!"

"You're not a monster, love." Mae ran her fingers through his hair. "You're just young, and you have some things to figure out. That's all."

"The fact that you're beating yourself up so much about this proves you're not a monster," Jack said. Milo looked at him, sniffling, and I thought Jack might have gotten through to him.

"Have you ever done anything like that?" Milo asked him, sounding hopeful. If Jack had behaved somewhat like this, then it would make it okay that Milo had done this.

"Well... no," Jack replied hesitantly.

"And you haven't even bit *anyone*, so you have no idea what I'm going through," Milo said to me, making me feel like an idiot and a loser.

I really hated that he had more experience in all of this than I did. I wanted to be able to advise him and comfort him through this, but like everything else in life, he knew more about it than I did. I was completely useless to him as an older sister.

"I have," Mae said reluctantly. Milo and Jack looked at her with surprise, and she gave Jack a weird look out of the corner of her eye. "It was a long time ago, but I remember it very clearly. I know how terrible it feels, knowing that you almost took a life. But I also know that it's something you can get past."

"So what happened?" Milo asked. The tears were drying under his eyes, and at least Mae had been able to distract him from his misery. "Was it with Ezra?"

"No, he was a human, but he didn't die, and that's what matters." Mae forced a smile, but there was something pained about it.

"How come I've never heard about this before?" Jack looked confused. They had been very close, and Mae loved sharing things. "Was it before I turned?"

"Yes, it was." Mae shifted in the bed and tucked a curl back behind her ears.

She sat up more and refused to look at Jack. Right now, he only felt bewildered and intrigued, but I got the impression that there was something that she wasn't telling us, and it made me nervous.

"Did he need a blood transfusion too?" Milo asked.

"No, but it doesn't matter how he survived. The point is that it doesn't make you a monster for drinking too much." Mae purposely turned more towards Milo, so her back was more to Jack. "It's easy to forget how fragile humans can be, and that's why it's important to always be careful."

"Well, how bad was he?" Milo started to doubt her story since she couldn't provide any details, but I knew she told the truth. She just left something out. "Did he lose a lot of blood?"

"Yes, he was almost dead." She closed her eyes and rubbed at her forehead. "His heart had completely stopped beating."

"So what did you do?" Milo sat up straighter, and Jack looked very interested in her story.

"We were... gone, and Ezra wasn't there." Mae sighed and shook her head. "It was a long time ago. I don't know why all of this matters so much to you."

"I just don't understand what happened. If he was that bad, how did he live? Did you take him to a hospital or something?" Milo asked.

"No, there wasn't enough time." Mae opened her eyes, but she stared intently at the bedspread instead of looking at any of us. "It's so easy to lose control, and that's why I only drink bag blood anymore. I never want to feel that way again."

"Mae, what happened?" I demanded as gently as I could. A sick feeling was building up in my stomach.

"We..." Mae exhaled shakily. "Peter turned him."

Mae closed her eyes tightly, and for a second, nobody said anything. It felt like all the air had been sucked out of the room. Milo's brown eyes were even larger than normal, and he looked back and forth between Mae and Jack.

Jack didn't seem to feel anything. Then this shocked, nauseated panic spread out over him. His heart hammered in his chest.

"What are you talking about?" Jack demanded, his voice quavering.

"Jack, love." Mae reached out for his hand, but he leapt up off the bed before she could touch him. Tears formed in her eyes. "It was a long time ago."

"No," Jack shook his head, refusing to believe or understand what she said. "I followed two girls into the club, and then…" He ran a hand through his hair and stared off, trying to think. He'd never really remembered much about turning. "You told me that you found me in the alley, that they left me for dead."

"Nobody left you for dead, love." She got up off the bed and took a step towards him, and he took a step back.

"What really happened to me?" Jack shouted. She flinched at the anger in his voice.

"You were at the club, and…" She trailed off. "You know how these things happen."

"No, I want you to tell me exactly what happened," Jack glared at her. "I deserve to know what you really did to me!"

"You were at the club, and I was hungry. I picked up people there a few times before, and I didn't think anything of it. So I took you to one of the back rooms," Mae said hurriedly, and Jack closed his eyes. "I didn't mean to, Jack! Honestly! I never meant to hurt you! I didn't even realize what I had done until it was too late! You weren't breathing and your heart had stopped!"

"I thought you couldn't turn if you were dead," he said but didn't open his eyes.

"I don't know why it worked, but it did." Mae walked closer to him, and he didn't move. "I called for Peter, and he said the only thing we could do was turn you, so he did. And then we took you back home and took care of you and loved you."

She put her hand on his chest, and he let her, but he was visibly shaken. His heart beat erratically, and the color drained from his face.

"Why didn't you tell me this before?" Jack asked as evenly as he could.

"The last thing you remembered was following the girls, and everything was confusing and frightening enough in the beginning," she said. "We didn't want to add to it, so we let you believe that the girls had done it."

"So you lied to me?" When he opened his eyes, they had gone icy. "You lied to me for the past sixteen years? You thought that was a better alternative?"

"No, we just... I didn't know how to tell you," Mae floundered.

"Whatever." He pushed her hand off him and stormed out of

her bedroom. I went after him because I felt I should, but I had no idea how I could help him.

"Jack!" Mae called, running after him. She tried to touch his arm, and he jerked it back from her. "Jack! Please! It doesn't change anything!"

"It changes everything!" Jack made it as far as the living room before he whirled on her. "You killed me! You…" He ran his hands through his hair, and he couldn't process what she told him. "And you covered it up! How could you lie to me about something so important? What else have you been lying to me about?"

"Nothing! This was the only thing, and it wasn't lying!" Mae looked away from him and shook her head, her eyes swimming with tears. "We just let you believe what you wanted."

"Bullshit!" Jack yelled. "You let me believe what you wanted me to believe! You didn't want to tell me that you had almost left me for dead! And if Ezra had been there, instead of Peter, you would have! He never would've let you turn me!"

"What's going on?" Ezra asked, coming down the stairs at precisely the wrong time.

Sometimes, it really sucked being able to feel everything Jack felt. He had his arms wrapped around himself, and he was very close to throwing up. He'd always thought they'd been so moved by his plight that they saved him, when really, he had just been a casualty.

"Why didn't you ever tell me Mae killed me?" Jack shouted, turning his anger on Ezra. "You made me live a lie the entire time!"

"You're being melodramatic," Ezra said calmly. "Nothing has been a lie." He gave Mae a disparaging look, and she shied away from it. Apparently, he didn't approve of the way she told Jack.

Cautiously, I took a step towards him. Jack wasn't mad at me in particular, but he felt kinda mad at the world. He stood in the middle of the living room. Ezra and Mae were in the living room doorway, and Mae started crying. Milo had smartly decided to stay behind in Mae's room to hide.

Somehow, Milo's pep talk had turned into this, and I felt sorry for him. He probably didn't feel any better about his situation when he saw Jack reacting this way.

In fairness, I don't think Jack was that upset about what happened. Or at least, he would've gotten over it a long time ago. He just didn't like knowing he had been lied to about something that was such a major event in his life.

"Jack, you know they love you," I said, and he looked at me uneasily.

"How do I know that? How do I know anything they ever said was true?" Jack asked me honestly.

"You know how much you mean to us!" Mae insisted. "Look at everything we've done for you and tried to do!"

"You know what? I really don't wanna hear from you right now," Jack snapped at her. He turned and headed for the stairs. "I don't wanna hear from anybody!"

When he ran up to his room, I followed him. He had no reason to be mad at me, but he didn't really feel like he wanted me around. He paced in his room, and I stood awkwardly in the open doorway, so I wouldn't be intruding on his space quite so much.

"Why would they all lie about this?" Jack ran his hand through his hair. "Why couldn't they just tell me the truth? Is it really that hard?"

"Kinda. I'm sure Mae was really ashamed of what happened, and you didn't remember," I said. "They probably just thought it would be easier for everyone."

"I could've died!" He stopped pacing so he could look at me. "Mae almost killed me, and she never thought it was the right thing to tell me? And I don't get why I don't remember. Everyone else remembers when they turned so vividly. Why can't I? Did she do something to me?"

"You died, that's why," Peter said, startling me.

He must've been in his room when he heard Jack yelling, and we had been too distracted to notice him coming out into the hall. I glanced back at him, then crossed my arms firmly over my chest and moved closer to the wall, away from him.

"You were dead for almost five minutes," Peter said. "We weren't even sure the transformation would take, but you've always had a strong heart."

"Well, thank you so very much," Jack said, his voice heavy with sarcasm.

"I know you're upset, but you're making too much of this." Peter sounded almost weary.

He walked into Jack's room, moving much closer to me than I would've liked. He barely looked at me, but I stared down at the ground. Supposedly, Peter was trying to comfort Jack, and that made me uncomfortable. Being around Peter and Jack together made me feel guilty.

If I had been able to think clearly or actually speak, I would've been wondering when Peter started caring about Jack's well-being. I know that they had once been very close, but I had never seen Peter ever say anything encouraging to Jack. Today, at this moment, Peter suddenly decided to repair their relationship.

"Peter, I really don't need your shit right now," Jack said. "You're no better than anybody else."

"Really? Because it was my decision to save your life." Peter looked at him, and Jack lowered his eyes to the floor. "But that's not the point. Mae was a wreck about what happened to you, and we did everything in our power to save you and take care of you. So don't act like we don't care."

"Out of guilt!" Jack shook his head. "And it doesn't matter! I just can't believe that you'd all lie to me all this time!" He sighed. "But I guess I shouldn't have expected much different from you. You're the most self-serving person I've ever met."

"What does that mean?" Peter narrowed his eyes at him.

"You are so selfish! You *never* think about anybody else!" Jack shouted at him. "You guys didn't want to tell me because you thought I'd be upset!"

"You sure proved us wrong," Peter replied dryly and crossed his arms over his chest.

"I never lie to you guys! Not ever! And I can't believe that you would all conspire to lie to me about something so big!" Jack yelled, and the knot in the pit of my stomach only tightened. "It's so weak, and even though you're a massive dick, I never thought you were a coward."

"I *saved* your life! And I have sacrificed so much of my own happiness for you!" Peter growled at him. "And that makes me a dick and a coward?"

"If you had to lie to do it, then yeah, it does!" Jack stared directly at Peter, and something flashed in Peter's eyes.

"Hey, you know what? I think that, um, we should just take a breather," I stammered.

"So you don't want me to ever lie to you? About anything?" Peter had a bitter smile on his lips, and it confused Jack. "That's the only way that I can overcome being this selfish asshole who has stupidly put your wants in front of my own for the past sixteen years?"

"I hardly think you've done that, but yeah." Jack didn't know what he was getting at, but it made him nervous.

"Peter, I think that Jack doesn't know what he's saying," I interjected breathlessly. Jack's eyes flitted over to me for just a second, but by then, it was too late. As soon as I said Peter's name, Jack realized something was up.

"I know *exactly* what I'm saying," Jack glared at Peter.

"Yeah? Well, then, just so I can absolve myself from all the sins I've done against you, like saving your life and running away to Finland so you could live in peace, I'm gonna tell you the truth." Peter leaned in a little bit closer to Jack and lowered his voice. "I kissed Alice. Three days ago."

"Peter!" I shouted because that was the only defense I had.

We both suspected some kind of reaction out of Jack, but for a minute, there was nothing. A weird buzzing feeling engulfed his emotions, and I couldn't get a read on any of them. His face was blank, and then finally, he turned to me. That's when I felt how much it hurt him, and it was like being punched in the gut.

"Jack," I said lamely.

"Fuck you all," Jack looked at Peter, then back at me. "Seriously. Fuck you all." Then he looked away from us and walked out of his bedroom.

- 24 -

Going after Jack would not be an option. When he left, I felt how badly I disgusted and hurt him, and he didn't want anything to do with me. He might never want anything to do with me again, but I had to give him time. So I stood in his room, reminding myself to breathe.

"Alice, I'm so sorry," Peter said genuinely. "I didn't mean to say that. I never meant to tell him anything, but he-"

"Shut up!" I snapped. "Just shut up!"

Peter left me alone, and I sat on the bed. I trembled horribly, but I managed to keep from crying or vomiting, so it was almost a win. Over and over again, I just kept telling myself that he wouldn't leave me forever. Not over this.

I had kissed Peter before, and he had gotten over it. Admittedly, I hadn't really been dating Jack at the time, and he had still been hurt by it. But he only hurt because he loved me, and it had just been one stupid kiss.

I tried to think of how I would explain this all to Jack. When he came back, he'd want to know why, and I had better have a good excuse. Unfortunately, I didn't have one. There was no good reason for what I did with Peter. I couldn't even explain it myself, and I had been trying for days. What I felt for Peter was nothing like what I felt for Jack... but I couldn't deny that I did feel something for Peter.

As much as I had been minimizing it, there was still this connection and pull I had towards him. Maybe I would have it forever, but I only acted on it because of weak impulse control.

That's not what I could tell Jack, though. He would never be okay with that. And he was just starting to get along with Peter again. Why did I always have to ruin everything?

When Jack still hadn't come back several hours later, I called and texted him. Multiple times. But he never answered. I could hear Bobby waking up in the next room, so I decided that helping him out would be better than feeling sorry for myself and worrying about Jack. Bobby wanted food, so I made him a sandwich and grabbed him a Diet Cherry Coke.

Milo was moping about the living room, and I'd had enough of it. Grabbing him by his arm, I drug him upstairs. He complained the entire time, but he didn't fight me that hard. I managed to get him and Bobby's food in his room without damaging any of them.

As soon as Milo saw Bobby sitting up in bed, he started crying. He ran over to him and they embraced. He apologized a million times, and Bobby forgave him a million times. Just like that, they were back to normal. I hated them.

Jack still wasn't home when Matilda and I finally passed out, but that didn't worry me that much. When I woke up, and he still wasn't there, I got more concerned. After another thirty ignored calls from me, I decided I had to try a different tactic.

Jack was pissed at nearly everybody in the house, except for Milo and Bobby. In fact, he was ridiculously fond of them. I woke up Milo and demanded that he text Jack, just to make sure he was okay.

Two minutes later, Jack replied with, "Yeah, I am okay." So I made Milo follow-up asking when he would be home again, but that text, Jack never answered.

I lay in bed, feeling certain that he was never coming home. He had left with a Lamborghini and credit cards with no spending limit. He felt betrayed by almost everyone living in this house. If I were him, I'd probably run away forever too.

What could he possibly still want with me? All I ever did was complicate and hurt him. He was better off without me, but selfishly, I wanted him still.

The ache I felt at being apart from him only seemed to be growing. Jack was either getting farther away, or ... I don't know. Maybe his feelings were ebbing away, and I could feel it, like a painful tear spreading down my middle.

I wanted to cry, but I couldn't. I just stared at the ceiling, and let the pain consume me. After all, I deserved it. This was my fault.

"Alice?" Peter knocked on the open bedroom door, but I didn't turn to look at him. I refused to do anything that didn't involve being immobile and suffering.

"Go away."

"You're pissed at me, and you should be," Peter said. "I never should've said that."

"For once, you didn't do anything wrong," I sighed. "I never should've kissed you, and after I did, I should've told Jack about it. I screwed up."

"I shouldn't have let you in my room that night. Or maybe I should've..." He trailed off. "I never should've come back in the first place."

"No, this is your home. *I'm* the one that ruined everything, but I always do."

"No, Alice, you don't ruin anything," Peter took a step into the room, but I held my hand up to him.

"I need to be by myself, okay?" I could see him out of the corner my eye. He debated whether he should listen to me, but finally, he nodded and left me alone.

If I wanted any chance of a future with Jack, I was going to have to spend the rest of my life avoiding Peter. For the first time, I really understood why Peter was always taking off. It was impossible for us to be around each other. It was just strange that Jack was the one that left and not Peter. I shivered and hoped that that didn't signify anything.

All around, everything seemed to be falling apart. Bobby was recovering, but Milo was still shaken up. Peter sulked about the house, and he tried to talk to me several times, but I always shut him down.

Mae and Ezra were completely unraveling. I could hear them shouting at each other constantly, about Jack, about Daisy, about anything. Matilda just lay by me and whined, and I buried my head under the pillow. I didn't know how much more of this I could take.

"Alice?" Milo knocked on the door tenuously, waking me up. It was the second night Jack had been gone, so I hadn't really slept. "Alice, wake up."

"What's in it for me?" I grumbled and poked my head out from under the pillow. When I saw Milo, I blinked, assuming that I was dreaming. He was wearing some kind of getup that included black angel wings and excessive amounts of eyeliner and glitter. "Okay, what the hell are you wearing?"

"It's Halloween!" Milo smiled and walked over to the bed. Matilda growled at him, and I totally agreed with her.

"What are you supposed to be? Some kind of dark fairy?" I sat up so I could inspect his costume, but it didn't make much sense to me. Other than being entirely black, there wasn't any rhyme or reason to it.

"No," Milo laughed. "I just wanted to wear wings, and black is Halloween-y. And slimming."

"Oh my god, I can't *believe* I didn't know you were gay growing up," I flopped back down on the bed. Every holiday ever was an excuse for Milo to dress up. The signs were ridiculously obvious when I thought about it.

"You can be a little slow sometimes," he agreed. "Now come on. Get out of bed and get ready. We're going out!"

"I can't go out," I said. "Jack's not home."

"I'm pretty sure you've left the house without Jack before." He sat down on the edge of the bed next to me. "And it's a holiday. You can't stay cooped up in your room forever."

"Maybe not, but I can't leave with Jack still gone. It doesn't feel right."

"He'll be home soon," Milo said without conviction. "Or maybe he won't. I don't really know. But either way, you can't just stay here until he gets back."

"I can't go out! That's like... I don't know. Sacrilegious or something." I looked over at him. "I mean, he left me here to punish me. So I should be properly punished."

"Jack doesn't punish anyone. That's not how he works," he waved off the idea. "He just needed time to clear his head, and he's giving you time to clear yours too. Since you can't seem to stop kissing his brother, I'm sure he thinks you need time to make up your mind about what you really want."

"I have made up my mind!"

"Well, good, then you have time to go out with us!" Milo said brightly. "So come on! Get up! Get dressed! Let's dance!"

"No, I really can't," I repeated. "Not until Jack comes back. I just have to stay here and wait for him."

"What if he never comes back?" Milo asked, and I shot him a glare. "Sorry. But you know, what if it's a really long time?"

"Then I'll just wait forever if I have to," I decided. "I'll be like Snow White, and you can just put me in one of those glass cases until Jack comes and gives me true love's kiss."

"Oh, Snow White, that's a good costume for you." He touched my hair. "With your pale skin and dark hair, we could totally make that work."

"Milo!" I groaned.

"Is she coming with?" Bobby asked, appearing in the doorway behind Milo. He was wearing a white shirt, unbuttoned down his chest, with a black vest and tight pants. I was about to guess for some kind of pirate, and then I saw the laser blaster in his belt.

"Are you Han Solo?" I raised my eyebrow at him.

"Yeah, I wanted him to be Princess Leia, but he wouldn't go for it," Bobby gave Milo a pouty look, and I was momentarily relieved that Jack wasn't around so he couldn't try out that exact idea on me. Then I realized that Jack wasn't here, and I got sad again.

"I am not going to wear a gold bikini," Milo said. "Even I'm not gay enough for that!"

"So you're like half a costume?" I asked Bobby.

"Yeah, I was gonna be Andy Warhol, but I looked really terrible with the white wig. My complexion is all wrong for it," Bobby gestured to his skin, then an idea dawned on him, and he smiled wickedly at me. "Hey, if you don't have a costume, you could always go as Leia!"

"No! No way!" I shook my head. "Even if I wasn't too busy being suicidal, there is no way you can talk me into that. No gold bikini's or cinnamon bun hair-do's."

"Fine. Costume or not, you really should come out with us," Milo said, looking at me with concern. "It's not good for you to just lay in bed all the time like this. You're not even watching TV or listening to music. You're just lying in the dark. It's not healthy."

"I don't care." I smiled wanly at my brother. "I'm okay, though. Honest. I'll get up and do something tonight. I just... I can't go out. But thanks for inviting me. I really appreciate it."

"Okay," Milo relented. "But you better be out of this bed when I get back. Or else."

Milo smiled sadly at me before leaving with Bobby. On the sheets next to me, he left behind a trail of glitter and black feathers.

I did not want to get out of bed, but I didn't really want Jack coming back to me being a big, stinky mess, so I decided that if nothing else, I should keep up my hygiene, so he doesn't break up with me for that. I showered, styled my hair, put on makeup, and got dressed. For the sake of Halloween, I even painted my nails green. I don't know why I went through all that trouble, but it felt like something to do.

Matilda needed to go to the bathroom, so I went downstairs to let her outside. She was the only real consolation I had. As mad as Jack might be at me and everyone else, he would never leave her behind. Not for good.

While she was outside doing her thing, I glanced down the hall. The door to the den was open, and Ezra sat at the computer, the screen glowing blue on his face. He probably still slept on the couch in there, and I wondered if he and Mae were ever going to make up. And if they weren't, I wondered why neither of them left.

My cell phone started ringing, and my heart skipped a beat until I realized it was Milo's ringer and not Jack's "Time Warp." I briefly considered not answering it. He probably just wanted to talk me into coming out with him. But then again, he might be in trouble, so I figured I should take it.

"Hello?" I answered, and I had to hold the phone away from my ear because the music was so loud.

"Hello?" Milo shouted over the music. "Hello?"

"Milo?" I yelled back, so he could hear me. "Milo? Where are you?"

"I'm at *V*!" Milo shouted, and I could barely hear Bobby saying something in the background about a girl. "You've got to come down here!"

"No, I already told you I'm not going," I sighed. Matilda started barking at the French doors off the kitchen, so I went and let her in. "Thanks anyway."

"No, I mean you *really* have to come down!" Milo said.

"She's going in the room with him!" Bobby shouted plaintively at Milo. "Tell her to hurry and get down here! We've gotta do something!"

"I'm not leaving you alone to deal with her," Milo told Bobby, and I really wished I understood what was happening or the music behind them was quieter.

"What is going on?" I asked.

"Jane is down here, and she looks like a corpse! For real! Not like a zombie Halloween costume or anything," Milo said. "She looks really, really terrible, and she just went into the backrooms with that Jonathan guy she was with before. I can't go after her and leave Bobby alone, so you need to get down here. If she doesn't get out of here tonight, she's probably never getting out of here."

"This better not be some trick to get me to come out!" I said, but deep down, I knew it wasn't. Both Milo and Bobby sounded genuinely frazzled, and I hadn't been doing enough to get her to stop being a bloodwhore.

"I would never lie about something like this!" Milo yelled, and he wouldn't. I don't think he ever lied about anything.

"Fine! I'll be there as soon as I can! Wait for me by the dance floor!" I told him, then hung up the phone. Immediately after doing so, I found a giant flaw in my plan: I didn't know how to drive.

- 25 -

I realized that there was somebody here that always fixed everything *and* knew how to drive. "Ezra!"

"Yes?" Ezra answered, and I walked to the end of the hall so I could see him. He looked up from his computer. "Something is the matter?"

"Milo's at a club, and Jane's there. She's a bloodwhore, and he says she's in really bad shape. I need to get her before something bad happens," I said. "Would you be willing drive me down there?"

"Absolutely." Ezra hit a button on the computer and stood up. "Milo told me he and Bobby were going out to the clubs tonight, and Bobby was looking quite well, so I told them to have fun."

"I think they're having fun," I said sourly as he met me in the hall.

"At least I get to go out on Halloween," Ezra smiled at me, and we walked towards the garage. "I haven't done that in years." He noticed his teasing falling flat on me, and he nodded solemnly. "We'll get your friend out of there." I nodded and followed him out to his Lexus. "And Jack will come home. He does love you very much."

"I know," I lied. "I just wish I knew where he was."

"He'll turn up soon," Ezra assured me. "He's not the kind to stray very far."

Ezra said very little else on the car ride to *V*. Downtown was a madhouse. People were everywhere, dressed in all sorts of wacky garments. Most of the girls' outfits could barely count as "clothing," and it seemed like everyone was drunk or high or just certifiably insane.

I had to jog to keep up with Ezra, and I felt strange going to the clubs with him. He dressed more fashionably and appropriate for a club situation than I did, but it was weird thinking of him clubbing. Even as attractive and as young as he looked, he never seemed like the kind of person that would frequent a place like this.

In the block before the club, he had to fend off several very drunk girls. I mean he literally had to push them off of him, and by the looks of the last one, she wasn't exactly drunk. The fading pink marks on her neck meant she was just leaving the club we were going to.

A couple guys made a pass at me, and I didn't really care, except for the fact that I was starting to get hungry. I hadn't even really felt it until we were in a crowd of people.

Ezra held the door open to *V* for me, and the two giant bouncers were still manning their post. They nodded at Ezra and exchanged some kind of look with him. It made me wonder if he was acquainted with him, but I didn't really have time to ask. Jane was in trouble, and it didn't really matter who Ezra did or didn't know.

The dance floor was completely packed. Michael Jackson's hit song "Thriller" blasted out over the stereo, and at least half of the floor was doing the dance that went along with it. It would've been a sight to behold, but Milo and Bobby waited by the doors for us, reminding me of the business at hand. One of Milo's wings looked damaged, but with the floor being as crowded as it was, I was surprised that his costume had stayed as intact as it had.

"It's crazy here tonight!" Milo shouted over the music.

"I don't understand how they all know the moves," Bobby said, watching the Thriller dancers with some fascination.

"Yeah, great. Where's Jane?" I asked.

"In one of the backrooms." Milo gestured across the dancehall to the vampire bar section of the club. Blue lights flashed overhead. "I don't know which one for sure, but I thought you could find her."

"As long as she's still alive, I probably can," I said.

Milo grabbed Bobby and made his way across the dance floor. I went into the crowd after him, but they were impossible to get through. Apparently, I wasn't even as forceful as Milo.

Ezra came up behind him, and putting his arm around my waist, he started pushing our way through them. I was strong enough to do it, but I felt bad about pushing people out of the way. Not that any of them seemed to mind. Humans and vampires alike seemed to enjoy being touched by Ezra a little too much.

The dim lighting and muffled sound of the smaller bar came as a huge relief. Even in here, it was incredibly packed. Usually there were just a handful of couples, but tonight, every available surface was covered with vampires feeding on people or making out with each other. There were even two vampires lying on the bar in the corner, grinding in a very provocative fashion. Milo, Bobby, Ezra, and I stood out for the simple fact that we were not kissing or biting.

"Which hall did she go down?" I asked Milo quietly.

There were seven different hallways that went off the main bar,

251

and I'm not even sure how many rooms were down each hall. I went down one before, and it seemed to go on forever.

"I think that one." Milo pointed to one on the far side of the room.

"Are you sure?" Bobby squinted. The red lights in here weren't the best for his eyesight. "I thought it was the one just to the left of that."

"You've got be kidding me," I groaned.

"Ezra Townsend!" Olivia squealed, and pushed an unconscious girl onto the floor. She moaned a little when she hit her head, but that was the only sign she gave that she was still alive.

Olivia's tight leather uniform seemed much more appropriate with the Halloween crowd, and she was smiling widely at Ezra in her usual drugged out way. I expected him to look appalled by her, but instead, he smiled back at her, and when she reached him, they actually hugged.

"It's so good to see you!"

"Likewise," Ezra agreed when they stopped hugging. I glanced at Milo and Bobby to see them gaping at him too.

"It really has been too long." Olivia touched his arm and laughed. "I didn't even know you were still in the area! I thought you would've moved on years ago."

"Well, I tried, but the wife has roots down here," Ezra shrugged.

"She's not-" Olivia looked at me distrustfully.

"No, no, Alice isn't mine. She's my brother Jack's," Ezra said, and Olivia nodded and smiled again at me.

"She's a little tart, isn't she?" Olivia was looking at me in a way that would've made me blush if I wasn't busy trying to figure out how we'd find Jane.

"Perhaps," Ezra looked at me, and I was pleased to see it was affectionate. I think I had been kind of expecting him to hate me after all the trouble I caused between Jack and Peter, but Ezra didn't seem to be one to hold a grudge either.

"You should've told me you were with Ezra," Olivia said and touched my arm. "I would've given you the special treatment." I had a feeling she was already giving me special treatment, but I just smiled.

"Sorry. I didn't realize you two knew each other," I said. I didn't want to talk to them anymore, but I wanted Ezra to help me, and I didn't want to be rude to her. After all, she had helped me out a couple times.

"That's just like Ezra," she rolled her eyes. "He never talks about his past."

"I don't mean to be rude, but we've got a missing friend," Milo interjected, saving me from some long, semi-drunken conversation. Olivia might not be able to drink alcohol, but she drank more blood than a vampire needed too, leaving her to act and feel rather drunk.

"Same one as before?" Olivia raised an eyebrow.

"Yes, and we've got to find her. So, if you'll excuse us." Milo had Bobby's hand in one hand and he took mine in the other. Olivia nodded at us as we started making our escape, but Ezra stayed with her. I wanted him to come with us, but I couldn't force him.

"So you know which hall it is?" I asked as Milo drug me to the other side of the room.

"Nope, but it's got to be one of these two halls." Milo let go of my hand, but he still hung onto Bobby's. In another circumstance, it would've been a very funny sight to see a black glittery fairy leading a rather short Han Solo by the hand.

They led the way, but once we were in the hall, they slowed down considerably. Milo didn't really know how to track Jane, not as well as I did anyway, but it was going to be impossible. There were too many people tonight.

Everything smelled like blood, and I was incredibly impressed with my current level of self-control. My stomach burned a bit, and I was really thirsty, but it was nothing I couldn't handle. It did, however, make it hard to distinguish different scents and sounds. Blood overpowered everything else.

I was about to give up on the whole thing when I finally got something. I froze in the middle of the hall, and Bobby bumped into me. It was too dark for him to see that I had stopped moving. Very faintly, I could smell her perfume. Her blood wasn't as distinct to me as I thought it would be, but her perfume was.

"It's this one," I whispered, gesturing to the door in front of us. Milo moved in front of Bobby, putting himself between him and any possible attack.

After the way Jonathan had reacted the last time we busted in on him with Jane, I figured we should take the necessary precautions. This time, I decided against busting in. Very slowly, I turned the knob and pushed the door open.

Jonathan didn't hear us because he was feeding on Jane. He knelt on the bed, her body hanging limp in his arms, and he gnawed on her neck. It wasn't the gentle bites that Olivia always gave her girlfriends, or like the ones I'm sure Milo gave Bobby.

This was intensely animalistic, reminding me of the shark attacks I watched on TV. Jane appeared completely unconscious, and when I listened for a heartbeat, I couldn't hear one. Only the sounding of his, pounding strong and fast.

Without thinking, I flew at him. He was killing her, and I had to stop him while there was still time, *if* there was still time. I jumped onto his back, and he snarled and threw Jane to the ground. It would've been easier for him to just drop her on the bed, but he purposely chucked her away, like a piece of garbage.

I wrapped my arms around his neck, but he reached back and grabbed me by my hair. He lifted me by it, and I screamed. I kicked and clawed at him, and he threw me against the wall.

The pain stopped instantly. Hitting the wall hurt like hell, but it was over right away, and I was back on my feet. I dove at him again, punching at him. I had never been in a fight before, so I was just doing whatever I could think of.

Theoretically, I should be really fast and strong, but I did not feel like it. He blocked every move before I even made it, and when I was resorting to simply scratching and kicking, he turned me around. He wrapped his arms tightly around me, pressing my back to his chest, and I couldn't move.

"Drop the meat!" Jonathan roared at Milo, and I looked over at him. Milo had carefully picked Jane up off the floor, but he didn't want to leave me alone with Jonathan.

"Get out of here!" I shouted. I didn't really want him to leave me, because I had a feeling that I couldn't win this fight, but this was his only chance to save Jane. "Go!"

Milo was indecisive, and Bobby stood in the hallway right out the door, looking pale and afraid. I struggled against Jonathan but didn't accomplish much. He tired of the standoff, and in a ridiculous move, he bit into my shoulder.

I yelped, and I could feel the blood flowing hot and strange from the wound, but he didn't drink from me. He could've bitten my throat and caused real damage, but he was doing this just to hinder and annoy me. Losing blood weakened me, and I wasn't that strong of a fighter to start with.

"Alice!" Milo shouted.

"Drop the girl!" Jonathan snarled, and threw me to the ground. My shoulder had already stopped hurting, and it tingled from healing, but I could feel the blood seeping out of me. It was incredibly nauseating.

"Run, Milo!" I yelled, and Jonathan turned back to glare at me.

He stood right by me, where I lay on the ground, and an idea occurred to me. He kicked me, and I let him, and Bobby shouted at me to get up. If Jane wasn't unconscious, Milo probably would've handed her to Bobby and helped me himself.

As soon as Jonathan turned back to Milo, I moved forward and bit into his ankle as hard as I could. I tore through his Achilles tendon, and Jonathan screamed in pain and fell back on the ground. Even though the pain would stop soon, the damaged ligament would slow him down.

I got to my feet. Jonathan, still on the floor, grabbed my ankle. I stomped on his hand before he would get the chance to bite me the way I had done him, and he hissed but wouldn't let go. He bared his teeth like he was some kind of animal, so I kicked him hard in the face. At the same time, he pulled my leg, so I fell back onto the ground.

His mouth was full of blood from me kicking him, and when Jonathan laughed, some of it sprayed on me. The worst part was that all the blood still smelled like Jane. I kicked him in the mouth again. He finally let go of me, and I scrambled to my feet.

Milo had started setting Jane down on the bed, preparing to help me fight off Jonathan, but Jonathan was busy holding his mouth to stop the blood from spilling out. I rushed over to help Milo get Jane, even though he wouldn't need any help. She was little more than skin and bones. Her throat was torn open, and Jonathan had really gone to town on it when he had bit her. It was like a dog bite and not the usual small incision vampires made.

I swallowed back vomit and lifted her up in my arms. I couldn't feel a pulse, and her head and limbs just dangled. Milo stared down at her with a look of dull horror. If she was still alive, she wouldn't be for much longer. Out of the corner of my eye, I saw movement, and Bobby gasped. I looked up, but it was already too late.

Jonathan had Bobby in his clutches.

26

Milo lunged after them, into the hall where I couldn't see anything. I wanted to throw Jane on the bed, but if she was dying, I didn't want that to be the move that killed her. All I could hear was the sound of growling and flesh hitting flesh and Bobby screaming.

Finally I decided saving Jane's life wasn't worth my brother or Bobby dying, so I set her on the bed.

"Sorry, Jane." I pushed her short hair off her forehead, and she felt completely cold under my touch.

I got to the hall the same time as Ezra. I'm not sure how well the fight between Milo and Jonathan had been going, but Ezra flew in and grabbed Jonathan by the throat and pinned him back against the concrete wall.

Milo's costume was in tatters and he was out of breath, and he just stood across from Jonathan, glaring at him. Jonathan fought against Ezra, but then Olivia appeared behind Ezra, and he completely stopped.

"*Enough*," Ezra boomed, and let go of his throat. Jonathan licked the blood from his lips and straightened out his clothing.

My mouth had blood on it from when I'd bit him, and I wiped at it with the back of my hand. I could almost taste it, but I refused to. It was Jane's blood, and I didn't want any of it.

"I don't want to see you around here anymore," Olivia said, and her voice sounded surprisingly commanding. "Is that clear?"

Jonathan didn't say anything. He looked at the ground and started hobbling down the hall. His tendon hadn't healed yet. I couldn't quite figure out why he'd listened to Olivia, but I didn't have time to think about.

"Are you okay?" Milo knelt on the ground next to Bobby.

Bobby slumped against the wall, and he was bleeding, but I'm not sure from where. He nodded, and I could tell he was fighting back tears, but otherwise he was alright.

I would've like to stay and make sure they were both okay, but I had to get Jane. I ran back in the room and scooped her up in my arms, and she hung like a rag doll. Her sheer, tiny dress revealed all her ribs, and I felt her spine. The wound on her neck had started clotting, which meant there had to be some life, but that was the only sign I had.

"That's your friend?" Ezra looked in the room at her, and his expression was grim.

"Yeah. Can you help her?" I held her out towards him, like I was a small child and she were a broken toy I expected him to fix.

"We'll take her back to the house," Ezra said simply. Gingerly, he took her from me, and I felt better just knowing that he had her. In my mind, he could fix anything.

"Take the back way out," Olivia suggested when she saw Jane. "You remember how to get there?"

"Yes. Thank you for all your help," Ezra said.

"Anytime," Olivia smiled at me. "You take care of yourself. Try and stay out of trouble, okay?"

"I'll try," I nodded, but I was already walking down the hall, following Ezra. Milo and Bobby came more slowly behind us. Milo tried carrying Bobby, but he kept insisting that it wasn't necessary, even though it kind of was.

When we left the club, the alley around us was deserted, and Ezra had planned ahead because he had parked right next to it. He commanded Milo and Bobby to go straight home, and we'd meet them there.

He laid Jane in the backseat of the Lexus, and I climbed in back with her, resting her head on my lap. Very slowly, her neck wound was healing, and I could feel her breath coming out faintly. Somewhere in there, she was still alive.

"Why'd he bite her neck like that?" I asked, more to myself than Ezra. I brushed her hair back, trying to get the blood out from it, and held back tears. "Was he trying to kill her?"

"Not exactly," Ezra said and looked at me in the rearview mirror. "He was trying to get more blood, and she was running out." I sniffled and looked back down at Jane. "Are you okay, Alice? Did that vampire hurt you?"

"No, I'm fine." I glanced at my shoulder, and it was almost entirely healed. "What about you? Are you okay?"

"Yes, I am." Ezra didn't appear to have a mark on him, but he had come in for the last minute of the fight. Although, I couldn't help but wonder if it would've gone on longer if he hadn't had Olivia with him.

"Why did that vampire seem so afraid of Olivia? She doesn't seem that scary to me," I said. Most of the time, Olivia seemed too drunk and hazy to be anything but harmless. But this was the second time she'd saved my life.

"Well, for one thing, that's her club, and for another, she used to be a vampire hunter," Ezra said. "Although, she tries to keep it quiet on both accounts."

"Wait. What?" I looked incredulously at him. "She *owns* the club, and she's a vampire hunter? But she is a vampire! That doesn't make any sense!"

"People can't possibly take down a vampire, not with a wooden stake or an uzi," Ezra said. "You could barely hold your own against one, and you are a vampire. So the only ones that can police us are other vampires. We don't have a system of laws, but every now and then, vampires get too renegade, and someone needs to be called in. That someone used to be Olivia, but she retired years ago and bought the club."

"Why do I feel like you're making this up?" I asked.

"Because Olivia is easily underestimated, but that's part of her strength," Ezra said. "She's one of the strongest and oldest vampires I've ever met. She must be... nearly six hundred years old." He looked at me in the rearview mirror. "And she's quite taken with you."

I might have found that more amusing, but Jane made a sound in my lap. Ezra sped up, probably deciding that there might actually be hope for her. He carried her into the house, shouting for Mae as soon as we got in the door. For the second time in a matter of days, Ezra's expertise with blood was called into action.

Much to Peter's dismay, Ezra kicked him out of his room, and

Mae and Ezra went about making Jane comfortable in there. I tried to help, but I was too upset to be useful, so they sent me downstairs. Milo was in the main bathroom, tending to Bobby's lacerations, and I went in under the guise of helping, but really, I wanted a distraction.

I sat on the edge of the bathroom tub and watched them. Bobby had a few minor scratches across his chest and shoulders, and a bite wound on the back of his neck. The bite was already healing, thanks to vampire saliva's healing properties, but it hadn't been that bad in the first place. Still, that was the wound that concerned Milo the most. He rinsed off all the rest of them, but he cleaned off Bobby's neck with peroxide.

Bobby winced. He sat on the bathroom counter with his head tilted over the sink as Milo scrubbed mercilessly at the swollen bite mark on the back of his neck. The peroxide fizzled white, and Milo rubbed at it with a damp rag.

"That really stings!"

"It needs to be clean," Milo said through gritted teeth.

"I don't think it's that dirty," Bobby grimaced. "You bit me all the time and never washed them at all." Milo didn't say anything, and Bobby tired of it, so he pulled away from Milo. "It's clean enough."

"No, I don't think it is!" Milo reached up for Bobby's neck again, but Bobby grabbed his wrist and stopped him. Milo could easily overpower him, and he looked like he was considering it. "Please. Just let me clean it a little bit more."

"Milo! No! It hurts, and it didn't hurt until you started messing with it!" Bobby held onto Milo's wrist because if he let go, Milo would immediately start cleaning his neck again.

"That's because I'm getting all his saliva out!" Milo pushed Bobby's hand back, but Bobby jerked back in the corner and pressed his back against the mirror so Milo couldn't reach it. "Bobby! Just let me clean it!" If he got any more aggressive, I'd have to intervene. "You still smell like him, and I have to get it out!"

"*No!*" Bobby shouted. "You'll have to deal with it! I just got attacked by a vampire, and I'm feeling bad enough without you clawing out the back of my neck!"

"Fine." Milo sighed and threw the bloody rag in the sink, then he had a change of heart. "You're right. I'm sorry. You had a really bad night, and I'm just glad you're alive and that you still want to put up with me." Ashamed of his behavior, Milo stared down at the sink.

"I'll always want to be with you," Bobby smiled at him and gently touched his face.

Milo lifted his head and they kissed, just long enough for me to feel embarrassed that I was in the same room with them. I cleared my throat, and Milo blushed when they stopped.

"Sorry about that." Milo dried the cuts on Bobby's chest and shoulder so he could apply giant Band-Aids.

"So all those scratches, those are from Jonathan's fingernails?" I nodded at Bobby's chest.

"Yeah, I think so," Bobby said, watching as Milo bandaged a particularly nasty one that ran down his collarbone. Hopefully, none of them would leave scars, or they would damage his tattoos.

"That's weird. Clawing at you seems like such a girlie thing to do," I wrinkled my nose. Sure, that is how I had fought against Jonathan, but *I* was a girl, and I was openly a terribly fighter.

264

"Maybe, but our fingernails are more like claws," Milo said absently. "It's a weapon we have, so why not use it?"

It wasn't until he said something that I looked down at my own nails. Before I had turned, I had bit them all the time, but I lost the urge. They were longer than I had them before, but I hadn't really thought about them being stronger. I tested one out on my arm and winced.

Milo and Bobby continued talking, getting more flirty and lovey, so I tuned them out. Milo had gotten awfully freaked and possessive because Jonathan had bit Bobby, and he hadn't even drank his blood. It surprised me because Milo had never been the possessive type, but I suppose that had nothing to do with who he was as a person. It was all part of being a vampire, but I had never gone through it because nobody else had bitten Jack since we'd been together.

Or at least that I know of. I had no idea what he was doing now. For all I know, someone could be biting him. Lots of someones could, or he could be biting lots of people. He could be doing anything, and I had no idea when or if he would ever be back.

After Milo finished getting Bobby cleaned up, they went back up to his room so they could change out of their costumes, and Milo needed to wash off all his makeup. Ezra and Mae were still up in Peter's room with Jane, so I sat on the steps and waited for someone to tell me what was going on. The night seemed to drag on forever, but finally, Ezra descended the stairs towards me.

"How is she?" I got up but held onto the wall, bracing myself for bad news.

"I don't know," Ezra shook his head. "She's been doing this for too long. Part of the reason her bite looked so terrible was because she had scar tissue building up. He had to gnaw through it to get to her veins."

"Oh my gosh!" I gasped, feeling disgusted.

"But the good news is that she hadn't lost as much blood as I'd originally thought." He gave me a weak smile. "I didn't give her any blood, although we did give her IV fluids."

"You have IV fluids just lying about?" I asked with a raised eyebrow.

"In a houseful of vampires and the occasional human, someone is going to lose too much blood eventually, and its best to be prepared," he said. "Your friend is resting now, but only time will tell how well she will do. Mae is giving her vitamins and plenty of water, and that's the best we can do."

"Why didn't you give her a transfusion? Wouldn't that have fixed her right up?" I asked.

"No. Like I said, she's been doing this too long," he said. "Her blood wouldn't mix or coagulate right with fresh blood. She has too much vampire saliva in her, messing with her body. That might actually be to her benefit. Our saliva can be very helpful in the healing process, and the only thing that has been keeping her alive the past few days is how much she has in her system."

"So the fact that she's getting bit too often is killing her *and* saving her life?" I looked at him dubiously.

"So it would seem," he sighed. "You can go up and see her if you like, but she's unconscious."

"Unconscious like sleeping or unconscious like coma?"

"Only time will tell," Ezra said

"Really?" I had been asking more as a lark, but if there was a possibility that she could be comatose, it didn't seem right that we were just keeping her in an upstairs bedroom. "Shouldn't we get her to the hospital or something?"

"If I thought there was anything they could do for her that we couldn't, I would've already taken her there. She just needs to rest and rebuild her blood."

"No offense, but you're not a doctor. How can you possibly know? If she's dying, they can put her on life support," I said.

"She's not dying, not yet, but if you think she would be better suited at a hospital, or she would be happier living out the rest of her existence on life support, I will take her there," he said, not unkindly. "But I have spent most of the past 300 years trying to keep the human victims of vampires alive. I doubt highly that anybody at the hospital can make that same claim, but yes, they do have more advanced medical equipment than I do."

"I understand." I looked down at the steps. "As long as she's stable now, I say we leave her here. But I reserve the right to take to her the hospital if her condition worsens."

"You've always had that right, whether it worsened or not." Ezra touched my shoulder, trying to comfort me and alleviate my shame. "Why don't you go see her?"

I argued with him just to avoid seeing her. Ezra would always do what was best for everyone, and I knew that. If he couldn't take care of Jane here, he wouldn't have brought her back.

But I didn't want to see her, knowing how sick and frail she looked. Jane had often been superficial and a bitch, but she was always powerful. She carried herself with purpose, and the last thing she'd ever want anyone to see is her being weak and small.

Slowly, I pushed open the door to Peter's room. In his huge bed, Jane looked even smaller. Mae sat next to her, monitoring her pulse and blood pressure, all by ear and touch. Jane was just a thin little line down the center of the bed. Her arms lay over the covers, and they were nothing but skin and bone.

Her normally manicured nails were broken and chipped. A bandage covered the bite mark on her neck, so at least I didn't have to see that again. She kept her hair short, but her roots were showing. Jane wasn't even making time for hair appointments anymore.

Mae had changed her out of her designer dress to put her in more comfortable pajamas, and left her dress discarded at the end of the bed. It looked dirty and faded. The only thing in life that had ever really mattered to Jane was her appearance, and she had completely let it go.

Mae said a few comforting things to me, but nothing could really make me feel any better about this. When I saw Jane at the club before, I should've just dragged her away, no matter how much she fought me.

Or better yet, I never should've told her about vampires, or let her see Milo after he turned. If Milo had never bit her, if she'd never found out, if she'd never even met me. I know I wasn't the one that made her go to the club night after night, looking for a fix, but I had set this course of events in motion. If I had made a different decision any number of times, she wouldn't be here, knocking on death's door.

I stood at the end of the bed, watching her chest rise and fall with each breath. Every time she exhaled, it felt like forever before she breathed in again, and it was an eternity between heartbeats. Every second she was alive, I was certain it would be her last. I barely even noticed when Peter came in the room. That's how hard I concentrated on Jane.

"Sorry. I just came in to grab a few things," Peter said and hurried into his bathroom. Since Jane had taken over his room, he was going to sleep on the couch tonight, and if he was getting ready for bed, it meant that it must be late.

"You should probably go get some rest yourself," Mae told me. "I'll stay with Jane and make sure she's alright. It won't do her any good if you stay up all day exhausting yourself."

"You'll let me know if something happens?" I chewed my lip. For some reason, I thought that when I stopped watching her, that's when she'd stop breathing.

"I'm just across the hall from you," Mae smiled at me. "She'll be just fine, love. I can feel it."

Reluctantly, I went out into the hall and shut the bedroom door behind me. I stood right outside it, listening for a minute, and when her heart kept beating, I started to believe that maybe she wasn't going to die right then.

I let out a sigh of relief that sounded suspiciously like a sob, and I took another deep breath to try to keep back the tears. Peter came out of his room and almost bumped into me, since I hadn't bothered to a step away from the door.

"Oh, Alice, sorry!" Peter put his hand on my back, as if I was stumbling and needed him to stabilize me.

"No, it's okay." I shook my head and swallowed hard.

"Are you alright?" He lowered his head, trying to look me in the eyes, but I looked away.

"Yeah, no, everything's great." I forced a smile, and my vision blurred from the tears. "I mean, why wouldn't it be? I almost got my best friend *and* my brother's boyfriend killed. Not to mention, I have no idea where my own boyfriend is because I drove him away. But yeah, everything is just great!" Tears slipped down my cheeks, and I wiped them away.

"What happened to Jane isn't your fault," he said quietly.

"Yes it is! I'm the one who introduced her to vampires!" I gestured widely to the hallway. "Everything I touch gets destroyed! I mean, you had this stable family, and I came in, and I'm just tearing it apart! You and Jack, and now Mae and Ezra, and I know that's not directly my fault, but it is! It's my fault by association! I'm the harbinger of doom!"

I expected Peter to tell me that I was being melodramatic and tell me in a very condescending way that none of that was my fault. Even I knew it was pretty egotistical to assume that the only bad things that happened in life happened because of me.

But instead he looked at me with the utmost sympathy and affection. I had never seen him look so gentle, and whenever he softened, he was almost blindingly attractive.

When he reached out and pulled me into his arms, I knew that I should pull away, but I didn't really have the strength for it. He held me to him, and I buried my face in his chest. I just wanted to sob, and I wanted someone to hold me. Peter's arms were wonderfully strong, and it felt so good and safe that I almost lost myself in them.

"Honestly, Alice, everything is going to be alright," he murmured into my hair.

"I wish I could believe you," I whispered. My tears were calming down, but I left my head pressed against his chest, listening to his heartbeat.

"Peter!" Ezra suddenly boomed, sounding as if he was standing directly at the bottom of the stairs.

He broke whatever moment I had with Peter, and I realized how incredibly inappropriate and dangerous it was to let him hug me, even if I needed a hug. I pulled away from him and looked at the ground. Peter just turned and went downstairs to see what Ezra wanted, and I slunk back to Jack's room.

Matilda lay on Jack's bed, looking very sad, and I climbed in next to her. I rested my head on her back and ran my fingers through her thick white fur. She whimpered a little, and I knew that she missed him too. But there was nothing I could do about it.

Although, I was starting to think it was maybe for the best that he left. Clearly, I wasn't good enough for him.

Mae woke me up a few hours later. I sat up with a start, but she smiled wanly at me in the dark. "Jane is awake."

27

Jane didn't look any better, and she didn't seem entirely alert. Mae had helped prop her up with a couple pillows. Her eyes were dull blue, almost glassy, and her expression was completely blank. She didn't look happy or angry to be alive, but she watched me with kind of a subdued fascination. I think it was still hard for her to get used to the idea that I was prettier than her, even when I'd just woken up.

"Hey," I said. I stood awkwardly off to the side of the bed and pushed a dark strand of hair behind my ears. "How you feeling?"

"How does it look like I'm feeling?" Jane asked.

"Oh, she's doing just fine," Mae said before I could reply. A glass of water sat on the nightstand, and Mae handed it to Jane. She gave Mae a bored look, but she took it anyway, taking a long drink. "She's been through a lot lately."

"Yeah, I know," I said. Mae pushed the hair off Jane's forehead, and I didn't appreciate the way she fawned all over her. Jane did need extra care, but I didn't like the way Mae made me feel incompetent.

"You don't know anything. We haven't spoken in months," Jane snapped, glaring at me.

"That's not my fault." I was indignant. "I tried calling and texting you a million times. You were the one who didn't want to talk to me!"

"Yeah! Because you turned into a vampire!" Jane sat up

straighter in the bed, and Mae looked annoyed that I was upsetting her.

"You don't need to get worked up," Mae said, taking the water from Jane before she spilled it all over the bed.

"So what if I'm a vampire?" I asked, ignoring Mae entirely. "You seemed just fine spending so much time with them that it almost killed you!"

"Yeah because they were fun and they had something to offer me. You're the most boring immortal on the whole planet. I mean, look at you!" Jane gestured to me with a skinny arm. "You're wearing a blink 182 tee shirt and sweat pants!" I looked down at my clothes, pulling a ball of Matilda's hair off my band tee shirt.

"It's pajamas!" I crossed my arms defensively over my chest. Then I pointed to her. "Did you see what you were wearing to the club tonight? Your dress was dirty and covered in stains!"

"I hadn't had a chance to change." Jane dropped her eyes.

"Girls!" Mae said. "You really need to calm down! Jane doesn't need all this excitement."

"Whatever." Jane rubbed her eyes. "Can I just get my clothes and get out of here?"

"You can't go anywhere, love," Mae told her gently. "You're sick. You need to get well first."

"And I can't get well at home?" Jane tried to sound angry, but she was already relenting and leaning back in the bed. "Does Jonathan know I'm here?"

"Um, kinda." I exchanged a look with Mae. "Did you tell her how she got here?"

"I told her that you found her at the club, and she was in bad shape." Mae once again deftly avoided the truth, and I wondered how often she lied to us.

"He won't be happy when he finds out I'm here." Jane wasn't threatening us, and from the look she gave Mae, I'd say she was actually just trying to protect us. Her "boyfriend" definitely had an anger management problem.

"We know, but we wanted you to be safe," I said.

I didn't really understand the animosity between us. She had been living a reckless, dangerous life, and I wanted to help her change that, and maybe get back to being friends again. It would be neat to be friends with someone that didn't live in the same house as me. Although, she probably would be living here, at least for a little while.

"I understand." Jane picked at her chipped nail polish and stared down at it for a minute. "You look really good. Your hair is longer."

"Yeah, our hair grows really fast." I played with a strand of my hair and smiled at her. "You look... Okay, I can't lie. You look pretty bad right now."

"I know." She shrugged her bony shoulders. "But I'm here now. So I guess that's something, right?"

We talked for a few more minutes, but she was obviously getting tired. Mae sent me away, saying that Jane needed her rest. It had been awhile since I had been bit, but I remembered being exhausted for days afterward. Jane had to be stronger than I was just to be able to sit up and talk.

As soon as the sun set, I enlisted Milo to make a run to the store with me. We picked up groceries for Jane, namely things heavy in fat and red meat, and energy boosters, like Red Bull and vitamins. Before we left I went to see if there was anything in particular she'd like to eat, and she said no, but requested we get her some hair dye.

When we got back, Milo made her food, and she came downstairs to eat it. Bobby joined her, and she seemed semi-interested in him until she found out that he was gay and dating Milo. Then he became almost a nonentity to her. It was good to see the old Jane back in action.

Half-way through her steak (which seemed unnecessarily rare, even by my standards, but Milo was the chef), Peter decided to make an appearance. It wasn't really intentional. He had been back in the den, working with Ezra on something, and he wanted to go up to his room to grab a shower.

As soon as Jane saw him, she locked her lasers on him. Naturally, he ignored her, but she almost tripped over herself trying to get up after him. Milo managed to assure her that Peter was completely off limits, but that probably only made her want him more. She realized that she wasn't up to getting a new suitor just yet, so she let him go without chasing him down.

Jane downed about ten Red Bulls, then went upstairs. I finally convinced Mae that Jane would be safe in my hands, even though I felt a bit thirsty. Jane wasn't appetizing because she didn't have healthy blood, and what she did have was tainted by another vampire's scent. But I knew I'd have to eat before I went to bed.

"So, I don't really understand," Jane said. She strolled through my closet, looking for clothes to borrow since I hadn't thought to stop and pick hers up. I had a new and improved wardrobe, and for the first time in our friendship, I had clothes that she actually approved of.

"What's not to understand about clothes?" I sat down on the small bench by the shoe rack.

It was overwhelming being in the closet, surrounded by all of Jack's things. I had to go in here every day to get clothes, but I hurried out as quickly as I could. I lay back on the bench so I could stare up at the ceiling instead of Jack's stuff.

"Half of this closet is Jack's stuff," Jane touched one of his shirts. "But nobody's made any mention of him since I've been here. Where is he?"

"I don't know." My phone was in my hand, and I looked down at the screen, willing him to call me.. I hadn't tried calling or texting him today, but I hoped giving him some space would make him come home. Absence makes the heart grow fonder and all that.

"What do you mean you don't know?" Jane had moved on to leafing through my clothes, and she looked at me sharply. "Aren't you two like in love or something ridiculous like that?"

"Something like that," I muttered and lay my phone face down on my belly, so it couldn't taunt me anymore. "We got in a fight, and he left."

"What'd you fight about? Who left the lid off the toothpaste?" Jane asked dryly.

When she found something she liked, she just took off her top. She'd just been wearing an oversized tee shirt, having kicked off the pants a long time ago. While she straightened out my dress before putting it on, she stood there, dressed only in lime green panties, but at least they were bikini cut and not a thong. Her spine stood out rigidly, but I looked away before I could think too much of it.

"No. It was a little more serious than that," I sighed. Peter's emerald eyes flashed in my mind, and I shook my head.

"I can't imagine you doing anything serious," she said absently.

Her focus was on her reflection in the mirror, modeling the strapless cocktail dress she'd slipped on. Even though I had lost weight, so had she, so my clothes were still too big on her. I'd say they were too short too, since Jane was still two inches taller than me and the hem fell way above her knee, but that was probably just right for her.

"What do you think of the dress?"

"It's great," I lied. For once, I'd look better in something than she did. Her shoulder blades stuck out like wings, and the top was made for a larger chest, so it was drooping weird in the front.

"Do you have any heels to go with this?" Jane turned, admiring herself from a different angle in the mirror. "Every good dress needs a good shoe."

"Somewhere, probably. Dig around." I gestured to the expansive shoe racks.

"So what did you do that made Prince Charming run away?" Jane wasn't quite ready to get shoes yet and returned to the task of stealing my clothes.

"Kissed Peter." I closed my eyes and grimaced.

Instantly after I said it, I don't know why I told her the truth. It wasn't something I was proud of, but since it had happened, I hadn't really been able to talk to anyone about it.

Milo had said very little on the subject, mostly because he'd been too wrapped up in Bobby drama, and Mae and Ezra had never mentioned it. Besides that, Jane was really the only friend I had. Everyone else was family. Or Bobby.

"What?" Jane wheeled on me, her eyes wide. "You kissed Peter? That really incredibly foxy guy I saw earlier? You *kissed* him? I didn't even realize that was an option!"

"It's not." I shook my head. "It was just a stupid mistake. I don't even really know why I did it."

"I do. That boy is irresistible." Jane looked wistful thinking of him. "If I were you, I'd say good riddance to Jack and move on to Peter."

"I don't want to move on to him!" Too late, I realized that telling Jane was a really bad idea. I sat up and shook my head again. "I love Jack, and I want to be with him. Peter was an accident."

"Okay. Fine, I believe you," Jane said dubiously. She kept staring at me though, chewing her lip. "So... does that mean he's single?"

"Jane!" I groaned. "Peter is bad news! And you need to stay away from vampires for awhile. Look what they've done to you."

"Yeah," Jane shrugged, "but look what they've done to *you*."

She had a point. Vampires were literally sucking the life out of her, but me, they had given immortality, beauty, power, and money. In fairness, those were all things that Jane already had, except for the immortality part.

"But I'm still miserable. So there." I stuck my tongue out at her, and she shook her head.

"Oh, Alice, you'll always be miserable no matter what you have."

Jane turned back to my clothes, picking out something hot pink and skimpy that I had never worn. "That's your lot in life."

"Maybe," I exhaled resignedly. "But what's yours?"

"My lot in life is looking beautiful." She held the dress up in front of her and looked at herself in the mirror. "Do you have any accessories?"

Sure, Jane was irritating and self-absorbed, but it was oddly comforting having her around. I always knew exactly what I was getting with her. Despite myself, I actually sort of enjoyed her.

For the hour I spent with her, I didn't check my phone at all to see if I missed a call from Jack. I didn't forget about him, exactly. The dull ache in my chest wouldn't let me, but I wasn't quite as obsessive as I had been.

After Jane went to bed, I went downstairs to get something to eat. The slow burning spread from my stomach, and soon it'd gnaw all over me. Jane didn't entice me at all, but Bobby was starting to, so it was time to eat. I gulped down the bag of blood, then went back to my room and curled up in bed.

I was having a dream about this incredible warmth growing inside me. It wasn't a burning, like a fire, but something different and more wonderful. Like a bright white light spreading out over me, until it became so much I couldn't stand it, and I opened my eyes.

When I woke up, my breath was ragged, but the feeling from the dream hadn't dissipated. I sat up, and I nearly screamed. Someone stood at the end of my bed, but when I saw who it was, I couldn't even speak.

"I didn't mean to wake you," Jack said quietly.

- 28 -

I couldn't breathe. Jack was pensive, his lips pressed tightly together.

The more alert I became, the more his emotions washed over me, and they were nothing pleasant either. Mostly, he felt nervous and hurt, and I didn't blame him. After apologizing for waking me, Jack just stood there, arms crossed over his chest and stared at me. I sat up farther in bed and tried to think of something to say, but my mouth refused to work.

"I have to admit, I was a little surprised I didn't find you in Peter's room," Jack said finally.

His words were cutting, and all the more so because they were from him. He never said things to hurt people, but he wanted to hurt me now.

"I was never with him." My mouth worked numbly, and my heart hammered in my chest. "What happened was a stupid mistake. It didn't mean anything."

"What exactly did happen?" Jack's normally soft blue eyes were like ice, and they pierced straight through me. "I don't know." All the rehearsed speeches I had explaining the kiss completely vanished. I had nothing except a blank expression.

"You don't know what happened?" He gritted his teeth and took a deep breath. "How do you not know what happened when you kissed Peter? Kissing really isn't that hard! I'm sure it started with you putting your lips on his-"

"No, I know what happened!" I held up my hand. Rubbing my forehead, I exhaled shakily. "I just don't really know why it happened."

"Well, maybe if you start telling me what exactly happened, I can help with the why," he suggested coldly.

"We kissed!" I shouted, feeling exasperated already. I just wanted to get to the part where I sobbed and apologized, and eventually, he forgave me.

"Who kissed whom?"

"I-I don't know," I stammered and looked down. I pulled my knees up my chest, and I wanted to bury my face in my hands.

"Really? You have no idea? Just one minute you're standing there and then next you're making out with him? That seems pretty spontaneous."

"Nobody was making out." I couldn't even look at him. This was much harder than I thought it would be.

"So... who kissed whom?" Jack repeated, and when I still didn't answer, he got louder. "Alice?"

"I think... I-I might've," I mumbled and swallowed hard.

I could've lied but I knew he'd see it on me, and that would just make things worse. I rested my hand on my forehead and leaned on my knees. He had to take a few moments to process what I'd told him, and his hurt was even rawer now.

"Are you in love with him?" His voice was so low I could barely hear it.

"God, no!" I shouted fiercely and looked at him. "No! I love you, Jack! And that's all!" A wayward tear slid down my cheek. I wanted to crawl over to him and kiss him, but I knew he'd push me away.

"So why would you kiss him? After everything we've been through!" He was almost pleading with me now, and it made me cry.

"I don't know! Honestly, Jack! I wish I did!" I wiped at my cheeks. "I was really thirsty, and I was trying to hold off on eating so I could get more self-control. And I just went into his room to talk, to distract myself, and ... I don't know. We were talking, and I just... I just kissed him. It was only for a second, and then I stopped it and I said that I couldn't do it.

"And I am so sorry, Jack! I am so sorry! If I could take it back I would! I never wanted to do anything to hurt you!"

"I've just been thinking about it over and over in my head." He rubbed his temples and looked at the ground. His eyes were moist, but he wasn't crying. "I kept thinking, if you kissed him, could I forgive you? And if you slept with him, could I forgive you?"

"I never slept with him!" I insisted and sat up on my knees.

"No, I'm just telling you what I was thinking." He shook his head. "And you know what I realized? I'd forgive you of anything!" What he was saying sounded good, but he didn't feel good. He was completely agonized, and I had done this to him.

"I'm not giving you permission, but you could do anything, and I would just forgive you. I couldn't *not*." Jack stared off at nothing, thinking. "I don't know if you know what that's like. Even if what you do kills me, I would..." With bated breath, I watched him.

"You could kill me, Alice," he looked at me seriously. "That's how much you mean to me. As foolish and masochistic as that makes me, you are so much to me that even if it destroys me to be with you, I'll be with you!

"And I don't care why you kissed him or what you did. I don't even really wanna know. But I am begging you to please never do anything like this again. Because I love you so much, and I am trusting you with far too much, but I don't know how to be any different! You just... you can't do this to me anymore, okay? Please?"

"I promise! I'll never do anything!" I got up off the bed and ran over to him, unable to contain myself anymore. Putting my hands on his cheeks, I looked into his wounded blue eyes. "I am so sorry. I never wanted this, and I'll never, ever do it again. I promise you. I love you so much, Jack."

"You better," he whispered.

Finally, he kissed me. I had thought that I had truly lost him, and there was this panicked insistence to the kiss. I wrapped my arms around his neck and held him to me. His mouth was warm and wonderful, and I knew nothing in the world tasted better than he did.

My thirst peaked at that, and my heart pounded hungrily in my chest, but I denied it. I just wanted to be with him, physical and present, in the moment.

"Run away with me." He rested his forehead against mine and knotted his fingers in the thickness of my hair.

"What?" I asked, thinking I'd misheard him.

"Run away with me," he repeated and moved back a little so he could look me in the eyes. "I don't wanna stay here anymore. Everyone lied to me. Peter is still going after you, and Mae tried to kill me. There's no reason for me to stay. Let's run away together."

"What about Milo?" My mind scrambled. There was something exciting about the idea of just running off with him, but I couldn't just pick up and leave like that. "And Jane?"

"Jane?" His brow furrowed. "What about Jane?"

"She's here, in Peter's room." I had forgotten that Jack hadn't been around. "Milo saw her on Halloween, and she was doing really terrible. So we're helping her out, I guess."

"Peter's room?" Jack looked appalled.

"Yeah, he's sleeping in the den. Everyone is playing musical beds," I waved it away.

"This house is too small for this many people," Jack pointed out. "And that's just another reason why we should move out."

Running away might be too extravagant for me. I didn't have a job, and Jack worked with Ezra and Peter. I didn't want to leave Milo, but I didn't think that Jack couldn't support the four of us, since I'd probably have to include Bobby in the equation. Maybe he could, but if we were running away from Peter and Ezra, I wasn't sure if that meant he'd quit his job too.

Not to mention I was still having issues with bloodlust, ones that could prove potentially fatal to everyone.

"What are you thinking?" he pushed a strand of hair off my forehead.

"I don't care if we leave Peter, but I don't think I'm ready to leave everyone else," I said finally.

"I can't live with Peter anymore, and I don't think you should either," Jack said. "And I don't really want to be around Mae."

I chewed my lip and looked up at him. He'd just come back, and I really didn't want to lose him again, but I wasn't ready to sacrifice everything else just to be with him.

"Okay," he said. "How about this? I keep working with Ezra, and we start looking for a place of our own in the Cities, with room enough for Milo and Bobby to stay with us as often as they want. We'll still be close to everybody, and Milo can go back and forth if he wants, but me and you will finally have some privacy."

"Okay," I nodded, but the idea made me nervous.

After seeing what Milo did to Bobby and Jonathan did to Jane, I wasn't so keen on the idea of privacy with Jack. Yes, I really, really, really wanted to do things with him, but I loved him too much to kill him.

"I have barely slept in three days," Jack yawned. "And it's not even noon yet. What do you say we get some sleep?"

"Sounds good," I smiled and gave him a kiss on the lips.

He pulled off his tee shirt and shorts, opting to sleep in his boxers, which was fine by me. Few people in the world looked as amazing in their underwear as Jack did. I crawled into bed, and he climbed in after me. He lay on his back so I could curl up in his arms, resting my head on his chest.

"I missed you so much," he said, running his fingers through my hair.

"Me too." I squeezed him tightly, then thought of something. "Where did you sleep for the past three days?"

"Hotel," Jack chuckled a little. "I just got a room at a hotel downtown, and I didn't leave until an hour ago. I couldn't take being away from you anymore, so I came home."

"You should've came home the first day."

"I know, but I had some thinking to do," he sighed. "And it worked out okay. I mean, I'm here with you now, aren't I?"

"That you are." I kissed his chest, then lay my head back down.

Jack must not have been kidding about not getting any sleep, because within seconds, he was sound asleep. I stayed awake longer than him, thinking about all the things he said, and trying to come up with a solution.

I promised him that I would never hurt him again and living with Peter might be too great a temptation for me. I couldn't explain it, but that made it all the more dangerous. If Jack thought it was best to leave, it might actually be. And even if it wasn't, it was what he wanted, and after everything I've put him through, didn't I owe him that much?

Nobody seemed that surprised to see Jack when we got up. Unlike me, they had all known he was coming back. Jane greeted Jack with a shocking amount of indifference, and that's the same way Jack treated Mae. Mae rushed over to apologize, and he all but pushed her back. Her face crumbled afterwards, but I couldn't really encourage him to forgive her. He had to do it in his own time.

Peter had stepped out for the evening, but nobody really knew where. I suspected that he had known Jack was around and disappeared before things got ugly.

Jack took Ezra back to the den so they could "discuss" things in a very mysterious fashion. It was probably business talk and about moving out, but apparently, Jack didn't want everybody else to know of his intentions yet.

Mae got over being snubbed by Jack because she had Jane to distract her. In the dining room, she had thrown down a giant towel on the floor and set up an impromptu hair salon. Mae always cut everyone's hair.

Jane sat in a chair with foil and dye in her hair, and she languidly flipped through an issue of *Cosmo*. While waiting for Jane's hair to set, Mae cut Milo's hair. For the first time in weeks, Mae seemed to brighten up. A discussion about lip-gloss had done what the rest of us couldn't.

"Would you like a haircut too, love?" Mae smiled up at me over the top of Milo's head. Her own hair was clean and pulled back neatly. Jane made some comment about shoes, and Mae laughed, her eyes sparkling. "What do you say, Alice?"

"Um... no, I'm good," I said.

"Girls' shoes are so much better than boys' shoes," Milo lamented. He lifted his head to steal a glance at Jane's magazine, but Mae gently pushed his head back down so she could trim his hair.

"At least you don't have to wear heals," Jane said. "I mean, they may look fantastic, but they kill to walk in. They're like little feet torture chambers." Mae laughed again, the second time in two minutes.

Taking in the scene in front of me, it finally occurred to me what was happening. Mae had a daughter, and a granddaughter, and a sick great-granddaughter, but all she ever took care of were boys. Peter and Ezra needed nothing from her at all.

When I came around, she had been so thrilled because she

thought she'd finally have a girl to pal around with, but I spent most days lounging around in jeans. Jack was back, so I tried to look extra pretty today, and I had still gone for jeans with a fancy green top.

Maybe that was why Mae had bonded so much more with Milo than she did with me. He was probably more feminine, and in a weird way, needier than me, even though he was also far more self-sufficient.

Enter Jane, the walking Barbie doll. All clothes, boys, fashion, and a constant need for attention, the exact thing Mae needed. I'm not sure if this solved Mae's crisis over what to do about her terminal great-granddaughter, but it lifted her spirits for a while.

For her part, Mae seemed to be making a massive improvement on Jane as well. She had already put on some weight, not enough for Jane to complain, but enough where she could almost pass for someone that wasn't anorexic.

The wound on her neck had healed, leaving a mangled scar. Vampire bites usually don't leave scars or marks of any kind, but if the tissue is damaged often enough, it's going to scar. Eventually, her father would probably have to pay for some cosmetic surgery to fix that, but for now, even she wasn't whining about it.

I felt weirded out watching the three of them laugh and titter about boys and clothes. Mae and Jane getting along I could understand, but I had never imagined that Milo and Jane could really enjoy each other.

One of the positive side effects from Jane spending so much time in the company of vampires was that she had grown more immune to the charms of our pheromones. She wasn't tripping over herself to be with Milo or Jack or Ezra the way she would've been before, although she did seem to be nursing a crush on Peter.

I moved onto the living room to wait out Jack's discussion with Ezra. Bobby sat cross-legged in the middle of the living room with a sketch pad on his lap and stared up at the television intently. This was the first time I'd seen anyone watching the new flat screen, other than the dog. Instead of watching some action packed blockbuster that got the most out of the HD, Bobby had the TV on CNN.

I assumed he was trying to seem smarter in some way. He had on thick black glasses that I had never seen him wear before. On closer inspection, I saw a fairly nasty black eye from the fight the other day, and he tried to mask it with fashion glasses and side bangs. He had another smaller bruise on his chin, but the worst of them were hidden under his shirt on his chest and abdomen.

"What are you watching?" I flopped back on the couch. The news wasn't my favorite thing, but it had to be better than watching the re-imagining of *Steel Magnolias* going on in the dining room.

"*Anderson 360*," Bobby replied absently. "It's for school."

"How is it for school?" I raised an eyebrow. "And I didn't think you still went to school."

"I go to school during the day, when you're sleeping. A whole lot of things happen during the day that you don't even know about," Bobby said. Still staring at the TV, he sketched furtively on the pad. A box of charcoals lay next to him on the floor, and he had the sleeves pushed up in his shirt, so he was getting black smudge marks all over his tattoos. "I'm supposed to watch the news for an hour and draw how it makes me feel."

"How does it make you feel?" I asked.

"Like the whole world is coming to an end." He didn't sound that upset by it. I sat up straighter, trying to see what he drew, but I was at the wrong angle to really see his sketch pad, so I flopped back on the couch.

The TV, I could see, so I watched it to see what had Bobby worrying. The screen had been divided into two boxes. The smaller one had news correspondent Anderson Cooper explaining the story, which took place in the big box. It showed a giant boat, like an ocean liner or a tanker, that appeared to have crashed into the shore. The boat tilted to the side as helicopters and smaller boats swarmed around it. The bottom of the screen said "Cape Spear, Newfoundland," but other than that, I didn't really understand what I was looking at.

"So what's going on?" I asked Bobby.

"An oil tanker crashed into Canada," Bobby nodded to the screen. "The hull was ruptured, but hardly any of the oil leaked out. They're saying it's a miracle, because if it had, it would've been like four times as bad as the Exxon Valdez cause this boat is much bigger."

"I don't know what that is." It sounded familiar to me, and considering the context of the conversation, I should've gotten it.

"It was an oil tanker that crashed by Alaska in 1989." Bobby glanced back at me. "I didn't really know that off the top of my head. They were just talking about it a lot."

"But there isn't an oil spill, is there? Not really?" I squinted at the TV, trying to see a sheen on the water around the tanker. "So what's the big deal? How does that make you feel like the end of the world?"

"Because of *why* the tanker crashed." He stopped sketching and stared at the TV in kind of amazement. "The whole crew died."

"What do you mean?" I sat up more. "Like when they the hit land?"

"No, they were all dead before that. Nobody was driving it, and they just crashed. The radio transmissions coming from them weren't right, and they sent boats out to check up on them, but nobody knows what happened. Finally, two days ago, they lost all contact with them, and then boom! It drove right into the island," Bobby nodded at the screen. "It's the creepiest, most bizarre thing I ever heard of, like in *Aliens* when they go to rescue that deserted ship or whatever. But real."

"What are you talking about? How did the crew all die? Did they run out of food or oxygen or something?"

"They didn't run out of oxygen. They're on Earth. You don't run out of oxygen," Bobby rolled his eyes at me. "But nobody knows why they're dead. Some of the crew is still unaccounted for, but both the lifeboats are still attached, so they don't know how they could've gotten off.

"Officials are trying to keep it under wraps, but rumor has it that they were all mutilated. Like really gory, horror movie stuff. Throats ripped out and all that. Anderson was talking to a guy that had been there, and he was just about puking talking about it."

"Holy hell. Really?" I leaned forward, staring more intently at the TV. "No way. That kind of thing doesn't happen in real life. Do they think the crew had something to do with it?"

"Maybe, but they're not counting on having any survivors at this point," Bobby said. "They had a crew of thirty, but only twenty-four bodies."

"That's pretty messed up." A chill ran down my spine, and I shook my head. "It's really creepy."

"Yeah, I know," Bobby agreed somberly.

"Where was the tanker coming from?"

"I don't know," Bobby shrugged. "I think like Europe or Russia or something."

"Okay, so be honest," Milo said, walking into the living room and breaking up our intense fascination with the television. "How does my hair look?" He ran a hand through his dark brown hair and did a little twirl, but it didn't look that much different than before. Mae had mostly just done a trim.

"Sexy, as always," Bobby grinned at him. He set his sketch pad aside, momentarily forgetting about his homework assignment. Milo sat down on the floor next to him, and in between kissing and flirting, they started talking about the tanker crash on the television.

Personally, it creeped me out too much, so I decided to go outside and play with Matilda. I had to bribe her with three dog treats to get her to leave Jack's side, and I was starting to think maybe she loved him more than I did.

The stone patio out back was slick from a slushy snow that was coming down. It was November, and this was the first snow of the season, so I knew it wouldn't last long. Matilda skidded through it, but she didn't seem to mind. Very little in life seemed to upset her, other than Jack's absence.

I couldn't shake the news story. I glanced back through the French doors at Mae and Jane talking and laughing, and spending time with them might've been almost as creepy as hearing more about the dead crew. I let the snowflakes melt in my hair and tried to forget all about it.

Jack went back to sleeping in the den, but he woke me up while it was still light to see if I wanted to go apartment hunting with him. I knew that I should, but daylight was still hard on me.

Besides, I didn't really want to. The thought of moving didn't thrill me, but I pretended it did. I told him to take lots of pictures for me and fell back to sleep.

I kept having dreams about the oil tanker crash in Canada. An unseen monster slaughtered them, tearing them apart. Everything was splattered with blood and viscera. It was horrendous. I wanted to scream and throw up.

The crew members were crying and pleading for their lives, but nobody listened. They could do nothing to save themselves. After all the crew was dead, total silent blackness enveloped the ship. That turned into an image: huge brown eyes, ones just like Milo's.

I woke up and wanted to scream, even though the last thing I saw hadn't been scary. It freaked me out, though, in the worst way.

As I tried to catch my breath and remind myself that everything was okay, I thought about how weird it was that vampires had dreams. *The Lost Boys* had not prepared me for this. In fact, I was starting to think that whoever wrote it had never met a vampire in his life.

Since I couldn't shake the dream, I got up to enlist some

assistance. I considered Jane, but she needed her rest. Mae was probably with her anyway, and, I didn't feel like talking to her. I went next door to Milo's room, and I went in without knocking. I made sure to listen in first, and Bobby wasn't there, so I knew it was okay to intrude.

"Hey, wake up," I said, walking into his room.

It was a little messier than I expected it to be, but that had to be all Bobby. The clothes strewn about appeared to be his, and his art supplies clogged up the floor. Milo lay in bed at a weird angle with his feet dangling off the side.

"Why?" Milo mumbled, his face buried in his pillow.

"Cause." I jumped on the bed next to him harder than I needed to, making it bounce him up.

"Why are you even up? You're *never* up before me." He rolled onto his back so he could face me. "What time is it?"

"It's six. It's not that early," I said. "Where's Bobby?"

"School. He has a night class," Milo yawned. "Where's your better half?"

"He's... out," I answered vaguely. Milo didn't even notice I tried to be secretive, but I decided I couldn't keep it from him anyway. "Okay. If I tell you something, you promise not to tell anyone?"

"No." Milo wasn't intrigued by the prospect of a secret, and I hated him for it.

This happened all the time growing up. I wanted to tell him a secret, but he never cared, so he never had to agree to any provisions. His apathy was pretty tricky.

"No, you actually do wanna know this, but you can't tell anyone.

Not yet. I'm just not ready for people to know," I said.

"I'm still telling Bobby," he said, stifling a yawn.

"Fine! Tell Bobby," I sighed. "But come on. You have to pretend to be excited about this."

"Why?" Milo raised an eyebrow. "I can't imagine what you'd tell me that was exciting. My room is right next to yours, and I know that you slept alone last night, so… it can't be that good."

"Ugh!" I groaned. "Good. Now I'm glad that we're moving out. I'm sick of your attitude."

"You're what?" That got him. He sat up, propping himself up with his arms, and looked at me. "What did you say?"

"Jack wants us to move out," I lowered my voice so Mae wouldn't be able to overhear. "He's out looking at apartments right now."

"When you say 'us' you mean…." He waited for me to fill in the blank.

"Me and him, and you and Bobby, if you want to." I tilted my head. "Does Bobby actually live here? Or does he have a residence somewhere else?"

"He technically lives in a dorm, but he hasn't spent the night there since we met."

"Don't you think you're moving a bit fast?" I asked. "You're incredibly young to be living with a boyfriend."

"Did you really say that to me with a straight face?" Milo raised an eyebrow at me.

I thought about trying to make some kind of point about how his situation was different than mine, but I just forgot about it. If we were normal kids living a normal life and going to high school and living with our mom, yeah, this would probably be weird and wrong. But we're not.

"Never mind. That wasn't the point."

"So you're really moving out?" Milo asked.

"I don't know. Jack really wants to, and he has a lot of good points. This house is getting too small for all of us, as crazy as that sounds, and neither of us should be living under the same roof as Peter."

"Yeah but... you want us to move with you?" Milo asked carefully.

"Yeah. Jack's looking for places in the area that would be big enough for all of us."

"But... what about you?" He looked at me seriously. "I know that you're still having problems getting your bloodlust under control, and you don't trust yourself enough to even sleep with him. How is that gonna work living together? Without Ezra to fix everything if something goes wrong?"

"I don't know," I sighed. "I've thought of that too. But I don't know what else we can really do."

"Not move out," Milo suggested.

"I just don't see how staying here could really work." I resigned myself to moving out even though I wasn't sure that's what I really wanted. It just didn't make sense to do anything else.

Milo lay back in bed and didn't say anything for a bit. He was always better at coming up with logical solutions. My actions were based more on my heart and temper, which is probably how he managed more success as a vampire than I did.

It still shocked me that he had been the one that nearly killed his boyfriend, and not me. That actually happened because he had so much more control than me. Everyone gave him too much credit. The fact that I had no impulse control is what actually kept me from murdering Jack. Nobody trusted me to be alone with him, so I never had the chance to bite him, not like Milo and Bobby.

"No, I do not require your assistance," Peter said wearily from out in the hallway, and I heard his bedroom door close a second later. "Jane, I suggest you just go back to the room and rest." I glanced over at Milo, and from his expression, I could tell he was listening to them too.

"I don't need any more rest. I'm bored," Jane put on her baby talk voice that vacillated between slutty and whiny. Peter must've gone to his room to get something, and she followed him out.

"Try reading one of my books," Peter said. "Or, if you cannot read, you can try one of Jack's movies. Or perhaps you can pester one of the six other people living in this house to entertain you."

"Come on, I bet you know plenty of ways to entertain me." Jane was out in the hall, so I couldn't see her, but I had enough experience with her to know that she was touching him in some way. Running her fingers down his arm or putting her hand on his chest.

"I can assure you that I am no good at entertaining anyone." Peter sounded uncomfortable, and Milo smirked.

"Well, maybe I can entertain you." Her voice went lower and sultrier.

"That's why I got a book. I can entertain myself," Peter said, his words clipped.

"Don't you get sick of entertaining yourself?"

"Jane, just go back to your room," Peter sighed. If she was touching him, he had just taken her hand away.

"Not unless you join me," Jane said, oblivious to his rebuff.

"No, I most certainly will not," Peter snapped. "This slutty little girl act may work for some people, but I can't see how. You are so filthy and dirty that I wouldn't bite you if I was starving to death. The only reason I am allowing you into my room is because of how much you mean to Alice, although, for the life of me I can't see why. You are insipid and vain beyond what I had understood humans were capable of, and it would serve you well to steer clear of me."

"Jeez," Milo whispered.

Jane didn't say anything, but I heard the door open, and she had started crying before she shut behind her. When Peter started walking away, I went into the hall to give him a piece of my mind. I should've gone out and defended her earlier.

"Peter!" I said quietly, so Jane wouldn't overhear. Sighing, he turned to look at me. "Don't you think that was a little harsh?"

"Not really, no," Peter said, but he wouldn't meet my gaze. I heard the shower in Jane's bathroom, her attempt to cure her crying, so I walked over to yell at him. "I didn't mean for you to overhear that."

"I don't know how that makes it okay." I crossed my arms on my chest and glared up at him. "Jane is annoying, but she's harmless. And she's recovering. We're supposed to be helping her and encouraging her, not bringing her down."

"I didn't want to bring her down." He rubbed his eye. "But you didn't see how she was around me. It was constant and more than annoying."

"God forbid someone have a crush on you, Peter." I rolled my eyes. "You were such a dick to me when I was into you, too. You can't handle anyone gawking at you for like five seconds?"

"No, I can. I handle it all the time," he said defensively. "Everyone I meet is like that, and I manage."

"Oh, what a rough life!" I scoffed. "You know, Jane isn't the only one that's vain and egotistical." It was Peter's turn to roll his eyes at me. "So you're saying your curse in life is that everyone finds you irresistible?"

"If I say yes, I sound like an ass, but it's true." He rubbed his temple and shook his head. "I am sorry if I am not doing well with tolerating her. She just won't stop staring at me, and... you won't even look at me."

"You're punishing Jane because you're mad at me?" I raised my eyebrow at him. "That's not even remotely fair."

"Life isn't fair, Alice!" Peter looked at me intensely, his eyes glowing green. "If life were fair, you wouldn't be with Jack!"

"No! You don't get to be mad at me for that!" I shook my head. "You had your chance! I wanted you first, and you wouldn't have anything to do with me!"

"I *never* had a chance!" Peter shouted. "You always wanted him! I saw you in the hot tub with him!"

"What are you talking about?"

"The night we met, you came up to my room, and I didn't want to meet you. I didn't want to want you, but the instant I saw you…" He looked away from me. "Before I even saw you. I felt you as soon as you walked in the house, and it was overwhelming.

"I reacted poorly when we met, so Mae took you away, out to the hot tub with her and Jack. I watched you when you weren't looking. You were sitting with him, laughing, and the way you looked at him… You've never looked at me that way."

"How did I look at you?" I asked thickly.

"Like you had to, like I was a magnet you were pulled to. There was no choice," he said. "And when you look at Jack, it's because when he's around, why would you want to look at anything else? You love him the way you could never love me."

I swallowed hard, knowing that was true. While that should have been comforting, it was painful. I felt like I had hurt Peter without ever giving him a chance.

"But I love you in a way that he never can."

"No, Peter, you don't love me," I shook my head.

"Alice, I am many things, but I'm not naïve," Peter said breathlessly. His voice had changed to something I had never heard before, desperate and earnest, and I looked up at him. "I love you, more than I've ever loved anyone, even Elise. As much as it kills me to do it, I can't stop."

"I can't be with you." My voice quavered.

His eyes were so beautiful and pleading. Part of me really wanted to be with him, but I could never hurt Jack again. I refused to. And Peter was right. Despite anything that I might feel for him, I still loved Jack more.

"I would never ask you to," he whispered.

"But you would love it if I offered," I smiled sadly at him.

"Yes. I would." He stared at me a moment longer, then exhaled shakily. "But you can't." He finally lowered his gaze and ran his hand through his hair. "I can't do this anymore, either. I suppose I should start packing up my things."

"No, you don't have to go." I reached my hand out, meaning to touch his arm and comfort him, but I realized how dangerous just touching him would be, so I dropped it. "This is your home. We have no right to keep kicking you out of here."

"What do you mean?"

"Jack and I are moving out. You can stay here," I smiled, trying to be hopeful, but his expression changed to one of dismal understanding. I had expected this to be at least kind of good news, but he didn't take it that way.

"Of course," Peter looked at Jack's room, *our* room, with jealousy and disgust. "This had already been planned. You're going to run away and live happily ever after, and I will stay here. With them. Forever."

"It's not meant to be a punishment!" I said, surprised that I was somehow hurting him even when I meant to be helping.

"Neither is my existence, and yet, it is." He shook his head and took a step toward the stairs. "I should go. We shouldn't even be talking. If Jack caught us, that would be disastrous, and I don't want to put a damper on your honeymoon."

"Peter!" I shouted, but he just kept walking. I stood in the hall for a moment, trying to catch my breath and clear my head.

"So…" Milo poked his head out of his room. I blushed, forgetting that he was in his room and had been able to hear everything. "I guess you really do need to move out."

"You think?" I laughed hollowly.

Peter vanished after my conversation with him, but I was grateful for it. I couldn't handle anymore run-ins with him, especially with Jack around. Milo, Jane, and I camped out in the living room watching bad chick flicks until Jack and Bobby made us stop.

When I had a moment alone with Jack, I asked him how the apartment hunting went, and he hadn't found anything exciting yet, although he had some promising ones to look at tomorrow. He told me to cross my fingers about them, but I wasn't sure if I wanted to.

Jane never mentioned her fight with Peter, but she was acting weird. All fidgety and twitchy. She complained of being hot and cold more than usual, and she added complaints that didn't even really make sense. Like the fabric on the couch was too rough for her skin, or that the air in our house was making her itchy.

Her mood swings were intense, too. One minute she'd be laughing, and then next she was threatening to smother Bobby with a pillow.

Bobby had put *Sid & Nancy* on the TV in the living room, because he claimed it was a love story that we could all relate too. I think Gary Oldman is a fox in it, so I didn't protest. I curled up next to Jack on the couch to watch it.

Milo laid a blanket down on the floor, and Matilda tried to take it over, but Jack convinced her to lay by his feet instead. Since Milo wasn't that interested in the film, he laid out long ways on the blanket, and Bobby rested his head on Milo's stomach, facing the TV.

Jane sprawled on the chaise lounge, with her current lament being that bracelets were too confining. Mae didn't want anything to do with the movie, so she opted for a bubble bath instead.

"Are all the doors locked?" Ezra appeared in the living room. He didn't seem anxious, but something wasn't quite right.

"Uh, I don't know?" Jack shrugged looking at him. "Do we ever even lock the doors?"

"You *have* to lock the doors!" Jane yelled, sounding tremendously worried. "People will steal your stuff!" Our stuff must really have meant a lot to her.

"Maybe, but someone is always here, and we're vampires, so…" Jack trailed off.

"I locked the French doors after I let Matilda out," Milo said.

"Why? They're glass. Anything that really wants to get in can get through them," Bobby pointed out.

"Regardless, I want you all to start locking everything," Ezra said.

"Alright. Don't we have an alarm or something?" Jack asked. "You had one put in when you built the place, didn't you?"

"Yes, I did." Ezra nodded and scratched his head. "I turned it off immediately after we moved in, and I can't remember the codes. I'll have to reset it and give everyone new numbers."

"That seems like a lot of trouble to go through." Jack had his arm around me, and it tensed. "Did something happen? What's going on?"

"No, it's probably nothing." Ezra shook his head. "There's just been a string of robberies in the neighborhood." I don't know how I knew, but he was lying.

"Oh my god," Jane gasped and put her hands to her mouth.

"We're still vampires," Jack gestured to himself, me, and Milo. "I'm pretty sure that we could take whoever broke in here."

Jane was over-the-top terrified, but Bobby didn't look concerned at all. When you're human, vampires seem extra invincible. But as a vampire, I knew that I wasn't anywhere as strong or amazing as everyone else.

"It's always better safe than sorry." Ezra nodded, as if that settled that. "I'm going to go look for the alarm manual, and I'll get back to you when I have codes."

"Alright." Jack gave me a weird look, and he was as skeptical about Ezra's intentions as I was.

"I don't how you guys can just sit here!" Jane got to her feet after Ezra left the room.

"Jane, relax. Nothing's gonna happen to you," Milo tried to reassure her.

"No! I don't mean that! It's just so *boring* here!" She pulled at one of the bangle bracelets she had taken from me, and her eyes darted all around the room. "You just sit here all the time!"

"Jane, its four in the morning. What do you suggest we do?" Jack asked her honestly.

"And we don't sit around here all the time," Bobby said. "I went to school, Jack went out, Milo goes places too, I'm sure. But you're not because you're still not feeling well."

"I'm feeling fine!" Jane stomped her foot and tried to take off the bracelets. "If it weren't for these damn bracelets! They're like handcuffs!"

"Jane! Just calm down and watch the movie," I said. "We'll go somewhere tomorrow night. Okay? But right now, it's too late. So just relax."

"Whatever." She managed to get off the bracelets and chucked them to the other side of the room, startling Matilda into barking.

"Is everything alright in there?" Ezra shouted from his den at the end of the hall.

"Seriously. What's going on?" I looked at Jack. "Is there like a carbon monoxide leak? Everybody is being a total freak today."

"I am *not* being a freak!" Jane protested, then collapsed heavily back onto the chaise lounge. "I'm fine. Let's just watch the movie. I wanna see what happens to this Sid guy."

Before the credits started to roll, Jane fell asleep, but she twitched a lot in her sleep. It was actually super creepy. We all watched with mild fascination until Mae came out of the bathroom and yelled at us for just staring at her. She carried Jane up to Peter's room, and Mae came down because Ezra enlisted her on his search for the missing alarm manual. It was the first time they'd really interacted in awhile, and she seemed to bare a grudge about the whole thing.

The rest of us watched movies for awhile longer, until Ezra tried to get us to search for a manual we'd never seen. We headed up to our respective rooms to avoid the whole thing.

"You know, Ezra's in the den," I said to Jack when we got to our room. He had already taken off his tee shirt in preparation to put on pajamas, but when he turned to look at me, I started slipping off my jeans in the most seductive way I could manage. "So you can't really sleep there."

"Here's the funny thing." Jack grinned as he walked over to me. He'd come into the room and gone straight to the closet to change, but I had other plans for the night, so I stayed next to the bed. "I'm not really all that tired anymore."

"Really?" I took a step back, so my butt hit the bed. "You wouldn't want to crawl into bed at all?"

"Oh, no, I definitely wanna crawl in bed," Jack smiled wickedly. He took another step towards me, so he was right in front of me, and put his hands on my bare thighs. Slowly, he slid them up under my shirt and let them linger on my waist. "God, you're beautiful."

I looped my arms around his neck and stood on my tiptoes so I could kiss him. He kissed me deeply, cupping his hands on my butt and holding me to him. Gently, he pushed me back onto the bed. I wrapped my legs around him, pulling me closer to him. He pushed against me, and I moaned. His mouth trailed to my neck, and suddenly, I wanted it.

"Bite me," I breathed, burying my fingers in his hair.

"What?" Jack stopped kissing me so he could look at me. He tried to play it cool, but his excitement was unmistakable. "Seriously?"

"Yeah," I looked up at him. Being bitten felt amazing, and he was in control enough where it wouldn't be that dangerous. I'd be the weak one, but I'd just fed so I wouldn't be ravenous.

"When was the last time you ate?"

"Jack!" I said. "Don't break the romance with logic. I'm fine, okay?"

He bit his lip and looked down at me. He was making sure that I was completely okay with it, but he obviously wanted to do it. I could feel his hunger, hot and eager, flowing over me. His heart pounded heavily, and it was just above mine, so I could almost feel it. His eyes faded translucent, the way they did when he really wanted me. The more passionate he got, the lighter the color of his eyes.

When his lips pressed against my veins, I moaned involuntarily, and I arched my back, pushing closer to him.

"Alice!" Mae screamed and threw open the bedroom door.

"You've gotta be fucking kidding me!" Jack yelled incredulously and sat up, and I agreed. He turned to glare at her. "There's nothing wrong with what we're doing!"

"I don't care about you," Mae said. She looked stricken, so I sat up and pushed Jack back out of the way. "Jane is missing! I think something's happened to her!"

- 30 -

In the panic over a possible Jane-napping, I didn't think to put on pants and Jack didn't put on a shirt, so we both got dirty looks from Milo. He'd rushed out of his room when he heard Mae screaming. I returned his dirty look since Bobby was shirtless and guilty looking.

We were all crowded inside Peter's room, investigating Jane's disappearance. Mae had tired of her pursuit of the alarm manual, so she had gone upstairs to bunk with Jane again, but when she'd come in the room, Jane was gone. That was all her evidence.

"Did somebody ransack the room or something?" Bobby asked, admiring the disheveled state of Peter's room. Somehow, half of my wardrobe had migrated over here and had been strewn around everywhere.

"No, it always looks like this," I said. I hadn't seen her room lately, but this was her natural state of being.

"Not to sound like a dick," Jack said, "but you just dragged us out of bed to show us Jane's messy room? That's not really an emergency, Mae."

"She's not here!" Mae gestured to the mess around her. "That's the emergency."

"Again, not to be a dick, but that's not really an emergency," Jack said.

"Something could've happened to her!" Mae insisted. "She

wouldn't just leave like this!"

"She might," Milo said. "She was bitching downstairs about how boring we are."

"But she didn't tell me where she was going." Mae looked at us all with disbelief. Jane had really gotten to her, and she wasn't willing to let her go so easily.

"You know what? I'm sure she has her phone on her," I said. "I'll call her, and we can figure this out right away."

"Good idea." Mae was slightly relieved at that.

"Well, I'm going back to bed," Milo yawned. "I'm sure she'll turn up."

I hurried across the hall to my room, and Jack trailed behind me. Mae stayed behind in the hallway to argue with Milo about how innocent Jane was while I pulled my cell phone out of my pants pocket. Jack rubbed his bare arms and shook his head.

"You don't really believe something happened to Jane?" Jack asked quietly.

"I don't really know, and I'll feel better making sure." I scrolled through my phone for her number, then hit call.

The phone rang in my ear, and I watched as Milo and Bobby slunk back to their room. Mae looked at me expectantly, and I started to tell her that Jane wasn't answering when Jane picked up.

"Yeah, what?" Jane sounded bored.

"Jane?" I asked tentatively. "Where are you?"

"Out. Your place was a drag," Jane yawned.

"Really? You're calling us a 'drag?'" I asked. Mae peered at me with concern, but Jack rolled his eyes and walked to the other side of the room.

"No, you're not." Jane sighed. "Look, I know you guys have been really good to me, and I appreciate all your hospitality. But… the thing is, I need a bite."

"We have food here, Jane. You didn't need to-"

"No, not a bite to eat," Jane cut me off. "I need to be bitten."

"But… No," I shook my head. "We just got you out of there. That life is bad for you, and you know it."

"Jonathan is bad for me, and I got a little carried away on Halloween." Jane made it sound like she had a drink too many at an office party. She had almost died because a vampire was eating her throat. "But I still love the way it feels, and I've just been craving it."

"Jane!" I shouted, incredulous. "No! You will die if you keep it up!"

"I don't think I will, but so be it." There was noise behind her, and Jane sounded in a hurry when she spoke again. "I gotta go. Thanks for everything, though, Alice. I'm sure I'll see you again."

"No, Jane! Wait!" I said, but she'd already hung up.

"What's going on? Where is she?" Mae asked.

"I don't know." I shook my head and tried calling her again, but it went right to voicemail. "Dammit. She shut off her phone."

"What did she say? Why did she leave?" Mae asked.

"She, um…" I considered lying to Mae, but what was the point? "She wanted to go get bit. I guess she's going back to being a bloodwhore."

"*No!*" Mae's eyes widened with terror. "She can't! She'll die!"

"I know. I told her that." I was taken aback by her intensity, and

313

I looked to Jack for help.

"Mae, she's a junkie," Jack said, not unkindly. Considering how much he currently disliked Mae and Jane, he was handling this quite well. "The last high had worn off from being bit, and she had to go out and get another fix. You can't keep her here for a couple days and expect to cure her."

"No. She was doing so well," Mae shook her head fiercely. "I refuse to believe she willingly went back out there. I've got to find her."

"Mae, the sun is about to come up." I gestured to the windows. No light ever spilled in around the curtains, but I could feel when the sun rose and set. It was a weird vampire tick. "She's probably crashing somewhere for awhile. She won't even be able to find a vampire until night fall."

"You don't know that!" Mae insisted. "I'm going out after her." With that, she walked out.

"Mae!" I went to stop her as she left the room, but Jack put his hand on my arm.

"Let her go," Jack said. "She's not going to listen to reason any more than Jane will."

I ran my hands through my hair and stared out the door. Across the hall, Mae had left Peter's bedroom door open, and I could see into the empty disaster that had been Jane's space.

"Do you think we should go after Jane?"

"Where?" Jack stared across the hall at the same thing I was. "Do you know where she went?"

"No. It feels weird just letting Jane go, though." I chewed my lip.

"You can't save her if she doesn't want to be saved," Jack smiled sadly at me.

I knew he was right, but I just hated the way it felt. We had gone through a lot of trouble to get her here, and Bobby had risked his life. I thought Jane had really seen the error of her ways, but she just needed a place to crash. Jack put his hand on my back, and I leaned into him, resting my head on his shoulder.

"I probably say this way too much, but it's going to be okay, Alice. Honest."

"I know." I wasn't sure if I really believed it, but I had to hope it was true. Jack kissed the top of my head and pulled away from me. "Hey, where are you going?"

"Taking a rain check on tonight." He went over to the closet and changed into his pajamas. When he walked out, he was still pulling his shirt on over his head. "The mood is kind of destroyed."

"I can reset the mood," I offered with a smile, but it felt plastic even to me. I wanted to want him, but my heart wasn't really in it just then. He walked over to me, and I put my hand on his chest, amending my sentiments. "It could be a really good distraction."

"Probably," Jack agreed, smiling. "But I'd like to be more than just a distraction." He kissed my forehead before heading out of the room. "I'll be in the den if you need me."

I stayed awake long after Jack left. I should've convinced him to stay with me, even if we didn't do anything. In a house overflowing with people, I felt strangely lonely. After everything I had tried to do for Jane, it had inevitably been a failure.

Even if I saved her today, what about tomorrow? Or the day after? Eventually she would die, and all my efforts would amount to decomposing in the dirt. Everything suddenly felt really pointless, but I tried to shake it off and get some sleep.

Jack once again started the day with an apartment hunt, which I once again declined. It had taken forever for me to fall asleep, and I wasn't up to it. I wasn't even sure that I wanted to move out, but by now, I knew that I didn't have a choice.

Peter had made it perfectly clear that cohabitating with him would be impossible, and considering Jack had actually been alive for over forty years, it was about time that he started living on his own.

I hadn't been awake for that long when Jack returned. I decided to take a shower, but I noticed the state of our bathroom. Mae was still gone, determined to rescue Jane, and I thought as a nice treat for her return, I'd get all our towels down and actually clean the bathroom.

I pulled my hair back in a messy bun and grabbed the Comet and got to work. I was scrubbing dried toothpaste and shaving cream off the sink when I heard Jack bounding up the stairs.

"Alice!" Jack shouted. "I've got great news!"

I came out of the bathroom, and I know I looked hot. I had on yellow rubber gloves to keep my hands from getting all mucky, and I held the Comet soaked sponge. My pajamas had water and soap splattered on them, and my hair fell out of the bun.

"What are you doing?" Jack gave me a perplexed look, but his delight was unmistakable.

"Cleaning, but never mind." I tossed the sponge back in the

bathroom, since I doubted I needed it to converse with Jack. "What's your great news?"

"I got us a place!" Jack beamed, and it was struggle for him to keep from jumping up and down. I smiled because he was, but the nerves in my belly tightened.

"Already?" I asked, and somehow managed to keep the unease out of my voice.

"Yeah! I know you haven't seen it, but it's perfect! It's absolutely perfect! You'll love it!" He'd already fallen in love with the place. "I had to put money down because it's so hard to find a place that matched all our needs, and it would get scooped up crazy fast. But I set up a time for you to see it tomorrow, and if you don't like it, the deal's off. I won't make you move anywhere you don't want to, but this place was just so *perfect*."

"No, I'm sure it's great. If you love it, I know I will too." That was completely true, so I didn't understand why I didn't feel that way. His happiness was taking me over, but a bit of doubt still gnawed at me.

"They allow Matilda, and it's *really* hard to find a place that allows big dogs, and there's a dog park real close by. It's three bedrooms, one for us, one for Milo, and one for... I don't know. Cause why not?" Jack shrugged. "And it has this fantastic balcony!"

"Do we even use the balcony now?" I asked. All three of the upstairs bedrooms had balconies, but I'm pretty sure that I had never been on one, and the only person I'd ever seen use them was Peter. After we kissed. That reminded me that I had to move out. "I'm sure we'll use it more since we don't have a yard."

317

"I know we'll be giving up some space and some creature comforts, but I think it'll be great." Jack had calmed down some, and he looked at me sincerely. "We'll be able to have a life of our own, you know?"

"Yeah, totally." I nodded.

"I stopped and got some boxes on my way back, so we can start packing some stuff up." He edged away to the door. "I'll be right back."

"Okay. I think that I'm gonna take a quick shower and get all the cleaning gunk off of me," I said. Jack barely heard me because he was already darting down the stairs.

Once he was gone and took his emotions with him, my anxiety had a chance to kick in. I tore off the stupid rubber gloves and went into the closet to get a change of clothes. I needed a moment to catch my breath. It all felt so sudden, and I couldn't explain what terrified me so much about it.

We were just moving out, not that far away, and Milo and Ezra and everyone would still be a part of our lives. Jack made decent money working with Ezra, although I was too embarrassed to ask the exact dollar amount, but I'm sure he could afford to take care of us. There was nothing to fear really.

Except being alone. As much as I wanted to be with him, it scared the hell out of me. On top of all these vampire hang ups about possibly murdering him, I still had the normal teenage girl insecurities. I had never been with anyone before, and Jack had. And if something were to go wrong, we were on our own. Milo wouldn't know how to handle anything, and Ezra couldn't get there in time.

As I leafed through my drawer of undergarments, it finally dawned on me. Without a doubt, I wanted to spend the rest of my life with Jack, and I definitely wanted to have sex with him. It would happen someday, and probably someday very soon if we were living on our own. So why not now?

Ezra was downstairs in the den, and Milo was next door. If something happened, I could easily get help. And really, I was sick of waiting. I was sick of interruptions. I loved him, and it was time.

- 31 -

I purposely held my clothes close to me when I came out of the closet so Jack wouldn't notice, but he probably wouldn't have noticed if I were waving them on a flag in front of me. He put some mix CD in the stereo that he claimed had lots of "upbeat jams" that got him in the mood to pack.

Normally, I would've argued with him about why he had to have a mix CD to get him in the mood to do something as specific and rare as packing, but I was on a mission. When I went into the bathroom, I left him grooving to Robert Palmer while tossing some of his graphic novels into a cardboard box.

After the shower I slipped on my sexy lingerie. Last month, Mae had given me a credit card and let me loose on the internet. I went to Fredricks of Hollywood, and I spotted this little number. Dark purple, lacy, and sheer, it had a baby doll top with matching panties. My stomach twisted with excitement and nerves, and I opened the bathroom door.

The wall was open, revealing the secret closet where Jack had his thousands of DVD's. He filled up a box with his movies, and he was too busy singing and dancing along to the music to notice me. I did a sexy lean up against the doorframe, and I didn't really want to move and ruin it, so I had to wait for him to notice me.

"I'm probably gonna have to buy like a massive entertainment center for all these movies," Jack said, staring up at his DVD's. It overwhelmed him for a minute, so he sighed, and finally turned back to look at me. I have no idea what he was planning to say, but his jaw fell open and his eyes widened. "Holy hell."

"Is that a good holy hell?" I blushed deeply, and I had never felt so self-conscious in my entire life. Maybe this was a really bad idea.

"Yeah." He seemed to recover a bit and smiled at me. "What's all this for?"

"You know." I bit my lip and looked up at him, hoping he would catch the gigantic hint and wouldn't make me spell it aloud. I took a step closer to him, but Savage Garden singing "Truly Madly Deeply" threw off the mood. "Can you change the song?"

"Oh, yeah." He clumsily grabbed the remote off the bed, almost dropping it, and flicked the song to the next track. It was Panic ! at the Disco's "Lying is the Most Fun," and while I wasn't sure how it was an upbeat jam, I liked it a lot more. "Better?"

"Much," I nodded.

Jack walked over to me. The butterflies in my stomach made it hard for his emotions to overpower me, but they finally managed to. Intense and yearning, his hunger radiated off of him like heat. He stood in front of me, taking me in a way that made me uncomfortable, and he exhaled deeply. I couldn't take it anymore, so I crossed my arms over my body, trying to cover myself up.

"No, don't do that!" Jack protested more loudly than he meant to. I lowered my arms, and he touched my cheek, then moved his fingers back to my hair. "You are so gorgeous. What are you doing with me?"

"I love you," I whispered.

"I am a very lucky man," Jack murmured then bent in to kiss me.

As soon as his mouth found mine, I felt this surge rush through me. This was Jack, and I loved him more than anything else. I had gotten so caught up in being afraid of sex that I forgot why exactly I wanted to do it.

Kissing him, his familiar taste, the way his lips worked against mine... I wanted him desperately. I pulled him tightly to me, and we stumbled back towards the bed. I fell back on it and looked up at him.

"Are you sure you want this?" Jack asked huskily.

In response, I reached up and pulled off his shirt. He was breathtaking, and I kissed his bare chest and smiled up at him. His skin already smoldered hot on my lips, and that was all the encouragement he needed.

The weight of his body pressed against mine. His heart hammered in his chest, and I could feel it pounding in time with mine. Instinctively, my body pushed against his, and I tightened my fingers in his hair, pushing his lips harder to me. Fervently, he kissed me, and I trembled with anticipation.

His mouth trailed down my neck, and I moaned breathily. It wasn't until I felt his lips pressed against my veins that I realized how badly I wanted him to bite me. He was so hungry for it, for me, so I tilted my head back, exposing more of my throat.

The sharp pain of his teeth was over before I felt it, and hot ecstasy spread away from my neck. I felt his heart thudding in my own chest, above my heart, that double beat that made it feel like he was inside me.

In some kind of twisted pleasure, I could taste him in my mouth, the tangy, honey taste of his blood, and my own bloodlust for him surged. Wanting him that badly while he had me, it was agony and bliss all rolled in one. I could feel the edges of myself waning, blackening. My body threatened to lose control, black out and give into the thirst.

What kept me from giving in was feeling how much he loved me. It flowed through my veins. It came from him, but it felt like it came from inside me. I was everything to him, and he was pure joy. I had never felt closer or more in love with him.

A tiny jolt ripped into me, and I gasped painfully. My body suddenly felt cold and alone, as result of the separation when he stopped biting me. Before I could even tell how empty I felt, his mouth was on mine. I could taste my blood on his lips, and that did strange things to me. I pressed him even tighter against me, desperate for the burning heat of his skin.

I felt his hand, strong and sure on my hip, and his fingers looped in my panties, sliding them down. I sat up a bit so I could peel off the negligee, and his arms were around me, pushing his bare skin against mine. His intensity was overwhelming, but it only made me want him more. I lay back down on the bed, and he looked me in the eye.

"I really do love you," Jack said breathlessly, brushing my hair back from my forehead.

Then I felt him, sliding inside of me, and my breath caught in my throat. It hurt more than I expected it to, but within seconds, any pain was a forgotten memory. I buried my fingers in his back and pushed him against me. He kissed my mouth, my neck, my shoulders, everything he could reach, and I moaned against him.

Never in my life had I felt as whole or complete as I did then. I felt as if I had been made just for him, just for this. Pleasure exploded inside of me, and I bit my lip to keep from screaming.

Gasping for breath, he relaxed, but he propped himself up so he wouldn't put the full weight of his body on me. He rested his forehead against my shoulder and tried to gain some composure. When he gently kissed my collar bone, my skin trembled underneath his lips.

My whole body glowed happiness, and I felt dazed and weak. My vision was blurred and hazy, and I knew that my stomach should ache with hunger, but I just couldn't feel it.

"Was that okay?" Jack asked, looking at me.

"Yeah. That was the most incredible thing I've ever felt." I smiled up at him and touched his face. He suddenly looked too marvelous to be real. "Did you enjoy it?"

"Did I?" He laughed, sounding wonderfully exhausted. I had worn him out, and his laughter sent tingles all through me. "Oh my god, Alice. I didn't know it could be that good." He collapsed back on the bed next to me, and he pulled me into his arms, so my head would lie on his chest. "Oh man. I can't believe I've been missing out on *that.*"

"I know," I giggled, feeling girlie and buzzed. I snuggled up as close to him as I could, loving the way my skin felt pressed to his.

"Wow," Jack laughed tiredly again. "You may not know this, but you are the single most amazing person I have ever met, and I am *crazy* in love with you."

"Good." I kissed his chest and smiled up at him. "Cause I feel exactly the same way about you."

The loss of blood and the exhaustion of pleasure left me drained. My vision started to clear from the haze of lust, and the pain in my stomach kicked in, but I was too tired to deal with it. I just wanted to stay in Jack's arms forever and listen to the sound of his heartbeat. Our bodies were slowly returning to their normal temperature, and Jack pulled the blankets up over us, tucking them neatly around me.

I just stated drifting off to sleep when I heard my phone ringing. It sounded like it was coming from the bathroom, so I decided it was faint enough for me to ignore. It stopped, so I settled back into his arms. A second later it started ringing again, and I groaned.

"Should I get that?" Jack asked.

"No, it'll stop," I said, hugging him even closer to me. If he got it, that meant he would have to be away from me, and I wasn't ready for that.

It did stop, only to immediately start ringing again.

"Sorry, I gotta get that." He untangled himself from me and I grumbled in protest, but I let him go. He slipped on his boxers, and I watched him as he walked to the bathroom, following the sound of the ringing.

For one second, watching how gorgeous he was, my heart swelled as I realized that I got to be with him. *He* belonged to *me*, and it delighted me endlessly.

The phone stopped ringing again, and Jack sighed. "I'm still getting it, in case it starts to ring again. Where is it?"

"I don't know." I sat up, holding the blankets over my chest.

"Of course it stops when I look for it." He poked around the hamper, since I had a tendency to leave my phone in my pants pocket, but it started ringing again. He went over to the medicine cabinet and opened it. "Alice, why is your phone in the medicine cabinet?"

"Maybe when I got the mouth wash?" I shrugged. "Just shut it off and come back to bed."

"Uh oh." He came out of the bathroom, holding my phone out to me. "It's Jane."

"I should probably answer that." I held my hand out. I answered it just before it went to voicemail, and Jack sat on the bed next to me. "Hello?"

"Alice? Oh thank god you answered!" Jane sobbed in relief, but her voice was shaking. "I've run into some trouble, and... Oh god. I am sorry. I don't know-" She sounded absolutely terrified, and she knocked any of the warm fuzzy feelings out of me.

"What are you talking about? What's going on?" I asked.

"I don't know! They just made me call you!" Jane said, then she shrieked and her voice got farther away.

"Jane? Jane!" I shouted.

"No, it's not Jane," a male voice returned to the phone, and the hairs on the back of my neck stood up. It was strong and deep with an accent I couldn't place. Almost British, or maybe German, but softer. "This is Alice, I presume?"

"Where's Jane?" I demanded, refusing to answer his questions until he told me what was going on. Out of the corner of my eye, I saw Jack getting dressed. I'm not sure if he could overhear the conversation, or if he just saw my panic.

"If you want to see her again, I suggest you come and get her," the voice said. There was something sinisterly playful in his voice, and I heard Jane crying in the background. "Where are we? You need to tell us if you want your friend to come rescue you."

"You son of a bitch!" I growled. "Leave her alone! When we find you, we'll kill you!"

"We?" He chuckled. "Even better." Jane screamed behind him.

"Loring Park!" Jane sobbed in the background. "We're at Loring Park! But Alice! Don't come! They're going to-" She screamed again, cutting off the rest of her sentence.

"As you can tell, we're in a hurry, so act accordingly," he said, then the phone went silent.

- 32 -

Immediately after the phone hung up, I tried calling back, but it went straight to voicemail. Jack had already pulled on shorts and a tee shirt, and he was struggling to put on his Converse. My stomach lurched, and panic and hunger were mixing together, making me feel volatile and frail.

"Alice?" Jack asked. "Where is she?"

"Loring Park," I told him numbly. "I don't know who has her, but I think they're going to kill her. And they want me to come. She's bait for me." He pursed his lips and looked at me thoughtfully for a moment.

"You stay here. I'll go get her," Jack decided and made a step for the door.

"No!" I jumped up, holding the blanket around me. "If this is about me, there's no way you're going without me."

"Alice, it isn't safe."

"Exactly!" I ran to the closet to put on clothes before he left. I don't think I'd ever gotten dressed so quickly in my life. "I'm a vampire now. I can take care of myself." This I said while struggling to put on a pair of jeans and nearly falling over. "I beat up Jane's boyfriend or whatever before. If you can handle it, I can handle it."

"No. I'm much more skilled than you are, and you just lost blood." He crossed his arms over his chest and tried to look resolute.

"I don't care." I slipped on my shoes and walked up to him. "We're together now, forever. That means if you're in danger, *I'm* in danger. Jane needs help, and we're going together."

"I don't like it," Jack relented.

"I don't care." I pushed past him, knowing that we had to hurry to save her, and I had to hurry before he changed his mind. He couldn't stop me from going, but he could slow us down with unnecessary arguing.

"Alice?" Milo opened my bedroom door before I could even get to it. He had a bewildered, frantic look on his face. "Is everything okay?" He pushed the door open wider and stepped inside. "What's going on?"

"Nothing. Why? What's going on with you?" I narrowed my eyes at him.

"Nothing! I just... I thought something was wrong," Milo floundered.

I realized what had happened. Just like I was tuned into his heart, he was tuned into mine. It had been beating in a panic for the last few minutes, so Milo was concerned. He probably would've come in right away, but he misread it at first as being part of me and Jack fooling around.

"Jane's in trouble." I chewed my lip, looking at him, and Jack gave me a weird look. Milo was my little brother, and I'd do almost anything to protect him. But he was a vampire, more powerful than me, and from the sounds of it, Jane had more than one attacker. We needed all the help we could get. "She's in the park. I don't know who has her, but I think they want to kill her, and they want us to hurry."

"What are you talking about?" Milo tensed up, and I could see his muscles flexing under his shirt. Someday, he'd probably even be more powerful than Jack, especially since he had so much control.

"I don't know. And I don't have time to explain. If you want to come with, we have to go now." I looked insistently at him, and I knew my invitation surprised Jack. He'd expected me to demand Milo stay here, and maybe I should've. But Jane might die. I didn't think I had much of a choice.

"I'm in," Milo nodded once. "Let's go."

We'd barely made it out the bedroom door when we ran into another snag. Bobby was in the process of pulling a sweater on over his head when he came out of his room. He saw us in a hurry, so he caught up with us.

"What's going on?" Bobby asked.

"Nothing. Go back to the room." Milo tried to make it down the stairs, but Bobby wouldn't stop following him. Jack and I paused at the bottom, but I wouldn't be able to wait long for either of them.

"Where are you going? Why do you all look so freaked?" Bobby's hair had been mussed when he pulled on the sweater, and he tried to smooth it out while keeping his eyes fixed on Milo. "What happened?"

"Look, just go back upstairs," Milo said. "You can't come with!"

"Why?" Bobby was only getting more and more freaked out. "What are you doing?"

"It's too dangerous for a human. Just go!" Milo pointed up to the top of the stairs like Bobby was a disobedient dog.

"*Dangerous?*" Bobby blanched. "No! If you can get hurt, I'm going with you!"

"We don't have time for this! We're going now!" I waved my hands of it and walked to the garage. Jack was a step of ahead of me, but Milo trailed behind us with Bobby at his heels.

"Bobby!" Milo snapped at him when we reached the garage. "You can't come with!"

"No!" Bobby grabbed onto Milo's arm and looked as if he might cry. I wondered if this is what I had looked like when I was mortal. "I'm not gonna stay here while you go off -"

"Get in the car," Jack said, looking over the Lexus at Bobby.

"What? No!" Milo protested. Jack refused to meet my gaze, and I knew he was thinking something, but I couldn't tell what it was.

"Just do it," Jack said and got in the driver's seat.

Milo and Bobby did as they were told, although that didn't stop Milo from arguing about how idiotic it was for Bobby to come along. I agreed with him, but I kept my mouth shut. Jack started the car, and we sped out of the garage, on the way to the park.

It wasn't until I was trapped in the enclosed space of the car with Bobby that I realized how hungry I was. He was afraid, so his heart beat even faster, and my mouth started to water. I had to grip onto the door handle to keep my hand from shaking. Jack noticed, and he frowned at me and rolled down the window. The cold night air helped some, but there was nothing more that either of us could do.

Thanks to the ridiculous weather, the roads were slick, and Jack wasn't keen on slowing down. When we came to a stop in front of the park, the car skidded sideways, and Jack jerked the wheel. The Lexus lurched over the curb, and slid across the slush covered grass before finally coming to a stop two inches away from hitting a tree.

"Is everyone okay?" Jack asked, looking around. Bobby had hit his head on the back of my seat, but otherwise everyone was okay.

"You're a really terrible driver," I muttered. I opened the door and stepped out of the car, instantly slipping in the grass. I grabbed onto the door just before I fell to the ground, but I wasn't boding well for how I would do in battle.

"Careful," Bobby said as he got out of the car.

"No!" Jack shouted. He'd already gotten out, and he pointed at Bobby. "You. Get back in the car."

"What? No!"

"No, if you come with, you'll only hinder us," Jack said. "Stay here so you don't get us killed." Bobby wanted to argue, but he had to realize that Jack had a valid point.

"I'll be back as soon as I can," Milo promised. Grudgingly, Bobby climbed back in the car, and Milo leaned in to give him a quick kiss.

"I love you!" Bobby said, but Milo was already hurrying after Jack and me. We went down a winding pathway through the center of the park. It had been salted and sanded so it was much less treacherous than walking on the grass.

"Where is she?" Milo asked when he jogged up to us.

"We don't know," Jack glanced over at me, hoping I'd have more information.

Milo was about to ask something logical, like how did we plan on finding her, but I shushed him. I was trying to get a read on her, but it was hard. Even late at night in bad weather, downtown Minneapolis still had tons of activity. It was hard to separate sounds.

On top of that, I was getting really hungry. I kept getting focused in on the wrong smells and sounds because they were far more appetizing than what I was looking for.

"Ugh." I wrinkled my nose, catching onto something. It smelled dirty and not quite right.

"What?" Jack froze and looked at me.

"I don't know. I just smell something." A cold wind came up, blowing it away, and I shook my head. "It was probably the dog park. But it definitely wasn't Jane."

We walked a little further down the trail, but then I started noticing the smell again. It wasn't even a dirty smell so much as it smelled like dirt, like the ground and trees. A hint of pine, and something else, something familiar. It reminded me of when the fair came to town, and I always spent too much time feeding the goats in the petting zoo.

I kept walking, and I had started following the scent, but nobody questioned me about it. Even when we veered off the trail, they didn't say anything to me.

Finally, too late, I placed it. I froze in my tracks, and my heart stopped in my chest.

"What?" Jack asked in a nervous whisper.

"Reindeer." I could barely even say it aloud.

"*What?*" Milo asked incredulously, and even Jack gave me a confused look.

Neither of them understood what that meant, but I scanned the trees frantically. I knew how fast they could move. They were probably here. We might be surrounded already. I turned in a circle, slipping in the slush, and Jack caught me before I fell to the ground.

The wind picked up again, taking the scent away from me, and that was the only hint I had to where they might be. Thirst mixed with my panic, and the edge of my vision blurred red. My hands trembled, but I couldn't say for sure if that was from hunger or fear.

Milo looked around, trying to figure out what exactly had me so freaked. Jack still had his hand on my arm, steadying me, and the scent became stronger behind me, so I turned around.

Only thirty yards from us, a vampire stood on a bench. I had just been looking at it a few seconds ago, and nobody had been around, but here he was. His dark blue work jacket hung open, revealing his bare chest covered in dark hair. His jeans were filthy and ragged and hadn't been washed in months. Despite the cold slush on the ground, he was barefoot.

The wind blew his black hair across his face, but I could still see his black eyes staring right at me, giving me the same chill they had when I first saw him in Finland. It was Stellan, the lycan that wouldn't speak English, and he'd already spotted us.

"I never should've brought you here," I said, both to Jack and Milo. Letting them come along had been a death sentence, but I didn't realize it until was too late.

"What is going on?" Milo asked.

"Who is that?" Jack followed my line of vision, where I was staring at Stellan, and Milo turned to look at him too. Stellan was by himself, and he didn't look that threatening, but I knew more of them were nearby.

"Lycan." I couldn't look away from Stellan because I knew he would move as soon as I did, so I couldn't see Jack's reaction, but he instantly tensed.

"Go back to the car," Jack said through gritted teeth. I thought of Bobby, sitting unguarded in the car, and I choked back vomit. They probably had already found him.

"No." I glanced back at Milo. The car was a deathtrap, and I couldn't have him going back there. "Run, Milo."

I looked back at Stellan, but he was already gone, and my heart sank. We didn't stand a chance. Milo would never be able to outrun him.

"Get out of here!" Jack shouted. He had just seen Stellan's disappearing act, and he just learned what we were up against. "Alice, Milo, get out of here!"

"I'm not leaving you!" I grabbed his arm and looked up at him. He wanted to protect me above all else, but we had already been ambushed. "They want me anyway!"

"No, they don't want you!" Jack shook his head. "They want Peter! You're just the thing that's most important to him! They're trying to flush him out."

"How astute." The voice on the phone interrupted us, standing in front of us.

Shirtless, his upper body was pure muscle. His dark hair was pushed back from his face, revealing brown eyes, but they were so cold and empty, like an evil doll. Just by looking at him, I knew he was Gunnar, the leader of the lycan.

He took a step towards us, his bare feet crunching in the grass, and Jack moved in front of me. Milo tried to step up next to him, but Jack held up his arm in front of him, blocking him. Gunnar laughed at his feeble attempts to protect us. He was alone, so his comrades must be hidden amongst the trees around us.

"Where's Jane?" I asked, barely keeping my voice even.

"Around here somewhere." Gunnar glanced darkly around us, smirking. "It's so easy to misplace things in the city. That's why I've always preferred the intimacy of the country."

"We don't know where Peter's at," Jack told him. "He doesn't know we're here."

"I'm aware. I know he would never let a pathetic attempt like you out to greet us." His expression changed, growing dark and angry, and rather terrifying. "There's no sport in going after you, and Peter would never bore his guests."

"Don't go after us, then," I said. "Just give us Jane, and we'll be out of your hair."

"You know what I think would be fun?" The devilish grin returned to his face. "Is if we made you find her, and bring her to us."

"Don't you already have her?" I asked, growing confused.

"Yes, I do, because I know that a good guest always brings something to share with his host," Gunnar said, his dark eyes sparkled. My stomach twisted, knowing that whatever made him happy would horrify me. "You're looking quite famished, Alice, and I know that your friend is a very tasty treat."

Dodge came out from behind a pine tree a few feet from us. His blond hair was messy, and he looked much less amused than when I met him in the woods. He had Jane in his arms, and he held his hand over her mouth to keep her from screaming.

Her heart pounded franticly, and I would've noticed it sooner if I hadn't been so distracted by Gunnar. Her eyes were wild, and she fought at Dodge as hard as she could, but it didn't do anything. He restrained her with ease.

"I'm not going after her!" I glared at Gunnar. "You can't make me!"

"That is true, but I can make it more tempting." Gunnar nodded at Dodge, who responded by dropping Jane to the ground.

"Alice, I'm so sorry!" Jane cried. She was barefoot in that short green dress she'd stolen from my closet and fell onto the frozen grass. "I didn't want to call you, but they made me!"

Her clothes were torn and her knees and cheeks were scraped and dirty. She kneeled on the ground with her hands pressed down in the icy slush. As cold as it that must've been for her, she was too weak and too afraid to get up.

"Its okay, Jane. Don't worry about it," I tried to reassure her. I wanted to go over to her, but I knew Gunnar wouldn't allow it. Jack and Milo didn't know what to do anymore than I did, so we all just stood there, waiting until Gunnar told us what he wanted.

"Dodge, make the food more appetizing," Gunnar commanded. Dodge reached into his pocket, and before I knew what was going on, he'd bent over and sliced open her arm from elbow to wrist.

338

- 33-

"Jane!" I started to run towards her to save her, but Jack wrapped his arm around me and stopped me.

"Alice, no," Jack hissed in my ear when I fought him. His grip was like an iron bar, and I was disappointed with how little I could do against it. I was even weaker than I thought.

I would've kept fighting against him anyway, but I smelled her blood. She held her arm up, trying to stop it, but it was flowing hot and sweet. My hunger intensified, a painful burning that shot through me.

I closed my eyes and swallowed it back. I did not want to bite her, and I wouldn't. Within a few seconds, I calmed down enough where Jack could let go of me, but he didn't.

"Put pressure on the wound," I said to Jane, and it surprised me how calm I sounded. "Tear your dress and put a tourniquet about the elbow, or you're gonna bleed out."

Jane did as she was told, her hands trembling and tears streaming down her cheeks. She struggled tying it around her arm, and Dodge moved to stop her.

"No, let her do it," Gunnar said, and Dodge straightened back up. He stood right over, watching as Jane sobbed and almost fell over onto the grass. "It's not fun if she bleeds to death first."

"I'm not going to bite her," I said, looking back at him. "None of us are."

"I feel a challenge growing," Gunnar grinned at me, showing his teeth.

I heard footsteps approaching, and I turned towards the trail. None of the lycan would be dumb enough to make a sound walking. This was a human, taking a stroll through the park at midnight. Admittedly, it was a stupid human, but he was definitely innocent of any involvement in this. Just a chubby guy in his twenties with dark glasses.

He was walking one of those ridiculous puggle dogs, and it sensed trouble before he did. The dog had been sniffing along the path, but then it looked at us and barked. No sooner had the guy looked toward us, then Stellan burst out from nowhere and dove on him.

I wanted to scream, but I opened my mouth and nothing came out. The guy didn't even have a chance before Stellan ripped out his throat. Jane screamed, and she was the only one that made a sound. His little dog barked angrily but realized the danger was too much for him and took off down the path.

Stellan was gnawing at his throat, and I could see the blood spurting out around him, as well as smell it. His body convulsed and shook, and I heard the sounds of bone tearing as Stellan completely tore through his neck, and the guy's body stopped moving.

I shrank back from the sight, but I couldn't look away. I wanted to throw up, and I hated myself for getting thirsty over the scent of blood. When I felt Milo's hand, I almost jumped. He put his hand in mine and squeezed.

I had never seen anything so horrific in my life as Stellan ripping apart a living person, and when I finally managed to look away, I saw that Milo had tears in his eyes. Suddenly, he looked so young and scared, and he moved closer to me. I wanted to hug him, but I was afraid of how Gunnar would react, so I settled for holding his hand.

"It'll be okay," I lied, looking Milo in the eye. "At least it happened really fast. I'm sure he didn't feel anything."

"He probably didn't," Gunnar admitted. "But he could've. Stellan was a little hasty with him, but he can do it much slower. Shall I have him show you?"

"No!" I said too quickly, and Gunnar laughed. Jack moved to block both Milo and me from Gunnar, and we stood behind him, holding hands and shivering like two scared little kids.

"Stellan!" Gunnar shouted without looking at him.

Stellan gave up on eating the guy and lifted his head. His face and chest were covered in blood, and he wiped at them absently with the back of his sleeve as he walked over to us.

"What do you want from us?" Jack asked. He was as scared and sick as I was, but he could almost pass for calm and confident.

"How about… a game?" Gunnar smiled.

Stellan returned to his side, leaving the corpse in the middle of the trail like a discarded piece of trash, like a half-eaten apple. Gunnar's eyes moved to something behind me, and when I turned, it was already too late.

A giant vampire had somehow crept up behind us, and he wrapped his massive bare arms around Milo. He yelped in surprise and fought against the vampire, but it was completely useless. He was the largest person I'd ever seen in my life, and he had vampire strength behind it. Milo was still gripping my hand, and I clung onto him tightly, trying to pull him from the vampire.

"Alice!" Jack had his arms around me, refusing to let me be dragged along with Milo as the vampire pulled him away, but I wouldn't let go. "Alice! Let him go! Alice!"

"*Milo!*" I screamed, but my fingers slipped, and I let go of him.

Tears streamed down his cheeks, and he was still reaching his arm out for me. His huge brown eyes had never looked so sad or scared in his life. I kicked at Jack, but he wouldn't let me go.

"Alice, as you can see, my good friend Bear isn't hurting him," Gunnar interrupted.

Bear, the gargantuan vampire, had Milo firmly secured in his arms, but he didn't even appear to be squeezing him. Milo still squirmed and fought against him, but he didn't look like he was in any real pain, just terrified.

"Milo – that's your name, yes?" Gunnar asked. Milo didn't say anything and kept fighting. "Milo, are you in any pain? Is he hurting you?"

"No," Milo grunted and settled down in Bear's grip. He was saying it for my benefit, so I would stop fighting against Jack. He looked over at me and nodded. "I'm okay."

I did finally stop struggling against Jack, but smartly, he didn't let me go. I would've taken off towards Milo the second he did.

"Let him go!" I yelled and turned to Gunnar. "He has nothing to do with this! Just let him go! Peter doesn't even like him!"

He laughed at that, but I'm not sure how that was amusing. Jack said nothing, but he was gauging the situation. He knew Gunnar had some plan going on, and he was trying to figure it out. I knew that too, but I couldn't keep my emotions under control.

"Mmm, yes, I'm sure, but Peter might not be arriving for awhile," Gunnar said with faux sadness. "So I thought we would play a game until he joined us. Can you guess what it is?" I glared at him. "Tag – vampire style.

"You see, it's just like normal tag, except you have to kill whoever you tag. Since you're new to this game, we'll keep it easy and start with two players. How about... *you*," he pointed to Jane, "and *you*," he pointed to me. "And since you're the vampire, you're It, Alice."

"No! I already told you I'm never going to bite her!" I yelled at him, disgusted.

"But you don't even know what the prize is yet?" Gunnar smiled widely at me. "It's that Milo fellow. If you win, you get him back. If you lose, then Stellan gets him, and we all know how he likes to play." Gunnar nodded to the corpse on the trail. "But since I am such a giving guy, I'll give you a parting gift. After Stellan eviscerates Milo, I will personally give you his heart."

I just gaped at him for a moment, unable to do anything but try not to vomit. Either I would have to murder my best friend, or they would murder my brother. The only good thing was that I wouldn't live very long to regret my decision, no matter what it was.

"No," Jack said. "Let me play. I'm much quicker than Alice." I'm not sure if he had a plan to save Jane, or if he was only trying to save me from killing her by doing it himself.

"Well, Jane doesn't seem much in the running mood, so I don't think speed is really an issue." Gunnar had a point.

Jane had tied the tourniquet around her arm but not before she lost quite a bit of blood. Her only consolation is that her body was used to running on less blood, and she had spent the last few days building her supply back up. But she was barely even holding herself up, and she hadn't screamed or protested when Gunnar told me to kill her. Her skin was completely ashen, and the blood had started freezing on her arm.

"There has to be something else!" Jack shouted.

He let go of me so he could step forward to Gunnar, challenging him. Stellan stepped towards Jack, defending him, but Gunnar held his hand out to him. His hand was the only thing preventing Stellan from ripping out Jack's heart, and we all knew it.

"I have other ideas, but I'm certain you wouldn't like them anymore than this one!" Gunnar growled.

I exchanged a look with Milo, his eyes wide and uncertain. If I had to choose, I would pick him. Without a doubt, I loved him so much that I would do anything for him. But I didn't want to kill Jane. She hadn't done anything to deserve this, and I couldn't imagine taking anyone's life, let alone someone I cared about.

"Just do it, Alice," Jane mumbled, her voice barely audible. Her heart was beating so slowly, I didn't know how she was still awake. She propped herself up with her good arm, and she held the wounded one up, trying to keep the cut above her heart. "I'm dying anyway."

"No. I can't." I shook my head and tears filled my eyes. "I can't do it."

"So be it." Gunnar shrugged and nodded to Milo. Stellan stepped towards him, and I shouted.

"*No!* Wait!" I shouted. Bear tightened his grip around Milo, and Milo clawed at him. "Milo! No! Stop! Let him go! I'll do it! *Milo!*"

"Do it, and we'll let him go," Gunnar said through gritted teeth.

"Fine! Just stop hurting him!" I begged. "Stop!" Gunnar rolled his eyes, and nodded at Bear again. Instantly, he loosened his grip on Milo, who gasped for breath.

My panicked screams for my brother had carried farther than I thought. I heard him before I saw him. Bobby was racing through the grass towards us. He fell and slid on his ass, and I wanted to scream at him, but I prayed he wised up and realized what he was up against.

"Milo!" Bobby shouted, and I winced. His only hope for survival had been going undetected, but he had just drawn attention himself. He scrambled to his feet. "Milo!"

"*Run!*" Milo screamed as loudly as he could, but it was already too late.

Stellan had started moving towards Bobby, but only a split second before he got there, another lycan came out and wrapped his arms around him. Bobby screamed in surprise, but the lycan held him tightly. Stellan growled in protest. If he had caught Bobby first, he would've gladly torn him apart.

Then the lycan holding him looked at me. His brown eyes were sad and disappointed. It was Leif, the kind lycan that had helped Ezra and I find Peter. I realized exactly what he'd done. Leif had just saved Bobby's life by intercepting him before Stellan did.

"This has all gotten rather tedious," Gunnar said wearily and looked at Bear. "I've tired of this game. Kill the boy."

Before Jack could stop me, I dove at Bear. I jumped onto his back, clawing and biting at him. Dodge came towards me, but Jack managed to fight him off. Milo bit into Bear's wrist, and in a bold move, started drinking his blood. Bear howled, and even though he was weakened, I could do little against him.

Stellan was on me instantly, pulling me off Bear. He threw me onto the ground and sat on top of me, pinning my wrists back. His mouth was stained red, and he bared his teeth at me, showing his bloodied incisors with bits of flesh still clinging to them.

"Stellan! Don't kill the girl!" Gunnar shouted. "We need her! Just scent the ground with her blood!" Keeping his dead black eyes locked on me, Stellan yelled something back at Gunnar in Finnish.

I tried kicking at Stellan, but he refused to budge, and he had my wrists locked into the cold slush. Dodge and Jack were still fighting, but now Dodge was holding Jack back from getting at Stellan. Milo had managed to get Bear to the ground, but he wasn't free yet.

Through it all, Gunnar didn't enter the mix. He just stalked around, observing our futile attempts at escape. Bobby was screaming at us, but I doubted that Leif was hurting him.

Stellan bent down and head butted me incredibly hard. Shooting pain shot through my skull and everything went black for a second. Had I been human, I'm sure he would've killed me with that. I could hear him saying something to me in Finnish, but I couldn't see him or understand him.

When my vision started clearing, I was holding my head, my

natural reflex. Belatedly, I realized that that meant he'd let me go. He was standing over me, repeating the same word over and over again.

"He's telling you to run, Alice," Gunnar told me. I was curled up on the ground, and I could see Gunnar through Stellan's legs. His expression was blank, and that was strangely disturbing. "I suggest you listen to him. Stellan loves a good chase, and believe me, you want him happy when he catches you."

I didn't give a shit what Stellan wanted, but if I ran, he would chase me. I was what they were really after, so maybe they would all follow me away. They would leave Jane and Bobby behind for sure, since carrying humans along with them would just be cumbersome, but maybe even Milo and Jack. And even if they didn't, it was the only plan I had.

My head stopped hurting, but I still felt dazed. I tried staggering to my feet, and immediately slipped and fell onto my knees. Stellan laughed, so I tried again. This time, I got up, and I ran.

- 34 -

Sliding through the grass, I fell more than I actually ran. Stellan was clearly giving me a head start, because I wasn't making it very far. He was going to be awfully disappointed when he caught me, but I didn't know what more I could do. I was running as fast as I could. If he hadn't head butted me so hard and the ground wasn't so slushy, I might've actually made it somewhere.

I only made it about twenty feet before I felt him pounce on me. It was how I imagined a tiger attack would be. His claws dug into my back, and then I was down, the wind knocked out of me. He pressed my face into the ground, so I was drowning in the watery snow and grass.

When he finally let my head up, I spit out chunks of grass and dirt. I tried to push myself up, with him on my back, but he was too strong and the ground was too slippery.

In the distance, I heard police sirens wailing. It seemed very far in the distance, but that was because my level of consciousness was changing. The adrenaline and panic changed my thirst into something different. I wasn't blacked out exactly, but I felt like I was fighting underneath water.

Stellan laughed, and I felt the weight move off me. His hand went between my legs, and I scrambled to crawl away from him, but that just made him dig his fingers into my inner-thigh.

When I say "dig into" I mean literally dig. His claws and fingers tore through my jeans and flesh into the muscle. I screamed as the searing pain shot through me. I turned around to fight him off, and he jerked his hand back, taking a massive chunk of my leg with him. He laughed, showing me his handful of flesh, and then disappeared.

I tried to sit up and look down at my leg, and it was then that I realized what he'd done. The femoral artery runs through the inner thigh, and if severed, a human would bleed out in a very short time. Unfortunately, it's not that much different for vampires.

In an ordinary situation, my heart would be beating much slower, which would give my body a chance to heal before things got out of hand. But I was scared as hell and my heart was beating to match that. My blood was spilling out all over the ground, and I could feel it.

When I bled as a human, it had never felt like this. It was pressure and pain and weakening. It was almost like a vacuum, and I could feel my life being sucked out of me with every drop of blood.

Jack appeared at my side. I might've noticed him approaching if I wasn't so focused on the blood. I held my hands over it, trying to stop the flow, but there was a big gouge in my leg. My hand wouldn't cover it. The blood just flowed out over it, and it was coming too fast for me to heal.

"Oh, hell, Alice."

"Where's Milo?" I asked, and my voice sounded weak. Jack put his hand over mine, trying to stop the blood. "Is he okay?"

"Yeah, he's with Bobby. They're fine," Jack bit his lip and looked back over his shoulder. "The lycan took off when the cops showed up. We gotta get out of here before they find us."

After the lycan attack, dealing with the cops didn't seem like that big of deal. Except that I was bleeding like crazy. They would take me to a hospital, where everything would get very, very complicated, and I couldn't handle that.

The wound itself wasn't deadly. Or at least I didn't think it was. I tried to remember if vampires could die from blood loss. I knew starvation could kill them, but it had to be a very long time. But by looks of the puddle growing underneath me, I had lost almost all the blood I had in me.

My insides felt like they were burning and shriveling up. I had this weird painful sense of being deflated. My mind had fogged up so much I couldn't understand anything Jack was saying to me, and everything I could see had blurred completely into a red haze.

I couldn't feel actual bloodlust because I was too weak. All the strength had seeped out of me, and it was replaced with some of the most intense pain I had ever felt. I started screaming until Jack put his hand over my mouth. I could smell and taste my blood on his hand, and my stomach lurched.

The ground seemed to move around me, falling away. A cold wind blew over me, but I could barely feel it. I couldn't see anything. There was just the pain.

I could smell blood, and that frantic animal part of me was barreling in. I tried to move, to fight to get at the blood, but my arms wouldn't work. They were shaking violently, and I wondered dully if I was having a seizure.

The world swayed and bowed around me, and I was about ready

to kill Jack to get his blood. The pain was so excruciating that I would've killed anyone to make it stop.

"Alice, drink." I heard Jack's voice in my ear, but I didn't know what he was talking about.

I could smell him, but it wasn't his blood. It was warm and fresh and pounding quickly. I wanted to drink it, but I couldn't find it. I couldn't speak or move.

Warm skin pressed against my lips, and I felt the pulse of veins throbbing on my mouth. Without thinking, I sunk my teeth and drank. Almost instantly, my strength picked up, and I grabbed onto whoever I was drinking. I pressed them closer to me and drank furtively.

My mind flashed onto when I saw Milo biting Jane and how he had looked like an animal, and I knew that I was eating like that, but I didn't have a choice.

The pain stopped, then pleasure slowly trickled in. Delirious heat spread over me. Pleasure exploded all through me, and I drank more deeply. I could feel how kind they were, and the acidic aftertaste from the adrenaline. They had been afraid, but they weren't now. They trusted me and cared about me, even though I was drinking them dry.

Some part of me knew I should stop. I had already drank enough where I would be alright, and it was almost more than a human could spare.

But the rest of me refused. I couldn't stop. It felt too amazing and tasted too wonderful. I *needed* this, and I couldn't stop, not until I had it all.

"Alice!" Jack shouted. A sharp pain grew in the back of my head, but I didn't care, not until that pain started pulling me back. He was pulling me by my hair, so I'd let go, but I wouldn't, and if he pulled too hard, I would end up tearing out the throat. "Alice! Let go!"

"Jack!" Milo wailed. "Make her stop!"

Jack kept pulling on me, and I literally growled at him, like a dog with a bone. He wrapped his hand around my throat, squeezing down on it. I couldn't breathe, but more importantly, I couldn't swallow.

I let go, simply so I could bite Jack and get him to leave me alone, but as soon as I separated, I could think again. I felt dizzy and drunk, but I didn't feel animal crazy anymore.

Jack didn't know that though, so he wrapped his arms around me to keep me from going after the blood. The neck had already been pulled away from me. It had been the instant I had stopped biting. Milo cradled Bobby in his arms, sobbing, and that's how I found out.

"Bobby?" I mumbled. The familiar tired haze I got after eating settled in on me. My inner thigh tingled and itched like crazy, meaning it was healing.

"You nearly killed him, Alice!" Milo yelled at me.

"She had to do it, or she would've died!" Jack shouted. He was still holding me in his arms, but more gently. He just wanted me near him.

I wiped Bobby's blood away from my mouth and tried to sit up. We were on black top next to a white building, and when I looked up, I realized it was a massive cathedral near the park. Jack had carried me over here, away from the police, and fixed me up.

I felt like passing out, but I was fighting it. We weren't safe here, not with the lycan after us, and I had to do something.

I could hear Bobby's heart beating, and it was still strong, I hadn't killed him, but he had completely passed out. Not to mention the fact that he belonged to Milo, and vampires hated sharing their humans with other vampires. Even though he loved me, it had to be driving Milo crazy to let me bite him.

"I never should've let him come with." Milo stroked Bobby's hair.

"That is *why* I let him come with," Jack said.

"What?" Milo glared at Jack. "You brought him along to feed her?"

"He saved your sister's life, didn't he?" Jack shot back. "She wouldn't have died from the blood loss, but she'd have been too weak to do anything against the lycan. She needs to be strong to fight."

"I'm sorry," I apologized weakly. I tried to sit up again, but that was all I had in me. Jack's arms were strong and warm, and I finally gave into them. Darkness rolled over me, and I passed out.

I awoke on the floor. After everything I'd gone through, I felt surprisingly good. When I opened my eyes, all I could see were the beautiful gold and white ceilings of the cathedral.

Bobby was lying next to me, sound asleep himself, and I felt this strange pulling in my heart for him. Not like love or even a crush, but just a connection. He had shared himself with me, and in return, he'd gotten some of me as well. I had never fed on a human before, and I was surprised to find that I felt anything for him afterwards.

I didn't have time to ponder the details of our relationship, though, because I heard voices talking.

I got to my feet, still feeling kind of dazed and drunk. We were in the balcony of the church, surrounded by pews and crosses, and Jack, Milo, Peter, Ezra, and Olivia were standing at the other end. They had been trying to let us sleep, which was ridiculous. I needed to be awake and strong for this. Their voices were hushed, and I tried to sneak over to them, but I stumbled and bumped into a pew.

"Oh good. She's awake," Milo muttered, so apparently he wasn't ready to forgive me yet.

"What's going on?" I asked when I reached them. They stood in a circle, and I squeezed in between Jack and Ezra. "What are you guys doing here?"

"We called them," Jack said, and I couldn't believe that he'd called Peter. Ezra, I understood, but I was pretty sure he hated Peter now more than ever. "We couldn't get to the car because of the police, and we didn't want the lycan to follow us back home."

"I called Olivia because she's the only one really equipped to deal with them," Ezra said.

"And I'd do anything for you, sweetheart," Olivia winked at me.

She wore leather pants and a tiny leather vest with nothing underneath it. On top of that, she had donned some kind of crossbow apparatus. The leather satchel on her back was filled to the brim with metal arrows.

"Titanium is strong enough to break through a vampire's sternum and go right through the heart." She saw me admiring her

355

weaponry and smiled. "The old wooden stake would never work, and even this isn't fool proof, but it'll at least slow them down."

"Great," I sighed and looked around. It dawned on me that someone was missing. "Where's Jane?" Jack pursed his lips and nobody said anything. "Jack? What happened?"

"The lycan took her with them," Jack said quietly.

"Oh my god." I ran my hands through my hair. "This is a fucking nightmare."

"We'll get her back," Peter promised. His green eyes met mine, and I felt Jack bristle, but he did nothing. "We'll make the trade, me for her. They can't deny it."

"We are not sacrificing you," Ezra said firmly.

"Why not?" Jack scoffed. "It's his fault we're in this mess! He almost got Alice killed, and who knows what's happened to Jane!"

"We're not giving them anybody," Ezra said, looking at Jack sternly. "We will stop them."

"What if we can't?" Peter asked. "We should all die for my mistakes? No. I won't let that happen. This is my fault. This is my war."

"We're all involved in it now," Ezra said. "Do you think they'll really just let us walk away if we give them you? That would be too easy for them."

"You should've just let me die in Finland!" Peter shouted, his face raw with pain. "I told you to leave me there! Why wouldn't you listen?"

"I'm more than happy to let you die here," Jack offered.

"Nobody is dying here today!" I held up my hands to silence

them. "We'll figure something out! I don't know what but… We'll do something."

"See? Firecracker," Olivia smiled at me.

"We need a better plan than arguing with each other," Ezra said. "The lycan will track us soon."

"Maybe sooner than you thought," Olivia said, and she reached back for her arrows.

As she set her crossbow, I peered down over the balcony. A dirty, disheveled lycan was walking down the center of the aisle of the church. I heard the click as she set it, and then he looked back up at us, his brown eyes wide and innocent. I can't explain it, but as soon as I saw him, I knew he wasn't with them.

"Stop!" I shouted, my voice reverberating off the ceilings, and I held my hand up in front of her crossbow. Leif stood in the center of the church, staring up at us. He would willingly take whatever fate we dealt him.

"What? Why?" Jack looked at me like I was crazy.

"No, she's right," Peter agreed. "He's not like the rest of them."

"Leif!" I leaned over the balcony, as if I thought that would help me speak to him.

"I'm not with them!" Leif yelled back. "I came here to warn you! It'll be harder for them to find you with me. I'm the best tracker they have, but you're so close, and Stellan tasted your blood. I've beat them by a matter of minutes."

"Why would you help us?" Ezra asked. Leif looked at Ezra for a moment, then looked back at me.

"Really?" Milo scoffed. "Does every vampire in the whole world want to tap my sister?"

That wasn't it, and I knew that, but I couldn't explain it. There was nothing sexual about the way Leif looked at me, and I wasn't even remotely attracted to him. It was something else entirely.

"No, I don't want to … 'tap' anyone," Leif looked unsure of the word. "I've just had enough. They are cruel and sadistic, and I've seen that vampires can live another way. I don't want to stay with them anymore. They shouldn't even be alive. They are abominations."

"How do you propose we stop them?" Ezra asked.

"Honestly, I don't know," Leif said sadly. "But I will help you anyway I can. Even if you just want me to bait them. If I can save you, I will do it."

"Do you trust him?" Jack looked seriously at me.

"Yes," I said, and Peter nodded in agreement.

"I think he's okay," Milo said.

"Hey, how did you find Jane?" I asked, looking down at Leif. It made sense to me that they'd be able to find me since they had met me before, but I didn't understand how they'd even know she was associated with us.

"She was wearing your clothes walking around downtown," Leif said, sounding ashamed. "I smelled you on her. We tracked you down to Minneapolis by asking around. Gunnar knew people that knew Ezra." His face flushed guiltily. "I never should've come with, but if I hadn't they would've killed me, and they still would've killed you. When we got on the boat, though, I knew I had to find a way to help you. That was a complete massacre."

"Oh my gosh." My jaw dropped as it hit me. "That was *you*? On the tanker that crashed into Newfoundland?"

"I'm not proud of what they did, and I will pay for my sins," Leif raised his chin when he looked at me. "I assure you that I will make amends."

The cathedral echoed with the sound of broken glass, but Leif stood his ground. The stained glass windows shattered, sending bits of broken glass raining down all around him, as the lycan crashed in through them. The lycan walked slowly in the pews towards him with Gunnar leading the way.

- 35 -

"Bear told me you were Judas," Gunnar said to Leif. "I thought he might be right, but I knew that you would still lead us right to them. You failed at killing them and at saving them. You're absolutely useless, aren't you?"

"Dying now would be far better than serving you," Leif growled at him.

"Stop!" I shouted, hanging over the balcony. The lycan already knew we were there, so it wasn't like I was giving away our position, but Jack glared at me anyway. "He's not the one you want!"

"You have no idea what I want," Gunnar looked up at me. His face was that of pure evil, and a shiver ran down me.

He walked to the center aisle, and the other three lycan moved in closer to Leif, but he didn't run. They were going to slaughter him, but he just stood his ground and held his head high.

"They're going to kill him," I said, looking at Ezra. "We've got to do something!"

He looked at me helplessly. We hadn't yet figured out how we were going to save ourselves. Jack was looking down at Leif, and I could almost see his mind racing. He wanted to think of something, but he was taking too long.

I launched myself over the balcony and heard Jack calling my name. When I hit the ground, I expected my legs to snap, but they barely even hurt. I even landed on my feet, and if the situation weren't so incredibly terrifying, I would've felt pretty damn cool for making a landing like that.

None of the lycan looked back at me, but then again, I wasn't much of a threat. I stood up and I heard the sound of Olivia's crossbow click back as she loaded an arrow, but I wasn't the only one.

Dodge and Stellan cocked their heads at the balcony, but Bear kept his attention fixed on Leif. Dodge moved first, but he wasn't as fast as Stellan, so the arrow sliced straight through his heart. He collapsed to the ground, and I thought he might burst into flames like in the movies, but he just laid there.

Stellan was standing in front of me, smiling, and in a blur, he was gone. Olivia fired an arrow at him, but it flew through the air behind him and landed in a pew. Using his speed as momentum, Stellan leapt from off the back of a pew up into the balcony. No other vampire moved as fast as he could, not even Ezra, and even with the five of them up there, they could barely hold their own against him.

In the moment of distraction, Leif took his chance to counterattack Bear, sending him crashing into the pews. Wood splintered everywhere, and I realized too late that Leif had the situation under control.

I looked back up at the balcony, feeling helpless as they struggled to keep Stellan at bay. Ezra was trying to defend Olivia so she could load her crossbow, but even when she did manage to get a shot off, Stellan was impossible to hit.

"Hello, Alice," Gunnar whispered, and his voice was right in my ear.

I had been too busy watching Stellan that I hadn't noticed him coming behind me. I tried to look up at him, and his hand was around my throat, one of his razor sharp nails pressing into the skin over my jugular. I fought to pull his arm free, and he started dragging me backwards, towards the altar.

I thought about screaming, but I didn't want anybody to know. They would stop and look at me, and that's exactly what would get them killed. Milo was crouched over Bobby, trying to protect him, and I could smell Jack and Peter's blood from fresh wounds. Only Olivia had yet to be wounded, but she was dodging and diving almost as quickly as Stellan.

So I let Gunnar drag me away. I knew that he would probably kill me, but whatever he did to me, I had to endure it silently. That was my only chance of saving them.

Leif was still fighting Bear, but he seemed to have the upper hand. He knocked Bear back to the ground and grabbed a broken piece of the pew. It had been the back rest, but it had been snapped in half, giving it a sharp edge. Leif held it high over his head, then plummeted it down against Bear's throat.

There was this awful gurgling sound, but I closed my eyes to keep from seeing the blood. I heard the crunch of bone, and Bear's heart fell silent. Leif had decapitated him.

"Everyone is so busy right now," Gunnar clicked his tongue. "It's so boring and dull with just the two of us, don't you think?"

"Gunnar," Leif said, keeping his voice low. Blood stained his shirt and face, and he carefully stepped over the pews towards us.

"Let her go. She's not what you want."

"You are quite right," Gunnar sighed. "But she is what everyone else seems to want, and if you take a step closer, I'll slice her throat wide open." Leif stopped where he was, glaring at him. When Gunnar spoke again, he was shouting loudly, so everyone would hear him. "What do you think, Peter? How much blood can sweet Alice lose in one day?"

Peter and Jack froze instantly, but Stellan went for Jack. He tackled him roughly, crashing into pews, and falling below the balcony wall, so I couldn't see him. Olivia aimed her crossbow, but I doubt she could get in a clean shot if they were rolling about together. Ezra jumped into it, trying to catch Stellan, but he moved too quickly, even with Jack in his clutches.

"No, Peter, help Jack!" I shouted. "He needs you more than I do!"

Peter stared at me, his eyes burning, and I knew that he wouldn't save Jack.

Peter leapt off the balcony, his eyes never leaving me. He walked deliberately slow down the aisle, and I looked up at the balcony. I could hear them fighting, Jack grunting, and how fast his heart pounded, but I couldn't see him.

Milo was just trying to keep Bobby from getting killed. I saw Ezra go flying across the balcony, landing hard against the wall, and tumbling down next to Olivia. At least Jack's heart was still beating. At least he was still alive.

Gunnar made it closer to us than Leif had, but he stopped just below the steps leading up the altar. Gunnar had us stationed right below the cross. When I looked straight up, all I could see was the emaciated corpse of Jesus. It was rather disturbing, and it didn't help that a vampire was about to tear open my throat.

"Let her go," Peter commanded.

"Why would I do that?" Gunnar laughed. "It's just so much fun watching you suffer!"

"I know what you're doing," Peter put his foot on the first step of the altar. "You still think that you're going to get out of here alive, but you don't really care if you do. You only care about winning, and winning for you is destroying me."

"Very true," Gunnar admitted, then nodded at Leif. "Then destroying him. The rest of them don't really matter to me." His grip tightened on me. "But you know why I can't let her go."

"She's the means to destroying me." Peter took another step up, and Gunnar pressed his nail into my vein, breaking the skin just enough to draw a little blood, and Peter froze. "You want to make her suffer, so you can make me watch. Killing her is your way of torturing me."

"Yes, and so far it seems to be working," Gunnar smiled, but there was an unease behind it.

"If I die, you lose." Peter bent down, picking up a titanium arrow off the top step of the altar. Olivia had been shooting them all over, and a stray one had landed a few feet from us. I felt Gunnar's confidence falter for the first time. "I want to die. If I die before she does, I don't see anything. I don't suffer at all."

"I'll still kill her," Gunnar insisted nervously.

"You're gonna kill her either way, according to you." Peter

pointed the arrow towards his own heart, pressing the tip against his chest. "But this way, I'm not destroyed. I've gotten exactly what I've wanted, and you haven't."

"You'll die knowing she's going to, and that might be enough for me," Gunnar said with false cheer. Peter's idea unnerved him. Testing him, Peter pushed the arrow into his chest, not deep enough to hurt but enough to draw blood. "How do you propose I make you suffer then?"

"Let her go, and we'll battle it out, hand to hand," Peter said. "The way real men fight. If you catch me, then you can let your surviving henchman do away with her while I watch. I'll suffer even worse because it's my idea."

It was a horrible idea, and that's exactly why it appealed to Gunnar. I saw no way that it could work out where either of us lived, but Peter was just buying time. He really didn't care if he lived or died, but he wanted to give me a chance to run away. I wouldn't, though, not when he and Jack and everyone were still here risking their lives. I would never leave without them.

"Peter, no! This is stupid," I said. Before I had been fighting Gunnar, but now I hung onto his arm, trying to keep me to him.

"That's why I liked you, Peter," Gunnar laughed. "You were brilliant. If only you hadn't killed my right hand man. We would've been so happy together." With that, Gunnar threw me and I landed roughly in the pews.

Leif helped me to my feet, and I shook off the pain. It faded quickly, but things still hurt. Peter and Gunnar were squaring off, staring at each other as Gunnar taunted him. Peter showed little emotion, and I hoped that he was planning something.

The noises in the balcony hadn't gotten any better, but from what I could tell, everyone was still alive. Leif and I stood unsurely in the broken pews, neither of us knowing how we could really help the situation.

"Oh, come on, Peter!" Gunnar groaned. "I didn't spare the girl so we could have a staring contest."

"I'm sorry to disappoint you," Peter said dryly.

Peter stood on the altar steps. Gunnar wanted Peter to come to him, but when he wouldn't, he tired of waiting. He dove at Peter, more to get the fight going than to actually hurt him, and Peter deftly jumped out of the way. He leapt over the sacrament table, and as soon as he landed, he jumped up again, grabbing onto the giant cross hanging on the wall. He scrambled to climb up, using Jesus as footing, and Gunnar just stared at him.

"Really, Peter? Are you that much of a coward?" Gunnar looked dubiously at him, and I was wondering the same thing. "I had expected so much more than this."

Gunnar had his back to us, so I took a step forward, planning to attack him, but Leif put his hand on my arm. I looked at him, and he mouthed "not yet." Apparently, he had a better understanding of Peter's plan than I did.

Peter climbed higher up the cross, and to my confusion, he started pulling at the bolts that held it to the wall. He started on the right arm of the cross, and then when they were free, he moved onto the top.

"What are you doing?" Gunnar asked. "Is this some kind of

suicide attempt?"

"Something like that," Peter said and climbed to start loosening the left arm.

"I can slaughter the girl right now, if you like," Gunnar offered.

Peter glanced back at me, but he didn't stop trying to free the bolts. The cross started to sway and groan, but he kept pulling at it. Once he got broke the bolt from the arm, there was nothing attaching it to the wall except for the bolts at the foot of the cross. Peter hung onto the arm, with his feet pressed against the wall and started to push off.

Because the cross was still connected at the bottom, it should've just swung down, moving like the hands of a clock until it hung upside down, with top resting on the floor at the 9 o'clock position. But Peter pushed hard against the wall, forcing it swing down and away from the wall. The cross groaned and as it swung down and out, like a crazed pendulum.

Gunnar took a step back, so Leif growled and jumped towards him. He didn't actually attack him, but Gunnar stepped closer to the cross again and his attention was diverted to Leif.

Peter jumped off the cross, and Gunnar turned around to see what was happening just as the top of the cross flew through his neck, cutting his head off. I shrieked as his head flew across the room, and his body collapsed a moment later. Peter barely jumped out of the way as the cross swung back, and he ran over to me and Leif.

"Gunnar!" Stellan shouted.

He paused and Olivia fired another arrow at him, but she

narrowly missed. He made a play for the edge of the balcony, and Ezra tackled him before he could make it over.

While Ezra held him back, Jack jumped off the balcony. He landed on the ground and did a roll thing, that made him look much more badass than I ever knew he was. When he stood up, he was holding one of Olivia's metal arrows in his hand, holding it pointed towards the balcony.

Out of nowhere, Stellan came to a halt next to Jack, the arrow protruding right through his chest. He had jumped down from the balcony with his eyes fixed solely on Peter, meaning to avenge Gunnar's death, and he hadn't been paying attention to Jack standing in the middle of the aisle. He had impaled himself on an arrow, and he sputtered, blood coming from his lips, then collapsed back on the ground.

I rushed over to Jack and threw my arms around him. He hugged me tightly, and I pressed myself to him.

Olivia jumped off the balcony and walked over to Stellan. She kicked him once with her foot, then pulled a machete out of the back of her belt. With one fell swoop, she sliced off his head, and blood splattered onto Jack and me.

"Sorry," she smiled at me. "I just had to be sure. You don't want any damn vampires coming back on you."

Honestly, I didn't even really care. I could feel Peter's eyes on me, and he had saved my life. I wasn't angry with him, but I didn't love him. I loved Jack and I was thrilled to be in his arms again. I stood on my tiptoes and kissed Jack softly.

"What the hell happened?" Bobby shouted.

Jack laughed, pulling away from the kiss. I didn't mind, though, because I loved hearing him laugh. Apparently, Bobby had just woken up, and he was surveying the carnage in the church.

"Hey. That guy tried to kill me! Why is he here?" Bobby pointed to Leif, and Milo tried telling him that Leif was our friend now. The answer seemed to satisfy him, but he still looked confused. "Where is Jane?"

- 36 -

After scouring the cathedral, Milo stepped out the front doors, and that's what we had needed to do all long. Jane was lying on the front steps. She was shivering and completely out of it but still alive.

The park across the street was swarming with cops and ambulances, thanks to the mangled body the lycan had left there. Milo had on a zippered hoodie over a tee shirt, so he took it off and laid it on top of Jane. He made an anonymous 911 call saying there was an injured girl on the front steps of the church.

This time, I thought the best solution for her was staying away from vampires. She needed more help than we could give her.

After that, we left in a hurry. Olivia went back to her place, and Leif disappeared into the night. I'm not sure where he'd go, but he assured me he'd be alright and he'd see me again. Peter had driven his Audi, and Milo and Bobby volunteered to go with him. It was only a two-seater, but Bobby didn't mind sitting on Milo's lap.

Since Jack had taken the Lexus, Ezra had been forced to take the Lamborghini, which he generally thought to be too flashy to drive around. Jack sat shotgun, and I curled up on his lap, resting my head against his chest.

On the ride home, I realized that the cathedral had constant staffing. Ezra explained that when he'd arrived, he'd charmed them into leaving. With his charisma and good looks, he could convince humans of anything. I suspected there might be vampire glamour along with that, but I didn't ask.

"Oh my god, it's never felt so good to be home," I sighed when we walked into the house. Jack grinned at me, squeezing my hand. The night had felt longer than any other one before. I just wanted to go up to bed with him.

"Tomorrow is going to be another long day," Ezra said, following us in. "I'll have to spend all day trying to convince the police we had nothing to do with this." Ezra went over to the fridge and got a bag of blood out of the bottom of the drawer of the fridge. All the blood used to be kept in the basement, but Milo and I were pretty lazy.

"Why would they even think we were involved?" I asked. I had my back to Jack, and he wrapped his arms around my shoulders. I leaned back against him, and he kissed the top of my head.

"Because the Lexus is still there." Ezra opened the bag of blood and took a long drink. "I'll have to get it from the impound. I just hope that I have chance to sleep before they come looking for us." His expression changed, growing perplexed. "That's funny. I saw Mae's car in the garage. I thought she'd be wondering where we all were."

"Maybe she's in bed," I shrugged. The sky had already started to lighten slightly already.

"Maybe," Ezra didn't look convinced. He finished his blood quickly, then cocked his head. I listened, but I couldn't hear anything. Not even Mae, but the night had left me exhausted so all my senses were dimmed.

I heard the garage door open, and a few seconds later, Peter walked into the kitchen, rubbing his eyes. Milo and Bobby followed right behind him, and thanks to that nice, long nap Bobby had, he didn't seem to feel any of the weariness the rest of us did. He was following right on Peter's heels, asking him a million questions.

"So you cut off his head using a cross?" Bobby was completely wide-eyed. "I'm Jewish, and even I think that's pretty damn awesome!"

Bobby noticed me in the room, and he gave me a weird look. It wasn't adoration, exactly, but I returned some of the sentiment. It made Milo bristle and put his arm possessively around Bobby.

"I just need to take a hot shower, and be done with this night," Peter grumbled and walked out of the kitchen. He hadn't looked at me or Jack since everything had ended, and I wondered if he ever would again. I had nearly been killed tonight because of how much he loved me, but then again, that wasn't the first time.

"Me, too," Milo said. He looped his arm around Bobby's waist to start leading him out of the kitchen, but Bobby stopped and looked confused. "What?"

"Where's the dog?" Bobby asked. "She's always knocking me over when we get home."

"Where is the dog?" I echoed, and Jack tensed up. She *always* greeted Jack after he'd been away. I couldn't keep her away from him.

"Matilda?" Jack called her and stepped away from me. "Mattie? Where are you, good girl?"

Matilda barked loudly, and it was coming from Mae and Ezra's room. She scratched at the door, and Jack and Ezra exchanged a look. Mae shushed her, and she opened the bedroom door, letting Matilda come charging down at us, and Mae immediately shut the door.

"That was weird," I said. Jack had bent down to start praising Matilda, but he looked just as surprised as the rest of us.

"Something's going on," Ezra said, more to himself than us. He tossed his empty blood bag in the garbage can and walked down to his room. "Mae?" He started to open the door, and she pushed it shut. "Mae? What is going on?"

"Nothing!" Mae shouted. "Go away!"

"Mae, open the door *now,* or I'll open it for you," Ezra said. When he talked like that, his voice was one of the most intimidating sounds I'd ever heard.

Slowly, the bedroom door opened, and Ezra stepped inside. There was complete silence, and Bobby took a step forward, trying to get a better look. Milo stopped him from going farther.

I looked up at Jack to see if he had any insight, but he just shook his head. We all waited expectantly, but Ezra never said anything. A minute later, he just turned and stormed out of the room.

"Get that out of my house!" Ezra growled walking away.

"She's not a *that!*" Mae ran after him, almost pleading. "And we can't travel right now! Not when she's like this."

"I don't care!" Ezra roared, and he wouldn't even look at her. "I want her out!"

"We just need two, three more days tops, and then we'll be out of your hair forever!" Mae insisted desperately. He had his back to her, seething. "Ezra, please! If you love me, you can give me three more days! *Please!*"

"Fine," Ezra said grudgingly. "But if you stay one day longer, I'll take care of her myself." He walked back towards the garage. "I'm going to the station now to deal with the car. Don't wait up."

"What happened to you?" Mae gasped, noticing us for the first time. We were all tattered and bloody, and Bobby had scratches and bruises.

Milo started explaining the night to her, but I brushed past him. I thought I knew what was in her room, but I had to see it for myself. Mae tried to pay attention to Milo, but I felt her watching me as I walked by. I pushed open her bedroom door, and it was exactly what I thought.

In the soft mass of Mae's bed, a small girl twitched. Her blond curls were sticking to the sweat on her forehead. She was pale and sick, but she was still adorable. She looked like a pint-sized version of Mae, with cherub cheeks.

She was still in the first phases of the turn, and the worst of it hadn't hit her yet. Matilda ran past me and jumped onto the bed next to her, licking the little girl's clammy face. She smiled a little at that, and Matilda settled down next to her.

"She really likes Matilda," Mae said from behind me. She walked over to the child. Jack stood behind me, taking the whole thing in, but he didn't say anything. "I'd like you to all meet my great-granddaughter, Daisy. I'm going to be taking care of her now."

"Oh, Mae," I looked at her sadly.

"No, don't do that," Mae shook her head. She sat down on the bed next to the girl, pushing her hair back from her forehead. "I did the right thing, and I know I did. I had to save her. After Jane left, I realized I wasn't upset about her. I had to save Daisy."

"Well, Jane is fine, by the way," I sighed. "But… you did what you had to do."

"I did. Isn't she precious?" She looked adoringly at the child, and I could see that there had really never been any choice for her. Even if she had to give up Ezra and everyone else, that child meant so much more to her.

"You're not taking my dog," Jack said finally. "Come on, Matilda." Reluctantly, Matilda jumped off the bed and followed him out of the room.

"So you're leaving?" I asked.

"It seems that way," Mae said wearily. "I thought Ezra might change his mind when he saw her, but… It's alright, though. I already have a plan."

"What's that?"

"Australia," Mae smiled at me. "I've never been. Vampires don't like it there because it's warm, but it's comfortable enough, and there's plenty of uninhabited outback for us to hide away. There's active blood banks in places like Sydney, though, so with a drive, we can get stocked up."

"So, the two of you are gonna spend the rest of existence hiding out in the outback?" I raised an eyebrow. I had always wanted to go there, but it just seemed like a horrible scenario for this.

"For awhile." Mae nodded and went back to staring at her bundle of joy. "But we won't be alone, at least not at first. Peter is going with us."

"Peter?" I hadn't realized that Peter really wanted that much to do with Mae, but then again, he did like running away from me and suicidal missions, like caring for a child vampire.

"He offered a few days ago," Mae said. "We'll be okay, love. Don't you worry about us."

She might've been talking to me, but she was looking at Daisy, and I think that was all meant for her. The second she got Daisy, the rest of us really ceased to exist for her. I watched her for a moment longer, fawning over the child, but I had somewhere to be.

When I went upstairs, Jack was already taking a hot shower. I was desperate for one myself, so I got undressed and climbed in with him. He smiled at me, but I just wrapped my arms around his waist and pressed my head against his chest. There was nothing sexual about it. I just loved being that close to him, his bare skin on mine, his heart beating in my ear.

He kissed the top of my head and held me to him. After everything the night had brought, I couldn't help but cry. Out of sadness and exhaustion and relief. I had never seen anything as brutal as what I witnessed tonight, and I hoped to never see it again.

"It's going to be okay, Alice," Jack assured me, rubbing my back gently.

"How can you say that? After what happened tonight?" I looked up at him. His soft blue eyes were full of nothing but love and optimism, and he smiled at me.

"Because you're here with me," Jack said. "Any night that ends with that can't be that bad."

"I can't argue with that logic," I admitted, and he laughed, sending delighted tingles all through me. I held onto him tighter, pressing my head against his chest, and relished the feel of his arms around me. There was no place in the world I'd rather be.

Read an excerpt from the fourth installment in the *My Blood Approves* series:

Wisdom — available now!

Terror ripped through me.

I had no idea where I was. I woke up expecting the familiarity and safety of my bedroom, and this wasn't it. It was hot, almost unbearable. Sweat soaked my skin, but I shivered. Disoriented, I stumbled out of bed.

I tripped over my own foot and fell onto the floor with a heavy thud. Cursing myself, I rubbed my knee, even though the pain had stopped. I'd been training hard to work on my strength and grace, and I hated when my clumsiness returned.

The light flicked on in the room. I sat on the floor and squinted up in the brightness to see who turned it on Peter stood in the doorway, wearing only ripped jeans, and he stared down at me.

I finally remembered where I was, but I still couldn't shake the panic. My heart pounded like crazy, and that's what summoned Peter.

"What are you doing on the floor?" Peter asked.

"I tripped."

"Are you okay?" He walked over to me and bent down so he could help me up.

I took his hand, and when he pulled me to my feet, I noticed the sweat gleaming all over his chest and his arms. If I hadn't been so distracted by my own terror, I might have taken the time to hate how perfect and gorgeous Peter looked. Every time I saw him, I wished he would get less attractive.

"What's going on?" His voice had taken on a protective edge that I was unaccustomed to hearing from him. He'd been working on showing me his gentler side, but it still surprised me.

"I don't know." I shook my head.

"Alice, you're terrified." He heard the panicked racing of my heart and no matter what I did, I couldn't slow it. "What happened?"

I bit my lip and pushed my hair behind my ear. He put his hand on my arm, and his bright emerald eyes managed calmed me a bit. I wanted to tell him everything, but I couldn't explain what freaked me out so much.

"It was like a bad dream," I said. "But it wasn't a dream. It was more of a … *feeling*."

"What kind of feeling?" Peter asked

"Just fear, this really intense fear."

"You were just sleeping, and then you were afraid?" He dropped his hand from my arm and studied my face. "No images that went along with it?"

"No." I furrowed my brow, trying to remember what exactly woke me up. "There weren't images, but I felt paralyzed. Right before I woke up, I felt really scared, and I couldn't move." I shook my head again, this time to clear it. "It's over now, and I'm done talking about it."

"As long as you're okay." Peter sounded reluctant to let the topic die.

"Yeah, I'm great." I forced a smile. "Except I'm really hot. Why is it so hot in here?"

"The central air is broken. I've been out back trying to fix it, but the sun is really getting to me. And, as it turns out, I know nothing about air conditioning units," he sighed. That explained the grease stains all over his jeans and the smudge that ran just above his naval, on the hard contours of his abdomen.

"That really sucks," I said and looked away from him.

"I'll call a repairman, but I don't know how long it will take them to get here." Peter ran a hand through his dark hair. He'd been wearing it shorter since he moved, probably because of the continuous heat. "It's the drawback of living out in the middle of nowhere."

"Yeah, I bet," I said. "I think I'm gonna take a shower."

"It's only noon."

"I doubt I can sleep anyway," I shrugged.

"I'll see if I can find a fan for you," he offered and stepped towards the door.

"Alright. Thanks," I smiled at him. He nodded, then left me alone in the room.

I went over to the closet to look for clothes. It was mostly bare since I hadn't packed that much for my ten-day stay. As soon as we'd gotten here, Mae insisted on putting my things away and doing my laundry.

I would've been fine with living out of a suitcase, but Mae wouldn't stand for it. With Daisy around, her maternal instinct seemed to be in overdrive. Really, I wasn't sure how Peter tolerated it.

After Mae had gone against Ezra's wishes and turned her great-granddaughter into a vampire, he'd given her three days to get out. They'd left in two. Peter chartered a private plane, and he, Mae, and Daisy had escaped to the Australian outback.

Even though they were gone, Mae still kept in contact with us, particularly with Milo. She'd been sad we spent the holidays apart, and after Christmas, she began plotting to see us.

Milo started school next week, so he decided now would be the best time to visit. Jack didn't think it'd be good for him to come with because he didn't really want to see Mae or Peter. He didn't even want me to go, but he didn't try to stop me.

It was just my younger brother Milo, his human boyfriend Bobby, and me spending a week and a half with Mae, her child vampire Daisy, and Peter. With a broken air conditioner.

Milo told me that January was summertime here, but if I had understood exactly how hot that could be, I might've put off visiting until July.

Peter bought a huge farmhouse about an hour away from Alice Springs in Australia. From what I'm told, it's a nice town, and Sydney's supposed to be divine, not that I've seen much of either of them. Sydney's a four-hour flight away, but that's not what stopped us from going. Daisy can't go out in public. She's only five and has almost no control over her bloodlust.

Milo'd tried to spin this as a trip in celebration of my eighteenth birthday last week, and in a way, it kinda was. Mae threw a little party for me, with a cake that only Bobby could eat. She gave me a lovely dress, and Daisy made me a card.

I got in the shower, and the cold water did wonders for me, but I couldn't shake the trepidation. Something was off, and I couldn't put my finger on it.

I thought about calling Jack back in the States, but I hardly ever got any reception. Besides, I didn't want to alarm him. He'd been convinced that this trip was a horrible idea, but it hadn't been that bad. A little dull, maybe. Jack's real fear, of course, was Peter.

When I got out of the shower, I went over to the dresser and pulled open the top drawer. Amongst my bras and underwear, I'd hidden Peter's present to me. A beautiful diamond encrusted heart-shaped locket. I loved it, but I had no idea how to explain it to Jack.

Nothing was overtly wrong with Peter giving it to me, but Jack wouldn't approve. For my birthday, Jack had a Muppet specially made to look like me and taken me scuba diving with the sharks at the aquarium. They were pretty awesome gifts and I loved them, but they weren't the same caliber as expensive jewelry.

Then again, Jack had also given me immortality, so he kinda had Peter beat.

"Is it cooler in here?" Milo opened my bedroom without knocking, and I dropped the necklace in the drawer and slammed it shut.

"Um, I don't know," I said, taking a step away from the dresser.

"I think it's hotter in here," Milo groaned but walked into my room anyway. Like Peter, he had decided that shirtless was the way to go. "It's got to be at least a hundred degrees here!"

"Have you tried the pool?" I asked.

"Yeah, right." Milo wrinkled his nose and flopped back on my bed. "The sun's still out, and even if it wasn't, you've seen the pool."

Something was wrong with the filtration system, so skeavy green moss covered the pool. There seemed to be something wrong with everything in the house. Apparently, it had been even more rundown when they bought it, but Peter and Mae were fixing it up. But the pool didn't work, the air went out, the wrap-around porch sagged, and the roof needed replacing.

I went over and pulled back the heavy curtains, looking outside. The sun stung my eyes, and I stared out at the emptiness. They didn't have a neighbor for miles, and everything looked dry and faded. I slid open the window and a hot breeze wafted in, but at least it was better than nothing.

"I'm starting to think this was a bad idea," Milo said wearily.

"It's not that *bad*. I mean, other than the heat." I sat on the bed next to him. Beads of sweat stood out on his chest, and he looked up at me, his big brown eyes dejected. "You've had fun seeing Mae, right?"

"Kinda," he shrugged and looked away.

Milo had been the baby, the one that had garnered all of Mae's attention until Daisy came along, and she required a lot more than he did. He wasn't a real jealous person, but this struck a nerve with him.

Being ignored by our real mother had been bad enough, let alone her replacement.

"What's Bobby doing?" I asked, hoping to cheer him up by talking about his boyfriend.

They'd been together for four months, and they weren't "meant for each other," not the way vampires are, but there was still something there. Bobby made Milo happy, and he was a good guy.

Bobby mostly lived with us back in Minneapolis, and despite my initial hatred of him, he'd really grown on me. Some of that probably had to do with the fact that I'd bitten him, bonding us together slightly. It tended to drive Milo nuts, but we couldn't do anything about it.

"He's sitting in front of a fan in our room," Milo said, scratching absently at his arm. The spiders here were crazy about him. The bites didn't really hurt him, but they left irritating, itching bumps for hours. "Even the heat is getting to him, so you know it has to be bad."

"He's probably just used to living in our climate," I yawned. We hated being hot, and we constantly kept our house at frigid temperatures. Plus, we had just come from winter in Minnesota. "Ugh! It's too hot sleep!"

"Tell me about it." Milo looked up at me. "What time is it back home? Maybe Jack's up."

"I don't understand the time difference. You tell me."

"I don't know what time it is here," he said and made no effort to find out. "Have you talked to Jack lately?"

"The other day. The reception here is so shoddy, it's hard for me to get through."

My heart ached at the thought of him. I was bonded with Jack, so it was painful to be away from him. It had lessened a bit over the last few months, but it still wasn't anything where I'd enjoy not being around him.

"How are things there?" Milo asked.

"The same, I guess. Ezra is moping around the house, and Jack can't wait for us to get back."

"I still can't believe that Ezra hasn't talked to Mae," Milo looked a little wide eyed over it, and I felt the same way.

No matter how mad or frustrated I might get with Jack, I couldn't imagine going *months* without talking to him. It would be like going months without eating.

Bobby shrieked from his bedroom down the hall, but Milo and I were slow to react. Spiders had been infesting their room since we arrived, and Bobby screamed like a girl every time he saw one. Admittedly, some of them could actually kill him, but most of the time, he'd already stomped on them by the time Milo or I came to the rescue.

I heard a door slam, followed by a bizarre clawing sound. Bobby's heart beat frantically, but his wasn't the only one. Another heart pounded hard and fast, but it was quieter and not as rapid as a human.

It was the sound of a vampire's heart. A very small, very hungry vampire.

By the time Bobby yelled again, Milo and I were already running out of my room. His room was way at the other end of the hall, but we could see Daisy, clawing at the door with her bare hands. She was strong enough to tear the wood, leaving bloody trails as it splintered out around her fingers.

Before we had a chance to reach her, she managed to tear a hole in the door big enough for her little body to wriggle through, and Bobby started screaming like hell.

Other titles by Amanda Hocking:

My Blood Approves series

My Blood Approves

Fate

Flutter

Wisdom

Letters to Elise: A Peter Townsend Novella (Christmas 2010)

Trylle Trilogy

Switched

Torn (coming Fall 2010)

Ascend (coming January 2011)

Connect with Amanda Hocking Online:

Twitter: http://twitter.com/amanda_hocking

My blog: http://amandahocking.blogspot.com/

Facebook Fan Page: http://www.facebook.com/amandahockingfans

Made in the USA
Lexington, KY
15 March 2011